THE ROOSTER TRAPPED IN THE REPTILE ROOM

A BARRY GIFFORD READER

THE ROOSTER TRAPPED IN THE REPTILE ROOM

Edited by

THOMAS A. McCARTHY

SEVEN STORIES PRESS
New York | Toronto | London | Melbourne

A Seven Stories Press First Edition

Seven Stories Press
140 Watts Street
New York, NY 10013
www.sevenstories.com

In Canada:
Hushion House, 36 Northline Road, Toronto, Ontario M4B 3E2

In the U.K.:
Turnaround Publisher Services Ltd., Unit 3, Olympia Trading Estate,
Coburg Road, Wood Green, London N22 6TZ

In Australia:
Palgrave MacMillan, 627 Chapel Street, South Yarra, Victoria 3141

Library of Congress Cataloging-in-Publication Data

Gifford, Barry, 1946–
The rooster trapped in the reptile room: a Barry Gifford reader /
Barry Gifford; edited by Thomas A. McCarthy.--Seven Stories Press 1st ed.
p. cm.
ISBN 158322-525-0
I. McCarthy, Thomas A., 1975– II. Title.
PS3557.I283A6 2003
813'.54--dc21
2003005742

9 8 7 6 5 4 3 2 1

College professors may order examination copies of Seven Stories Press
titles for a free six-month trial period. To order, visit www.sevenstories.com/textbook,
or fax on school letterhead to (212) 226-1411.

Printed in Canada.

"The pure products of America go crazy."
—William Carlos Williams, "To Elsie"

"Literature does not lead men astray."
—Fortune found in fortune cookie by
Barry Gifford in Chinatown,
San Francisco, 1970

CONTENTS

I WISH I'D MADE IT UP

SAILOR AND LULA

OUT OF TIME

ON THE RECORD

POETRY

FOREWORD

Giffordia

Barry Gifford's writing keeps: it stays fresh every time you re-read it and what's more you want to re-read it because his characters feel like old friends. His fiction is just as vivid as his memoirs, as heart-filled as his poetry, as workmanlike as his essays, and vice-versa da capo: vivid essays, heart-filled memoirs, workmanlike fiction. It isn't that Gifford disrespects genres by letting them leak into one another. Quite the contrary: the specific engine of each genre is powered by something ineffable: the Gifford style. Like Hemingway, Saroyan, Kerouac, Salinger, Brautigan, and Bukowski, Gifford has a style. He is a great comic realist who does with the turn of a phrase what a Zen master does with a brushstroke. Gifford's universe is Giffordian. It's an unmistakably American universe, too, populated by a huge and loveable humanity propelled on a tragic river of excess energy. Once brought to life on the page, they cannot be removed, they will live forever. Wherever Marble Lesson, Sailor, Lula, Baby Cat-Face or Consuelo come from, they aren't going anywhere: they are a permanent part of our literature.

Gifford has rightly noted that the "human comedy" of Balzac Saroyan, and Kerouac is his project as well, and, like them, he has staked out a specific humanity that is solely his. The lesbian jail-birds, drifters, outlaws, star-crossed lovers, charlatans, preachers, and lumpen-spiritualists who populate the mythical (but geographically precise) Gifford-world, are neither puppets nor cartoons, (though they have the seductive swiftness of comic strips or shadow theater), but real-life spawns of the demented last-half of the American century. Gifford, however, is not primarily a social critic. He is foremost a benevolent and involved deity who looks with curiosity and compassion on his creations. Which is to say, he is foremost a writer and an original who has seized the still-live vein of that American realism which began with Mark Twain and has not been exhausted by theory of any kind.

Writers like Gifford come big, to the chagrin of academics. The insurgent life that powers his prose is unwieldy and generative, manifest in marginal and violent characters whose genius for language and depth of inquiry is sublime but saves them neither from tragedy nor absurdity. If their marginality doesn't distress the pencil-pushers of our Sahara of the Bozarts, their prodigal speech certainly does, as does Gifford's clearly joyous disregard for the ongoing fads. This wouldn't even be worth mentioning in the context of this foreword if it wasn't in itself a guarantee of authenticity. The great family of American writers to whom Gifford belongs is one of outsiders. Among the ones mentioned above, only Hemingway and Salinger are canonized, and the effort seems to have sapped the dainty energies of our exegetes. Others, such as Tom Robbins, Ken Kesey, and Jim Harrison, have captured the allegiance of readers while still being treated like live serpents by the literary establishment.

I mention this because it points to a paradoxical failure: America delights itself and the world with the joyous products of a popular culture that is complex enough to generate its own distinctions of greatness, from genuinely luminous creations such as Sailor and Lula, to outlandishly marvelous television creatures like Homer Simpson and Hank Hill. The self-selecting critical instinct of people who think of culture as their quotidian right, like hot water and Stop'n Go, is still suspect to the fading guardians of "high" culture. European critics don't have that problem, at least not with American culture, which they value precisely for its irreverent freedom. It makes sense then that Gifford, like the other writers mentioned, is better respected in Europe than in his native country. The analogy, of course, is jazz, which thrived for a time in Europe before returning in triumph to its native land.

Barry Gifford is both a "cult" writer and a great one. In Europe, where his cult and his prose are not in conflict, he is read as an American original who meets his readers' expectations of America's violent pioneering spirit. Eventually, he will be read the same way here. Critics will have no choice but to abandon their terror of fertility and genre-crossing and read his work for the purposes of delight, just like real readers do.

Andrei Codrescu

"You're no writer," said Nathan.

"What do you mean?" asked Franz.

"When do you work? You never work."

"All the time. Writers work all the time. They're always working, that's what Gertrude Stein said."

"Fuck Gertrude Stein."

Franz couldn't say anything to that.

—from *Port Tropique*, 1980

INTRODUCTION
The Thrill of a Writer's Lifetime

from
El País
(2003)

I RECENTLY RETURNED to Cuba for the first time in more than forty years, since I was a young boy. My mother and I spent most of our time in the early and mid-1950s in Key West and Miami, Florida, interspersed with frequent visits to Chicago, my father's headquarters, and our alternate residence. My father stayed regularly at the Hotel Nacional in Havana, where he had business dealings; and for a time my mother kept a house at Varadero, on the beach near the DuPont estate, about two hours from the capital. I have a snapshot of myself playing on *la playa* at Varadero when I was three years old or so, and a great picture of my dad with his cronies at Oriental Park racetrack in Havana. After Castro took over, however, my family no longer spent time in Cuba. My father died in December of 1958, in Chicago, and my mother, who lives in Phoenix, has never gone back to the island.

I was invited to participate in an international symposium sponsored by a Brazilian organization to talk about life and its risks. My qualifications for speaking on this subject, it was explained to me, were simply that I had lived my life as a writer, not ever taking an academic route but taking the chance that I could support myself and my family on the basis of my (mostly) literary efforts. I have been writing stories and poems since the age of eleven—when my mother and father and I were still visiting Cuba—and it is true that somehow I have been able to survive and provide for others by virtue of earnings derived from novels, screenplays and journalism. I am now fifty-four years old, and I was told not long ago that only one percent of writers are able to support themselves solely by their writing. If this is true, I certainly must consider myself a lucky man, because writing has been my abiding passion for longer than the lifetimes of Kafka or Rimbaud.

It was in Cuba that something so exquisite occurred that I consider it to be one of the greatest thrills of my life. One afternoon during my recent visit I was taken with a few others on a private tour of the Cohiba cigar manufacturing plant in Siboney, a *barrio* of La Habana. While we were walking around the nineteenth-century mansion observing the workers sorting and culling and rolling tobacco leaves, I asked our guide if Cohiba still employed a *lector*, a person to read to them to help pass the time. The tradition of *lectores* dates back to mid-nineteenth century Spain and continued thereafter in Cuba and then Key West and Tampa, Florida, which became the cigar manufacturing capital of the United States after refugees of the Spanish-American War settled there. I began spending time in Tampa in 1959, after my Uncle Les, my mother's brother, moved there, and the old cigar factories were still operating, although by that time the readers had been replaced by radios and the rollers by machines.

Our guide at the Cohiba plant asked me if I wanted to meet their *lector*, and I said, of course. While we waited for her I thought about the history of these readers, who read everything from newspapers to Tolstoy, Dostoevsky and potboilers. A large black woman named Zaida greeted me, introducing herself as *la lectora*. She asked me what my profession was and I explained that I was a novelist and screenwriter—"*Yo soy un escritor de las novelas y películas*"—and that I was pleased to learn that the tradition of the reader still existed in Cuba. Zaida asked me what I had written that she might have heard of. I told her that the most likely story of mine would be my novel, *Wild at Heart*, in Spanish *Corazón salvaje*, which had been made into a popular film. *La Lectora*'s eyes lit up and she grabbed me and gave me *un gran beso* (a big kiss) and *un abrazo* (a hug). "*Corazón salvaje* is one of my favorites!" she exclaimed. "I love *Corazón salvaje*! Sailor *y* Lula!"

I assumed that she must have been referring to the movie rather than the novel—the Cubans lift American films off satellite and broadcast them on national television. It didn't matter to me, since I'm very fond of the film version.

I then mentioned to Zaida that my practice is to carry with me to foreign countries a copy of a book of mine in the language of that country whenever possible, to use as a kind of second identification in case I lose my money and passport; this way I can at least prove who I am—especially if there is a photograph of me on the book cover—and get someone to loan me money until I can wire for more. I happened to be carrying with me in my pack that day a paperback copy of *Corazón salvaje*. I took it out and Zaida snatched it out of my hands. She kissed the front cover and insisted that I sign it for her, which I did. Zaida said that she read each day to the workers for an hour and a half, she was on the final chapter of a romance novel at the moment, but she promised that when she finished she would read *Corazón salvaje* next. I told her I would be honored if she did this.

Zaida took my arm and proceeded to take me around, introducing me to her special friends among the workers, ` them know that I was the author of *Corazón salvaje*, the next novel that she would be reading for them. As we passed from room to room, most decorated with photographs and portraits of Che Guevara and signs reading "*Seguimos en combat*" ("We are still in the fight") and "*Viva la revolución*!," Zaida handed me a selection of cigars, which I gratefully accepted.

Later, as my friend José Pinto and I were descending the steps of the Cohiba house, waving goodbye to Zaida and others, José, who lives in Madrid, said to me, "My God, Barry, that was amazing. What a great coincidence that not only did she know your work but that you happened to have a copy of the book with you. What a thrill."

What had happened hadn't quite sunk in yet, but I acknowledged that this sort of unexpected event validated my efforts in a way I never could have imagined. I shivered a little in the heat. "José," I said, "what more could a writer ask for?"

Q & A

McCarthy: *You began your career as a poet, with the book* The Blood of the Parade, *published in London in 1967, followed by a number of poetry books published in the U.S. through the 1970s. Then all of a sudden you began publishing novels almost exclusively. When did you stop seeing yourself primarily as a poet?**

Gifford: I've never stopped seeing myself as anything but a poet. The point of writing poetry was to figure out the language. I wasn't so conscious about that at first, then gradually I became conscious of writing poetry to learn how to write a sentence. I'm not the first person to say that but it's true—it was true in my case.

Where did you first get the idea that you could be a writer?

Nobody encouraged me to be a writer. My father was dead by the time I was 12 so he never had a say in the matter. My mother was distracted, involved with her own life and so she really didn't have anything to say about it, either . . . Nobody really challenged me.

But when I began reading the stories of Jack London, and then Joseph Conrad—because I thought these were adventure writers—I began to see a way, that they were men who got out, and saw the world, and had things to write about. And they had their own way of observing and recording the events, and that was really what inspired me—reading those stories.

*Interview conducted by Thomas A. McCarthy, June 30–July 2, 2002, in Berkeley, California.

My idea of being a writer was in that traditional sense, being a merchant seaman, working on the railroad, hitchhiking, doing whatever it was, just to be out there in the world and experience as much as I could experience, a classic approach to it. School was not part of my plan.

You got the idea from the books themselves.

I got the idea that it was possible to make a living, and to have an interesting life. I figured that I'd never get married, I'd never have children or a conventional life, really—which I did eventually have. I never lost this wanderlust, or whatever you want to call it. I wanted to do it in the way these guys had done it. It meant a lot to me. To experience as much as I could experience.

Are there writers in the family, besides yourself?

Not that I know of. On my mother's side there were a couple of artists, painters. And musicians, certainly. There were always musicians. And that's basically how I began writing poetry, as song lyrics.

You worked as a musician for a little while.

I did. I was a musician in London in the mid-1960s, then later when I came to California in the early 1970s, I was writing songs. I must have written a couple hundred songs. I still write songs sometimes. I was never a very good musician. But I could write songs.

Poems began coming out of the song lyrics. So I began seeing that some of these so-called songs that I was writing really were poems.

These weren't exactly pop tunes?

No, the songwriters that I admired the most were more the Tin Pan Alley songwriters: Hoagy Carmichael, Harold Arlen, and later, guys who could write anything, the Brill Building people like Doc Pomus and Mort Shuman. Really, I admired anybody who could write good songs: Kurt Weill, Johnny Mercer, Agustín Lara.

And all this, the songwriting and poetry, was part of getting to know the language, to figure out how to use it, eventually to write prose?

Expanding the vocabulary.

You know, the real story here begins well before all of this. As a child I grew up mostly in the company of adults. I traveled a lot with my mother and my father, separately, most of the time. I was virtually an only child, in my early years certainly. Since we traveled so much, I grew up in hotels. We were living at the Seneca hotel in Chicago when I was born, then moved to a hotel in Key West, Florida, a hotel in Miami, a hotel in New Orleans, a hotel in Jackson, Mississippi, a hotel in Havana, Cuba, in New York, then back to Chicago. Growing up this way, as I became a conscious child, I had to be quiet and listen to what the adults were saying.

So the thing was I had to listen to people talk, that was the key. I heard a lot of people speaking, like my father's associates, many of whom spoke in different dialects, and they spoke often in a symbolic kind of language. If somebody said, "Chicken Charlie's down in two," I had to figure out what they were saying—what the symbolism of that was. But it was a very creative, inventive, and colorful language.

The role of the child was to listen and to observe. And then of course I was meeting people all the time. New people. Fresh faces. People from everywhere. And so I would meet them in the lobbies, around the swimming pool, on the street, wherever it happened to be, and I'd hear their stories. And then I would invent my own stories. After a while, instead of telling the same old thing of who I was, I really didn't know who I was or what was going on . . . My father had a rather shadowy profession. I mean he was involved in the rackets. So nobody was ever very specific about what was going on. I used to make up stories about my own life. I used to tell people that I had this house in a small town somewhere with a dog, that I had brothers and sisters, this and that, which was totally untrue. And then they would meet my mother, and my mother was, well, *interested* to know what I'd said.

So this business of fiction—you know, Proust said, "Fiction is the finest kind of lying"—came early to me.

You've written poetry, novels, essays, reviews, journalism, short fiction, plays, screenplays . . . Is any one form most important to you?

I do cover a spectrum, from poetry to the movies. I'm not saying that I'm wonderful at all of the forms or any of the forms in that sense. I really am no judge of that and I'm not very analytical. All I know is that, except for work that has been assigned, early journalism, screenwriting jobs—if I'm self-generating, if I'm generating the story, the expression entirely on my own, I really find that it's the subject, the way it comes to me that inspires the form. A thought may come and it may be best expressed as a poem, or it may be best expressed as an essay, or a short story, or maybe it takes a long time for me to get at a novel . . . hard to say. The great thing about it all is, since I have experience now in a great many forms, I have these to choose from.

You've said that the short story is the most difficult to write, and also your favorite.

Often my favorite. It is tough to put so much into relatively few pages. To get three acts into a small space. I always admired the great short story writers, Kafka, Chekhov, James, Salinger, others. I did write a lot of short stories but they were all contained in the novels. Or what I chose to call novels. You know it's a kind of arbitrary term, too, in that there are a lot of books called novels that aren't continuous narratives. It's a marketing term, these days, more than anything else.

Have you changed your definition of the novel over time? Your novels certainly have changed.

No, to me a novel is just a longer form of a story. I can't define it any more clearly than that. That's why I like the form of the novella. It falls somewhere in between. It might be 50 pages, it might be 100 pages. I take as much space as I need to tell the story and when the story's done, that's it. When the voices stop talking, it's over.

What do you mean by voices?

When the characters have said enough, or when I determine that they've said enough, that's it. It's finished.

Do they let you know or do you let them know?

Oh, they always let me know. They absolutely let me know. This is not automatic writing. Or taking dictation, as Yeats' wife pretended to be doing in order to impress him.

So you don't actually hear them?

Well that's a funny thing. I've told the story before. I began writing *Wild at Heart*, the first of the Sailor and Lula novels, in a little hotel in Southport, North Carolina, right on the Cape Fear river.

Which is where the book itself starts . . .

Where it starts. I was doing something completely different, I was down there to write about deep sea fishing.

I woke up one morning and I heard these people talking in my head, and I sat down and started writing it down, and it was the voices of Sailor and Lula having a conversation. At first I thought that this was just a little story, a fragment, or a short story, I didn't know what it was. But they kept talking, they wouldn't leave me alone.

I had to be responsive to it. So I decided not to write the book on deep-sea fishing, on billfish tournaments, and instead wrote *Wild at Heart.*

Where did the voices of Sailor and Lula come from? Can you trace it to a person, a couple you had seen? These were people's voices you'd been hearing your whole life.

No, I'd never heard their voices before.

But you'd lived where they live in the novel, you'd heard people who spoke that way.

I had never before really written out of the Southern side of myself. Not in fiction. There was a bit of it in *Port Tropique*, where the protagonist comes to New Orleans at the end. But I'd never really written out of that side of things, using those voices. And that's what Sailor and Lula represented. It began a cycle of novels that I wrote for ten years. So that's really what happened.

Many of your characters speak in dialects, from the bayou to the barrio. They talk in different ways.

Just like real people.

I'm just trying to honestly reflect the way people talk. Nothing more, nothing less. For example, I have a lot of black, African-American characters. I've had people at readings, always young people, college students, give me this politically correct argument: "How can you, a white male"—and these are always white people asking this question—"presume to write with an African-American voice, or out of an African-American perspective?" First of all, they don't know shit about me, that I helped to raise two African-American boys. But that doesn't matter. What really matters is that I can identify with people to a certain extent, or accurately or closely reflect the way that people really do speak.

I write about white characters who speak in different dialects as well. I don't speak that way, I don't have to speak that way. I can mimic them, I've always been interested in the way that people speak.

I love H. L. Mencken's book, *The American Language*, a great document of what became disappearing language. Writing down how people spoke entering Ellis Island. How English was transformed. This is still fascinating to me.

In New Orleans, if you know the way people speak there, you say oh, this person must be from the ninth ward. Because that's how they speak, they're Yats. "Where yat?" If you write about a certain neighborhood in Chicago, at a particular time in history, then you're going to reflect the way people speak there and then. And that's what I'm doing. And I'm identifying these characters by the way they speak.

Some of the characters talk like they're straight from the Bible, the fire-and-brimstone part.

I have for many, many years been a big reader of the Old Testament. I've always thought this was a very interesting book, all these versions of these events. As Allen Ginsberg said about *Jack's Book*,* "My god, it's just like *Rashomon*—everybody lies and the truth comes out!!" With the

**Jack's Book: An Oral Biography of Jack Kerouac*, Barry Gifford and Lawrence Lee (New York: St. Martin's Press, 1978).

Bible, you could turn that around: Everybody gives their version of the truth. And what is it really? Is it all lies?

Kerouac you've named as a literary influence, along with B.Traven, Jack London, Conrad, Flaubert, others.

Kerouac was a great inspiration. Not his autobiographical style, but he was a great inspiration. And he was another one who had his own universe to inhabit and to write about, and he created his own legend.

Kerouac said of his work, "The whole thing frames an enormous comedy . . . the world of raging action and folly and also gentle sweetness seen through the keyhole of his eye." Does your work form one big whole?

I think the novels that I wrote, beginning with *Wild at Heart*, those six novels and novellas: *Perdita Durango, Sailor's Holiday, Sultans of Africa, Consuelo's Kiss, Bad Day for the Leopard Man*, and then continuing with what I call the Southern Nights trilogy, harder-edged books—*Night People, Arise and Walk, Baby Cat-Face*—and then finally *The Sinaloa Story*, all of these written within a decade, they certainly form a coherent whole, for me. I was dealing with the things that were bothering me in America. Religious fundamentalism. Racism, which is the biggest wound of all. And basically I was dealing with relations between men and women, women and women, men and men. In other words I was really playful at times, but writing a kind of violent satire, to better make my point. I think that there definitely is a connection among all those books.

Kerouac uses the particular word comedy—

Yeah, but he was taking from Balzac, the *Comédie Humaine*. And William Saroyan, who was another great influence on Kerouac, also wrote *The Human Comedy*.

And the word suggests that these writers wanted to capture a particular quality of existence, of the human predicament, and that is why they wrote. Is that why you write?

Well, I suppose I'm just trying to make sense out of everything, a futile enterprise. Certainly I think that many of my books are comic novels. Not everybody sees it that way. But there's a lot of funny stuff in those books. I mean even with violence, and strange sexual goings on and what not, these books are full of comedy.

In Kerouac's case, being a Catholic Buddhist as he was, and knowing that the motto of his family was "Live, Work, and Suffer," you're seeing everything through a veil of tears, so you'd better laugh to keep from crying.

You're reflecting the world around you, what you see. B. Traven was a profound influence on me, too, early on.

Traven was famously self-abnegating, believed that the life of the writer meant nothing, that the work was everything. Do you see it the same way?

That professed opinion of Traven's was slightly disingenuous. I believe he was not entirely sincere if and when he said this. He was living in Mexico and had an interest in covering up his tracks, disguising himself due to his own radical political past in Germany.

The work is what always matters certainly. Because we're here now, I'm alive, you're alive, we can sit here and we can talk and that's worth something. But no matter what I say I can't explain all of this. The work is either going to survive for a while or it's not. Either I've made a contribution that makes sense to some people, enough people to keep it alive, or not. I've been pretty lucky so far.

So writing started out for you as a means of seeing the world. But then the writing takes over, outlasts, supersedes experience.

Is that a question?

No.

Certainly, what you do, how you spend your time, all of that, sometimes intrudes on the writing as well as informs. Fiction means you made it up. And there are no rules here. It doesn't matter if you took six weeks, six months, six years, sixteen years, or sixty years to write a book. It's either good or it's bad. It either works or it doesn't. The world isn't waiting for the next great book. You really have to have a passion, you have to be obsessed, this is what it comes down to.

The tough part about this is if you don't have any chops, if you don't have any talent, if you don't have any luck—all of these things—if you get sidetracked by drugs, women, horses, whatever it happens to be, you don't do it.

So there's passion and there's discipline.

Exactly. There's passion, there's discipline and you do need a certain amount of good fortune. But I think that you basically make your own fortune, good or bad. I'm not exactly a big believer in predestination, the way Conrad seemed to be. And I'm not very analytical about the writing itself. I'm not very good talking about it.

You don't know what the next book will be?

I don't plan these things, to tell you the truth. Probably some people would say well, it shows. But that's part of it for me. I like to be surprised, I like the mystery of it all. I'm really as curious as anybody else about what comes next, and how it's delivered.

How extensively do you roadmap, plan the interlocking characters and themes? How much is on the fly?

One thing leads to the next. That's the best way I can describe it. When I came toward the end of *Wild at Heart*, Perdita Durango, one of the characters, began taking over. She was such a strong presence that I had to do everything I could to suppress just dropping Sailor and Lula and writing about Perdita, but I was able to bring her in at the end of *Wild at Heart* and then go on and write a whole novel about her. One thing just led to the next.

Then finally one day, six or seven hundred pages later, because it really is one book [*The Wild Life of Sailor and Lula*], even though I at first published them separately, I saw a very tiny little item in the newspaper. And it said, "Sailor dies in car wreck."

I see it, it's right here, on the wall [in BG's studio].

That's all it took. That was the sign. I saw it, and then I knew how the last novella, *Bad Day for the Leopard Man*, was going to end. However, I did bring Sailor and Lula back again, in *Baby Cat-Face*, as a prequel to *Wild at Heart*, when they were younger. So there are all kinds of ways to do it.

An advantage of the Reader *is that people have parts from most of the novels in one place, and can go in the order they want. Where should one start?*

This is an impossible question for me to answer because, like I say, I've written in different forms; various readers are partial to certain books and not others. There's certainly a choice out there, it's not all the same. Where to begin is anybody's guess.

I always like to think that the *next* book is the best book, the next book that I'm writing is the place to begin.

I will say that my personal favorite among all of these books is *Wyoming*. I think there's the most truth in it, for me.

Wyoming is a state of mind. It's a dream. It's an idyll. It's a place where the little boy dreams of having a big ranch, a place to run with his dog, which he doesn't really have. He lives in hotels. His mother is generally unhappy with her life, and they're in this hermetic situation in this car, driving in the South and the Midwest in the 1950s. And so Wyoming is a place where neither of them has ever been. It's a mythic place for them. And they agree upon Wyoming as a place where perhaps they can go some day, and then they'll be happy. It's a panacea, a Shangri-La. Wyoming is not real. It's an idyllic state of mind, not the state itself. This novel was for me a way of not only recapturing time passed but reinventing it, to make it live again albeit with a difference, a different kind of truth.

What about within each novel? Do you do much revising?

When I write a novel, I don't necessarily plan it out, I don't know what's going to happen. But as I go, things occur to me and I note them down, on another piece of paper or in the margins, so that I'm going to get to that part. And that's as much as I'm willing to do. I've never made an outline in my life.

I'll say this much. I write in longhand. Then I reread it. As I reread it, I make changes. Those are two drafts. Then I move it to the typewriter. I still use a manual typewriter. On the typewriter it undergoes another change. Three drafts. Then I reread that. I make changes, by hand most of the time. Four drafts. Then I make a final copy, on the manual typewriter again. That's the fifth draft. If you then include changes which might be made in galley proofs—that could be six, even seven drafts.

Now people write on computers, people work in different ways. I never even owned an electric typewriter. I didn't like the hum; I didn't like the idea of being plugged into the wall. I didn't want the insistence of that. I don't want the computer staring at me. To me it's very tactile, writing is a physical event, it's a physical activity. I like to hold the paper and the pencil or the pen. It's corporeal. It's a living being, the manuscript. I wouldn't know what to do without it.

It's really much more like fucking, because my own feeling is if I wrote on the computer to me that would be like masturbating.

Not getting all that you could out of it?

Not getting the real thing. Although I know that Flaubert was considered a mad masturbator, would masturbate as he wrote, not to waste any time, have to get up from the desk—that's not what I'm talking about. You understand the difference.

Same thing with poems?

Same way.

Your writing contains numerous scathing depictions of organized religion. Especially in the Southern Nights *novels, with the likes of Dallas Salt and his Church on the One Hand, and Mother Bizco's Temple of the Few Washed Pure by Her Blood. Then Wig Hat Tippo Jr., a charac-ter in* Baby Cat-Face, *says "Shit, Jimbo, time peoples get a clue. Orga-nize religion be dangerous to dey health. Ought to da gov'ment put warnin' signs on churches, same as on cigarettes." Is this Barry Gifford talking?*

I would say that Wig Hat Tippo speaks for me.

Let's just say that the books are filled with fear and trembling. Or fear and loathing. There's so much hypocrisy. We've seen this in our lifetime so many times. The hypocritical acts of so-called religious men and women, people who supposedly have an answer, are guides through the wilderness, through belief or disbelief. And I don't buy any of it. I never have. I don't know where this cynicism came from exactly, but I saw the way the world worked very early, with my father and his friends. These were people who were trying to control others, and their circumstances.

I have no great ontological explanation for you. I don't believe in *any* answer, so I'm not looking for one.

It's not just organized religion in the books. Also there are the militant feminist groups, like Hilda Brausen's Brausenkriegers and Marble Lesson's Mary Mother of God group, and Big Betty and Miss Cutie's Raptured Holy Brides of Ms. Jesus.

You notice that the heroes of most all of these books are women. Heroines, I should say.

And the villains.

Yes, but they have an agenda that's more justifiable, in a way.

It's the women who somehow triumph, whether it's Lula Fortune, or Zenoria Rapides, or it's Marble Lesson. I don't know why that is exactly.

And anybody who's reading these novels . . .

Perhaps that's why so many of my readers are women, that they come to the readings . . . they have thanked me. This has been gratifying and unexpected. Certain people are relating to it, responding to it in a way that has meaning for them, not just for me, and that's important, it helps to keep me going.

What about all of these violent things that happen to the men in your books? Are you a man-hater?

Not at all.

They're getting "cantalouped," castrated, shot, beheaded.

Yes, but what's been happening to women, or people of color? I mean, I'm not the most politically correct person on the face of the earth. Nor do I ever hope to be. I'm just observing. This is not necessarily my philosophy. Like Hamlet says to Horatio—and Bram Stoker later used this in *Dracula*: "There are more things in heaven and earth than are dreamt of in your philosophy." Well, I take this seriously.

Are your novels topical? The section of Night People *entitled "The Secret Life of Insects" seems to make a case for abortion rights.* Arise & Walk *features the assassinations of two racist provocateurs.*

Everything I have to say about race and religion and politics is in the novels. I'm interested individually in what drives people, what motivates them, how they react in particular situations. I've seen all manner of behavior, good, bad and indifferent. We all have, it's just that some people choose to ignore or blind themselves to some or much of it.

In many of the books of modern fiction I read, people are scratching at scabs that are too insignificant to even bother about.

Which do you consider the greater conflict, that within the individual or that between individuals?

What's on the inside comes out.

I think that people are motivated by fear, they're insecure, and it's expressed in different ways. Some people have a mania to control others, to control their environment.

Look what happens when you have the religious zealots running the country. Look what's happening now. It's The Crusades all over again. They never quit, these fucking people! It's just fear and trembling all over again. And that's what I'm writing about in those books. That's why I changed, in a way, in 1997.

I can't inhabit that universe forever, I can't do it intellectually. It becomes a vacuum and you're just never gonna have a good time again.

*In a way your most recent books—*The Phantom Father *and* Wyoming*—represent a return to simplicity, to works of the self, writing like* Landscape With Traveler, *your first novel.*

I'm just writing [in the middle novels] about how certain people see the world. It's personal in another way. I'm always reminded of a quote from Pound's *Cantos*. He recounted a conversation between Aubrey Beardsley and William Butler Yeats. Yeats said to Beardsley, "Beardsley, why do you draw such horrors?" And the illustrator replied, "Beauty is difficult, Yeats." This told me, really, the truth about a lot of things.*

Is a gritty book, such as one of the Southern Nights *novels, a depiction of beauty?*

No, I think it's a catalogue of horrors. Not so much with Sailor and Lula, they're two innocents, naïve, going through the world, and the shit is raining down from the sky and some of it's gonna fall on them. And then they're going to be forced to deal with it. That's how most of us go through life.

However, beginning with *Night People* and going through *The Sinaloa Story*, the books get progressively harder.

What do you mean by harder? To read? To understand?

Less compromising, in certain ways. And in some ways really a kind of a catalogue of one unspeakable act after another. But if you inhabit that universe all the time, it starts to wear on you. It's like I used to hear when I was a kid: "If you walk like a duck and talk like a duck and you're seen constantly in the company of other ducks, I can only assume that you, too, are a duck."

Meaning?

[Author quack-quacks]

How do you spell that?

*See *Canto LXXX*

Q-u-a, Q-u-a, Q-u-a, as Beckett has in *Godot*. Qua qua qua qua. I want to see how you transcribe that one.

Me, too.

In a 1975 letter to your friend and literary confidant Marshall Clements, you wrote: "There are so many weird things that go on out there, you don't have to make it up. It's going on all the time."

In fact I say this all the time. Obviously [by 1975] I had already drawn my conclusions.

The books are realistic, however. These things do happen. I've had detectives in Oakland, New York, New Orleans, tell me the most horrifying stories of things that they've seen, first-hand, that I can't even begin to approach in these novels.

You told me once about a reader who found a particular scene in Arise and Walk, *where a rat bites the nipple of a breastfeeding mother, so offensive that he quit reading the book.*

This was an old acquaintance of mine; he thought I was being sensational, that I used it just to get a reaction. "How could you make this stuff up?" he said. Well, I didn't make it up. It was told to me by a painter who grew up in New York, in a tenement, and as a child had witnessed this very thing.

So how to say whether you made it up, or whether it's based on a story somebody told you, or something that you saw—it doesn't really matter. Was I complaining about poverty? Was I talking about man's inhumanity to man? What was I talking about? Rats have to eat too? He had a political agenda, and this was not consistent with his idea about how to proselytize.

In Arise and Walk *the escaped con, Ice D, reads a century-old poem written by another African-American desperado, Rufus Buck. Ice-D wonders, "How could a man, black, white, or brown . . . do such terrible things as Rufus Buck apparently did, and then express himself in such tender fashion?" Is this a question you answer in your writing?*

I'm just stating a fact. Because of circumstances in the world, Rufus Buck was forced to behave the way he behaved. He was put into a context in which he was in effect made to behave in a certain fashion if he wanted to survive—after his own definition of survival. And so it's no mystery at all that he could also be compassionate, be generous, be tender-hearted.

Do you have a favorite character from your books?

This is a very tough question. I really think that Lula is my favorite because she's a little nutty, she's not a hypocrite, and she's generous, and she's a survivor. I really care about her for this. She's really not a victim. And the fact that she is not a victim and never sees herself as a victim is in itself a victory. And people who see themselves as victims are anathema to me.

Do you believe in victimhood, ever?

Oh, it's a religion! I mean, forget those people. Keep them the hell away from me. That's all I have to say about that.

Are you taking more risks now?

I never thought I was doing anything but taking risks. But I didn't think of myself as particularly brave. I was just doing what it was that I could do. I tried at various times, certainly very early on, to write in different styles, to make money and what not. I found that I was an unsuccessful prostitute. I was really incapable of writing to order because I believed that writing was my vocation. I don't want to sound holier than thou, I'm not, it's just that I was really bad at it. One time somebody offered me $400 to write a little semi-pornographic soft-core paperback book. I had known a couple of writers, poets who had done this quite successfully, written a bunch of them under pseudonyms. I couldn't get past page two. I mean I really couldn't do it. It just bored me to tears. I couldn't imagine doing it.

Better to make money driving a truck, work on a ship, work in the pipeyard, work in the woods, something completely divorced from my real work.

Is writing a radical act?

There's nothing radical about it. It's part of the fabric of who I am, as I've been explaining all along. I don't think in these terms, radical or reactionary. When it occurs to me to tell a story, I do it. I write it. The form is dictated to me by the inspiration itself.

Is there a Barry Gifford style?

You tell me, you're the critic.

I've heard you deny it.

People have said there is, so there may be, I don't know. André Gide said an interesting thing. With each new book the writer should understand, and be almost intentionally willing to lose fifty percent of the audience that he had for the previous book. Because he's going to go on. And fifty percent of the readers that he had for the previous book didn't understand him in the first place. They bought the book for a multitude of reasons, but not really because they understood the writer himself, what he was saying, what he was doing. The thing is to not worry about it; the fifty percent that did understand you, and are interested in the way your mind works, will follow you to the next book, and you'll pick up the other fifty percent along the way. In other words, don't be afraid to change, don't be afraid to follow your own mind, your instincts. I guess that's what I've been attempting to do all this time.

I want to talk about your film work. You've written numerous screenplays and thus far have had two novels, Wild at Heart *and* Perdita Durango, *made into films. How did you first start working with filmmakers?*

In 1982, *Port Tropique* was bought for the movies. The producers asked me to write a screenplay, which I did, having never written a screenplay before. I got a couple of screenplays and I read them.

They didn't like what I wrote. Then the producers hired a couple of other writers to write two or three different screenplays after that. There was a director involved in the project who collaborated with the screenwriters, but each script was worse than the one before.

By the third screenplay, they'd changed the title of the novel, which they'd always professed to love, and was ostensibly untouchable, to *Oil and Water*, which was about as good a phrase I can think of to describe how I was getting along with the producers and the putative director for this movie.

Soon after that, a producer at 20th Century Fox hired me to be a consultant on [another] project, and I came up with different ideas for him.

You said you started reading screenplays more often. Did this reading influence your writing?

Not at all. It's odd that I never did read screenplays. Perhaps in those days there weren't so many easily available. I'd had this great affection for movies since I was a boy. I don't know why I hadn't read screenplays before.

And then, in 1989, *Wild at Heart* was bought for the movies and after that I was asked to write screenplays on a regular basis.

Did you have reservations about adapting your work to film? Were you worried that the filmmakers might degrade your work?

Nobody can degrade *my* work. The book is always the book, the book exists on its own. There is a certain danger, because more people see movies than read books, and they have a greater influence these days, that the film can influence people's thinking . . . but the book is always the book. David [Lynch, director of *Wild at Heart*] didn't do anything to my novel. The novel's still the novel—read it.

In the mid-1980s you started Black Lizard Books, which printed noir fiction, crime novels and the like. What's the story behind that?

Black Lizard began publishing in 1984 and ended in 1989.

In 1982, on a trip to Paris, I went into a bookstore and I saw all these novels by Jim Thompson in print. I had read Jim Thompson when I was a young teenager, and remembered *The Killer Inside Me* and others.

So I bought up a bunch of these books and read them. And then I started trying to find them in English. I went to a friend of mine, who was a publisher, Don Ellis, and suggested to him that we publish a *série noire*, books that have a very particular psychological edge, and that we ought to start with Jim Thompson, because he was out of print in America. He liked the idea, and Don became the publisher of Black Lizard Books.

I set about to obtain the rights, and I acquired thirteen Jim Thompson novels for next to nothing. Because we had nothing. We had fifty cents, a pencil and a telephone. And I was the founding editor. We decided to make them like the old fashioned Gold Medal paperbacks but with a higher quality. Only the rights to the *The Killer Inside Me* were owned already. We did all the others. And some were made into movies. *The Grifters*, which was produced by Martin Scorsese, a couple others. This popularized Jim Thompson all over again.

We also published Charles Willeford, Charles Williams, David Goodis, and a few new writers. We did eighty-two books in four-and-a-half years.

Black Lizard was an amusing but important sidelight for me, an area of interest, just like horseracing.

You said you were reading Jim Thompson when you were a young teen. How would you describe the influence of this kind of writing on your own?

Take writers like Jim Thompson or David Goodis, or Charlie Willeford. These were guys who wrote about a lower echelon of society, they wrote about the people who were downtrodden, the people who were usually ignored. Characters who might stick up a liquor store or rape their father. They lent these people humanity. They wrote about them not as stereotypes but as real, living, breathing human flesh. And this is what I admired so much about them. Mostly these people they were writing about were dismissed out of hand. And this gave them a voice. Not unlike what Nelson Algren did. With just a little difference, or less literary talent, Nelson Algren could have been one of these guys. Women were also writing in this field at this time, often using male pseudonyms.

What's the difference?

Algren was a better writer. I mean, Charlie Willeford could be a great writer. *The Burnt Orange Heresy*, which was one of the first ones we published, is a brilliant book, and very well written and as literary a novel as you'll run across. But the first time around these books were mostly published as paperback originals; they weren't reviewed very often, they were not taken seriously, for the most part, by the literary critics. I read them as a teenager, buying them on the wire rack at the drug store or the bus station. That's the only place you could find them. They had lurid, provocative covers.

Why is a book like *Night People* published as literature, or fiction, taken seriously, and why is a novel of Charles Willeford's, or Jim Thompson's, for example, considered crime writing? What's the story? Or Elliott Chaze's great novel *Black Wings Has My Angel*? That's a terrific novel. I mean, it's just a novel; but because of the form in which it was published it was just not seriously considered. That's too bad.

Are you concerned about the state of literature?

It's like the state of Wyoming, isn't it? In my novel. It's a kind of ideal, a place that we don't really know about. How could I be concerned about the state of literature? It's an absurd idea.

To me, the writing of so-called literature is really a very subjective thing. You can understand it or like it or appreciate it on your own terms. You have to be prepared to understand or appreciate it or not. Also, it's not a competitive sport. There are different voices for different people.

It's not my place and not my inclination, anyway, to make pronouncements about anything so grandiose as "the state of literature." If you ask me, do I think so-and-so is a good writer, I'll tell you yes or no and I'll tell you why, *if* I've read them. That's the best I can do. Other than that, I'm only concerned with my own work.

SOUTHERN NIGHTS

"There's something wild in the country
that only the night people know . . . "

—Tennessee Williams
Orpheus Descending

from NIGHT PEOPLE (1992)

APACHES

BIG BETTY STALCUP KISSED Miss Cutie Early on the right earlobe as Cutie drove, tickling her, causing Cutie to swerve the black Dodge Monaco toward the right as she scratched at that side of her head.

"Dammit, Bet, you shouldn't ought do that while I'm wheelin'."

Big Betty laughed and said, "We're kissin' cousins, ain't we? Sometimes just I can't help myself and don't want to. Safety first ain't never been my motto."

Cutie straightened out the car and grinned. "Knowed that for a long time," she said.

"Knowed which? That we was kissin' cousins?"

"Uh uh, that come later. About the safe part. You weren't never very predictable, Bet, even as a child."

Big Betty and Miss Cutie had spent the week in New Orleans, then the weekend in Gulf Shores, Alabama, and were headed back into Florida at Perdido Key. The Gulf of Mexico was smooth as glass this breezeless, sunny morning in February.

"Jesus H. Christ, Cutie, tomorrow's Valentine's Day!"

"So?"

"We'll have to make somethin' special happen."

"Last Valentine's we was locked up at Fort Sumatra. Spent the whole day bleachin' blood and piss stains outta sheets."

"Still can't believe we survived three and change in that pit."

"Don't know if I'd made it without you, Bet. Them big ol' mamas been usin' me for toilet paper, you weren't there to protect me."

Big Betty shifted her five-foot-eight, two-hundred-pound body around in the front passenger seat so that she faced Cutie Early. At twenty-four, Cutie was twelve years younger than Betty, and Miss Cutie's slim-figured five-foot-one-inch frame engendered in Big Betty a genuinely maternal feeling. They had been lovers ever since Miss Cutie had tiptoed into Big Betty's cell at the Fort Sumatra Detention Center for Wayward Women, which was located midway between Mexico Beach and Wewahitchka, Florida, just inside the central time zone. Cutie's curly red hair, freckles, giant black eyes and delicate features were just what Betty Stalcup had been looking for. It was as if the state of Florida penal system had taken her order and served it up on a platter. Big Betty brushed back her own shoulder-length brown hair with her left hand and placed her other hand on Cutie's right breast, massaging it gently.

"You're my baby black-eyed pea, that's for sure," said Betty. "We ain't never gonna be apart if I can help it."

"Suits me."

"Cutie, we just a couple Apaches ridin' wild on the lost highway, the one Hank Williams sung about."

"Don't know that I've ever heard of it."

"Travelin' along the way we are, without no home or reason to be or stay anywhere, that's what it means bein' on the lost highway. Most folks don't know what they want, Cutie, only mostly they don't even know that much. Sometimes they think they know but it's usually just their stomach or cunt or cock complainin'. They get fed or fucked and it's back to square one. Money makes 'em meaner'n shit, don't we already know. Money's the greatest excuse in the world for doin' dirt. But you and me can out-ugly the sumbitches, I reckon."

"How's that?"

"Just by puttin' two and two together, sweet pea, then subtractin' off the top, one at a time."

"I ain't sure I understand you, Bet, but I'm willin' to learn."

Big Betty threw back her head, shut her wolfslit green eyes and gave out a sharp laugh.

"Young and willin's the best time of life," she said. "You got to play it that way till you can't play it no more."

"Then what?" asked Cutie.

Big Betty grinned, threw her heavy left arm around Cutie's narrow shoulders and squeezed closer to her companion.

"Start cuttin' your losses," she said. "All that's left to do."

"Along with cuttin' throats, you mean."

"Why, Miss Cutie, honey, you way ahead of me."

BIG BETTY, HOW IT HAPPENED

DUBUQUE "BIG BOY" STALCUP, Betty's father, was fully grown at six-foot-six, two hundred thirty-five pounds by the time he was sixteen. He was raised on a south Georgia farm next to the Suwanoochee Creek close to the point at which the Suwannee River crawls out of the Okefenokee Swamp. The Stalcup place wasn't so much a farm, really, as a junkyard hideout for criminals. Big Boy's father and mother, Mayo and Hilda Sapp, maintained an infamous safe house for thieves, moonshiners and killers on the run. Whenever the law got up enough nerve to invade the Stalcup sanctuary, which was not often, the various fugitives in residence used a secret trail to the swamp, where they would remain until one of the Stalcup kids came to tell them it was safe to come back. The Stalcups made no real attempt to work their land, which had been homesteaded in 1850. The War Between the States passed the Stalcup clan by; they were too remote and the males considered extraordinarily crazy and too dangerous by those few who were acquainted with them to be pressed into service of the Confederacy.

Big Boy and his wife, Ella Dukes, had four children, of which Betty was the youngest and also the only girl. Her three brothers, Sphinx, Chimera and Gryphon—each of whose names were chosen by Big Boy from *Bulfinch's Mythology*, the only book other than the Bible that he owned—never left the farm. Betty, named by Ella after her grandmama, Elizabeth Hispaniola, a niece of the Seminole warlord Osceola, had run off at the age of fourteen with Duval and Sordida Head, a brother and sister from Cross City, Florida, who had robbed a bank in Valdosta and paid the Stalcups to hide them. Their descriptions of city life intrigued Betty, and she agreed to leave with them when they felt the time was right. Betty never said goodbye to her parents or brothers and never returned to the farm.

After Duval had used her several times, he tired of Betty and passed her to his sister, whose sexual proclivities involved mainly the participation of women and dogs. Sordida introduced the adolescent Betty, who at fourteen was already a rather large person, to the delights of female love, which Betty found preferable to the rough ways of the men who had handled her—namely her brothers, who had deflowered their sister when she was nine and subsequently took their pleasure with her whenever one or more of them felt the urge, and Duval Head. Betty told Sordida that Sphinx, Chimera and Gryphon really preferred cornholing one another anyway, and figured she'd hardly be missed.

Big Betty stayed with the Heads for a few months, during which time they knocked off dozens of convenience stores and gas stations and burglarized homes all over the state of Florida. Duval and Sordida went off one day to rob a bank in Fort Walton Beach, leaving Betty to wait for them in the Greyhound bus station, and they never returned. A man and his wife who were traveling to Miami gave Betty enough money for a ticket to New Orleans, a city that for no reason she could think of Betty told the couple was her destination. Betty never did learn that both Duval and Sordida had been killed in a head-on crash with an eighteen-wheel Peterbilt transporting commodes when Duval drove their 1972 Dodge Coronet onto an off ramp of Interstate 10 while attempting to elude a police car in hot pursuit.

Betty found work in New Orleans as an exotic dancer at the Club Spasm on Opelousas Avenue in Algiers. She was big enough to pass for twenty-one and nobody questioned her. Between her dancing gig and turning occasional tricks on the side, Betty did all right. She stayed away from drugs and alcohol, neither of which particularly agreed with her, and entered into a series of lesbian relationships with other dancers and prostitutes. Many of the women with whom Betty consorted were married or had boyfriends, a situation to Betty's liking; she was not interested in committing herself to any one person and discovered that she enjoyed living alone. Privacy, a condition she had never truly experienced either at home or on the road with the Heads, was her greatest pleasure.

Eventually, Betty moved on to Houston, then Dallas, where she took a small caliber bullet in her left ankle from a drunken patron named Feo Lengua, an illegal from Nueva Rosita, while she was dancing onstage at Rough Harvey's Have Faith Sho-Bar. After she was shot, Betty's days as an exotic dancer were finished, and she worked as a bartender, card dealer, waitress, seamstress, car wash cashier and hooker—just about anything and everything, as she drifted from Texas back through Louisiana and Mississippi to Alabama and Florida.

It was in Orlando, where she was working in a janitorial capacity, cleaning up a medical building after hours, that Betty was brutally raped and beaten by two male co-workers one night on the job. Betty reported the attack to the police, who several days later informed her that there was insufficient evidence to pursue the case. She bought a Beretta .25 caliber automatic at Emmett's Swap City off the Orange Blossom Trail near the Tupperware International headquarters, went to the apartment of one of her assailants, a glue-sniffing freak named Drifton Fark, found him in an olfactory stupor, and shot him just below the heart. She then hunted down Drifton Fark's companion, Willie "Call Me Israel" Slocumb, a black man who claimed to be a Miccosukee Indian and who had converted from Disciples of Christ to Judaism after reading Sammy Davis, Jr's account of his own conversion in his autobiography, *Yes I Can!*, and shot him once in the right knee and again in the groin while he sat at the bar in The Blind Shall Lead Lounge across from the Flying Tigers Warbird Air Museum.

After Betty shot Willie "Call Me Israel" Slocumb and watched him drop to the floor, writhing in pain and clutching at his affected parts, she laid the Beretta on the bar and told the bartender to call the cops. She sat down on the stool next to the one that had been occupied by her most recent victim, picked up the glass he had been about to drink from prior to the interruption, and drained the contents, a double shot of Johnnie Walker Black on the rocks. Just before the police arrived, Betty told the bartender, "You know, that's the first time liquor really tasted decent to me."

Betty was sent to the Fort Sumatra Detention Center for Wayward Women, where, until she met up with Cutie Early, she kept mostly to herself. Miss Cutie was the one for her, all right, Betty decided, the only person she could rely on forever and ever, her ideal friend. Betty had an agenda, of course, but Cutie, Big Betty vowed, would always rate just as high on the big chart of life as she did herself.

SNOWBALLS

"How about that five-hundred-pound man got caught at the Miami airport attemptin' to smuggle more'n three hundred grams of crack cocaine under the tremendous folds of his stomach? Dogs sniffed out the dope—shepherds. Boy'll lose most that weight in prison, prob'ly be the second best thing coulda happened to him. Come out a new man."

Vernon Duke Douglas glanced at his Timex. Only twenty minutes until the plane would land at Tallahassee and he would not have to listen any longer to the woman seated next to him. She was about his own age, rail-thin, a brunette with green eyes and not entirely unattractive, but she had not stopped talking since before the aircraft had taken off from New Orleans. Her name was Petronia Weatherby, and she had introduced herself to Duke by saying, "I'll tell you my name, but you've got to promise not to ask, 'What will the weather be?' Or, 'What be the weather?' I hear it all the time." She had told Duke the purpose of her trip but he had already discharged the information from his memory bank.

"Conversation makes a flight go quicker, don't it, Mr Douglas?" said Petronia. "You're not, now it occurs to ask, by any chance related to the movie-actin' Douglases, are you?"

"No, I'm not."

"Wouldn't I be somethin' lucky, you had. Couldn't control myself if I met someone really famous. I'd pee my pants in a whore's hurry, I know. I'm like that. Somethin' really wild happens? I just pee away. You know I ain't never seen snow, for example? Ice don't count; I mean real actual snow fall down. I ever do, I'll pee my pants. I'd die to throw a snowball, really I would."

"Comets are snowballs," said Duke.

"You mean those things shoot through the interplanetary air?"

Duke nodded. "They're composed of frozen gases, mostly carbon dioxide, methane or water vapor. Very little solid material. Their behavior is that of a ball of frozen gas being heated by the sun."

"I tell you, Mr Douglas, I figured you for a scientific type right off, but now I see you're even a deeper person than most persons I've encountered on planes. Mind if I ask you a particularly scientific question?"

"Go ahead."

"Do women think different from men? I mean, their brain work another way? Technically speakin', that is."

Duke laughed. "I can't say, Ms Weatherby. But I do know that dialogue between men and women seems to have about the consistency of a snowball. Some contain more ice than others, of course."

Petronia stared hard at Duke, her green eyes narrowing. He thought she was about to hiss.

"Now quick, before we land," she said, "I want to know the truth. Can there really be such a thing as a snowball in hell?"

MIDNIGHT EVERYWHERE

EASY EARL DROVE the Mercury Monarch slowly, no more than twenty miles per hour, along St. Claude Avenue in New Orleans. It was eleven fifty-eight P.M., almost Wednesday, raining again. Thunderstorms day and night, lately. Earl switched on his wipers. The personalized license plates on his fire engine red 1978 Merc read EZY EARL, not EASY because there could be only seven figures, not eight, but it was good enough for Earl, whose last name was Blakey, like the great jazz drummer's. Earl, who was forty-six years old and never married, was headed from his house on St Roch to his job at the post office on Camp Street, where he worked as a truck loader. His shift began at midnight and he knew he would be a little late, but he could blame the rain.

The car radio was tuned to WWOZ. Sam Cooke and the Soul Stirrers were singing "That's Heaven to Me." Terrible about Sam Cooke gettin' taken out like he did, thought Earl. Shot down by a old lady in a motel. Woman claimed he been abusin' a girl. Man sure did have a beautiful voice.

The record ended and the deejay said: "It's a new day in the Crescent City. From Florida comes news of two women being held on suspicion of a series of murders, all of men, dating back to last year. Bettina Stalcup and Carol Early were taken into custody today in Pensacola on murder charges ranging across the states of Florida, Alabama and Louisiana. Authorities say the women, both ex-convicts, claim to be brides of Jesus, whom the suspects insist was also a woman. 'Miss Jesus,' they say, ordered them to rid the world of the male species. 'Men is beyond the point of being reeducated. The disease has spread too far,' said Ms Stalcup. 'It is midnight everywhere for them.' "

Easy Earl shook his head, pulled a Kool from his shirt pocket, stuck it between his lips and punched in the dashboard lighter.

"Mm, mm," he mumbled, "sure as shit some righteous bitches out there."

JOHN BROWN'S WISH

BEATIFICA BROWN HAD FIRST HEARD the song about John Brown when she was a child, but the lyrics meant nothing to her until she found her vocation. Many times each day Beatifica sang to herself, "*John Brown's body lies a-mouldering in the grave.*" She kept among her few belongings F.B. Sanborn's book *Life and Letters of John Brown*, published in 1885, and had been for eight years making notes toward the composition of a monograph entitled *John Brown and the Divine Notion.* Beatifica's treatise was based on Wendell Phillips's identification of "letters of marque from God" as the foundation of John Brown's conviction that he was entitled to destroy slavery by violent means.

John Brown, a descendant of *Mayflower* Puritans, had been born in Connecticut and raised in Ohio, and at the age of forty-nine he moved to the state of New York, where he farmed land contiguous to that worked by black settlers. He had already made plain his hatred of slavery, and soon thereafter John Brown joined five of his sons in Kansas, the border state from which he launched his active campaign of opposition to the odious institution. Following bloody confrontations with pro-slavers in Kansas, John Brown led his followers to Canada, Massachusetts and finally to Virginia, where his plan was to establish a stronghold in which fugitive slaves could take refuge.

On the night of October 16, 1859, with only eighteen men, five of whom were Negro slaves, John Brown led an attack on a federal arsenal at Harpers Ferry. They captured the arsenal and took as hostages sixty of the town's leading citizens. The next two days saw the abolitionists laid siege to by a force of United States Marines, led by Colonel Robert E. Lee. The Marines ultimately overpowered the free-staters, killing ten of them, including two of John Brown's sons. Brown was captured, being seriously wounded after his surrender. Within the month he had been tried and found guilty of "treason, and conspiring and advising with slaves and other rebels, and murder in the first degree." On December 2, he was hanged. John Brown had fathered twenty children by two wives.

Beatifica felt a powerful connection to her nineteenth-century namesake, and was convinced that she also carried "letters of marque from God." Like John Brown, Beatifica had identified her immediate enemies, among whom was a militant pro-life New Orleans preacher named Dallas Salt, pastor of the non-sectarian Church on the One Hand, located on Elysian Fields Avenue. Dallas Salt's sister, Dilys, was an equally militant pro-choice preacher who had broken with Dallas over the abortion issue, and established her own ministry, the Church on the Other Hand, directly across the street from her brother's. Each Sunday, the Salt siblings exhorted their respective flocks to study against the opposition.

Beatifica had attended both congregations: Brother Dallas's Church on the One Hand in order to know her enemy at close quarters; and Sister Dilys's Church on the Other Hand to lend her support. It was Brother Dallas, of course, who had the larger ministry, and who was allowed access to the airwaves, broadcasting for an hour on radio station WGOD at midnight Sundays. The Church on the Other Hand was constantly under siege, its building regularly vandalized and its members, most of whom were women, threatened and terrorized. Sister Dilys was never left unguarded, her constant companions being several of the most rugged members of the Sisters of Clytemnestra Motorcycle Club.

Beatifica Brown knew that to be successful in her role she had to maintain a low profile, to carry out her mission with a minimum of attention. She was content to let others, such as Dilys Salt, carry on the fight in a public fashion, while she made her services available to all who were in need and proselytized as occasions arose.

On one wall of her room on Decatur Street, at the edge of the Quarter near Esplanade, Beatifica had hung a framed photograph of John Brown, his wild eyes burning in his bearded face. Across the bottom of her hero's picture she had written, "His Soul Goes Marching On." Beatifica knew it was she, the Unknown Warrior, who would assassinate Dallas Salt when John Brown spoke to her as she slept on her ninth night in New Orleans, their common number. Beatifica awoke, sat up in bed, shook her shoulder-length red hair, felt the length of her body shudder, nodded her head numerous times and said aloud, "Yes, yes, it is my wish also!"

VICTIMS OF RECEIVED INFORMATION

SISTER DILYS SALT STOOD at the podium in the Church on the Other Hand and surveyed her congregation. All 401 seats were occupied and another 100 people or so were wedged in around the sides and at the rear of the room. Loudspeakers had been set up outside to carry Sister Dilys's sermon to those forced by order of the Orleans Parish Fire

Department to remain on the church steps, at the foot of which were gathered approximately fifty protestors, anti-abortion activists who were present whenever Dilys spoke. A line of beefy Sisters of Clytemnestra insured that the demonstrators would not attempt to invade the premises, as they had done in the past.

"Sisters united!" Dilys began, as she always did. "And you all-too-few brothers in arms, welcome to the Church on the Other Hand. A warning to those of you out there who oppose us: Do not confuse body parts, namely hand with cheek. We will not turn or be turned! The neverending plague of ignorance is carried by victims of received information, unfortunates fallen prey to the Fear Riders. Be advised: The enlightened adherents to the beliefs of the Church on the Other Hand will not be trampled! We stand firm on the higher ground of free choice. There shall be no retreat to the shadows. No longer will it be our blood displayed on the swordblade! The One Hand falls as the Other Hand is raised! Then shall we say also unto them on the one hand, Depart from me, ye cursed, into everlasting fire, prepared for the devil and his angels."

While Dilys Salt's flock rocked to her pronouncements, Dallas Salt sat in his dressing room across the street, his eyes closed, as Fatima Verdad, a fifteen-year-old prostitute whom Sabine Yama had driven over from Algiers, stood behind him, massaging the preacher's ears and the back of his neck with her milk chocolate breasts while he masturbated. Fatima Verdad was extremely thin, in accordance with Dallas's preference, so her relatively large breasts were a bonus so far as he was concerned. Dallas pulled lazily at his semi-erect cock, completely relaxed, listening to Fatima hum.

"What's that tune, honey?" he asked.

"Wan' I stop?"

"No, no, baby. I like it. You know the name?"

"Be 'Things That Make You Go Hmmmm' by C & C Music Fac-t'ry."

"You sure do make me go hm-m. Lean over more, precious, put your sweet tits 'gainst my cheeks."

"I gon' be a singer, too," Fatima Verdad said, as she stood on her toes and lifted her breasts in her hands and rubbed the nipples on Dallas Salt's face. "A real one, though, not like some girl only dance an' preten' to sing."

The preacher stroked himself faster.

"I dance good as Paula Abdul, too. You like Paula Abdul? She cute but ain' got no tiddies."

"Come around now, baby," said Dallas. "Move quick, girl!"

Fatima, who was entirely naked except for a black velvet choker with a pearl cross on it that Sabine Yama had made her put on before bringing her in, knelt in front of Dallas Salt, as Sabine had instructed her to do when explaining the pastor's needs, and blew gently on the head of his penis as it grew fat and red. The prostitute kept her face still while Dallas Salt's semen pelted it, not flinching even when some flew into her left eye. After he had finished, the preacher rested for a few moments with his eyes shut, still holding his shrinking prick.

"You done fine, girl," he said, finally, looking at Fatima Verdad. "Sabine!" he shouted.

Sabine Yama came in from just outside the door, where he had been waiting.

"Show her where to clean up and give her some extra taxi money. How much time I got till the broadcast?"

"About fifteen minutes."

Sabine handed him a towel, which Dallas used to wipe off his hand and leg.

"Whew! Used to it didn't take so long gettin' primed," said Dallas, standing up.

He watched Fatima Verdad as she stepped into her panties.

"Bless you, honey," Dallas said. "Hope to hear you on the radio one of these days pretty soon."

Fatima smiled, showing big white teeth. "Be doin' it, with God's help."

Dallas nodded, and said, "Baby, He might could do worse."

NIGHTCAP AT RUBY'S CARIBBEAN

"SABINE, DARLIN', one more of these and I'll even go to bed with you!"

Jimmy Sermo and Sabine Yama were at Ruby's Caribbean Bar on Poland Avenue, drinking Bombay and listening to the jukebox. Little Johnny Taylor had just now wailed on "Love Bones" and Fabrice Dos Veces, the transsexual Cuban bartender, offered a free drink to whoever would play "Lookin' for a Love" by The Valentinos. Sabine hopped down from his stool, limped over, pushed a few quarters into the Rock-

Ola, and punched up Fabrice's request, along with "The Things That I Used to Do" by Guitar Slim and "Nite Owl" by Tony Allen and the Champs. By the time Sabine had climbed back onto his stool, there was a fresh Bombay on the rocks with a twist of lime waiting for him.

"*Gracias*, Sabine," said Fabrice, as Bobby Womack's sweaty voice surged into the room.

Jimmy Sermo slid off of his stool onto the floor and stayed there, curled up in a fetal position on the brown-and-white tiles. He was a short, thin man of thirty-one, with wavy blonde hair and hazel eyes that, due to his alcoholism, were bloodshot most of the time. Jimmy and Sabine had known each other since both had been child prostitutes, and they met occasionally at Ruby's Caribbean or the Saturn for drinks. Jimmy now worked in a laundromat on St Ann, his once angelic looks having deteriorated badly over the years. His disheveled and dissolute appearance disturbed Sabine, who had tried unsuccessfully to get Jimmy to seek the counsel of Dallas Salt.

The last time Sabine had suggested it, Jimmy Sermo said, "That faggot's your savior, not mine."

"Brother Dallas ain't a faggot," Sabine replied.

"All the more reason I ain't got no time for his mess," Jimmy said.

Fabrice Dos Veces, who was five-foot-two in her high heels and could barely see over the top of the bar, asked Sabine where Jimmy had got to.

"Sleepin' on the floor here, like a good boy."

"Tough for a man or a woman to get any peace these days," said Fabrice, wetting the tips of her index fingers with her tongue and smoothing down her thick black eyebrows before twisting them up at the ends.

Just as Guitar Slim gave it up to Tony Allen, the door opened and in walked Terry Perez and another member of the Sisters of Clytemnestra named Dogstyle Lou. Ruby's Caribbean was not a regular hangout for the Sisters, so Sabine and Fabrice were surprised to see them.

"You serve real women in here?" Dogstyle Lou asked Fabrice.

"We serve real drinks to real people who can pay for them," Fabrice said. "I don't guess you'd know a real woman if she squatted on this bar and pissed in your glass."

Dogstyle Lou, who was six-one and other than svelte, laughed hard and shook her close-cropped head.

"You know, Terry," she said, "that's what I love about New Orleans, the candor of its citizens. There really ain't another city in this country for tellin' it like it is, as old Aaron Neville never can quit remindin' us."

Dogstyle Lou looked at Sabine Yama and then noticed Jimmy Sermo sprawled on the floor.

"Nice place we done found here, though. Got a bartender don't know if it's Charo or Bela Lugosi, with a cadaver and a part-built dwarf for customers."

Terry Perez went over to Jimmy Sermo and nudged his head with the toe of her right boot.

"He's breathin', I think," she said.

Fabrice billyclubbed Dogstyle Lou so fast the large woman never saw it coming. Sabine grabbed Terry Perez around the throat with his one powerful good hand and squeezed until Terry lost consciousness, then allowed her to drop to the floor next to Jimmy Sermo and Dogstyle Lou. He swiveled back to the bar and finished his drink.

"Care for another, Sabine? On the house."

"No thanks, Fabrice. I'm drivin'."

Sabine twirled off the barstool, stepping carefully over the bodies.

"Be glad to help out here," he said.

"Not necessary, Sabine, but thanks. I can handle it. Do me a favor, though? On your way out."

"What's that?"

"Play 'Lookin' for a Love' again."

"You got it, Fabrice."

Sabine dropped in a quarter, pressed the letter *H* and the number *8*, and hit the street.

THE SECRET LIFE OF INSECTS

"You won't believe this, Brother Dallas."

"Believe what? Who's callin' on the damn phone at this ungodly hour, Sabine?"

"It's your sister, Dilys."

Dallas Salt took the portable phone from Sabine Yama and cradled it over the embroidered gold initials scripted on the breast pocket of his purple silk pajamas. He sat straight up in his bed as Sabine propped two pillows behind his back and head. Dallas cleared his throat before raising the receiver to his ear.

"Dilys? To what do I owe this pleasure? Do you know that it's three-thirty in the mornin'?"

"I know the time, Dallas, and there ain't no pleasure involved. I got bad news. Pillara's dead."

"How?"

"Mama said the people at the Thelma Cates Palestine House in Plain Dealin', where we been keepin' her these years, told her Pillara was on a picnic outin' to the Red River where a tarantula hawk flew into her left ear, got trapped and stung her. By the time they got to a doctor, Pillara was swole up worse'n a 4-H champion bull. Died at four P.M. this afternoon."

"Why'd you wait so long to call me?"

"Wasn't sure I was gonna call at all, seein's how you ain't paid no attention to our daughter since she was born. But I knew Mama would if I didn't, so I told her I would. Now I done it."

"Where's the funeral?"

"Ain't gonna be one. I told the Palestines to let Mama take her for burial in a field between Ida and Mira. That way Mama and her people can tend to the grave."

"What denomination is it?"

"What you suppose? Deep Bottom Baptist, like all Mama's folks."

"We should be there, Dilys. Say some words."

"Maybe be holdin' hands while the pine box is lowered, you think? Fuck you, Dallas."

Dilys hung up. Lightning streaked the sky outside Dallas's bedroom window, but there was no rain.

"Sabine?" said Dallas, passing the crippled Cajun-Pakistani the phone. "You recall that six-foot-tall quadroon female impersonator from Lake Charles moved to New Orleans last year? Name Mumbo Jumbo or somethin'?"

Sabine nodded. "Mumbo Degolas. She from Lake Arthur. Works at Chataignier's Monkey House in the Quarter."

"Call her for me, Sabine, if you please. See she can come 'round, do a favor. Tell her if I asleep when she get here, just start ahead, wake me up with them fat lips polishin' the knob."

"What about Dilys?"

"She never could give a decent blow job, Sabine. Teeth too big. You just go on, call Miss Mumbo."

Dallas rolled onto his left side and closed his eyes. He remembered a fellow he had been in the service with named Larry Lucca, an Italian boy born in Brooklyn, New York, who claimed he had an uncle from the old country who was afflicted with a disease called tarantism, a nervous condition characterized by melancholy, stupor and an uncontrollable desire to dance. Dallas wondered whether Larry Lucca's uncle had contracted his disease from the sting of a tarantula hawk wasp rather than from the bite of a tarantula spider, which the Lucca family believed had caused the malady.

As Dallas drifted off to sleep, he envisioned a young girl with slanted eyes and a broad, short skull sticking out her large tongue as she clumsily danced the tarantella.

PURPLE NOON

EVER SINCE JOHN BROWN'S VISITATION, Beatifica had eagerly awaited his return. Night after night she lay awake until exhaustion overtook her and she fell into a brief and troubled sleep. Beatifica thought it possible that the great man of her life had been waylaid by government agents fearful of the abolitionist's sworn intention to create "a host of Ossawatomies," violent actions directed against areas of recalcitrance concerning equality and progressive behavior. Since being recruited via telepathic communication into this resurgent force of enlightenment, Beatifica had meditated on the meaning of having been infected with the spirit of John Brown, and realized his desires now issued forth through her and others like her. Whether or not he came to her again, Beatifica knew she would rise to meet his expectations.

Every Saturday at noon, Dallas Salt kept an appointment at Dutz's Dancing Comb Barber Shop on Felicity Street. For weeks, Beatifica had surreptitiously observed the preacher's movements, and she decided that it would be in Dutz Sanglant's chair at the Dancing Comb that Brother Dallas's days were to be clipped short.

Following a particularly restless Friday night, Beatifica rose from her companionless sheets slightly after daybreak. It was a chilly, cloudy December 2, the anniversary of John Brown's hanging. The assassin assembled her weaponry, concealing the ordnance in a large canvas

Canal Place shopping bag. Beatifica dressed carefully, wearing a tie-dyed, 100-percent cotton T-shirt with the words WHEN DIPLOMACY FAILS printed on the front underneath a tan field-jacket liner. Over this she wore a night desert uniform with a random pattern of scattered dark olive drab splotches and grid lines on a lighter shade of olive drab. Around her waist Beatifica buckled a Type 13 nylon-webbed black aircraft belt, and over her head draped a polyester sniper face veil. She pulled on black Coolmax socks, Sta-Dri liners and a pair of olive drab breathable leather-and-cotton duck jungle boots with non-clogging Panama outsoles and web-reinforcement straps. She stood by the window and studied the sky, seeing no face among the clouds. Beatifica stayed in her room until eleven A.M., at which time she picked up her bag and began the trek toward Felicity Street.

Dallas Salt was in an unusually sour mood this morning. His sleep had been disturbed by a dream wherein Dilys, dressed in rags, approached him as he stood in front of his congregation on the stage of the Church on the One Hand, and when she opened her mouth as if to speak, a deformed baby emerged head first, falling to the ground at his feet. The baby uttered no sound, but twisted and writhed in apparent agony on the stage as Dallas's flock confronted him, chastising him for having committed an unholy act with his sister. At this point, Dilys was swallowed up by the advancing pack and disappeared. Dallas had awakened in a sweat, his arms stiff at his sides.

"Just a shave today, Dutz," Dallas said, as he assumed his position in the barber's chair. "I don't feel like sittin' for very long."

"Wad chew say, pasta," said Dutz Sanglant, a rail-thin, hairless man of fifty-five whose ocherous skin color betrayed his quarter-century addiction to Pernod. His childhood nickname had been "The Chihuahua."

As Dutz levered the chair backwards, Dallas Salt looked at the faithful Sabine Yama, who sat opposite him beneath the wall-length mirror, reading a back issue of *Soldier of Fortune* magazine, turning the pages with his one normal set of fingers. Dallas's stomach quivered and suddenly he felt nauseated, but he fought the urge to vomit and closed his eyes as the barber wrapped a hot towel around his face.

It was Sabine who first noticed the person, face swathed in see-through cloth, come through the door. Dutz ceased his ministrations as soon as he heard the crinkle of the shopping bag, and looked over just as the initial flash of metal disappeared into the preacher's pancreas. The next missile entered Dutz Sanglant's open mouth and penetrated through the rear of his skull into the wall behind him. A third arrow ripped part of Sabine Yama's face off, sending him to his knees. The fourth and final projectile pierced the leaking and listing pastor's heart, its tip sticking out the back of the chair, stabilizing the body.

As the shrouded figure turned away, the half-blind Yama managed to extricate from his belt a Beretta .25 automatic, which he directed the lethal end of toward the offender and fired as many times as he could before collapsing in pain and losing consciousness, his rent flesh resting on the worn, cool linoleum.

ALFONZO'S MEXICALI

Easy Earl Blakey cruised along Louisiana Avenue in his 1978 Mercury Monarch with all four windows down, his left arm hanging out to catch a breeze and his right hand on the steering wheel. It was Saturday night, just past ten, and Earl had decided to check out the scene at Alfonzo's Mexicali Club. He crossed La Salle Street, pulled over to the curb and parked. It was unseasonably warm for January in New Orleans, the temperature still in the mid-seventies and a humidity reading over eighty. At least two dozen black men of various ages lounged on the street in front of Porky Muette's Port in a Storm Liquor Store, drinking from or holding in one hand a short dog in a brown paper sack. Most of them eyeballed Earl as he got out of his car, which he did not bother to lock, leaving the windows down.

"Evenin', fellas," Easy Earl said, nodding in their direction as he walked toward Alfonzo's Mexicali, which was two doors over.

The men and boys who hung out here lived in the housing project across the street or in one of the several run-down transient hotels on the block. There were a few bad asses among them, but mostly they were just poor folks making time pass more easily with the aid of an inexpensive anesthetic.

"Got a extra dollar, Pop?" a young man of about eighteen asked Earl.

Earl stopped and handed him a five.

"Nothin' extra these days, son," he said. "But I like to find my car how I left it when I come back out."

The young man grinned and took the money.

"Enjoy you self, Cap. Ain nobody gon touch it."

Earl entered the Mexicali and sat down on a stool at the bar. There were a few people dancing, some sitting at the several tables lined along one wall, a couple of others on barstools. It was early yet for Saturday night. By one A.M., Earl knew, the place would be jumping.

"How you, stranger?"

"Just fine, Miz Alfonzo," Earl said to the heavy-set, middle-aged woman bartender who had greeted him in the same manner that she greeted every customer.

"Jim Beam and water?" she asked.

"Crown Royal and milk on the rocks, if you please, ma'am."

"JB's a buck tonight."

"Stick to my standby, CR and milk, thanks."

Miz Alfonzo laughed. "Ain't ever'body afford a extra fo' bits."

She left him his drink, picked up the two dollars he had laid on the bar, and brought back two quarters, which Earl waved away. Miz Alfonzo nodded and smiled, turned and dropped them into a glass next to the cash register, then walked down to the other end of the bar.

Earl sipped at his Crown Royal and milk and listened to the music. A deejay was playing old stuff. Right now was "If You Lose Me, You'll Lose a Good Thing" by Barbara Lynn, a local favorite. Hearing the song made Earl think of his ex, Rita. They had busted up right after her recent abortion. She had gone with her children to live with her sister in Baton Rouge and Earl had not spoken to Rita since.

The door opened and a large Latino man about thirty years old, dressed in an ice cream suit over a maroon shirt and beige tie, a young black woman hanging onto his left arm, entered the Mexicali. They passed Earl and paraded to the other end, stopping opposite Miz Alfonzo. Earl could not hear the initial exchange between them, but then Miz Alfonzo raised her voice, as did the young woman.

"You don't be draggin' yo tacky self in here with no greasy pimp!" shouted Miz Alfonzo. "Take it back out on the street!"

"Luis and me is down, Mama! Get used to it!"

"Get used to this!" Miz Alfonzo said, and pulled up a .38 revolver from behind the bar.

"Take the ho and go!" she yelled at Big Luis, pointing the gun at his chest. "She ain't no mo daughter to me!"

What happened next took place so fast that Earl could not quite follow the action. Several people surrounded Big Luis, whose white suit became visible only in flashes as the large Latino struggled with them. Somehow, Miz Alfonzo"s daughter gained possession of the revolver and tossed it along the top of the bar toward Earl, who made a big mistake: He picked it up.

Earl heard a weird noise coming from behind him, a loud, grinding sound. As he turned around to investigate the source, everything slowed down. White lights popped in Earl's eyes, as if a series of flashbulbs were going off. The floor tilted and Earl lost his balance. His first thought was that someone had kicked the stool out from under him, but he did not fall down. Then came the moaning—long, slow, unearthly noises unlike anything he had ever heard before. The air was full of multicolored feathers that covered everything.

Easy Earl had no idea how he came to be in his car, driving on Palmetto Street toward Metairie. His left cheek burned and he touched it, then glanced at the blood on his fingers. The .38 was on the seat next to him.

Back at Alfonzo's Mexicali Club, the policeman who had been wounded in the abdomen asked the woman kneeling by his head if his partner was all right. She told him that the other officer looked pretty dead and to lie still, an ambulance was coming.

"Who shot us?" asked the wounded man. "And why?"

The woman shook her head and said, "Honey, I just don't know."

NIGHT OWL

IT WAS SLIGHTLY after four A.M. when Earl Blakey drove into a Red Devil service station outside Tornado, Mississippi. He had driven north-northeast from Irish Bayou on the old two-lane highway, U.S. 11, across Lake Pontchartrain and the Pearl River, past Picayune and Carriere to Poplarville, where he had swung west on Mississippi State Road 43 and decided to stop for fuel before crossing back into Louisiana.

There was a light burning in the station office, and Earl hoped somebody was around so that he could keep going. He cut the engine, turned off the lights and got out of the car. A swarm of stinging insects descended on him in the darkness and Earl swatted at them as he walked toward the office. Through the glass in the door, Earl saw a white man seated on the floor, his back against a wall. There was a noose around the man's neck, a thick rope strung from a large hook that had been screwed into the ceiling. The man, whose Coke bottle–thick eyeglasses were askew and who was wearing an oil-stained white-and-black Ole Miss baseball cap, was either asleep or dead. Earl could not tell, although there seemed to be no discernible movement, no rise and fall of the man's chest.

Earl tried to open the door but it was locked. To enter, he would have had to break the glass, and he did not need any more trouble tonight. He looked again at the man, who appeared to be in his forties, wondering how he could be dead if he was sitting on the floor instead of hanging in the air. The rope was knotted at the top around the hook and had plenty of slack in the line down to the noose. Then Earl noticed the black letters on the floor at the ends of the man's outstretched legs, and that both of the man's feet were missing. He pressed closer to the glass and read the words that had been spraypainted there: EL MOCHUELO.

"Damn," Earl said. "Guess I got enough gas to get to Bogalusa."

He hurried back to his car, got in and drove away.

ROADRUNNER

"INTERESTIN' LICENSE PLATE you got there," the attendant in the 76 station in Bogalusa said. "EZY EARL. That you?"

Earl Blakey handed the kid a ten and a five.

"Used to was, an' maybe not even," said Earl.

The kid laughed. "I hear dat!"

Earl knew where he was headed now and he took 21 South out of town. At Covington, he'd take 190 West, stay off the interstate. As he sped past Sun, Louisiana, over the Bogue Chitto River, Earl considered the possibility that the last twelve hours of his life had been a dream; that he had not really shot two policemen in Alfonzo's Mexicali Club in New Orleans, and not seen a footless white man with his head in a noose on the floor of a Red Devil gas station outside Tornado, Mississippi. Maybe he was suffering from a medical condition and he could get a doctor to explain it. Rita and her sister, Zenoria Rapides, would help him, he figured, which was why he was on his way to Baton Rouge.

Earl still did not entirely understand why Rita had acted strangely toward him after her abortion. They had discussed the situation beforehand, agreed that it was the best solution, her being thirty-six years old and already having four children. Earl had paid for it, treated her kindly, but then Rita got bitter and took off quick up to Zenoria's. He was puzzled about that, but now it was himself, Mr Earl, who needed backup, and he hoped Rita would be there for him.

Earl turned on the radio.

"The long-lost gun tied to the assassination of former governor of Louisiana Huey P. Long fifty-six years ago has been found. James Starrs, a forensic scientist who plans to exhume the body of the purported assassin, Carl Austin Weiss, Sr., said in Washington, D.C., where he is a professor at George Washington University, that the .32-caliber handgun allegedly used to kill 'the Kingfish' in the Louisiana State Capitol in 1935 is in the possession of Mabel Guerre Binnings, the seventy-five-year-old daughter of the policeman who investigated the case. Binnings lives in New Orleans.

"Professor Starrs says he is certain the discovery of the apparent murder weapon will prove to be 'a bonanza of evidence.' The disclosure, however, has set off a legal battle over who owns the gun and the police files on the case, which also have been missing since 1940 when Mabel Binnings's father, Louis Guerre, retired.

"Louisiana State Police insist that both the weapon and the files belong to the people of Louisiana, and have delivered a letter requesting that Mabel Binnings hand them over. She has refused this request and has also declined to talk to reporters. Ever since the shooting in Baton Rouge, there has been speculation that Long, who was forty-two years old at the time, actually died from bullets fired by his bodyguards. The twenty-nine-year-old Weiss was gunned down by them on the Capitol steps."

Easy Earl lit a Kool, found a pair of dark glasses in the glove box and put them on. They were Rita's. Earl recalled the time he had bought them for her in the Walgreen's on Royal.

"In New Orleans," the radio news continued, "the manhunt for the killer of a metro police officer is underway. A second officer was wounded in the incident, which took place last night at Alfonzo's Mexicali Club on Louisiana Avenue. Details regarding the circumstances of the shootings are still unclear, said Acting Police Commissioner DuMont 'Du Du' Dupre. The suspect is believed to be a middle-aged black male with a pencil-thin mustache who may be driving a red late-1970s Mercury automobile. No further information is presently available.

"We have an appropriate tune comin' right up, people. 'I Am a Lonesome Fugitive,' sung by Ferriday, Louisiana's own bad boy, Jerry Lee Lewis. But first we have to pay a few bills."

Earl turned off the radio. He drove straight through to Baptist, where he stopped in a 7-Eleven and bought a Bic razor, a Snickers bar and a black corduroy Playboy bunny baseball cap. He dry-shaved in the car, using the rearview mirror, then ate the candy bar. This was the first time since he was sixteen years old, Earl realized, that he had not worn a mustache. He put on the bunny hat, adjusted his dark glasses, and hoped he could make it to Zenoria's house on Mohican Street in Baton Rouge before the cops caught him.

WOMEN ARE WOMEN BUT MEN ARE SOMETHING ELSE

ZENORIA RAPIDES HAD never married. Now forty-seven years old, she had lived alone, until Rita and the children arrived, in a two-bedroom house that she had bought and mostly paid for with her earnings as a grade-school teacher and seamstress. Her reputation as a dressmaker was nonpareil among the middle-class white women of Baton Rouge, and they brought her more work than she could adequately handle. Zenoria was pleased that her youngest sister, Rita Hayworth Rapides, had come to live with her, since Rita sewed almost as well as Zenoria herself and was willing to assist in the business.

There had been six children born to Althea Yancey and Zelmo Baptiste Rapides: Zenoria, Zelma and Zoroaster were named by their father; and Althea had named Lana Turner, Pocahantas and Rita Hayworth. Althea and Zelmo had perished sixteen years ago when their house on Evangeline Street, in which all of the children had been raised, caught fire due to an electrical problem and burned down in the middle of one night with them trapped inside. Zelma and Zoroaster, who were identical twins, were killed together in a car crash coming back from Port Allen, where they worked in a Popeye's, when they were sixteen. Lana Turner now lived in Memphis, married to a radical white lawyer named Lucius Lamar Bilbo, a great-nephew of the former Mississippi senator who had advocated deportation of all southern blacks to Africa. Zenoria and Rita seldom heard from her. Pocahantas had disappeared at the age of seventeen with a dishwasher from the Poteat Cafe in downtown Baton Rouge named Leopard Johnny, so called due to his peculiar black-and-yellow complexion, the result of a chronic, debilitating liver condition. The only word of Pocahantas that Zenoria or Rita or Lana had received in the last fifteen years was a picture card of the Monongahela River sent to Zenoria, postmarked Pittsburgh, Pennsylvania, that said, "Dere Sister, The Leopard has Lost his Spots. Hi to All. Love, Pokey."

Rita Hayworth Rapides's four children were the progeny of four different fathers, none of whom had Rita married, though at least two had proposed to her. Rita enjoyed her independence and insisted that each child carry her own surname. She had named them after four western states—Montana, Wyoming, Idaho and Colorado—none of which had she visited, nor was she particularly interested in visiting them. She told Zenoria that she just liked the sounds of the names.

Rita found that she usually had no use for men beyond occasional companionship. She preferred, also, to support herself; not that she ever refused financial help from any of the children's fathers, but Rita never depended on it. Until Easy Earl Blakey came around, she had not really been tempted to maintain a close friendship with a man. There was something uncomplicated about Blakey, Rita thought; not simple, exactly, but he was—true to his nickname—easy to be with. The termination of this recent pregnancy, her first abortion, had depressed Rita more than she ever could have anticipated. She had moved back to Baton Rouge just to have the comfort of her oldest sister, not to escape from Earl or New Orleans. Rita missed Earl, which surprised her; and when he turned up on Zenoria's doorstep that Sunday morning, clean-shaven and wearing a stupid Playboy bunny hat, Rita took him into her arms without a word and felt her entire body relax.

"They after me, Rita," Earl said, once they were inside the house. "Where Zenoria and the kids?"

"At church. I wasn't feelin' up to goin'. I ain felt up to goin' most places, lately. Oh, Earl, I am pleased to see you. Why'd you shave your mustache? And what you mean, they after you? 'They' who?"

"Po-lice. I shot a cop, Rita. Two cops. One's dead, other's wounded."

"Earl, you talkin' crazy. Easy Earl Blakey don't go around smokin' nobody, 'specially policemens."

"I know, honey, but it happen. I was havin' a CR an' milk in Alfonzo's Mexicali, by myself, thinkin' on you an' how much I been missin' us, when the incident just come about. That's all, it just come about. Next thing I find, I'm runnin'. I went to Miss'ippi firs', seen somethin' there so awful I ain sure I really seen it."

"Wait, baby. You talkin' too fast. How you so sure you shot anyone?"

"Had the gun with me in my car after it happen."

"You don't own no piece, Earl. Where's this gun?"

"Throwed it in Irish Bayou. It belong to Miz Alfonzo."

"Bad idea. Be some Cambo fish it out the bayou fo' long."

"That don't matter, Rita. Prob'ly a bad idea me comin' here, too, but I been missin' you so much. They bound to figure out where I am. They knowin' the car, said on the radio. Shit, Rita, this whole thing just some crazy accident, an' now my life be over."

"Earl, hush. We work it out."

"Rita, I love you." Earl kissed her softly on the lips. "But ain no way to deal with it 'cept run. You holdin' any green?"

"About ninety dollars. You can have it."

Rita went into another room and came back out with the money and handed it to Earl. He kissed her again, deeply this time.

"I been thinkin' about our baby," he said.

"Thinkin' what?"

"That we shoulda had it. Now I'm gone be dead an' ain no child of mine in the world to remember me. Also that if you ain move to Baton Rouge, which you wouldn't of if we ain kill the baby, I never would of been in the Mexicali Club in the firs' place."

"Earl, hold it. If you think runnin's the only way, go on ahead. I don't be stoppin' you or nobody, 'cludin' my children, they own time come, from doin' what they think they got to. But subtractin' out that way won't kick it. Look straight, Earl. You a good man, I know. I mighta had that baby, you'd told me to."

"You could come with me, Rita. Kids be safe with Zenoria an' we get 'em later."

"Go 'head, Earl. Don't need that nobody be lyin' to the police about not seein' you but me."

Rita kissed him and touched the tip of her right index finger above his upper lip.

"You get where you're goin'," she said, "grow that mustache back."

Earl grinned. "I will, baby."

Rita watched him drive away, then went into the bedroom she shared with Idaho and Colorado—Montana, her oldest, slept in the front room, and Wyoming with Zenoria—and lay down. Suddenly, she felt very tired. Rita remembered her mother, Althea, telling her when she could not have been more than eight years old, that just when things seemed almost to be makin' sense, a damn cow would jump over the moon. Rita had asked, "Whose cow, Mama?" Rita laughed now, lying on the bed, as Althea had twenty-eight years before in response to Rita's question, the only answer her mother had to give.

MARBLE

EARL HAD HEARD or read that when the Mafia kidnaps someone and murders him, they usually leave his car at an airport parking lot, so that's what Easy Earl did with his Mercury Monarch, abandoning it at Baton Rouge Metro and riding a bus downtown to the Greyhound terminal. He bought a ticket to Tampa, Florida, a city he'd never been to but one that he figured was big enough for him to find work in. His bus would not leave for forty-five minutes, so he bought a sausage and a Delaware Punch at a concession stand and took a seat in the waiting room.

A thin white girl, about thirteen or fourteen years old, wearing bluejeans and a powder blue LSU sweatshirt, carrying a small canvas bag, came in and sat down on the bench directly across from Earl. The girl's hair was white-blonde, she wore glasses, and she surveyed the waiting room calmly, her unmarked face expressionless. Earl noticed her but his thoughts were connected with his own situation. He ate his sausage and drank the punch and then went to the restroom. By the time he had used the toilet and washed his hands and face, the bus was loading and Earl climbed aboard. He took an aisle seat, three-quarters of the way toward the rear, next to the young white girl.

The bus was five minutes out of Baton Rouge on Interstate 12 when the girl said to Earl, "My name is Marble Lesson, I'm from Bayou Goula, though my daddy lives up in New Roads now, and I'm on my way to meet my mama and her new husband in Jacksonville, Florida. I was born in Miami County, Kansas, where my daddy's people had a farm outside Osawatomie, but they lost it, so we moved to Louisiana where Daddy's cousin Webb got Daddy a job in a refinery. Mama moved out of our house in Bayou Goula months ago, but I wanted to finish the semester since it had already started, so I stayed with Daddy for the time bein'. He didn't could use that big of a house, so he found him a place up at New Roads, in Labarre, actually, in Pointe Coupee Parish, as I said, and dropped me off just now at the bus station.

"My ambition is to be a writer of fiction. I never have got other than a A in English since the fourth grade. I am what is commonly called a keen observer, which means, of course, that I notice details most everyone else don't. Eyeglasses don't bother me. I got 'em five years ago, when I was nine, to perk up my left eye, which is lazy. But my own good guess is that it's the one sees the really important things and the right eye is mostly used to get me from here to there. The eye is a photoreceptor, which means a camera if you can capture what you see and store the image in the cortex, which is the outer layer of the anterior cerebral hemispheres of the brain. My cortex is overflowin' with captives, such as black vomit, one of the most serious symptoms of yellow fever, which I seen a film of victims of in the eighth grade and never forgot, nor will I. It's bound to come in useful for a novel or story before I'm through. Where are you goin'?"

"Tampa," said Earl.

"You'll have to transfer to another bus, then, because this one goes straight through to Jacksonville. Did they tell you that at the terminal? Sometimes people don't volunteer information very readily."

Earl nodded. "Uh huh. Change in Lake City."

"Did I tell you my name? Marble Lesson? Of course, I did. My daddy's name is Wesson, so people call him Wes. My mama's first name is Bird. Her first last name was Arden, like the forest. Then, as you know, it was Lesson. Now it's Doig, which she says nobody can pronounce properly when they see it, so she gets called Bird Dog a lot in Jacksonville. What's yours?"

"Earl."

"Oh my friends they call me Speedo but my real name is Mister Earl."

"Say what?"

"Song Mama used to sing me when I was little."

"Oh yeah, yeah. I kinda do remember it."

Earl closed his eyes.

"You appear to be tired, Mr Earl."

"Guess I am, Miz Lesson."

"Call me Marble, please."

"Miz Marble. You don't mind awfully, I'mo sneak on out here fo' bit, get some res'."

"I'll wake you up if you're asleep when we get to Lake City, though I doubt you will be since it's hours away."

Earl pulled the black corduroy bunny cap down over his eyes and drifted into a dreamscape where Rita, wearing black lace underwear, was standing over a fiery pit poking at something with a long stick. Earl tried to see what was in the pit, but he could not raise himself high enough. Rita kept jabbing with the stick, and then she speared an object and lifted it out of the pit, gripping the stick with both hands. She held up a charred baby, its limbs outstretched but motionless. Pieces of the corpse flaked off and were carried away by the wind until there was nothing left. Rita dropped the stick into the fire.

SOMETHING SPECIAL

BUS CRASHES, BURNS IN LIGHTNING STORM

GULFPORT, JAN. 21 (SNS)—A Greyhound bus, en route from Baton Rouge, La., to Jacksonville, Fla., was struck by lightning yesterday during a thunderstorm at approximately four P.M. as it traveled on Interstate 10 north of Bay St Louis, Miss. The strike caused the bus to crash into a roadside ditch, killing twelve passengers and the driver, who was identified as Dio Bolivar, 42, of Phenix City, Ala.

Witnesses said it appeared that the secondary channel of a double bolt of ground lightning struck the bus, which was several miles away from the primary channel that destroyed a railroad bridge-tender's shack just west of Waveland, Miss.

Ten of the eleven survivors were injured, some seriously, and were taken to nearby hospitals for treatment. The only passenger who emerged unhurt was Marble Lesson, 14, of Bayou Goula, La.

Interviewed at the scene, Miss Lesson, who was traveling alone, told rescuers, "A violet vein of hellfire reached down inside the bus and cooked them folks. There was a nice black man sitting next to me and all of a sudden he lit up like a Christmas tree. It was pretty spectacular.

"I don't know why I was spared, except perhaps the Lord has something special planned for me to accomplish in life."

JESUS SEES US

Dear Jesus,

There is no doubt in my brain that it was a direct act of God that I am alive and in fact did escape unscathed and unscarred from the bus crash that took so many lives of the innocent and injured so many others. That I am safe now in the home of my mama Bird Arden and her second husband Fernando Doig on Trout River Boulevard in Jacksonville Florida a town about which I know practically nothing at all since I am a recent arrival is without question a miracle. The Earth cannot turn fast or slow enough to disturb me as I am at this moment as of now undisturbable.

In case You may not know very much about me though I believe You observe us all let me explain just who it is is writing You this letter. I am Marble Lesson (no middle name) 14 years old. Until now I lived in Bayou Goula Louisiana the state where my daddy Wes still lives. Now I have come to live with my mama and it was while traveling here on the Greyhound that the accident occurred that convinced me of Your investment in me. Writing is how I have chosen to justify Your faith and commitment. You may ask what can a 14 year old girl of The South have to say that You should pay any attention to? I believe writing is a process of self discovery and each thought is my own. Stick with me Jesus You may hear something You never thought of Yourself.

I am concerned about the World Condition not only as things are in my own country of the United States of America but all over the globe. One thing I would like to know is if You see what is going on on other planets or just Earth? A few days ago before I left Bayou Goula on that fateful trip I wrote a song I wish You could hear me sing but maybe You can when I do anyway here are the words.

Jesus sees us even when we're bad
And every time I think of that
It makes me feel so glad
Gives me the finest feeling
That I ever have had
Oh Jesus sees us even when we're bad

In time I plan to add more verses but I thought as long as I have it this far and I am writing to You anyhow You would be interested.

There is a black man staying with our family now at the house who is a friend of Fernando Doig. The black man's name is Mr Rollo Lamar and he and Fernando are lawyers. They are working together for a women's group in the state of Florida that is pro choice which means they are for allowing women to decide for themselves as individuals whether or not to have a baby. I am only 14 but I do not understand how anyone can tell anyone else what to do with their own body. Personally I do not know what I would do if I was pregnant and did not want the baby either have an abortion or have the baby and give it out for adoption like Lástima Denuedo did back in Bayou Goula at the age of 15 however I would want to be able to choose for myself which is only fair. Others of course do not agree.

Last night at dinner Mr Lamar told Fernando and Mama and me about a trial up in Georgia where a man wore his Ku Klux Klan costume which includes a white robe like one You wore when You were here on Earth and a pointy hood and a mask. This man wore this outfit of the Klan which is a group who hate Jewish people (I know You are one) and black and other peoples of color and Catholic persuasion and are against abortion in any form I am sure to test a law that says it is illegal to wear a mask in public. Of course at Mardi Gras in New Orleans where I have been many times people always wear masks so it is no surprise to me that the Ku Klux Klan person won the case. The argument against him was that wearing the costume and mask was intended to strike fear and terror into the minds of the Jewish and Catholic and black people of the town where he did it. My thinking about masks is that if every person wore the same kind of mask and all looked alike then people would have to deal with who the other person really is on their insides and maybe it would not be such a horrible idea to try someday. That way you would not know if another person is even black or white underneath the mask it is just a person. What do You think?

It is very late at night now and I am pretty sleepy so I will stop here. My plan is to continue writing letters to You until I know where to send them or can deliver them in person. All for now.

Sincerely, your friend
Marble Lesson

THE GOOD SAMARITAN

WESSON LESSON STAGGERED out of the Saturn Bar into the street. After losing his job in New Roads, Wes had come to New Orleans to visit his brother, Webb, only to learn that Webb had been arrested and jailed for operating a tax scam involving false bills of sale for automobiles. This swindle landed Webb a ten spot at the Atchafalaya Correctional Facility, to which he was sent a week after Wes got to town.

Wes moved into his brother's house on Rocheblave Street and immediately thereafter fell off the wagon on which he had been a brief passenger. His heavy drinking and abusive behavior had cost him his wife, Bird, and their daughter, Marble, and any number of oil field jobs. He was thirty-nine years old, looked fifty, and was definitely headed down the road feeling bad.

Wobbling on the corner of St Claude Avenue and Clouet Street at two o'clock in the morning, Wes Lesson was suddenly overcome by feelings of guilt about having failed his family, and he dropped to his knees and wept. Marble, who was now fourteen, had gone to live with Bird and her new husband, an attorney named Fernando Doig, in Jacksonville, Florida, and Wes despaired of ever seeing his only child again. He knew he was no good, had mistreated the one woman he had truly loved, forcing her to leave him, and now his beloved daughter was also beyond his touch. Wes lay crumpled up on the broken sidewalk, sobbing, oblivious to the perilous position he was in.

"Best be gettin' on your feet, fella," a large, moon-faced man said, as he reached down to assist Wes Lesson. "You must ain't be up on the local geography. Natives have you skinned in fifteen minutes, spear through your ear, I leave you be."

The man, who appeared to be in his mid-fifties but was still built like a middle linebacker in his prime, lifted Wes with one arm and looked at his puffy face and bloodshot eyes.

"Bud, you in a ugly condition. I'll take you to home, you got one."

"Rochebla' Stree'," Wes said, struggling to stand on his own.

The big man guided Wes to a midnight blue Buick Roadmaster and stuffed him into the front passenger seat, closed the door, then went around to the driver's side and slid behind the wheel.

"Don't know how a man can let this happen to him," the driver said, as he pulled the Buick into the sparse traffic on St Claude. "You smell bad, boy. It's the stink of defeat."

All Wes Lesson could do was groan. He barely heard what his savior of the moment was saying.

"My name's Defillo Humble. Maybe you've heard of me. Wrote a book some years ago did a little. Twenty weeks on the *Picayune* best-seller list. *Negroes with Cars*. About how the African American's access to the automobile drove the final nail into the coffin of the Old South. I'm workin' on a new one now, *The Unnecessary Passing of the Southern Woman*. You can pretty much guess what-all it's about."

Wes Lesson was incapable of intelligent or intelligible response. He was only vaguely aware of what was happening, and when the car stopped in front of his brother's house, Wes could do no better than open the passenger door and drop onto the street. Defillo Humble got out and came around, picked him up and half-carried him to the porch, where he deposited Wes on the top step.

"Best I intend to do, pardner," said Defillo Humble. "Whatever it is you're afraid of, there's worse. Mister, unless you've been forced to eat rodent sushi from the scooped-out skull of a Liberian rebel soldier, like I have, or had a twenty-foot-long anaconda jump into your dugout and swallow half of your five-year-old son before you could put a nine-millimeter round through the serpent's ganglion, like happened to me, you ain't got a clean bone to pick, I don't reckon. I'll get back by some-time, check on you."

Defillo Humble walked to his Roadmaster, got in and drove away. Before the big man got to the next corner, Wes Lesson had fallen asleep right where Defillo had dropped him.

• • •

THE BLINK OF AN EYE

HUMBLE, WES AND MARBLE ACCEPTED Bunk's invitation to stay overnight at the Academy and return the next morning to New Orleans. On the ride back to Cuba from Meridian, Wes told Bunk that he would take the job but that he could not begin for a week, until Marble left for Jacksonville, and Bunk said that was all right by him. There was a small dormitory-type setup at the rear of the fifteen-thousand-square-foot Butler building, the remainder of which was divided into office and warehouse space, so guest accommodations were not a problem.

Once they were inside, Bunk noticed that the red light was flashing on his answering machine. He hit the message button.

"Black zero, black zero. Straight up, straight up. Hammerhead, hammerhead. Respond, Cuba, respond."

Bunk immediately punched up a number on the telephone and as soon as his connection was made, he said, "Cuba big, Cuba big. Lay down, black zero. Lay down, black zero. Zero in."

He hung up and told Defillo Humble, "Got a unexpected visitor comin' in at midnight. Better tell Lesson to put his kid to bed. I've got to set the lights."

At one minute past midnight, Humble, Wes and Bunk stood next to the landing strip watching a Learjet taxi toward them. The airplane stopped and idled while the passenger door opened and an aluminum stepladder was lowered to the ground. A man wearing light but sturdy casual clothing, dressed as if he were going sailing, and carrying a green duffel bag, climbed down the ladder, put the duffel on the ground, then lifted the ladder back into the plane. The man picked up the duffel bag and walked toward the reception committee as the jet taxied toward the far end of the runway. Bunk stepped forward to greet the visitor.

"*Bienvenida*, Señor de Estoques," said Bunk. "It's been a pretty little while."

They did not shake hands but the man, a handsome, clean-shaven Latino in his mid-twenties, smiled at Bunk, then turned and watched the Learjet rumble away, ascend in the north and describe a perfect 180° arc before disappearing into the sub-tropical moonlit sky.

"Mozo, this is Defillo Humble, a longtime associate," Bunk said, "and Wes Lesson, my new assistant. Gentlemen, meet Mozo de Estoques, from Medellín, a most highly valued member of the Colombian Boys Club."

Mozo de Estoques smiled again and spoke in close-to-perfect English.

"Señor Bunk, how can it be that you look younger now than you did when I first met you? That was what, eleven years ago? I was fourteen then."

"I remember. It was in Cali, and you'd just completed your first assignment for the Club."

"Broke my cherry, as you *norteamericanos* say."

Bunk nodded. "That's right. Mozo was no bigger'n your little girl sleepin' inside, Wes, when he embarked on his illustrious career. Just a kid."

"What little girl?" asked Mozo de Estoques.

"Wes's daughter," said Bunk. "She's asleep back in the dormitory."

"How old is she?"

"I don't know," Bunk said. "Twelve or thirteen."

"She's fourteen," said Wes. "What difference does it make?"

Mozo looked at Wes Lesson, reflections from the runway lights flickering like tiny flames in the Colombian's unblinking black eyes. He smiled with the corners of his mouth.

"Much," said de Estoques. "It makes much difference."

"Come on, men, let's go inside," said Bunk. "Take 'em back, Humble, while I kill these lights. Be right there."

Humble and Wes walked behind Mozo, who obviously had been there before. He tossed down his duffel bag and went into the restroom.

"Who is he?" Wes asked Humble.

"Jorge Muleta's top assassin. He's here to hit somebody big, you can bet. Mozo de Estoques don't travel for no good reason. He supposedly whacked the last two opposition presidential candidates down there. Runs a school for assassins financed by the Muleta cartel."

Bunk came in at the same time as Mozo emerged from the can.

"How much time you got, son?" Bunk asked him.

"A car will come in three hours or less. I'm tired, Señor Bunk." Mozo yawned and stretched his arms and back. He studied his oversized Rolex. "If I am still asleep at two forty-five, wake me up."

"You got it."

The assassin picked up his bag and headed for the dormitory.

"How about a drink, Bunk?" said Humble. "Got any of that Glenmorangie left?"

The three men were perched on stools around a stainless steel table in the kitchen area. Bunk and Humble were sipping single-malt Scotch and Wes held a can of Dr Pepper.

"Only time I was in Colombia," Bunk said, "Estrago Muleta—that's Jorge's younger brother who was executed by a firin' squad year before last in Venezuela, Maracaibo, I believe—he and I were out in the jungle when we come upon the biggest goddamn snake I've ever saw, sleepin' smack in the middle of the trail. Estrago said it was a bushmaster, a *serpiente muy peligroso*. Estrago handed me his Uzi machine pistol and snuck up on the viper, lopped off its head with a machete. Reptile didn't budge. Estrago hoisted the head on the tip of his long knife and carried it that way, like a Sioux with Custer's scalp, back to the camp. Boy was one fearless son of a bitch. Well, he's a government footnote now."

The gunshot came before the scream. There was a very loud pop that sounded like a deeply imbedded cork being removed from a goosenecked bottle, followed by Marble's long, wobbly howl. Wes was the first of the three men to reach her. Marble sat on the floor next to the cot on which she had been sleeping, clasping in her two hands a Colt Python pointed at the inert body of Mozo de Estoques, who lay draped across the cot, naked from the waist down, except for his white cotton socks.

Wes took the pistol from his daughter, who sat perfectly still, rigid, her eyes frozen open. He knelt next to Marble and hugged her to him. Humble pushed aside Mozo's black forelock, revealing reddish ooze where his right eye had been. Bunk came in last, took a look at the scene, started to say something, then stopped. Wes gently caressed his daughter's head as he held her, and after a minute or two, she blinked.

STICKING WITH JESUS

Dear Jesus,

It has been a while since I wrote I know but lots has happened during this time. I will begin with the big event and go back. I killed a man who tried to rape me in Alabama. You know I am fourteen and still a virgin child and intend to remain one until I decide to do it though I have to tell you not necessarily in the marriage bed. Anyway that is the big news now I will tell you how it happened.

Daddy and I went with a stranger named Defillo Humble to see about a job for Daddy at an airfield in Alabama by the border of Mississippi. This stranger had helped out Daddy I guess when he was drunk in trouble one night and when he showed back up at the house and said he might know about a job Daddy figured why not check it out due to his not having one and the work situation in his home state of Louisiana not being good at the moment. I did not have a very good feeling about this man Humble who is an extremely large person but who says he is a writer which did interest me. As you know I have ambitious desires in that direction.

So we went with Defillo Humble in his Buick up around Meridian to this airfield which is a school called Bunk Colby's Balloon and Airship Academy. It is run by an extremely strange man Bunk Colby who says he is 75 years old but looks almost as young as Daddy. There was one balloon there but nothing else of an air nature that I could see. This school was way out in nowhere and I did not think Daddy would accept work there but he did being so desperate and not drinking though he is not going to work there now of course.

That night we were there was when everything happened. Mr Humble, Mr Colby and Daddy and I went to Meridian to eat dinner and see a movie called Showdown in Little Tokyo. The dinner was OK at a barbecue restaurant but the movie was dumb and awful with really fake looking foot fighting, automatic weapons galore going off, and lots of naked women with mostly Japanese criminals. The worst part was where the leader of the Japanese criminals cuts off the head of a blond woman with a sword in one hand while he rubs her bare breasts with his other. He does this from behind her with no shirt on so we can see he is tattooed all over his chest and shoulders and arms and stomach. Later he is killed but you would not believe how horrible this movie is Jesus don't go see it.

After we got back to Mr Colby's place I went to sleep in a room with lots of small beds in it because it was too late to drive all the way back to New Orleans. I woke up with a man on top of me I did not know who he was. He put a hand over my mouth and pulled down my blanket with his other to get at me. I turned my head and saw a gun on the floor next to the bed and while he was doing things to himself I reached down and grabbed the gun and put the nose by the side of his face and pulled the trigger.

The man collapsed on me and there was junk everywhere not just blood but stuff from inside his head. I guess I screamed then and crawled out from under his body and would have shot him again if he moved but he was completely dead and did not. Daddy came and held me. I knew it was him but honest Jesus I could not talk or even move for a long time. Mr Humble and Mr Colby came in and saw the mess but they did not say a word.

Daddy held me in the back seat of Mr Humble's car all the way back to New Orleans in the middle of the night. I guess Mr Colby buried the body of the rapist who Daddy told me later was a murderer from South America who the US government was after and would be glad to know he was dead but we were not going to tell them or anybody else. I promised Daddy I would not tell Mama about any of this because she would never allow me to visit Daddy again not that she wanted me to anyway as you know. But I had to tell you Jesus you are the only one.

I am writing this on the bus back to Florida. Remember the last time I was on it a bolt of lightning hit us and every passenger except me was killed or hurt bad. I know for certain now that I was spared for a special purpose and probably for more than one. The first was to destroy the South American killer and rapist who beyond any doubt in my mind was an agent of the devil. More are out there Jesus and I am ready for them. There is a TV show that says 25 million people claim to have spoken with the devil and I believe it. I also believe there are others on the planet such as myself who can save the world from the devil and his agents. Stick close with me Jesus I am on your side forever.

Your friend,
Marble Lesson

from
ARISE AND WALK
(1994)

WET HEAT

WILBUR "DAMFINO" NOUGAT and Gaspar DeBlieux slumped down in their red leather easy chairs in their two-bedroom suite at the DeSalvo Hotel on Gravier Street, drinking rum and orange juice, waiting for the two hookers they had ordered from the Congo Square Escort Service to arrive. Nougat and DeBlieux—pronounced "W"—were white men in their mid-forties, in New Orleans for the annual national convention of dental supply salesmen, the profession at which each of them had been laboring for the better part of twenty years. Nougat lived in Nashville, Tennessee; DeBlieux in Monroe, Louisiana. They had become friends fifteen years before, when they had first shared a room at the Pontchartrain in Detroit. Since then, they had arranged to stay together whenever and wherever the dental supply salesmen of America gathered.

"More an' more I'm likin' dark meat," said Gaspar. "Used to it was only blondies stood Little Boy at attention. Why I married Dolly Fay, 'cause of her yellow hair, which now can't no way tell for sure what color it is. Changes every month or two. 'Bout you, Wilbur? What's your preference?"

"Damfino or care, Dublya. Long's it's hooters a pair an' wet heat below, she can be blue with white polka dots from hair to there. Stick it and lick it, that's the ticket."

DeBlieux laughed. "Sonesta hear what you say, she'd be after you with her magnum cocked."

"Only cock she get, too," said Damfino. "Woman size the

Goodyear blimp now. You ain't seen her in a year or two. Awful how she let herself go."

"Sorry to hear it. Sonesta was sweet-lookin' once."

"She claims it was havin' a fourth child did in her figure, but it's chocolate. Sonesta can't go a hour without she's chunkin' chocolate."

There was a knock on the door.

"Be our dates, Dub."

Damfino popped up, went to the door, and opened it. Two tall, lanky black hookers entered the room and stood together, unsmiling, in front of a large picture window opposite Gaspar DeBlieux.

"Drinks, ladies?" asked Damfino.

The hookers had tough faces; their heavily painted skin looked waxed. Both of them were quite beautiful, however; each had high cheekbones, full lips, and what appeared to be a perfectly sculpted figure barely contained by a tight leopard-skin dress. They wore red berets over their pressed black hair.

"Holy Infant!" chirped Gaspar, springing out of his chair. "Looks like we hit the right number tonight!"

He practically pranced around the hirelings, grinning, the contents of his hand-held glass sloshing onto the burgundy carpet.

"We don't use alcohol," said the slightly shorter of the two prostitutes. Her voice was very deep.

"If you don't mind," said the other, in a more feminine tone, "we'd prefer dispensing with the business side up front. Two hundred each, gentlemen."

Wilbur Nougat and Gaspar DeBlieux each extracted two crisp C-notes from his wallet and handed them over. The prostitutes took the money and deposited it in their purses, out of which they each then withdrew a .32-caliber Smith and Wesson revolver with a silencer affixed to the barrel. They pointed the guns at the men, who froze at the sight.

"Take off your clothes," said the tallest hooker.

"Just a hot damn minute," said DeBlieux. "What you doin'?"

"Take off your clothes or we'll shoot you," said the other hooker. "We be aim low."

The men removed their clothes and stood naked in the middle of the room.

"Suck his dick," the shorter hooker commanded DeBlieux. "Genuflect front your partner an' do 'im."

"This the buddy system," said the taller one.

Gaspar dropped to his knees, put his lips on the head of Damfino's penis, and closed his eyes.

"Suck it off!" the taller one repeated.

Gaspar DeBlieux did his best, but Nougat's penis remained flaccid. Tears rolled freely from both men's eyes.

"Maybe you do it better," said the tallest tormentor. "Trade places. We ain't goin' till the faucet starts flowin'."

The men did as they were told and this time Nougat got some results. Gaspar's penis hardened despite his fear.

"Stroke it," said one of the hookers, Damfino didn't know which, and after a few minutes he made DeBlieux come.

"Swallow it!" ordered the taller hooker.

Damfino dropped his head to the floor and sobbed. Gaspar stood, trembling, his depleted penis shrinking rapidly.

"Y'all get down again," the smaller hooker said to DeBlieux, who obeyed.

Both men bent forward, their eyes shut tight. The hookers lifted their short dresses with their free hands, took out their penises, and urinated on Nougat and DeBlieux.

"Surprise!" the prostitutes shouted, mirthful now, giggling like schoolgirls.

When they had finished, the hookers straightened their skirts, replaced the guns in their bags, and walked out of the room, leaving the men wet and shivering on the hotel room floor.

Outside the DeSalvo, Cleon Tone stood about ten feet from the entrance, wearing his HAND YURSEF A FRESH START BY LEND A MAN A HAND sign and holding his hat. As the regal, leopard-skin-clad hookers walked by, the taller of the two dropped a hundred-dollar bill into the disgraced pastor's fedora. Before the occurrence had registered on Cleon's brain, his benefactors had climbed into a taxi and sped away.

The Reverend Tone stared at the glowing C-note, shook his head, and said aloud, "The Good Lord got Him some sundry damn messengers, don't He?"

THE SECRET OF THE UNIVERSE

WHEN HE WAS a boy, Cleon Tone decided that he would be the one to discover the secret of the universe. His Southern Baptist parents took him to church regularly, he attended Sunday School, but Cleon did not entirely bite on the concept of creationism. At eight and a half years old, the future preacher inclined more to scientific reckoning than he did toward blind purchase of the idea of the Garden of Eden.

During a discussion of Adam and Eve one Sunday noon, the perspicacious Cleon announced to his class that it would be he who correctly ascertained the origin of man. His Bible studies teacher, an unmarried woman in her late thirties named Myrtis Wyatt, took a piece of bituminous coal the size of a hockey puck from the top drawer of her desk, pried apart the blaspheming boy's lips, and forced it between them.

"And the Lord said unto him," Myrtis Wyatt pronounced, her hands holding firm Cleon's birdlike shoulders, " 'Who hath made man's mouth? or who maketh the dumb, or deaf, or the seeing, or the blind? have not I the Lord? Now therefore go, and I will be with thy mouth, and teach thee what thou shalt say.' "

From that time forward, Cleon Tone never questioned the explanation for man's place in the universe or gave expression to his thoughts in regard to an alternative genesis. Myrtis Wyatt never did marry, and at the age of fifty-six, while pruning roses in her wheelchair-bound mother's garden, a mud wasp invaded the tympanic membrane of the spinster's right ear, where its sting proved fatal. Myrtis's paralyzed mother sat watching her daughter writhe in agony on the ground while the winged insect crawled deeper and deeper into the aural cavity. The old woman was entirely helpless in the face of death, a distinction that allowed her a momentary kinship with those persons more abled than she.

BUGS

IT WAS NOT Rebel Ray Bob's custom to return to his shop once he had closed it, but he had forgotten to take with him earlier in the evening a shortwave radio he intended to fool with. He was convinced that some of the languages he heard on it had to be coming in from outer space. There was no way, he figured, a human being on planet Earth could work their mouth around some of those sounds. It was eleven minutes past midnight when Ray Bob unlocked, entered, and then closed the front door. Three seconds later, before he could turn on a light, a blunt object—a chunk of heavy glass with the word MIZZOU decaled on it in gold letters over a black and gold drawing of a snarling tiger—permanently wrinkled the unsuspecting owner's right temple, causing his immediate collapse onto the brown-stained cedar board floor.

"Wad you hid 'im wid?"

"Ashtray."

Ice D knelt next to the prone pawn king and closely inspected his head.

"He fix, Spit. Fix permanen'. Maybe bes' we carry 'im out back way we come in."

"No," said Spit Spackle, slipping the murder weapon into the canvas sack that already held the several guns and ammunition he and D had swiped from the store. "Bugs be on him too quick. Cop scientists use insects now to establish time of the crime."

"Insex? How you know dis?"

"Read it in a magazine in the prison library. Dead body lyin' outside attracts enough blowflies and flesh flies to lay thousands of eggs in the mouth, nose, and ears within ten minutes of death. The eggs hatch about twelve hours later into maggots that feed on tissues. When the maggots is done, they crawl off the body and cocoon in the soil around it. Then comes more bugs, beetles usually, that chow down on the dryin' out skin. After them it's spiders, mites, and millipedes that feast on the insects. Best we just leave him."

"Damn!"

Ice D stood up and the two fugitives took off out the front, Spit slammed the door behind them, dislodging from the wall next to it a framed sign that flipped faceup onto Rebel Ray Bob's back. It read: IF ASSHOLES COULD FLY, THIS PLACE WOULD BE AN AIRPORT.

SMART MOUTH

"GOOD EVENING, PEOPLE, and welcome to *Prostitutes Talk to Christ*. I'm your host, Roland Rocque, the Smartest Mouth in the Deepest South, and if you are a regular listener you know by now that opinions expressed on this program do not necessarily reflect the views of radio station WJEW or its sponsors. If you haven't tuned in to us before, well, now you know.

"It's one minute past midnight here in Kenner, Louisiana, and we're broadcasting from the studios of WJEW, located on Airline Highway, one-quarter mile from the New Orleans International Airport. We afford an opportunity to the denizens of the seamy side of life who work in the area to stop by between tricks and give voice to the Lord via the airwaves. *Prostitutes Talk to Christ* is strictly nondenominational and open to hookers of every race and sex whether or not either can be satisfactorily determined and/or verified by medical science. Listeners are invited to call in with their comments to our free access line. Here's the number: 1-800-555-WJEW. That's 1-800-555-9539.

"Okay, folks, here's our first guest of the night. Come right in and have a seat. There you go. Well, that's a conscience-raisin' outfit you have on. My! Lavender taffeta, isn't it?"

"Yeah, Rolan', it is."

"And your first name is? No last names on the air, please."

"Rosetta, from Sicily Isl', Louisiana."

"What is it you must tell Jesus, Rosetta?"

"Well, Rolan', firs' off I jus' wants to thank you fo' what you doin'. Givin' this oppatunity to airwave our inmost religious thoughts an' all."

"Rosetta, it's our pleasure and your choice."

"Righ', okay. I ain' rehearse nothin' now, you know."

"Don't be shy, dollin'. Go ahead."

"Lord, if you be listen, please unnastan' I wouldn' be doin' no nastiness 'less it necessary feed my babies, which there be two: Oprah Winfrey an' Paula Abdul, twin girls. They three now."

"How old are you, Rosetta? If you don't mind my askin'."

"Nineteen, Rolan'."

"And you've been working as a prostitute for how long?"

"Fo' years, almos'."

"Speak to Jesus, Rosetta."

"Jesus, I don' do no drug. I ain' never wan' my babies be strung up on the dope. Pressure be bad, though. Prince Egyp', he my man, he like his ladies go fo' it. Keep 'em control, you know. But Jesus, I tryin' keep my min' straight. I aks you an' yo' daddy help me an' my babies stay off it. Gi' me the strength, Jesus, resis'. That all I aks, Rolan'. Let me do my job without no jones."

"Thank you, Rosetta. I'm sure Jesus hears you. And if any of you out there in the Greater New Orleans area are hearin' Rosetta and have a thing to say, call in: 1-800-555-WJEW. That's 1-800-555-9539. I see the lines lightin' up already, Rosetta. You bein' hoid."

"Maybe one of 'em be Jesus, Rolan'."

"That wouldn't surprise me, Rosetta. One day pick up and there's the Son of God himself on the line. Let's take this one. Hello, this is Roland Rocque, the Smartest Mouth in the Deepest South, with Rosetta on *Prostitutes Talk to Christ*. Who's this?"

"Roland? You do better for that nigger whore just shoot her and her babies, too. Put 'em straight out they mis'ry. They just livin' off the good folks, folks right with God and country to begin with."

"Sir, I'm endin' you right now. Sorry, Rosetta, that's not typical of our listenin' audience, I know."

"That okay, Rolan'. I know what kinds peoples is roamin' free. They pays me let 'em come on my face, then go home to they wife 'cross the lake."

"Next caller, I hope you more enlightened than the last one."

"That was terr'ble, Roland. It's callers like him should be shot, not degraded victims of society such as little Rosetta there. It was up to me, anyone who wasn't in church on Sunday doesn't have a good goddam reason they shouldn't be deported. Send 'em to China, be force' to speak Chinese, nothin' but rice to eat, wear them plain-lookin' clothes. What you think, Roland?"

"I think it's time for a break here, Rosetta, pay some bills. I know you gotta get back on the street, sweetheart, so I want to thank you for comin' on the air tonight."

"Be my pleasure, Rolan'. Can I come back?"

"Certainly, Rosetta, any time."

Pace Ripley sat in a wicker chair on the deck of his houseboat in Delacroix, smoking a joint and listening to the radio. His wife, Tombilena Gayoso, came out, looked at the water shimmering in the moonlight, stretched her arms over her head, and yawned.

"You comin' to bed, Pace?"

"In a few minutes, Tommy. I'm listenin' to this call-in show, *Prostitutes Talk to Christ*. You wouldn't believe the shit people say."

"Mostly that's all people do say, is shit. Bein' more'n twice my age you must surely have noticed that by now."

Pace flicked his roach over the railing.

"Roland Rocque got nothin' on you in the smart mouth department, I'll go that far."

"Come inside, babe, you can go as far as you like. I won't stop you."

She switched off the radio. Pace stood up and took her in his arms.

"Guess I'd better, before you bring out that old shotgun of yours."

Pace kissed Tombilena softly on the lips. She put her right hand on his crotch and giggled as she felt him get hard.

"Am I scarin' you, mister?"

"Honey, can't you tell? I'm petrified."

MOTHER OF GOD

FOLLOWING THE DEATH of her husband, Pace Ripley, who was lost at sea and believed drowned during a hurricane, Tombilena Gayoso, age twenty-eight, childless, had relocated from Delacroix Island, Louisiana, to New Orleans. Though only forty-five minutes by car from her family—her father, Rodrigue, and brother, Campo, were fishermen in Delacroix—N.O. was, to borrow a phrase from the Rolling Stones, two thousand light-years from Tombilena's home. She felt the need to change her life after Pace slipped away, and a shift to the Crescent City, where she had lived previously for a short time—where, in fact, she and Pace had first met—was both a convenient and obvious move. Tombilena was the only Gayoso woman now, her mother having passed several years before, and she wanted to remain within hailing distance of her father and brother, both of whom she loved dearly.

In short order, Tombilena found an apartment at the edge of the Quarter above a bookshop on the corner of Barracks and Dauphine; and a part-time job answering calls at the Mary Mother of God Rape Crisis Center on Terpsichore Street. Established by women united in the belief that the mother of Jesus Christ, the so-called Virgin Mary, actually had been a rape victim, the Mary Mother of God organization functioned as an all-purpose assistance service for women burdened by any manner of difficulty. Tombilena dealt with the battered, the homeless, the assaulted, and psychologically adrift distaff of the Greater New Orleans area, the numbers of which, to her horror, were legion.

Also present at the center was a sixteen-year-old girl named Marble Lesson. A legend among radical feminists the world over, Marble's notoriety stemmed from her having shot to death the infamous Mozo de Estoques, an international terrorist and assassin, who had attempted to rape Marble when she was fourteen. Following this incident, which took place at a rural airfield near Cuba, Alabama, the teenager had been counseled by several of the women who were then in the process of forming the Mary Mother of God group. After a failed attempt to live in harmony with her mother and stepfather in Florida, Marble Lesson had come to live with her father, a construction worker named Wesson Lesson, in N.O., where she resumed her association with Mary Mother of God.

It was in the company and under the tutelage of these women that Marble developed her political and social manifestos. She read extensively those historical and philosophical texts that her helpmates made available to her, including the writings of Hilda Brausen, a German woman who had disguised herself as a man in order to fight at the front in World War I. Killed in France during a firefight—some believed by members of her own unit who had discovered Hilda's secret—Fräulein Brausen advanced a fundamental belief that all men were prone to a mental illness that expressed itself in the form of violence toward women. "The male human," Hilda Brausen wrote, "almost invariably will sooner or later be overcome by this disease, and therefore bears close scrutiny, so that at the first sign of derangement he can—and *must*—be eliminated. As grows the male prostate gland, so grows his proclivity for behavior dangerous to the female human."

Though medically unsound, this correlative theory of Hilda Brausen's was nevertheless embraced by an ever-growing number of feminist thinkers. Basing it on "the Brausen principle," Marble Lesson had created a radical faction within Mary Mother of God dedicated to the eradication of any man believed by their society to be guilty of exceptional abuse. This faction, informally called "Die Brausenkriegers," dealt literal deathblows to those men deemed diseased. They eschewed any possibility of rehabilitation.

Tombilena noticed that despite her youth, Marble Lesson was accorded inordinate respect and treated with the utmost deference by the other members of Mary Mother of God. Tombilena's own history was not devoid of violence—she had shotgunned down two men who were threatening to murder her husband—and from what information she could at this point gather about Marble, she thought that the two of them might prove not incompatible.

• • •

MARBLE LAYS IT ON THE TABLE

After Tombilena had finished speaking on the telephone to her father, Rodrigue, and learned that Campo's bail had been set at fifty thousand dollars, as it had for each of the accused, and that Rodrigue was about to put up the Gayoso house as collateral, she walked with Marble Lesson over to Tallulah's, a café on Religious. Tombilena was still stunned by the news of her brother's alleged involvement in the assault, and she hardly noticed when a waitress brought to their table the cups of coffee Marble had ordered for them.

"Your brother been known to be knockin' females around?" Marble asked, as she stirred a spoonful of brown sugar into her own cup.

Marble was short, about five foot one, with straight, sandy brown hair chopped off under the ears and bangs below her eyebrows. She wore schoolboy glasses that made her greenish blue eyes look even tinier than they were. Her lips were light pink, the same color as her cheeks. Tombilena looked at Marble bringing the cup to her mouth and was startled by how small the girl's fingers were. The sight reminded her of an old movie she and Pace had watched once on TV, *The Incredible Shrinking Man*; the scene where the guy who's fading away due to an undetermined malady is drinking coffee with a lady midget and they're both holding enormous saucers and bowl-like cups in their child-sized hands. It is shortly thereafter that the man, who has come to believe that the shrinking process has ceased, realizes to his horror that it's started again; suddenly, he's smaller than the lady midget. At this moment, Tombilena felt tiny, tinier than she had ever felt before in her adult life.

"I guess I don't really know," she said. "Campo's five years younger'n me, and I ain't closely kept up on his activities these last few years. I was livin' here in N.O. before I got married, then me and Pace, my husband who's now deceased, was mostly concerned with each other.

Bein' back in Delacroix, of course, I seen a lot of Campo, but I never heard about nothin' extra strange in his behavior."

Marble took out a pack of Delicado cigarettes and stuck one in her mouth.

"Mind if I smoke?" she asked, then before Tombilena could answer, lit it with an inch-and-a-half flame from a freshly polished Zippo that had two Oriental characters engraved on one side.

"What're them scratchin's on your lighter?"

Marble exhaled a bluish stream of Mexican smoke, looked quickly at her fire source, smiled, and dropped it back into the left breast pocket of her red sateen cowboy shirt. Because her breasts were so small, Marble never wore a brassiere, and she liked to feel the cool, smooth weight of the silver lighter against her body.

"Name of a Japanese girl, Take Ahike. She sent it to me from Japan. Writin's called *kanji*, she told me. Chinese, but the Japanese use it. She come to Mary Mother of God with her problem. Man much older'n her—Take was eighteen at the time—he maybe been forty or so, was her cousin, kept her prisoner in his house over in Gentilly Terrace. Love slave stuff. She come to New Orleans to attend the Pillara Salt Memorial Bible College, and her folks back in Osaka had thought they were doin' right arrangin' for her to board with their relative. Man owned a porcelain repair shop on Melpomene and South Tonti."

"He got her pregnant, I guess."

"Never even enrolled her at the college. Kept her locked in a soundproof bedroom for fourteen months. Made her write letters home sayin' how good she was doin' at school and how gracious a host their cousin was."

"How'd she escape?"

"Stabbed him through the right eye with a chopstick one night when he brought her supper. Man would watch her eat, then, before she could finish, Take said, he'd rape her. Seems her chewin' excited him so much he couldn't wait. Take told us he was like a rabbit, on and off real quick, but he done it to her six, seven times a day, sometimes more, every day, even durin' her period, for fourteen months. She said she woke up the middle of her first night in this country with his dick in her mouth."

"Did she kill him?"

Marble puffed a few times, then stubbed out her cigarette in an ashtray.

"No. Blinded him in the one eye, then run out with hardly no clothes on and no money, of course. Didn't know where she was. Happened Helga Grandeza was drivin' by at just that moment—she lives in that neighborhood—and Helga stopped and picked Take up, brought her directly to Mary Mother of God. We took care of everything, then she went back to Japan."

"Her parents know about what happened? The abortion?"

"Doubt it. Take said her folks'd freak if they did, prob'ly all commit *seppuku* 'cause of the humiliation."

"They could've revenged theirselves."

"Die Brausenkriegers took care of that. We waited till after Take had gone home. Her cousin never even tried to find her, far as we know. We told Take to tell her folks that he'd had a heart attack and died."

"What really happened?"

"Night she left, we paid the man a visit. Tied him down to the bed he'd abused her on and invaded the orifices of his person repeatedly with a variety of power tools. Then, before Take Ahike coulda said *sayonara*, we served him his last meal. One natural guess'll get it."

"Penis sushi."

Marble grinned. "You got a future with this company, Ms Gayoso, but first we gotta agree on the deal involves your brother."

"Marble, before Die Brausenkriegers go into action, let me talk to Campo, see in fact he participated."

"Observin's same as doin' if he done nothin' try to stop it."

"I'll get the details. Campo won't lie to me."

"All right, Tombilena. They ain't no way these boys is escapin' our attention."

"What about the woman? You know who she is?"

"Victoria China Realito, forty-five, from Port Arthur, Texas. She was in New Orleans settlin' the estate of her brother, a pawnshop operator, who was murdered a while back. She met this one of 'em, Gallo Viudo, in Phil's Lounge on St Roch, then accompanied him to Delacroix. That's all we know right now. Ms Realito is under heavy sedation at the Hôtel Dieu. Madonna Kim and Junebug are over there, waitin' on her to counsel."

Tombilena's eyes suddenly watered up, and she said, "Marble, I know you're a lot younger than me, but somehow it seems you're way older. This world's so terrible, but it appears you got better'n a hog grip on things."

Marble reached across the table and clasped Tombilena's trembling hands with her own.

"As Jeremiah said, when he was in the *juzgado*: "The Lord is with me as a mighty terrible one: therefore my persecutors shall stumble, and they shall not prevail: they shall be greatly ashamed; for they shall not prosper: their everlasting confusion shall never be forgotten. But, O Lord of hosts, that triest the righteous, and seest the reins of the heart, let me see thy vengeance on them: for unto thee have I opened my cause." There's comfort there."

"Oh, Marble, dear Marble, it's so hard not to suffer."

"I know it, Tombilena. One of the reasons I'm on the planet, help spread the sufferin' around more evenly."

WHEN LIFE IS LIKE A CHEAP HOTEL ROOM

Dear Jesus,

Well this is sure it. This is letter number 666 that I have written to You over these past few years 666 is the devils number as You well know and I have dreaded coming to it but theres nothing to be done other than show him how his name and number mean nothing to a Believer on the Righteous side so consider this only another letter from me to You. We have a Situation here at Mary Mother of God. There is a problem that I thought it best to share with You before deciding on. One of the women who has come lately to work with us her name is Tombilena Gayoso she is an Isleño as is her brother who participated in an attack on a girl in Delacroix. This girl was raped by six men with poolsticks. A bunch of fishermen not unlike some of the ones You run with back in the days. The difficult part concerns this woman who is among our organization and her desire to spare her brother from the wrath of the Righteous she knows is coming to be visited upon each of these men done the devils work. There was lightning here today Jesus that struck close to the roof of our building out of an anvil-shaped cloud and continued to spark for twenty minutes or more. I was not frightened so much as surprised and impressed by the display of Your Daddys power. Watching the electric sky my mind kinda wandered back to when I was much younger and my Daddy was all the time drunk a time when he would fall in the road any old place even in the path of truck traffic and sleep. People would rescue him and he would not even know later what happened. He recovered and said he was so twisted up in his brain about the divorce from my mother Bird who lives now in Florida that he did not care what befell him. But the difficult decision here is should we let Tombilena deal with her brother herself. I am tempted to let her as a way of testing her commitment to our cause at Mary Mother of God. Die Brausenkriegers as I told you before are already set to take care of the other five in fact before there can be a trial. A good guess is they would leave the country on boats and never have a day in court. I saw on the TV news yesterday about a 6 year old girl who was stole out of her house in the middle of the night. They found the man who done it after he returned her to the home after molesting her in all kinds of ways and had shot the girl up with drugs and burned her body with cigarettes. This man had tattoos one of a lizard on an arm and a skull I think on the other that he cut off after she had told the police about them and this information was printed in the newspaper he must have read it. He had been kidnapping and having sex with girls down to the age of 9 months old Jesus I sometimes cannot even believe the sickness that is walking around loose out the door. If this is a test of us it is a severe one only You know why. I am thankful to be such a strong young person but I feel older than almost everybody aint that weird? My daddy Wes has fell off the wagon too which is the other terrible news. Last night I discovered him passed out from beer on the front porch so I pulled him inside the house where he woke up and said over and over Im not dyin in some cheap hotel room Im not dyin in some cheap hotel room. Jesus I hate to say this but life can get more awful the more a person sees of it.

Sincerely Your faithful
Marble

BLACK KISS

THE NIGHT BEFORE Tombilena left for Delacroix, Marble had handed her a seventeen-shot nine-millimeter Glock pistol and a copy of *Magnificent Female: An Intimate Memoir of Hilda Brausen* by Eva von Blutvergiftung, translated from the German by Irma Zunge.

These items were on the front seat beside Tombilena Gayoso as she drove east in her Toyota 4-Runner on Louisiana State Highway 46.

Finding herself too agitated to sleep last night, Tombilena had read several chapters of *Magnificent Female* before finally falling out for a couple of hours. Eva von Blutvergiftung had been Hilda Brausen's governess from the age of four until Hilda turned thirteen, at which time Eva, then in her early thirties, introduced her precocious charge to the carnal delights of Sapphic culture. This sexual liaison continued secretly for four years, until the pair were discovered engaged in an act they referred to as "releasing the pythoness" on the pantry floor of the Brausen family summer home in Blindheit by Hilda's father, Bruno. Horrified and enraged, Herr Brausen beat both women with a mop handle so severely that they required hospitalization.

Bruno Brausen, a beer baron whose brewery empire extended from Munich to Mexico City to Shanghai, disowned his seventeen-year-old daughter, casting her into the world with a subsistence-level stipend to be doled out to her by his lawyers only until she reached the age of twenty-one. Those same lawyers brought charges against the woman their client perceived as a heinous corrupter of youth, and succeeded in providing her—subsequent to a highly publicized trial—a six-year prison sentence for the practice of deviant behavior with a child.

It was during her incarceration at the women's penal colony on the island of Schwips that Eva von Blutvergiftung wrote the first part of her memoir. She then set it aside until after Hilda's death. Because of Hilda Brausen's notoriety as a polemicist prior to World War I, and the public controversy that ensued concerning the circumstances of her death, Eva—who had not seen or corresponded with her former lover since the details of their relationship were served up to the masses by the European press in the most scandal-inducing fashion—completed her book, including in it not only material of a personal nature, but an eccentric analysis of female sexual urges and responses later acknowledged by Wilhelm Reich as having proved extremely useful to his research for *The Function of the Orgasm*.

Suppressed by the governments of Germany and Austria for more than a decade following its initial publication in Zurich in 1920, *Magnificent Female* became an international best-seller, and had never been out of print in the German, French, Italian, and English languages during its author's lifetime. Eva von Blutvergiftung died in 1960 in New York City, where she had been the proprietress of a vivarium on Second

Avenue that specialized in pythons. She was believed to be at least ninety years old.

Tombilena found the book difficult—in part due to Irma Zunge's stilted and dated translation—but fascinating. Aside from the story of the love affair between the woman and the girl, Eva von Blutvergiftung's copious classifications of sexual dynamics mystified Tombilena. She never knew there was so much to say about fucking. What she did know, she decided, was that reading Eva von Blutvergiftung's exegesis served to suppress in her sexual desire of any kind. Not that she had been up for much these days, anyway, but old Eva, Tombilena thought, was as weird a turnoff as ever there was likely to be.

Tombilena glanced down at the Glock, admired its contours, and lifted it with her right hand. She balanced the gun in her palm as she returned her gaze to the road, then was suddenly startled by the lethal feeling implicit in the pistol's weight. A blackness crept up her arm and Tombilena dropped the weapon onto the seat. She pressed hard the inside of her right wrist against her lips and kissed its heat, then managed to pull the 4-Runner off to the side and kill the engine before blacking out.

THE PASSION

PARSHAL LEE CRACKED open the monkey's skull with a ball peen hammer, picked it up, and drank the fluid from the deceased simian's hypothalamus gland. He was a determined individual. If this was what it took to regain the exclusive affections of Hypolite Cortez, damn straight he'd do it. It and anything else that seemed logical to Miss Consuelo Yesso, Parshal's advisor in matters involving love and finance.

Parshal Lee was an artist, a portrait painter who set up shop daily next to the north fence of Jackson Square in New Orleans. He was thirty-eight years old, a native of Meridian, Mississippi, a place to which he had no desire to return. Parshal had not been in Meridian since his mother, Zolia Versalles Lee, was buried four years before across the street from the Dixie Boys Field. He had no living relatives that he knew of other than an eighty-four-year-old bastard uncle named Get-Down Lucky, who was part Gypsy and sold Bibles door-to-door in Dothan, Alabama. It was this uncle who had informed Parshal at Zolia Lee's funeral that the meaning of life was based on a simple concept. "It ain't what you eat," said Get-Down Lucky, "it's the way how you chew it."

Parshal's father, Roy L Lee, had disappeared the day before his son's fourteenth birthday. Roy L—he had no middle name, only an initial he'd taken himself so that he would have something to write in on forms that requested one—was believed to have fled Meridian in order to avoid prosecution for grave robbing. He and a one-armed Salvadoran refugee named Arturo Trope, who had worked as an undertaker's assistant in a Meridian funeral parlor, had been apprehended exhuming newly buried bodies in order to steal rings, necklaces, and other valuable items decorating the corpses. Both men had skipped town on bail, and two months later Arturo Trope had been shot to death during the commission of an armed robbery of a jewelry store on Capitol Street in Jackson. Roy L had not been seen or heard from since the cemetery scam. Parshal considered his daddy dead and himself a free agent. All he had to make his way in the world was his God-given artistic talent. Roy L, Parshal figured, had nothing to do with that.

Parshal sat on the porch of his rented bungalow on Spain Street in the Marigny, chasing the bitter taste of monkey gland fluid with Rebel Yell. His brain was obsessed by thoughts of his erstwhile girlfriend, Hypolite Cortez, and the fact that she had abandoned him in favor of a woman. Hypolite now lived with an exotic dancer named Irma Soon, a Panamanian-Chinese who simulated copulation with a rock python six nights a week at Big Nig's Gauchos 'n' Gals Club on Pelican Avenue in Algiers. Parshal was hoping that Miss Yesso's prescription would inspire Hypolite to return to her senses and to him. She had given no reason for her defection, merely left a note on her red sateen pillow embroidered in yellow with intertwined initials *P* and *H*, that said: "Parshal you took care of me best you could but I have fallen for Irma Soon who I believe is my destiny. Our two years together have been good however love is got to be better than good and only with Irma Soon have I felt what is commonly called ecstasy. I hope one day you will know for yourself with someone the way I feel with Irma. Luv to you and I mean it, Hypolite."

Parshal Lee had given Hypolite's note to Consuelo Yesso, who rolled the paper into a tiny ball, dipped it into a powder made of flywings and lizard tongues, and told Parshal to swallow it, which he had. By ingesting Hypolite's note, garnished with these purposeful ingredients, Miss Yesso explained, Parshal would cause his beloved to dream of him and force Hypolite to reconsider her situation. Miss Yesso had handed him the monkey's skull wrapped with aluminum foil and promised to continue her efforts toward accomplishing Hypolite and Parshal's reconciliation. Parshal paid the *bruja* what she asked, and tried to put a hopeful spin on his thoughts, but he knew that it would take more than Miss Yesso's powers to bring back Hypolite Cortez.

"Hey, Parshal! Parshal Lee!"

Parshal broke out of his trance and saw Avenue Al, a neighbor, standing on the sidewalk. Al was wearing a dyed-purple mohair suit, which he called his "goat coat," and was propped up on crutches, necessitated by his having taken a hard fall and broken both knees while leaving Teresa's Tite Spot Lounge in the Bywater two months before. Avenue Al, a sixty-year-old former professional wrestler whose claim to fame was that he had bitten off one of Dick the Bruiser's earlobes, was suing Teresa for damages. His plan, he told everyone, was to take the money and retire in Cebu City, the Philippines, where he had once wrestled an ape. "Fell in love a dozen times in six days," he claimed, "and never even got the clap."

"Come on, Parshal," Avenue Al shouted, "let's go! Trumpet Shorty havin' a funeral for his pit bull, Louis Armstrong, jus' passed. Be the firs' dog have a second-line since dat rabid Airedale, Dagoo, hads to be put down in '71."

GREAT EXPECTATIONS

"Nobody cares *what* you do in New Orleans, but everyone wants to know what it is."

"I like for folks to know what I'm up to, so they know what to *expec'*."

Parshal Lee sat at the bar in Teresa's Tite Spot, nursing a Bombay on the rocks, half-listening to Beverly Waverly and Caspiana Pleasant, two café-au-lait transvestites, converse. Mostly, he contemplated his unhappy circumstance.

"Parshal. Parshal, baby," said Caspiana. "Why you so morose?"

"What's morose?" asked Beverly.

"Unnormally quiet and broodish," Caspiana answered. "What's up, Parshal? You might can tell us girls."

"Hypolite left me."

"Aw, honey," said Beverly, putting a meaty, hairy forearm around

Parshal's neck, "ain't that a bitch. Some women just don't got good sense. No man she could get better'n you."

"Didn't leave me for a man. Took up with an exotic dancer over in Algiers. Woman name Irma Soon."

Caspiana gasped. "You mean the China girl porks her ownself with a snake? Used to she work at Tickfaw Fouquet's Crawl Inn?"

"Half Chinese. Half from Panama."

"Shit, baby," said Caspiana, "that's rough. You need it, me an' Beverly, we zoom ya."

"Ain' be pussy, 'xactly," said Beverly, "but it defi'tely da nex' bes' thing."

" 'Preciate your concern, ladies, but I'm workin' on this in my own way."

"Okay, baby," said Caspiana, "but we here for ya."

"I hoid such a terr'ble thing, today," Beverly said. "Was on the TV news."

"What dat?"

"Russian man was sentence to death for killin' more'n fifty people. Men, boys, women, an' girls. Ate parts their bodies, mostly tips of their tongues and genitalia."

"Saint Rose of Lima!" cried Caspiana, crossing herself.

"Man was fifty-six years old, and impotent. Only way he could complete a sexual act was by torturin' an' killin' someone. Russian papers called him the "Forest Strip Killer," after the place where he dump mos' the bodies."

"Lord have mercy. He jus' cut folks apart, huh?"

"What da news say."

"An' some people thinkin' *we* weird!"

"If everyone was so well adjusted as you two," said Parshal, "wouldn't never be no more wars."

Caspiana smiled, leaned over, and kissed him on the left cheek.

"Bless you, baby," she said. "But you jus' seen us on our best behavior. We might can be some tacky bitches sometime."

"You want Hypolite back," said Beverly, "best you stay in her face. Let her know you there for her."

Caspiana shook her curly gold wig. "Don't believe it, sugar. Liable push the lady further away. Besides, she an' this snake charmer in the first flush of their love. No way to buck that. My advice, darlin', wait it out. You a good *man*, after all. Hypolite come back aroun'. She don't, somethin' turn up."

Parshal finished off his Bombay, thanked Caspiana and Beverly for their commiseration, and walked outside. It was a hot night; the air was even heavier than ordinary in July. He went to his car, a two-year-old blue Thunderbird, unlocked the driver's side door, and was about to get in, thinking to cruise over to Algiers, check out his rival Irma Soon's terpsichorean snake act, when Parshal felt a cold, hard object enter the outer part of his left ear.

"Y'all don' min'," a high-pitched voice said, "my name is Carjack Jack an' I gon' be y'all's designated driver tonight."

Out of the corner of his left eye, Parshal saw a skinny, balding white man in his mid-thirties, wearing a blue Hawaiian shirt decorated with yellow parrots and red flowers. A bright purple scar the width of a trouser zipper ran down the center of his nose from bridge to tip. Parshal started to turn toward him but as he did the man inserted the gun barrel deeper into Parshal's ear, forcing his head away, then removed the weapon briefly before bringing the butt down hard on the soft spot at the back of Parshal's head. Parshal collapsed against the car and the man opened the door, shoved Parshal's limp shape into the backseat, took the keys from the door lock, climbed behind the steering wheel, and closed himself inside. He cranked the engine and grinned, exposing a row of rotten teeth.

"Hellfire!" Carjack Jack screeched, shifting the T-Bird into gear and tearing away from the curb. "We got us some *miles* to go before we sleep. *Miles*. Course, y'all're already sleepin', ain't ya? Well, as them pussies out in California say, this here's the first day of the rest of our lives, an' a life is a terrible thing to waste. Or is that a mind is bad to waste? Hell, *I* don't mind! Waste not, want not. Two peas in a pod. Damn the *Defiant!* Ain't *no* business like *show* business. Fasten your seatbelt, buddy, this gon' be a *bumpy* fuckin' ride."

THE BIG BITE

HYPOLITE CORTEZ SAT at a ringside table in Big Nig's Gauchos 'n' Gals Club, sipping sparkling water through a straw. She was twenty-two years old, a smidge more than five foot two, had never weighed a hundred pounds in her life, had huge black eyes, severely arched Chinese eyebrows, and permitted her midnight black hair to fall slightly below her seventeen-inch waist. Above the nipple of her left breast was a three-quarter-inch in circumference dark blue, star-shaped mole that Hypolite referred to as "where the Arab bit me." This mole Hypolite had inherited from her maternal grandmother, Ephémère Plaire, who told Hypolite that her own paternal grandmother, Pilar LaLa, had borne this identical mark. The first time Irma Soon saw it, she experienced a spontaneous orgasm.

The lights dimmed, a drum rolled, and from offstage a husky female voice, that of Bruma "Big Nig" Goma, the proprietress herself, announced: "Get ready, Eddie! Chase dat frown, Miz Brown! You ain't seen poon 'til you seen Miz Soon! Here she be, di-rek from Mandinga, Panama, da soipent princess, doin' an exclusive performance of "La Gran Mordedura"—a specialmost dance she create herself that been banned in most parts da Orient

"Miz . . . Oima . . . Sooooonnn!"

The lavender curtains parted, revealing a diminutive woman whose body was crisscrossed with several rivet-studded black leather belts. Miss Soon's most intimate part was fully exposed, however, while stretched across her tiny breasts and relaxed around her neck was a reticulated creature the color of Delaware River mud. The patrons of the half-filled Gauchos 'n' Gals Club howled and applauded at this sight. A slow version of "Little Egypt" emanated from the band pit, prompting the lithe Filipina to begin her routine, which consisted mostly of waving arms and undulating hips. This tepid dance continued for several minutes, during which time the reptile remained composed, placid, unstirred; until Irma Soon gently but firmly grasped its head with her right hand and placed it directly between her legs.

At this point the patrons, some of whom gasped audibly, froze in their seats. The dancer closed her eyes, thrust her pelvis forward, and bent backward incrementally, slowly, tortuously, or so it seemed to those in rapt attention, until her head touched the floor. To all appearances, the python's head had disappeared inside Irma Soon. Hypolite Cortez shivered as she watched her lover manipulate the reptile. As easily as Miss Soon had accommodated it, she withdrew the lubricated cranium and with an agonizing absence of haste, sinuously resumed an upright position. Holding the python by her right hand just behind the head, Irma positioned it face-to-face and flicked her own pointy tongue toward it. The music reached a crescendo and Irma twirled with the snake, the two creatures' tongues darting at one another until the dancer whirled them offstage.

The audience whistled and clapped their hands, hardly believing what they had just witnessed. Hypolite smiled demurely and sat still, proud and deeply in love, thoroughly enchanted.

"Dass it, gauchos 'n' gals," boomed Bruma Goma. "Ain't another performer like Irma Soon this side o' Subic Bay! Let her know y'all appreciate her art! Open up fo' dis Filipina baby!"

The patrons continued to shout, whistle, and applaud until the curtains closed. It was not Irma Soon's habit to take a parting bow. She had explained to Hypolite that once the connection with her audience had been made, she preferred to leave it unblemished, having no desire to break the spell or alter the feeling she had engendered. To her fans, Irma remained forever in character.

The band segued into a waltz-like treatment of "The Fat Man" and several couples, some of the same or similar sex, rose to dance. Hypolite dipped a hand between her gooey thighs and closed her eyes as she massaged herself, holding in her mind the impossibly beautiful image of Irma Soon and the python locked in their forbidden embrace.

TWO FOR THE ROAD

"YOU GONNA HARM me?"

Carjack Jack looked back over his right shoulder at Parshal, wrinkled his lips toward his zipper-nose, and laughed.

"Hell, pardner," he said, returning his eyes to the road, "I ain't no demon. Don't do no brutalizin' 'less it's essential. Sorry I had to sock you back there, but a man has to know what he has to do when it has to be done. Mack Daddy of all Mack Daddies told me that ten years ago. City jail, Montgomery, Alabama. Copperhead Kane was his name. Famous man, famous. Had him a escort network from Alabama to Illinois. Copperhead Kane, yeah. The man in*vented* phone sex. That's a fact."

Parshal lay on the backseat, still woozy from the blow to his head.

He noticed that neither his hands nor his feet had been bound. Carjack Jack sped the blue Bird along Chef Menteur Highway.

"What're you gonna do with me, then?" Parshal asked him.

"Ain't quite decided. You want me to drop you someplace in particular? I'm thinkin' on headin' up north, myself. What's your name, anyway?"

"Lee. Parshal Lee."

"Just call me C.J. Best you don't know my family name."

Parshal thought about Hypolite Cortez. He wondered whether the years she had worked as a teenage prostitute for the Hilda Brausen Charm School had unduly influenced her gender preference. He had to admit that despite his unselfish efforts of a sexual nature, Hypolite had never really responded to him as did other women. Something had been missing in their relationship. Parshal watched the blackness pass for a minute before he spoke.

"You don't mind, C.J., maybe I'll just tag along with you. Need to put some space between me and a kind of unhealthy situation here, anyway."

"Guess I could do with some comp'ny, Parshal. Ten to one it's a renegade female messed up your mind."

"How'd you guess?"

C.J. laughed. "It's a epidemic. Happenin' all over the so-called civilized world. Copperhead Kane predicted it back when. The people ain't starvin' for food are starvin' for answers. Things is got too complicated for words, or ain't you been payin' attention?"

"Not close enough, I guess."

"Take this show I seen on TV one night in the joint, called *Down to Earth*. You ever watched it?"

"No," said Parshal. "What is it?"

"See, these couples go out on a date for the first time, and one of 'em thinks it's the greatest thing. Usually they had sex of some type on the date. So they bring on the one of 'em thinks the date was great, all that. Then the other one comes on and totally tears up the date, hated it, had bad sex, bad breath, bad manners, the guy's hairpiece fell off while he was performin' cunnilingus on her. They'll say anything."

"Prob'ly it's in the script. They just sayin' what was wrote for 'em to say and ain't none of it happened."

"Wrong, Mr Lee. Nobody could make up this stuff. This guy had eyebrows took up half his face won with the best story."

"Wha'd he tell?"

"You won't believe it. Said he and this girl go out to a nice dinner. She has the lamb chops, eats the parsley, so he figures she's both classy and healthy, yeah?"

"Oh?"

"Yeah. So, they go to a movie."

"What movie?"

"A Spanish picture, somethin' European, where all the women got long noses and by the end the men are wearin' spike heels and lipstick and complainin' how they don't get enough sex."

"Ho!"

"They go next to the girl's apartment, where the guy says she's all over him like an electric blanket. Get this, the guy actually says this: 'I got my eel out and she's doin' the popsicle!' That's what he says! The audience is dyin'!"

"He got his eel out."

"His eel, yeah. Then it comes."

"His eel?"

"No, no. The good part of his story."

"The good part."

"He grabs her crotch, and guess what?"

"She's a guy, too."

"Right! Right! Of course, she's really a guy!"

"Is the guy who was supposed to be a girl on the show?"

"Yeah, yeah. And guess what? He comes on after Eyebrows gives his version and denies everything! You believe that, Mr Lee? Completely and entirely says Eyebrows is out of his goddamn mind!"

"Jesus."

"Now, here's the killer."

"Don't tell me."

"Shit, Parshal, can you guess? Can you?"

"She offers to prove she's a woman."

"Correct! Yeah, yeah! Right on the air! She pulls up her skirt an' shows her pelt! The audience is goin' batshit. The host is lyin' on the couch, chokin' to death. This Nancy starts paradin' up an' down the stage, like on a runway, got his jewels tucked up so nothin' shows. Man, you never, *never* seen nothin' like this."

"What's Eyebrows doin'?"

"Okay, get this: Eyebrows attacks Nancy."

"Eyebrows *attacks* Nancy?!"

"Tries to get at his dick."

"Holy shit."

"Nancy karate chops him in the back of the neck, and Eyebrows goes down hard on his nose, which bleeds."

"Holy shit."

"The security guys come out an' separate the two. Nancy is outta-hermind handsdown havin' the greatest time of her life! She's smilin', throwin' kisses to the audience."

"You have to admit, C.J., it's a special place would allow a program like that on the air."

Carjack Jack nodded his red crew-cut head several times and laughed.

"Mr Lee," he said, "I got no doubt in my mind but that there ain't never been and won't never will be another country like this one in the history of planet earth."

from
BABY CAT-FACE
(1997)

BABY AND JIMBO

"TAKE HERE DIS LADY in Detroit bludgeon her husban', chop up da body, den cook it. Talkin' 'bout payback! Whoa!"

"Baby, you oughtn't be readin' dem kinda lies is put inna newspaper. Ya know dat shit jus' invented, mannipilate y'all's min'. Make peoples crazy, so's dey buy stuff dey don't have no need fo'. Stimmilate da 'conomy."

"Wait up, Jimbo, dis gal got firs' prize. She skin him, boil da head, an' fry his hands in oil."

"What kinda oil? Corn oil? Olive oil?"

"Don't say. Lady be from Egyp', 'riginally. Twenny-fo' years ol'. Name Nazli Fike. Husban' name Ralph Fike. Police found his body parts inna garbage bag, waitin' be pick up. Whoa! Ol' Nazli was stylin'! Put onna red hat, red shoes an' red lipstick befo' spendin' hours choppin' on an' cookin' da body. Played Ornette Coleman records real loud while she's doin' it. Tol' police her ol' man put her onna street, shot dope in her arms, an' was rapin' her when she kill him in self-defense."

"Bitch was a hoojy, begin wit'."

"Jimbo, how you know? Plenty guys lookin' turn out dey ol' ladies."

"Was a hoojy."

"Aw, shit!"

"What?"

"She ate parts da body."

"Cannibal hoojy."

"Dis disgustin'."

"What else it say?"

"Can't read no more."

Jimbo Deal got up from the fake-leopard-skin-covered sofa and snatched the newspaper out of Baby Cat-Face's hands. He and Baby had been living together for six weeks now, since the day after the night they had met in Inez's Fais-Dodo, and he wasn't certain the arrangement was going to work out. She had a tendency to talk too much, engage him in conversation when he was not in a conversational mood. At thirty-four years old, Deal was used to maintaining his own speed. Since Baby Cat-Face, who was twenty-three, had come into his life, he had been forced to *adjust*.

"Woman ain' be clean fo' way back, Baby, you read da res'. Run numbers on guys since she come from Egyp', seven years ago. Car thef', drug bus', solicitin' minors fo' immoral purpose. A hoojy, like I claim. *Foreign* hoojy."

"Husban' put her up to it," said Baby. She lit a cigarette and stood looking out the window down on Martinique Alley. "She been abuse' as a chil', too."

"Dat's what dey all usin', now. Abuse dis, abuse dat. Shit. Says she be foun' sane an' sentence to life imprison. Shit. She prob'ly be queen da hive, have hoojies servin' on her in da joint. Big rep hoojy like her."

"Quit, Jimbo! Cut out dat "hoojy" shit, all ri'? Tired hearin' it."

"Troof, is all. Since when you don't like to listen da troof?"

Baby sucked on an unfiltered Kool, then blew away a big ball of smoke.

"Swear, Mister Deal, you da mos' truth tellines' man in New Orleans."

Jimbo tossed the newspaper on the coffee table.

"I got to get ready fo' work," he said, and left the room.

Baby Cat-Face smoked and stared out the window. The sky was overcast. It was almost six o'clock in the evening and Baby was not sure what she was going to do while Jimbo pulled his night shift at the refinery in Chalmette. She saw two boys, both about twelve years old, one white, one black, run into the alley from off Rampart Street. They were moving fast, and as they ran, one of them dropped a lady's handbag.

"Baby!" Jimbo Deal shouted from the bathroom. "You gon' make my lunch?"

Baby took a deep drag of the Kool, then flicked the butt out the window into the alley. It landed, still burning, next to the purse.

"We got some dat lamb neck lef', darlin', ain' we?"

THE DWARF OF PRAGUE AND THE DREADFULS

BABY CAT-FACE HAD not used her real name, Esquerita Reyna, since her second, and last, year of high school. Even then, most of her friends and all of the members of her family called her Baby or Baby Cat-Face, as they had since she was born. She had been nicknamed Cat-Face for the most obvious reasons: she had green feline eyes and a tiny snub nose. Esquerita was the youngest of three sisters and two brothers born to DeDe Benavides and Refugio Reyna in New Orleans over a twelve-year period, and so she was dubbed Baby.

She attended St Guerif of Rivages Grammar School, Turhan Bey Junior High, and St Phoebe of Zagreb High School, all in N.O. It was during Baby's second year at St Phoebe's, while on the class retreat, that Baby learned the legend of the Dwarf of Prague and the Dreadfuls. Sister Mercy Vermillion related the story of how in the fifteenth century A.D., a band of thugs and cutthroats called the Dreadfuls were terrorizing the good citizens of Prague. This group of murderous thieves specialized in kidnapping children of the rich and threatening to burn them alive unless their parents paid an enormous ransom. After the Dreadfuls had carried out this threat on two or three occasions, the families subsequently victimized quickly capitulated.

One day a gnomish dwarf named Desenfrenado appeared in Prague at the office of the mayor. Desenfrenado declared that he could rid the city of the Dreadfuls, but in return the citizens would have to build him a mansion behind the church in which he could live for the rest of his life, provide him with servants and funds adequate to a comfortable lifestyle, and allow him to go about the city naked during good weather. The mayor and most of his advisers were angered at the seeming effrontery of the dwarf, and were about to have him thrown into the street, when a member of the city council known as Raymond of Pest, a man who had come from the East and married a local woman, begged the mayor to indulge Desenfrenado. After all, said Raymond of Pest, there would be no harm in allowing the dwarf this opportunity to better himself, especially since the council had been unable to develop an effective plan of action. If the dwarf could eradicate the Dreadfuls, Raymond argued, Desenfrenado's request would be a small enough price to pay. The mayor and the other council member, having no immediate alternatives, thus sanctioned the dwarf's enterprise.

That night there was a full moon over Prague, and at ten o'clock Desenfrenado appeared nude in the town square. Mumbling to himself, the dwarf began to dance, gyrating wildly over the cobblestones around the deep well in the center of the square. Word of the dwarf's appearance spread throughout Prague, and soon most of its citizens were gathered in order to observe the event. Desenfrenado danced and danced, his movements becoming increasingly frenzied, his indecipherable mutterings growing louder, and—as Sister Mercy Vermillion delicately phrased it—his extreme maleness reaching a rather preposterous state. An hour or so into his mad romp, several of the audience, infected by the dwarf's dedication, themselves threw off their clothes and joined him in the dance. By midnight, virtually the entire population of Prague, including the mayor and his advisers, was whirling in intoxicated abandon around the dwarf.

Only nine men stood apart from the naked, swirling mass. Suddenly, the dwarf bolted from among the throng and began to run in a circle around the isolated men, shouting, "These are they! These are they!" The citizens turned their attention to the nine nonparticipants and advanced on them, mumbling and drooling as they came. The nine men, quickly surrounded, could not escape. They fell to their knees and begged forgiveness for their sins, confessing that they were indeed the Dreadfuls who had kidnapped and burned the children. No sooner had these words escaped their mouths than the furious crowd tore the men's limbs from their bodies, their tongues from their heads, and crushed their skulls on the cobblestones.

Desenfrenado was provided with his mansion and supported thereafter by the citizens of Prague. When in fair weather he chose to go about the streets of the city unclothed, the citizens greeted him as affectionately and respectfully as they did when he was clad. The dwarf, Sister Mercy Vermillion told her class, lived to be very old. Desenfrenado had not been accorded sainthood, she explained, due to his own choosing. Before he died, Desenfrenado declared that he wanted forever to remain a humble man, as ordinary in memory as he had been in life. Remember, he said on his deathbed, it is always the most dreadful among us who ultimately are revealed to be the most timid.

Baby Cat-Face never forgot the story of the Dwarf of Prague. She had told it to every man she had slept with more than once, all of whom, with the exception of Jimbo Deal, had said that it was the most ridiculous story he had ever heard. Jimbo had only nodded and said, "Baby, funny, ain't it, how there never be a dwarf around when you need one."

Jimbo, Baby hoped, would turn out to be the kind of man who never lost his sense of humor.

RAT TANGO

" 'WHAT YOU WANT, baby I got it. What you want, baby I got it.' "

"Say, what?" Baby Cat-Face said to the red-haired café-au-lait woman who was singing and dancing the skate next to the jukebox, her back to Baby.

"Huh?" the woman said, doing an about-face, keeping her skates on. "How come there ain't mo' Aretha on this box? 'R-e-s-p-e-c-t, find out what it mean to me,' " she sang-shouted, beginning to swim and shimmy. " 'Sock-it-to-me sock-it-to-me sock-it-to-me!' "

The woman wiggled and shook, causing Baby and another patron of the Evening in Seville Bar on Lesseps Street to grin and clap.

"Down to it, Radish!" shouted a fat man standing next to the pay phone. He banged his huge right fist on the top of the black metal box. "Be on time! Ooh-ooh-ooh!"

The dancing woman looked at Baby, and asked, "You say somethin'?"

"Thought you was talkin' to me, was all," said Baby. "You say 'baby.' "

"Yeah, so?"

"That's my name, Baby."

The woman smiled, displaying several gold teeth, one with a red skull painted on it. "Oh, yeah? Well, hello, Baby. I'm Radish Jones. Over here playin' the telephone's my partner, ETA Cato."

The fat man nodded. He was wearing a porkpie hat with a single bell on the top with DALLAS printed on a band around the front of it, and a black silk shirt unbuttoned to the beltline, exposing his bloated, hairy belly.

"Happenin', lady?" he said.

"ETA?" said Baby.

Radish laughed. "Estimated time of arrival. Cato's firs' wife name him, 'count of his careless way 'bout punctchality. Come we ain't seen you in here before, Baby?"

"Firs' time I been, Radish. My ol' man, Jimbo Deal, tol' me check it out."

"Shit, you hang wit' Jimbo? Shit, we know da man, know him well. Don't we, Cato?"

"Who dat?"

"Jimbo, da oil man."

Cato nodded. "Um-hum. Drink Crown Royal an' milk when he up, gin when he down."

"Dat him," said Baby.

"Where he at tonight?" Radish asked.

"Workin'."

"Well, glad you come by, Baby. We front you a welcome by."

"Rum an' orange juice be nice."

"Say, Eddie Floyd Garcia," Radish called to the bartender, "lady need a rum an' OJ."

The bartender mixed Mount Gay with Tang and water and set it up for Baby.

"Thanks, Eddie Floyd," said Radish. "This here's Baby."

"Hi, Baby," the bartender said. "Round here we call dis drink a Rat Tango, as in 'I don't need no rat do no tango at my funeral.' "

Eddie Floyd Garcia, a short, wide, dark blue man of about fifty, winked his mist-covered right eye at Baby. Up close, she could see the thick cataract that covered it.

ETA Cato traded off dancing with Radish and Baby to the juke over the next couple or three hours, during which time they consumed liquor at a steady clip, Eddie Floyd making sure to keep their drinks fresh. It was a slow night in the Evening in Seville. Other than a few quick-time shot and beer customers, the trio and Eddie Floyd had the place to themselves. Baby learned that Cato worked as a longshoreman on Celeste Street Wharf, and Radish did a thriving nail-and-polish business out of her house on the corner of Touro and Duels called The Flashy Fingers Salon de Beauté.

Sometime past two A.M., Radish decided that ETA Cato had danced one too many times in a row with Baby Cat-Face. Johnny Adams, "The Tan Canary," was seriously wailing "I Solemnly Promise" when Radish flashed a razor under Cato's right ear, cutting him badly.

"Damn, woman!" Cato yelled. "What you do that for?!"

Radish Jones shook a Kool from a pack on the bar, stuck it in her mouth, but couldn't quite hold her lighter hand steady enough to fire up the cigarette.

Eddie Floyd Garcia grabbed a rag, vaulted over the counter, and knelt next to ETA Cato, who had slid to the floor, holding his right hand over the cut. Blood was jumping out of his neck.

"King Jesus! King Jesus!" screamed Baby, backing away.

Eddie Floyd applied pressure to Cato's wound with the rag, but the bleeding did not abate.

"Call a ambulance!" Eddie Floyd cried. "Look like a artery be sever'."

Radish did not pay any attention to Cato's predicament, absorbed as she was in her attempt to torch the Kool. Baby grabbed the phone and dialed 911. When a voice answered, she started to talk, then stopped when she realized it was a recorded message requesting that the caller please be patient and hold the line until an operator became available.

Baby forced herself to look at Cato. He coughed, lurched forward, and fell back against Eddie Floyd. Cato turned toward Baby and opened his eyes wide. She thought he was going to say something, but he died with his mouth half open, staring at her. A human being came on the line and asked Baby, "Is this an emergency?"

ONLY THE DESPERATE DESERVE GOD

"In Yuba City, California, two severed hands were found in a K-mart shopping cart. The grisly discovery was made at about four P.M. Sunday by a clerk collecting carts, a Yuba City police spokesman said. The hands are being treated as evidence in a crime, but it will take a forensics expert to determine for sure that the body parts found are, in fact, human and whether homicide is indicated."

"There just ain't no end to human mis'ry," Baby said out loud to herself, as she switched off the radio next to her and Jimbo's bed.

Baby Cat-Face had spent most of the previous three days drifting in and out of sleep, depressed by thoughts of the incident she had witnessed in the Evening in Seville Bar. After Radish Jones slit the throat of her boyfriend, ETA Cato, who expired on the barroom floor, flooded by his own blood, Baby had gone stone-cold with shock. Jimbo Deal told Baby later that the police had brought her home and that he had put her to bed after feeding her the Valium mints the NOPD nurse had safety-pinned in a tiny plastic bag to Baby's blouse.

She had eaten sparingly during this time, only Rice Krispies and dry toast with tea. Jimbo had stayed home from work for two days, "Baby-sittin'," as he called it; but today he had had to go, afraid that he would be fired if he did not. Jimbo placed a loaded Ruger Bearcat in Baby's bedside drawer and told her to protect herself with it if she had to until he came home.

Baby reached over with her right hand and switched the radio back on, tuning it until she found an interesting voice and left it there.

"People, when I say you got to stand up to God, I mean you got to challenge his word!" said the voice. "You got to be bold enough for Him to pay you any mind. Only the desperate deserve God, don't you know? Hallelujah! Are you desperate yet? Are you ashamed yet? Are you frightened next to death yet? Well, well, well—you should be! Yes, you should, you should! This is the time, people, the only time you got to hear God's word. It don't matter what your name is, what color you are, what size or financial condition, no! You got to stand up to him right now or it's snake eyes for the planet! Yeah, we got to do this little thing together, people, make it work right. Get our neighbor to admit how desperate he or she is so we can get on with this holy war, 'cause that's what it is, a holy war! Standin' up to God means standin' up to the beast in the street, the one soon's spit poison in your eyes as look at you. You got to know what I'm talkin' about, people, or die stupid!"

"I know," Baby said. "I know what you sayin'."

"All right, then!" said the voice from the radio. "Stand up to God! Do what's necessary! Most of you desperate and don't know it!"

Baby turned off the radio. She heard the front door to the apartment open and then quietly close.

"Jimbo? Honey, that you home already?"

A short person wearing a red ski mask stepped into the bedroom. The intruder held a .45 automatic pistol with both black-gloved hands and pointed it at Baby. Baby threw a pillow at the gun and rolled off the bed onto the floor, pulling down the bedside table as she fell. She grabbed Jimbo's Ruger from the drawer, swung it toward the intruder, closed her eyes, and pulled the trigger twice. Baby opened her eyes and saw that she was alone in the room. She held the Bearcat straight out in front of her as she got to her feet.

"Come on, muthafuck!" Baby yelled. "I stand up to God now!"

Baby crept stealthily from the bedroom into the living room. The front door was closed. The kitchen, which was in full view from the living room, was empty. The only other place a person could be hiding was the bathroom.

"Come out of there!" Baby shouted, pointing the Ruger at the closed bathroom door. "Or sure as shit I gon' bust a cap up yo' butt!"

There was no sound from the bathroom, so Baby Cat-Face fired two rounds through the door. She kicked it open and charged inside, firing two more shots into the shower stall. Baby looked around: there was nobody but her in the bathroom. She saw her reflection in the mirror above the washbasin. Her eyes were slashes of red on her face.

"King Jesus," she said, "am I hallucinatin'?"

A police siren wailed and Baby heard a car screech to a stop in Martinique Alley. She sat down on the toilet seat and let the handgun drop to the floor.

"Maybe I be *too* desperate," said Baby.

• • •

BUZZARD'S LUCK

SISTER ESQUERITA TOOK the .30/06-caliber 1917 Enfield rifle fitted with a six-power Golden Hawk telescopic sight and held it up for everyone to see. As usual for Sunday night's sermon, more than five hundred people were in the temple to witness Mother Bizco's testimony.

"The very weapon, people, employed by the murderer Ezra Nuez when he struck down in the coldest blood our own Brother Sheshbazar. Thank you, Sister Esquerita. You may now return the instrument of destruction to safekeeping."

Sister Esquerita departed the stage as Mother Bizco continued.

"As most of you already know, we at the Temple of the Few Washed Pure by Her Blood have cleansed the world of this assassin Nuez. We take care of our own business, needing no service of outsiders."

"Amen!" chorused the congregation.

"Now there was a certain man of Elohim, of Mount Toil, and his name was Desire, the son of Love, the son of Vainglory, the son of Right-Thinking, the son of Over-and-Back, an In-Time man."

"Hallelujah!"

"And he had two wives. The name of the one was Honor, and the name of the other Pain. And Pain had children, but Honor had no children."

"Hallelujah!"

"And this man went up out of his city yearly to worship and to sacrifice unto the Lord of hosts in Denial. And the two sons of Offal, Fill-It and Do-Wrong, the priests of the Lord, were there."

"Hallelujah!"

"And when the time was that Desire offered, he gave to Pain, his wife, and to all her sons and her daughters, permission to take revenge when necessary."

"Hallelujah!"

"But unto Honor he spoke of forgiveness in all things. This way did Desire cover his ample posterior."

"Hallelujah!"

As Mother Bizco sermonized, Sister Esquerita, known to intimates by her nickname, Baby Cat-Face, locked away the rifle in the temple's weapons chest and stole out the side door of the building into Spain Street to light up a cigarette. She leaned back against the brown bricks and inhaled deeply. As she exhaled, tears flowed from her eyes. Late that afternoon, Baby had learned she was pregnant for sure, a situation that would not mix, considering the vow of chastity she had taken when she became a full-time sister to Mother Bizco. As a member of the temple's Almost-Perfect Flock, Sister Esquerita was expected to devote her entire being to the furtherance of charity as defined by Mother Bizco's book; to give herself up to pure works. Baby had instead given herself up, in what Mother Bizco would define as an unreasoning moment of unheavenly forgetfulness, to a funky piece of the devil's work called Waldo Orchid, an acquaintance of her former boyfriend Jimbo Deal.

"Jus' my luck," Baby Cat-Face confided to the wet air.

Esquerita's tears mingled with sweat hoovered from her pores by the unholy heat that crept up in the summer from the Amazon Basin to New Orleans.

"Buzzard's luck," she said, then took a long drag on her Kool and closed her eyes, letting the bitter water drip down her face and into her mouth as she moaned.

" 'My soul is continually in my hand, yet I do not forget the law. The wicked have laid a snare for me.' "

A giant cockroach scooted up the wall next to Baby and she scrunched it with the fiery end of the Kool.

WALDO REGRETS

WALDO ORCHID LIVED in a shotgun bungalow on Lapeyrouse Street with his widowed mother, Malva, and his spinster Tante Desuso, Malva's older sister. Waldo's father, Tosco Orchid, had died when Waldo, his only child, was six. Tosco, an electrician, had been rewiring the tower of the Lighthouse for the Blind building on Camp Street when a sepia-puce Norway rat the size of an average javelina exploded from a dark corner of the crawl space Tosco had wedged himself into and sank its diseased incisors into Tosco's carotid artery. The elder Orchid had bled to death even before he could extricate himself from the cubbyhole.

This paternal loss so enervated the juvenile Orchid that until the age of fifteen he barely ate. Waldo was such a skinny kid, and had such a prominent overbite, that, to his horror, he became known in the neighborhood as Rat Boy. In an effort to eradicate this image of himself, Waldo began to eat upon waking and continued until bedtime every day. By the age of twenty, the former Rat Boy stood five foot nine and weighed 325 pounds; even then, upon self-appraisal in a mirror, Waldo thought he could do with some fattening up.

It was a steamy gray morning when Baby knocked on the door of the house on Lapeyrouse Street. Tante Desuso, whom Baby had never met, opened up a crack and said, "What you wan'?"

Baby was startled by the old woman's eyes, which in the dimness appeared to be perfectly yellow.

"Is Waldo Orchid at home?"

"He is, he sleep. Who wanna know?"

"My name is Esquerita Reyna. *Sister* Esquerita."

"Sister? From what church?"

"Temple da Few Wash Pure by Her Blood, down Burgundy in da Marigny."

"Dat crackpot quadroon Mother Bizco's church, ain't it?"

"Yes, ma'am. But Mother Bizco ain' no crackpot. She help all sorts of folks."

"Our Lady da Holy Fantômes where we belong."

"Yes, ma'am. Can you see Waldo be in? Tell him Baby need to see him."

"*Baby?* Who dat?"

"Be me."

"Thought you was Sister Esquerita Raymon'."

"Reyna, mean queen. I am, but he know me by my familiar name."

Tante Desuso closed the door. Baby waited on the porch and thought about the night she had backslid and gotten nasty on Crown Royal with Waldo and his one-legged Hungarian-Creole partner, Balzac Kicz. Baby had encountered the two men in Elgrably's Grocery on Mandeville, around the corner from the temple, where she had gone to buy cigarettes. Waldo Orchid had introduced himself, reminding her that they had met once before at the Evening in Seville Bar on Lesseps Street, back when she cribbed with Jimbo Deal. Orchid and Deal had both belonged to the Lost Tribe of Venus Pleasure & Social Club on Claiborne before it burned down under mysterious circumstances two Christmases back. Baby remembered Jimbo saying that a former member named Bambola Schmid, who had been thrown out for welshing on card debts, was suspected of having torched the building. Bambola had disappeared from New Orleans after the fire and apparently found a haven with cousins who operated a hotel in the Swiss Alps named Die Müssigkeit. Nobody from the Lost Tribe had been able to get to Switzerland to verify this however.

Waldo then introduced Baby to his pal Balzac Kicz, and they invited her to join them for a beverage. The two men were extremely polite, and since Baby had no duties that afternoon, and no plans in particular, she went along with the strange pair to Enrique's Birdcage on Almonaster Avenue.

What happened after that Baby had mostly dismissed from her cerebrum. Blasted as she had been on Crown Royal, she now remembered only her mirthful reaction to Waldo Orchid's obesity necessitating that she mount him in order to sufficiently effect intercourse. Baby had not had sexual relations of any kind since she and Jimbo had split up, and Waldo caught her at a weak moment. She was certain, however, that she had not been intimate with the rail-thin and gimpy Balzac Kicz. As far as she could recall, Kicz had injected himself hypodermically in his remaining ankle with a purplish substance he referred to as "cobra come." The Magyar druggie then passed out in the bathroom of his apartment on General Diaz, to which the trio had repaired following the frivolities at Enrique's Birdcage.

Baby had dated Waldo Orchid twice since that night, and on one occasion he showed her where he lived, although they had not gone inside the house. Waldo told Baby that he and Balzac Kicz were weapons importers, most of their product coming from China, and the majority of their sales being made to the white religious right in Idaho and black separatists in California. After her last secret date with Waldo a month or so before, Baby had decided to end their association, such as it was, mainly because of her guilt about transgressing Mother Bizco's dictum that her Almost-Perfect Flock abstain from alcohol, drugs, and sex. The other reason was that Waldo had backhanded her across the mouth after she refused to give him *beso negro*. All she wanted of him now was money for an abortion.

The door cracked open and Tante Desuso said, "Waldo regrets he unable to talk today." Then she closed it again.

Baby Cat-Face stepped down from the porch and into Lapeyrouse Street. A few raindrops hit her, a breeze came up, and then a platinum bolt of ribbon lightning discharged about twenty-five coulombs of negative energy from the N-region of a cumulus cloud into the ground directly in front of her, the force of which knocked Esquerita flat but not out. Next came an almost deafening bang, followed by a torrent of water that totally soaked the prone *enceinte*.

Baby lay on the sidewalk with her eyes closed, allowing the rain to cleanse her body. She shouted out, "Deliver me, O Lord, from the evil man! Preserve me from the violent man who have purposed to overthrow my goings!"

There came another thunderclap, and Baby whispered, "I call heaven and earth to witness against you this day, Waldo Orchid, that ye shall soon perish from off the land. Ye shall not prolong your days upon it, but shall utterly be destroyed."

SNAKE HEADS

Dear Sugargirl.

Remember wen I rote you all that bout Mother Bizco mama name Virguenza bein blin an all an bein rape in St Louis cemetary well after this hapen to me wat Im gon tell you Mother an me hav a privat tak an she tell me it were not at all true jus a story she say giv strenth an hope to other yung womens. I bin wonder why somtim she tell difren storys bout hersef an she say it serv difren purpos. I gess she got the rite who am I say Mother Bizco ain rite all the good she do can be wrong. Yesterday we get 2 girls from China an I ask em they no Cris Chew but they don even spek english. Man who brot em to the Temple say they pay the snake heads in China lots of mony get em to America by smuglin. Then they end up a slave in som factory or lik these girls was made into hos kep uptown som big ol house an only forteen yers ol. Snake heads wat they call the Chinamen send em over on ol leekey boats so meny sink in oshen. We gon keep the China girls les they be made go back to China by the govmen. Also I here som news bout Jimbo sombody takt him in a mens room of a bar but he OK. They fin the guy don it witout no head an one leg missin in Irish bayou but Jimbo tell the cops he don no wat happen in the firs place. I no Jimbo he don lie. Now the mos real rezon I rite you is I bout to hav a baby an I am hopin an prayin you be abel com to NO an be wit me do you think you can? This be very mos import to me Sug I hav a dream an God tak to me also the baby. I no this so hard to belev but it a boy his name Angel de la Cruz mean Angel of the cross. I so friten wen my hol body flot in air Mother Bizco say it a maculat consepshun but truth be the father a man sick in his min name Waldo Orchid. I lik to kill this man sam as the China girls lik to kill the snake heads. I no it a sin even think it but these men got som dises in they brane, snake head a good nam for em. I hop you be here soon I tell you the hol story. I pray you com Sug.

Love Baby

SANCTUM

"Girl, am I glad to see you!" said Baby Cat-Face, embracing Sugargirl Crooks on the top step of the entrance to the temple.

"Look at you," said Sugar, double-eyeballing Baby's garb, a snow-white muumuu embroidered with dozens of tiny gold crosses. "Size of a house an' done up pure as Mother Teresa!"

"Ain' no mother yet. One mo' week, doctor say. Beside, dey calls me Sister aroun' here."

"Okay, Sister Baby, we gon' bring an angel into the worl', no doubt about dat!"

As Baby and Sugar were catching up on each other's news, Waldo Orchid sat in a green-banded lawn chair in his yard on Lapeyrouse Street. He wore only a triple-extra-large pair of chartreuse shorts, letting his enormous gut take the little sun New Orleans had to offer this mostly cloudy June afternoon. Waldo's mother, Malva, and his Tante Desuso had gone earlier to visit the tomb of his father, Tosco, at the graveyard of Holy Fantômes, today being the anniversary of Tosco's untimely death by rat. Visiting tombs was not Waldo's idea of getting a leg up on the morning, so he had declined his mother and aunt's invitation to join them. Gone be gone, the oversized Orchid believed. Life its ownself was tough enough to handle without tripping on tragedies passed by.

Waldo popped open the pull tab on a sixteen-ounce can of Pabst he had brought out to the yard with him, and drank half of it in one swallow. He sat still and listened to a trio of screeching blue jays argue, probably over a scrap of pork rind raided from the overflowing garbage cans by the side of the house. Waldo reminded himself that he had promised his mother to dispose of the waste. Later for that. The whole world is just like them jays, Waldo thought. What happened to Balzac Kicz, such as. Pitiful, way things go. That darkmeat toil in service of Mother Bizco, now she could make nasty nice and do it twice. But what come of it? Girl write a letter call me the devil. All I done she be party to. Could maybe made something fine with her, gone to Casino Magic a long weekend.

Six jets streaked overhead, vaporizing what was left of the sky. Waldo lifted the beer can to his lips, but just as he was about to finish off the Pabst, he felt a cold nudge on his right calf. He reached down to rub the spot without looking and froze at what felt like forty tenpenny nails simultaneously piercing his hand.

Waldo's scream was drowned under the residual thunder of jet engines. He turned and saw a six-foot-long alligator with its jaws clamped solidly below his right wrist. Waldo's attempt to pull away from the beast mostly succeeded. As he suddenly stood and stared at it, the leathery creature chunked twice on Waldo's severed hand before swallowing. When he looked at the bloody stump on his starboard limb, Waldo screamed again, and this time the noise was undisguised.

• • •

MARKED FOR LIFE

"PRETTY INTERESTIN', ANGEL, ain't it? Mean how you and me come to be cellmates after we both been busted at the same time on the same type beef, and got to serve the same amount of time."

"Only thing less interestin' than bein' alive, Sailor, is dead. That's a natural fact."

Angel de la Cruz Reyna and Sailor Ripley were inmates at the Pee Dee River Correctional Facility in North Carolina, where each man had been incarcerated for the crime of manslaughter. Sailor had killed a man named Bob Ray Lemon in a bar fight in his hometown of Bay St Clement, after the man had aggressively and repeatedly insulted Sailor's girlfriend, Lula Fortune.

In a remarkably similar circumstance, Angel, who had come to Corinth, North Carolina, from New Orleans, to visit his cousin Gracielita Pureza, had encountered in a bar Gracielita's erstwhile boyfriend, a Montenegran-Gypsy immigrant named Romar Dart, confronted Dart about his physically abusive behavior toward Ms Pureza, and then bested him in a Texas-style teardown, the result of which landed Angel a five-to-ten-mandatory two-year chill-out at Pee Dee and dealt Dart a permanent grounding of the literal persuasion.

Romar Dart had been working as a home-appliance salesman at Huge Huey's Discounteria. He was twenty-four years old, six months out of the army, in which service he'd done two consecutive stretches straight out of high school. Romar wasn't quite used to being a civilian, and he had a difficult time accepting the fact that Gracielita Pureza, who was only nineteen, could possess such an independent mind. Dart was emotionally adrift due to the loss of his parents in a car crash a fortnight before his discharge. Raimundo and Della Dart had been returning home from an evening of playing the slots at Poor Homer's Gates of Horn

Casino, when a pig truck blew its left front tire and toppled across the white line onto Raimundo and Della's Lumina, crushing the elder Darts inside. Pigs spilled onto the road around the wreck, squealing and scrambling, causing motorists to swerve and stop suddenly, resulting in not a few whiplash cases, as well as several casualties of a porcine nature.

Despite Gracielita's attempts at consolation, Romar could not shake the brutal feeling of having been abandoned by his parents. Gracielita put up with Dart's self-pity for a while, but finally told him to let it go and deal with the life ahead. Romar reacted violently, knocking her around his trailer and denting Gracielita's left temple with what had been Raimundo's favorite five iron. Angel de la Cruz had arrived in Corinth the day after this incident occurred.

Sailor lit a tailor-made and handed it to Angel, who took a drag and passed it back.

"We all of us lost sons of Cassiopeia, anyway," said Angel, leaning back on his bunk. "We marked for life."

"Sons o' who?"

"Cassiopeia, was an Ethiopian queen. This bitch was so vain, she claim she was better lookin' than the sea nymphs. That pissed off them bitches so much they commanded a sea serpent attack her daughter, the virgin Princess Andromeda, who the Oracle made her daddy, King Cepheus, chain to a rock in the water, so the serpent get at the girl."

"How you know all this?"

"Myths, man. You ain't read 'em?"

"No."

"Cat name Perseus rescue Andromeda. He the son of Jove, and a famous dragon slayer already had took out the Gorgon. So Perseus whips this sea monster, carves it up with his sword, and gets to marry the princess."

"Ethiopians is black, right?"

"Cassiopeia mostly was, I guess. Make Andromeda a quadroon, like my mama."

"What happen to her?"

"Cassiopeia? Or my mama?"

"No, Cassie, yeah."

"Oh, man, she be so mortify by the situation, trouble she cause, the word 'melancholy' be invented just describe her. After she die, Cassiopeia was sent to the stars because of her beauty, be the brightest light in her own constellation. But the sea nymphs still got the red ass about her and force the gods place Cassiopeia up top of heaven, near the pole, make her be humble by bendin' her neck."

"So what you mean by us bein' sons of her?"

"*Lost* sons. Mean we the kind of fools get too full of ourselves sometime, lose control. Look at us, man, where we are."

"You and me? Like in jail?"

"Not *like* in jail. In jail! We ain't paid nobody get here, have we?"

Sailor stubbed out the end of his cigarette on the wall and dropped the butt back into the pack for hard-ups.

"We just done what had to be done, Angel. What we had to do."

"And the man done what he had to do, too."

"You say your mama was what? Quadroon?"

"Right. One-quarter black. 'Bout like most the population of south Louisiana."

"And your daddy, what was he?"

"We don't talk about him."

"Assumin' he was white, what that make you?"

Angel's eyes turned red, blood spurted from the palms of his hands, and then he levitated, arms spread, feet together, floating until his back was flat against the ceiling of the cell. Sailor cringed on his bunk in disbelief, horrified, as he witnessed the blood dripping from Angel's stigmata.

A voice filled the cell, saying, "The Son of man shall come in the glory of his Father with his angels."

Sailor watched the blood stain the floor. He tried to speak, to ask Angel what was happening, beg him to come down, but his mouth and throat were paralyzed. Angel's body began to spin, and Sailor collapsed, falling instantly into a deep sleep.

When he awoke, Sailor saw Angel standing by the cell door, leaning against it, smoking a cigarette.

Angel looked at him, held up the butt, and said, "Hope you don't mind, man. Stole one of yours."

"Hey, what's goin' on?" Sailor asked groggily. "I fell out, huh?"

Angel nodded. "Yeah, all of a sudden, like you been hit with a hammer."

Sailor shook his head. "Had a crazy dream, man. You were in it, too."

"What was I doin'?"

"Flyin', man. You were flyin' around the room, and there was blood everywhere."

Sailor looked down but there were no bloodstains.

"Blood?"

"Yeah, comin' off your hands."

Angel laughed and stamped his right foot.

"Hell, Sailor, that just sounds like Saturday night."

from
THE SINALOA STORY
(1998)

SAINTS PRESERVE US

Ava had a thumbnail-sized scar high on her left cheek. When DelRay inquired about it she turned sullen and the pink mark became crimson. A shudder, visible to Mudo, passed through the length of her body, concluding with a brief facial twist and audible soft gasp. At the moment, the two were semi-entwined, standing under a xanthic desert moon in front of Ava's trailer.

"You know what day this is?" asked Ava.

"February twenty-ninth," he said. "Had a extra day before rent's due."

"El Día de Santa Niña de las Putas, the patron saint of Satan's prisoners. It comes only when there is a second full moon in the month on the final day of February in a leap year."

"Knew about the blue moon. Never heard of Satan's prisoners, though."

"Those are souls sold to Satan during the person's lifetime. People who reformed before their death and tried to undo the deal."

DelRay disentwined himself, lit a Lucky, inhaled, coughed. The night air felt chilly now that he wasn't pressed against Ava. He rubbed his hands together, then shoved them into his pants pockets, letting the cigarette dangle from between his lips.

"Who was Santa Niña?" he mumbled.

"A peasant girl, like me," said Ava, "born in Huehuetenango, Guatemala. Her father had bargained with the devil in order to save the life of his wife, who was dying from a cancer. Satan told him his wife would live only if the man promised also the souls of his three sons."

"Not the daughter?"

"Niña was not yet born. She was the youngest of four children. The father was horrified to do this but consented, thinking that later he could persuade Satan not to take his sons. The mother recovered and, of course, no matter how passionately her husband begged, the devil would not relent. The thought that he and his sons were doomed to hell destroyed the poor man, and he died of grief soon after the birth of his daughter."

"Did the mother know about this deal?"

"Not until her husband confessed on his deathbed. When Niña was twelve years old her brothers were killed when a donkey cart in which they were riding broke its axle on a steep mountain road and crashed with the donkey to the bottom of a ravine. Niña's mother then told her about the fate of the boys' souls, so the girl vowed to save them and her father."

DelRay spat out the cigarette. "Did she?"

"Yes. That night she called to Satan, telling him she could not live without her brothers, that she wanted to join them immediately. When Satan appeared she took his hand and allowed him to lead her to hell, where she became his mistress."

"No shit!" Suddenly DelRay no longer felt the cold.

"Satan's attachment to Niña was soon complete. She beguiled him in ways even the King of Cruelty had never imagined. In this way was it possible for her to gain a kind of power over the devil and convince him to allow her father and brothers to pass out of hell and enter into the Kingdom of Heaven. Niña, of course, had to remain in hell as Satan's whore. It is the prostitutes who honor her on this, the rarest of days, for her sacrifice."

"Saint Niña of the Whores."

"Our own and only. This is the one day no whore should feel ashamed in the eyes of God."

"But what about your scar? How did you get it?"

"After I was fucked by a man for money for the first time I cut myself on the face with the sharp edge of a rock."

"But why? You were so beautiful.—You still are, of course."

"To never be as beautiful again. I was marked inside and out."

DelRay embraced her. "My poor Ava."

She pulled away and glared at him. "No," she said, "there is nothing about me that is poor."

MOO YANG

AVA WAS GIVING HEAD to a seventy-one-year-old beet farmer from Big Spring named Euple Mapes when she heard the gunshot. Euple's prostate problems being what they were, he was about at the point that a fair piss beat hell out of having what could reasonably be considered a decent erection. Ava had been working on Euple's penis a good fifteen minutes without any discernible sign of blood gathering in the tissue when he lit up a cigarette and said, "Give it another few licks, missy, and if the old warhorse don't stir I'll settle for a high five in the rectum." The explosion came right after that.

Both Ava and the john jumped at the sound. Euple Mapes stood and pulled up his pants. Ava went to the door, opened it a crack, and peered into the corridor. Thankful Priest pounded past and barged into a room two doors down and across the hall. Ava threw on a terry-cloth robe and followed him.

Thankful was standing just inside the room, and Ava poked her head in next to his right shoulder. Moo Yang, a fourteen-year-old Thai-Chinese girl Indio had brought in the week before from Port Arthur, was sitting on the floor holding a .44 Ruger Blackhawk with both hands, wearing only a buffalo horn headdress. A man clothed in white buckskin and knee-high moccasins lay face down on the bed; the back of his head had mostly adhered to the wall directly above him. Ava, who had taken a liking to Moo Yang, squeezed past Priest and knelt next to the girl, who sat staring vacantly into space.

"*¡Madre de Díos, niña!*" said Ava. "What happened?"

Moo Yang lifted the revolver slowly and pointed it unsteadily at Thankful, who turned and fled.

"Pow!" she said, then lowered the big gun to her lap, resting the long black barrel along her smooth brown thigh.

"Moo Yang, *díme!*"

The girl smiled and looked at Ava Varazo. Her huge black eyes were glassy. She began to weep but kept smiling.

"America sucks," said Moo Yang.

A SHORT VISIT TO LA VIUDA

INDIO DESACATO controlled the steering wheel with the index and second fingers of his left hand. He guided his rainforest green Lincoln Mark VIII slowly through the dusty postmidnight streets of Ciudad Yeguada, six kilometers northwest of Tampico. Indio had heard about a house operated by a woman called La Viuda, "the Widow," who offered no whore more than twelve years old. He thought that a very young girl would be a special attraction in Sinaloa, especially if it were known that her residency was temporary. Indio had sent word to La Viuda and received a reply that she would be willing to rent out one of her *brotes* for a short time. She was expecting him.

At the end of what some dreamer or fool of a city planner had named Avenida de la Paz Eterna, as if such a backwater required or deserved an avenue, the predatory flesh merchant turned right, as he had been instructed, and brought the Mark VIII to a stop in front of a squat tin-roofed bungalow. Before getting out of the car, he opened the glove compartment and removed from it a nine-millimeter Glock automatic pistol. He put the pistol into the right side pocket of his safari jacket and surveyed the empty street. It was the time between Sunday night and Monday morning, *madrugada,* the hour between dog and wolf; and all of the dogs and wolves, the men who worked on the oil rigs, the men who worked in the bank or the courthouse, the cops, the ones who could afford to patronize La Casa de la Viuda, were obliged to honor the only night of the week that the establishment remained closed. Indio knew this and did not expect trouble, but he nevertheless felt more secure carrying a weapon. One never knew when an ugly dragon would appear bearing the unwelcome gift of fire breathing, especially in Mexico.

"Welcome, Mr. Desacato," said a handsome woman of approximately sixty years old, as Indio approached the bungalow entrance. The woman was dressed simply; she wore a long white cotton dress and had wrapped a black silk mantilla decorated with orange birds and scarlet flowers around her shoulders. "It's a pleasure to have you here."

"You must be La Viuda."

"I am, yes. Come in."

La Viuda closed the door behind him.

"You've come a long way," she said.

"The thought of what might be awaiting me kept me entertained."

The interior light was dim, but Indio could see that the Widow's face gave evidence of a grave history. The many lines in her cheeks and forehead looked like they had been cut with the thin edge of a finely honed knife. Indio had no doubt that not a single drop of the blood and tears she had shed had been or ever would be forgotten by La Viuda or by those who had caused the wounds, if any were still alive.

"I regret that I have only a short time," said Indio, "to avail myself of your hospitality."

There appeared out of the dimness by the Widow's side a sylph in a short black dress. The sylph's red hair was twisted together on the top of her head, knotted to stand up as if by force of electric shock. Her skin was red, too, but darker. She was about four feet tall and weighed no more than seventy pounds.

"We call her Perla Roja," said La Viuda. " 'Red Pearl.' For obvious reasons. She'll be twelve years old in three weeks."

Indio moved closer to the girl and studied her. He had never seen a child so exquisite, so unblemished. Her eyes were huge yellow-black spheres from which shone an eerie light, a flame from a time unremembered before this terrible and dangerous moment. The entire room glowed amber, burnished by Perla's presence.

"Sssssssssss," hissed Indio, as he circled the child. "Truly, Widow, this is something beyond dreaming."

He touched Perla Roja's round, perfect face with the fingertips of his right hand, then dropped to his knees and caressed her bare feet, toes, ankles, calves, thighs, sliding a hand over her tight, trembling buttocks before standing again.

"Name your price," Indio said.

The girl grabbed the Glock from Desacato's jacket pocket, pointed it at the Widow, and pressed the trigger. Four rounds invaded La Viuda's body before the tiny *puta* turned the pistol toward herself and fired. Indio staggered and fell as a bullet tore through Red Pearl's left eye socket, exited her posterior medulla oblongata, and creased Desacato's collarbone before burying itself between the almost-clasped hands of a genuflecting Juan Diego as represented on a wall calendar advertising Discoteca Orquidea Negra. Bathed in the blood of fallen females, the visitor shut his eyes and stared into the grinning face of a jaguar.

WILD COUNTRY

Elvin "El" País had promised to help her and he would. He was fifty-four years old, five foot six and a half with his boots on, and 239 pounds naked, but he had most of his hair, now a mixture of dirty brown and gray, and the use of his stumpy but sturdy limbs. His arms were heavily muscled from construction work and heavy-equipment operation. El País realized he had very little to show financially for more than thirty-five years of hard labor. He and his wife of a quarter century, Ginger, had only one thousand dollars in their joint account at Sinaloa Savings, of which Elvin had felt justified in withdrawing half. He should probably have taken more, he thought, but it was best Ginger not remember him as being greedy.

When Moo Yang first asked him about the possibility of their running away together, El País was confused. How could he, a fifty-plus fat man, make a life with a tiny fourteen-year-old Thai-Chinese prostitute? El was also thrilled by the idea. His childless marriage to Ginger had long since lost any reason to continue. About the only activity Elvin and Ginger shared an interest in anymore was eating, and his meager earnings precluded any real adventures of a culinary nature. Neither of them had much imagination in that department, either. Chicken-fried steak, mashed potatoes with brown gravy, lemon cream pie and Dr Pepper had been their staple diet for decades. Ginger, Elvin guessed, passed the three-hundred-pound mark twenty years ago and never glanced back.

The most recent sexual encounter between them that he could recall occurred on Elvin's fiftieth birthday. Ginger bought him an issue of *Juggs* magazine and while he perused pictures of huge-breasted women she masturbated him with a dish towel soaked in a mixture of grape jelly and motor oil. Her friend Earlene Weld had told her about an article in *Cosmopolitan* concerning spicing up married folks' sex life that suggested using honey and oil as a marital aid; so, using what she had on hand, Ginger gave it a shot.

This episode, however, had an unfortunate conclusion. After Elvin came, he fell asleep and Ginger went to the bathroom to wash her hands. While she was gone red ants got into the jelly jar, which Ginger had left open on the floor next to the slumbering birthday boy, and from there the fiery, aggressive devils made a swift assault on his slathered genitals. It took Elvin several weeks to recover from the bites, the first two in

Sinaloa Baptist Hospital, during which time urination was possible only through catheterization. This gruesome experience did little to inspire further sexual experimentation or research on the couple's part.

Thereafter Elvin availed himself of biweekly visits to La Casa Desacato for a blowjob. Until the arrival of Moo Yang, however, País was not inspired to move past this seemingly dead-end existence. Following the shooting incident involving Big Chief Buffalo Horn—for which action Moo Yang was found by police to be entirely justified—the Thai-Chinese teenager began plotting her escape. El País, she decided, was her nicest customer, as well as being the least complicated or sexually troublesome. When she asked him to run off with her, he agreed immediately. Moo Yang tried to give him a second blowjob that night but Elvin wasn't up to it. Every two weeks was his speed, he told her; that was enough for him. Moo Yang smiled then for the first time since she had left Port Arthur. El País was her man.

Moo Yang jumped out of a second-story rear window onto a mattress in the bed of Elvin's three-quarter-ton Ford pickup at five o'clock one morning. País sped away with the girl and all seemed right with the world until he realized that in his haste and excitement he had forgotten to fill the truck with gas. El stopped at Excello Pomus's Red Devil on the way out of town and was in the process of fueling the Ford when Thankful Priest cruised his vintage '69 Barracuda convertible into the station.

Priest pulled the 'Cuda alongside the Ford and said to País, "You got somethin' belongs to Señor Desacato."

Elvin dropped the gasoline hose and backed away. Indio's gigantic monocular henchman debarked, a hideous, dark, glinting object in hand.

"I was only tryna hep her out," País said.

"No hurt my hero!" shouted Moo Yang.

"Try this, hero," Thankful replied, and made *pad tai* of Moo Yang's guy with a street sweeper.

The girl leaped out of the truck and ran down the road. Thankful Priest caught up with her thirty seconds later, cutting in front with the 'Cuda.

"Come on, Moo Yang. Get in."

Moo Yang sank to her skinny knees on the cracked asphalt, holding her hands over her face. The sun was coming up. She started screaming.

RIFIFI

"MOST OF THE GIRLS are at a private party tonight," Ava told DelRay. "At a ranch outside of town. That's why it's so quiet."

Ava wore jeans, boots and a cowboy shirt. Around her neck she'd wound the green scarf with parrots on it that DelRay had bought for her in Nogales. She had two guns, nine-millimeter Sig Sauers, one of which she handed to DelRay.

"Where did you get these?"

"From a client. An arms dealer from Zip City, Alabama, named Farfel El Perro."

"How did you pay for them?"

"You really want to know?"

"Yeah."

"I let him in the back door without a raincoat. It's the easiest way to get AIDS, but I figured I'd take the chance for *la causa.*"

"La causa?"

Ava kissed him quickly on the lips. "*Vámonos*, baby. We've only got a small window of time."

DelRay followed her down the corridor, then along another until they came to rosewood double doors at what DelRay guessed was the far end of the house. Ava fished a key out of a pocket of her jeans and inserted it into the lock. She turned it slowly until they both heard a click, and Ava opened one of the doors.

Indio was sound asleep in the fetal position on his canopied four-poster bed. The couple crept up to him and Ava placed the nose of her gun against the pimp's exposed right ear.

"Time to rise, Desacato," she said.

He stirred. One eye opened.

"Easy now," said Ava. "No fast moves. Get up slowly."

Indio followed orders. He slid off the bed and stood next to it in his blue silk pajamas and fresh bandages.

"Push the bed aside, Del," she said.

"You don't want to do this, Ava," said Indio.

DelRay moved the bed and pulled away an oriental throw rug that had been under it, revealing a floor safe. He read the gold lettering on the black steel: HERRING-HALL MARVIN SAFE CO. SAN FRANCISCO.

"Open it," Ava told Indio, holding her Sig Sauer against his right cheek.

"You and your boyfriend are already dead."

"Open it."

Indio knelt down, spun the combination, and pulled the heavy lever.

"Stand up," Ava said. "Move away from there."

Indio stood and moved. She kept him covered.

"Take a look, Del. There's probably a gun."

DelRay stuck his nine-millimeter into his pants and bent to it. He reached in and pulled up an ugly hunk of metal.

"Big sucker. Weaver .300 H&H magnum."

"We'll take it with us. Is the money there?"

DelRay set the gun down on the floor and unearthed a large canvas sack. He opened it and peered inside.

"Christ, Ava. It must be a million bucks in here."

"Half a million," she said. "Right, Indio?"

The pimp kept silent.

"Hand me a pillow, Del."

He got up, took one off the bed and gave it to her.

"Put the Weaver in the sack and close it up."

DelRay did as she commanded.

"Get down on your knees," she told Indio. "Hold this pillow over your face."

The pimp took the pillow from her and held it.

"You're a whore from hell," he said.

"Stick your fucking face in the pillow."

As Indio's nose pressed satin, Ava shoved the barrel of her Sig Sauer into it and fired. The pimp jumped back a foot and collapsed on his left side. Blood gushed from what formerly had been his forehead. Ava picked up the pillow and placed it over Desacato's face.

Ava and DelRay walked out of the house with the money.

"Head south," Ava ordered DelRay as they climbed into the Cutlass. The sack was in the trunk.

DelRay drove south out of town. After they had gone ten miles, Ava said, "Pull over here."

Mudo eased the Cutlass to a stop next to the highway. He saw another car parked a short distance away. It looked like an '86 Thunderbird. DelRay turned toward Ava and saw that she had her pistol pointed at him.

"Give me your gun," she said.

"Ava, what the hell?"

"I don't want to shoot you, Del. I really don't. Give it to me."

He gave up the Sig Sauer.

"Now, get out of the car. Slowly."

DelRay opened the driver's side door and got out. Ava slid across the seat, taking the keys out of the ignition. She got out and stood next to him.

"Move," she said, motioning toward the rear of the car. She handed him the keys. "Open the trunk."

DelRay took the keys and unlocked it.

"Take out the bag and put it on the ground."

He did what she said.

"Get in."

"Ava. . . ."

"Get in, Del. Don't argue or I'll kill you, too."

DelRay climbed into the trunk. Ava tossed him the keys and closed the lid. He heard her dragging the sack; faintly, two doors slamming shut in succession; a car's ignition; wheels scraping purchase on dirt; then, nothing.

Twenty-five minutes before, DelRay thought, Ava had been sucking his cock.

THE CHANCE OF A LIFETIME

"CAN'T UNDERSTAND how Indio let that broad get the drop on him."

"He was a good man to work for. I'm gonna miss him."

Thankful Priest and Sonny "Mr. Nice" Cicatrice were cruising south on Texas State Highway 277 in Indio Desacato's Lincoln Mark VIII. Thankful was at the wheel. They were passing through Val Verde County and had just crossed Dry Devils, headed for Del Rio and the plunge into Old Mexico. Thankful Priest had telephoned Puma Charlie in La Paz, Arizona, and Charlie told him that Ava Varazo was from La Villanía, Mexico. Other than that, Puma Charlie said, he didn't really know a whole hell of a lot about her. Sonny insisted that since they had nothing else to go on, La Villanía was as good a place as any to begin the trackdown. If she had any family left down there, he reasoned, they might know where she was.

Thankful had shut down the house in Sinaloa for the time being, leaving Señora Matrera and Moke Lamer as caretakers until he returned. The girls had been given a holiday and told to contact Señora Matrera in two weeks. Indio's corpse was cremated, which had been his desire, and his ashes scattered by Moke Lamer into the languid, rust-colored creek called Rio Pestoso, with Thankful and Señora Matrera in attendance. Moke then played "La Golondrina," Indio's favorite tune, on a guitar, after which Thankful fired into the air a single round from his fallen *jefe*'s Glock pistol, and tossed the gun into the foul water. "*¡Un fuerte abrazo, amigo!*" Priest shouted, and the ceremony was over.

"After we get the money," Sonny said, "we kill her and whoever else is around. Agreed?"

Thankful nodded. "I go with you, *jefe!*"

"What's that?"

"Means I agree."

"Good. You know why I got the name Mr. Nice?"

"No."

"Tommaso 'Short Hair' Fabregas, remember him?"

"Uh-uh."

"An independent out of Tampa. Knocked off a casino on Paradise Island, the Bahamas. Big Tony sent me to find him. I was nineteen years old, never killed nobody. Caught up with Short Hair in New Orleans. Suite 1515, DeSalvo Hotel. I'll never forget it. He's in there with his wife. I confront Tommaso, tell him Big Tony don't want the money back. He asks me what then? Short Hair's on his knees. I got a hair-trigger .45 kissed to his forehead. His balls, I say. Tony wants the major stones he must have to done what he did. Tommaso tries to make a deal. I decline. He says okay, kill me, but don't touch my wife."

"What's she doin'?"

"Sittin' on the couch. Doesn't say a word."

"What'd you do?"

"I shot him. Just once. The bullet completely penetrated the skull, come out the back of his head. The wife don't peep. I took out a ten-inch blade I had in my pocket and gave it to her. Told her cut off her husband's balls."

"Christ, Sonny. She did this?"

"Gets down next to him, pulls down his pants. You know what she says?"

"What?"

" 'Should I cut off his dick, too?' "

Thankful almost lost control of the car. "No!" he shouted.

"Exactly the words. I said no, just the nuts. She handles the knife like a brain surgeon. I give her a plastic bag I had for the purpose. She sticks 'em in there, hands it to me. She wipes the blade clean on Short Hair's shirt, folds it, gives it back. Now guess what she says."

"Tell me."

" 'You'll be nice, won't you?' That's what she says. I say whattaya mean, be nice? Tommaso's request, she reminds me. He asked that I don't touch her. I say sure, I'll be nice, I ain't an animal. She's there on her knees. Before she can stand I shoot her right between the eyes, same as her bandit husband. Didn't touch her."

"Mr. Nice."

Sonny laughed. "Big Tony wanted to know the details when I bring him Short Hair Fabregas's balls. He hung the name on me."

"Was she good lookin'?"

"Who? The wife?"

"Yeah."

"Not particularly I can recall. Why?"

"Just wonderin' what kind of woman would do that, slice off her old man's nuts."

"She would've cut his cock, too. It was her chance of a lifetime, Priest, every broad's dream. I was really nice, I'd have let her."

DOWN TO EARTH

WHERE THE SOUTHERN CROSS' THE YELLOW DOG

Journal Excerpts
Mississippi & New Orleans 3/28–4/5/92

from
SPEAK
(1998)

3/28 NEW ORLEANS—Back in the city that care (and often sanity) forgot. Walking down Dauphine early A.M.—one-armed man, jacket sleeve stuffed into left side pocket—another man with some kind of leather and canvas contraption strapped to his left forearm (at least he's got one). The South's cripples and sundry afflicted have always cottoned to contraptions, strange-looking devices designed to facilitate utilization of various damaged appendages, substitute for absent limbs. For some reason, poverty probably, and inadequate medical care, amputees are more in evidence in the Deep South, it seems. I was always fascinated by this phenomenon, growing up in Florida. It's the '90s now, not the '50s, but it's still the same. N.O. displays an inordinate number of walking wounded & grotesques. Seeing the armless and rigged-out guy right away makes me feel at home. I know where I am.

I pick up a *Times-Picayune* and turn immediately to the Police Reports, always the most interesting section. I'm not disappointed. The first item: "Kidnapping—Franklin and St. Claude Avenues. A 14-year-old girl told police a man sat next to her on a Franklin Avenue bus Tuesday about 7 A.M. and put a gun against her side. He ordered her to get off the bus at Canal and Decatur Streets, then made her get on a Canal Street bus headed toward the lake. He made her get off the bus in the 3800 block of Canal Street and walk to the rear of a driveway in the

3800 block of Iberville Street. He ripped her blouse off and told her to strip or he would kill her. He then picked up a rock and tried to strike her with it, but she took it from him struck him in the forehead and ran away."

This was followed by a variety of colorful and tragic items, including one about cops named Thelonious Dukes and Wellington Beaulieu chasing two juvenile burglars through the Desire Street public housing project and carrying on a running gun battle; two men beating up a third man with handcuffs and then stealing his watch at 3:45 P.M.; a two-year-old boy named Djuan Hills being shot to death by his babysitter. The dead boy's father, an inmate at the Washington Correctional Institute at Angie, La., learned of the shooting while watching the noon news on television. For the two days prior to my arrival in the Crescent City, the Police Blotter reported the following totals: Murder 0, Rape 1, Armed Robbery 27, Shooting 3, Stabbing 3, Purse-Snatching 5, Burglaries 92, Car Burglary 7, and Car Theft 62. A relatively inauspicious count, seeing as how the local miscreants apparently outdid themselves during the recent Mardi Gras. These days are the calm after the storm.

Listening to Cuban salsa on WWOZ before I go to the Tennessee Williams Festival, where I'm to participate in a panel forum entitled, "Tie Me Up, Tie Me Down: Writers Talk About Sex and Violence." The dubious distinction accorded this event by the New Orleans weekly, *Gambit*, is a discussion of "the use of shocking material" in novels. "Well, get you, sister," Tennessee Williams might have said. Seems to me the *Times-Picayune* staff does as good a job as anybody when it comes to seeking out and describing bizarre behavior. In N.O. one needn't search very hard in order to stumble across some, or be stumbled over by it.

Speaking of which, I can't pass over this last item, also plucked from the perky pages of the *T-P*: "Agents of the Violent Crimes Task Force arrested Willie Webster, 20, no local address, at 6:10 P.M. at Annunciation and Terpsichore Streets. Webster was booked with first-degree murder in the shooting death of Derrock Ilsworth, 19, on Aug. 29 (Charlie Parker's birthday), 1990, at 2:30 A.M., at Foy and Duplessis Streets, and the attempted murder of Wayne Thomas, 22, Ellsworth's friend, who was paralyzed from the neck down after being shot nine times in the same incident. Ellsworth was shot five times. Police also booked Webster with aggravated battery in the shooting of Lawrence Hall on Aug. 19, 1991 (maybe the cops should just lock this guy up every August) at about 3:30 P.M. at an undisclosed location, police said. Webster had been the subject of a manhunt by New Orleans police and the FBI."

Other N.O. news: Mamie Braud Sturdivant, a homemaker, died at 88. Mrs. Sturdivant was born in Thibodaux, La., and lived in N.O. for 30 years. Cicero Sessions also died, at 83; as did Jesse Farris Kennon, aged 86. Just so you know that longevity is possible in this city. The weather is mostly cloudy, slight breeze, seventy degrees at 2 P.M. Rain is expected by evening. A sampling of river stages: the Mississippi at Cairo—flood stage 40, yesterday 38.4; at Natchez—40, yesterday 39.3; at N.O.—17/11. The Pearl at Bogalusa 18/14.7. The Atchafalaya at Butte La Rose—28/13.9. The Bogue Chitto at Franklinton—12/0. Never live next to a river.

3/29 New Orleans—My friend Iron Mike Swindle told me that night before last (his birthday) he was restless at 2 A.M., so he went down to the The Dew Drop Inn on LaSalle Street—the club where Little Richard, Ray Charles and James Brown and virtually every great r&b artist played during the '50s. A year and a half ago Mike and I and our friend Rachel Carner showed up at the Dew Drop—which these days is a rather low-rent bar, its glory days long gone—and the bartender told us we were the first white people to come in there on a Saturday night in fifteen years. The other night a black lesbian DJ named Engineer #3 was running the show for a less-than-packed house. One guy was passed out on the bar, Michael said, and a crack junkie burst in and tried to sell Iron Mike a vial of Anacin he'd lifted from a drugstore. Mike could not accommodate the frantic peddler—"I told him no," said Mike, "and I even had a headache."

Last night was a crawfish boil party for Iron Mike. Met John Sinclair, founder of the White Panther Party and MC5 rock group of the late '60s. He moved to N.O. last July from Detroit. I told him I read poetry at a benefit to raise money for his legal defense fund twenty years ago, after he was busted for possession of a marijuana joint. The Detroit cops wanted him in jail and they put him away where he did hard time. He's a gentle, bearded giant, teeth missing, hobbling on a cane after a recent accident in a restaurant; he fell and broke both knees. An old warrior who never lost his sense of humor, a sure indication of a brave heart.

Swindle and I go to The Fairgrounds racetrack for the feature race because I think I found a horse in the morning paper that can beat the odds-on favorite, a Mr. Prospector filly. We get to the track just ahead of a thunderstorm and just in time to get our across-the-board bet down on Desert Radiance, who goes off at three to one. The favorite is a gross underlay, one to five. Our horse gets up in the stretch—the distance is a mile and a sixteenth—but the favorite wins for fun and a thirteen-to-one shot edges out Desert Radiance for the place money. I pick a beer-soaked *Racing Form* out of a garbage can and dope out the next race, refusing to go home a loser. I find a seven-to-two shot named Louisiana Cookin' who's performed well on the turf before (this is a mile race on the grass), a stretch runner, so we throw back our show money along with some more, all on the nose, and then watch Louisiana Cookin' take it by less than a nostril in a photo finish. As Iron Mike and I are vociferously expressing our pleasure at the outcome, the jockey on the beaten favorite lodges a foul claim on our beast for a supposed infraction committed in the final sixteenth during the stretch duel. We wait (sweat) it out, until the claim is finally disallowed, and we collect, going home winners.

The thunderstorm hits, but it's brief and we swing by a bar in the Bywater, an Irish neighborhood, for a farewell party for the English girlfriend of Little Frank, a pal of Iron Mike's. On the way to the racetrack we'd passed a parade of black Indians, krewes decked out in feathery regalia.

N.O. is the paradise for costume queens of any color. It's truly a nonstop party town, if you want it to be. Tomorrow the party's over—we hit the road for the Magnolia State, Mississippi.

3/30 Jackson, MS—This is Iron Mike's and my 2nd Annual Tristram Shandy-Joseph Andrews-Sal & Dean Roadtrip. Last year we drove from N.O. to Key West, with various sidetrips in Alabama and Florida. This time we've decided to tour Mississippi, where Mike lived until he was six. We drive up Highway 49—remember Big Joe Williams's "Highway 49 Blues," old Delmark record. Around Star we pass by Jerry's Catfish Dome—looks like an abandoned nuclear power plant, apparently open only at night. Drove on 59 to Hattiesburg to connect with 49 (near Petal, the checkers capital of America). Three years ago at this same time of year I visited the writer Elliott Chaze at his home in Hattiesburg. He was author of the immortal ultimate noir classic novel, *Black Wings Has My Angel*. Elliott died a year and a half ago. When I was with him he took his pistol out of its holster from where it hung on the wall of his study, and showed me how he sat at his desk and held the gun to his head after he came home from the hospital following a prostate operation. He couldn't stand the pain, he said, but he couldn't quite manage to pull the trigger, either. In a couple of days the pain eased off, and he decided not to shoot himself.

We see the sign for D'Lo, Mississippi, and Swindle wonders how it got that name. Since it's the site of a water park, I figure the name has been anglicized from the French, *de l'eau*—of the water. In Jackson, we go immediately to John Evans's great bookstore, Lemuria, grab Johnny away from his work and go to the Mayflower Café on Capitol Street, one of my favorite restaurants since I was a kid. The Mayflower's been there for 55 years. My mom and I used to go there when we stayed at the old Heidelberg Hotel (torn down). She had a boyfriend who owned a girdle factory outside Jackson in the '50s. The Greek wife of the owner shows me photos of her native home in Patmos. She's in late middle-age, bored—shades of *Orpheus Descending*—she reminds me of Anna Magnani in the film version of the play, *The Fugitive Kind*.

We meet the photographer D. (for Diogenes) Gorton at the Mayflower—I'd called him from Lemuria—and he takes us after we eat to his studio, where he and his assistants are working on the prints for the Eudora Welty photo project. Miss Welty, who is in her eighties, has lived in Jackson virtually all of her life. Her father was in the insurance business and she, of course, became one of the finest writers of fiction in the world. She also took photographs, only eighteen of which will be included in the portfolio. Some of them are up on the walls of D.'s studio, and I tell him that they remind me of pictures taken by the late Kentucky photographer Ralph Eugene Meatyard. Gorton is amazed I've made the comparison—he says two other people have said the same thing. He tells a story about Miss Welty.

"Miss Welty came to my studio to look over the project. She asked me if she might have a drink of bourbon. 'But Miss Welty,' I said, 'it's ten o'clock in the morning.' She nodded, seeming to recognize the impropriety of her request, then raised her eyebrows and lifted her right hand as if there were a glass in it. 'Champagne?' she said."

Tomorrow we go to the Delta, where I've never been. In some places, Mike tells me, the alluvial soil is as much as 25 feet deep! Catfish and cotton country.

3/31 Greenville—Highway 49 West through Yazoo City—beyond the bluff is the Delta, stretched out in front of us. Punch in Muddy Waters tape—"She Moves Me"—"Took her to a funeral, the dead got up to run" sings Muddy, who lived and worked on Stovall's Plantation in the Delta—he was born in Rolling Fork, over on Highway 61. Reminds me of the old Clap tune (the band I played with in London in the '60s) "Down in the Delta"—written by Duke Pilkington: "Down in the Delta/Down in the Delta/There things goin' on/Ain't no one gonna tell ya."

Humphreys County—Catfish Capital of the World—Through Belzoni, by The Pig Stand barbecue restaurant where the catfish farmers hang out—Midnight, Mississippi, the Midnight Gin still in operation, cotton trailers lined up, wind blowing the strands stuck to the cages—Itta Bena up ahead. We stop in Indianola, where B.B. King grew up, cruise in on B.B. King Road and over to Hanna Avenue to check out the Club Ebony, where Iron Mike once hung out for the better part of a week. Nobody playing until Thursday night, The Dancin' Dolls from N.O.

Sunflower County—in Moorhead, "where the Southern cross' the Yellow Dog"—two trains running. "Where the Southern cross' the Yellow Dog" is a line from W.C. Handy's "Yellow Dog Blues"—Handy lived in the Delta just after the turn of the century—wrote about the intersection of the Yazoo Mississippi Valley Railroad (known as the Yazoo Delta or the Yellow Dog because of its yellow boxcars) and the Columbus and Greenville (called the Southern). In its heyday, Handy's time, eight passenger trains a day—the Yellow Dog—went from Yazoo City to Memphis.

Up the road from Greenville, at Tutwiler, is where the blues supposedly were born, where Handy heard the field holler. At nearby Dockery Plantation is where Charlie Patton worked—all that's left of Dockery now is a sign. Tonight we check out the Greenville clubs on Nelson Street—the Zodiac Lounge, Perry's Flowing Fountain Lounge, the Players Den—Tomorrow to Parchman Farm, the state prison; and Clarksdale, home of Robert Johnson, the greatest blues stylist of his day.

According to W.J. Cash's eccentric study, *The Mind of the South* (1941), between 1882 and 1938, there were 3,397 lynchings of Negroes in the U.S., all but 366 in the Southern states. It's impossible for me not to consider this while travelling through the Delta, just as it is rare to have a conversation with a citizen of Mississippi, white or black, without the subject of race entering into it.

One of my favorite places to go when I was a kid in Chicago (I grew up both there and in Florida) was Riverview, the giant amusement park on the North Side. What my friends and I were most fond of at Riverview was Dunk the Nigger. At least that's what we called the concession where by throwing a baseball at a target on a handle and hitting it square you could cause the seat lever in the attached cage to release and plunge the man sitting on the perch into a tank of about five feet of water. All of the guys who worked in the cages were black, and they hated to see us coming. Between the ages of thirteen and sixteen my friends and I terrorized these guys. They were supposed to taunt the thrower, make fun of him or her and try to keep them spending a quarter for three balls. Most people who played this game were lucky to hit the target hard enough to dunk the clown once in every six tries; but my buddies and I became experts. We'd buy about ten dollars' worth of baseballs and keep these guys going down, time after time.

Of course they hated us with a passion. "Don't you little motherfuckers have somewhere else to go?" they'd yell. "Goddamn motherfuckin' white boy, I'm gon' get yo' ass when I gets my break." We'd just laugh and keep pegging hardballs at the dip lever targets. My pal Big Steve was great at Dunk the Nigger; he was our true ace because he threw the hardest and his arm never got tired. "You fat ofay sumbitch!" one of the black guys would shout at Big Steve as he dunked him for the fifth pitch in a row. "Stop complaining," Steve would yell back at him. "You're getting a free bath, aren't ya?"

None of us thought too much about the fact that the job of taunt-and-dunk was about half a cut above being a carnival geek and a full cut below working at a car wash. It never occurred to us, more than a quarter of a century ago, why it was that all of the guys on the perches were black, or that we were racists. Unwitting racists, perhaps; after all, we were kids, ignorant and foolish products of White Chicago during the 1950s.

One summer afternoon in 1963, the year I turned sixteen, my friends and I arrived at Riverview and headed straight for Dunk the Nigger. We were shocked to see a white guy sitting on a perch in one of the cages. Nobody said anything but we all stared at him. Big Steve bought some balls and began hurling them at one of the black guys' target. "What's the matter, gray?" the guy shouted at Steve. "Don't want to pick on one of your own?"

I don't remember whether or not I bought any balls that day, but I do know it was the last time I went to the concession. In fact, that was one of the last times I patronized Riverview, since I left Chicago early the following year and Riverview was torn down not long after. I don't know what Big Steve or any of my other old friends who played Dunk the Nigger with me think about it now, or even if they've ever thought about it at all. That's just the way things were.

In Greenville, we have dinner at Doe's Eat Place—Charles, the owner, shows me the meat locker, piles of gigantic red slabs, the biggest steaks I've ever seen—Doe's is a white-owned and mostly white-patronized place in a black neighborhood. There's a big fat white security guard standing out front. Then we go down Nelson Street to Perry's Flaming Fountain Lounge—Malcolm Walls, an old friend of Mike's, and whom we met earlier in the day, comes in and we all talk and listen to blues records until after midnight. Malcolm is a smart, hardworking guy—he organizes the Delta Blues Festival held each year in Greenville—he was born in Clarksdale, lived in New York for awhile before moving back down south to the Delta. Iron Mike, D. Gorton and I are the only white people in Perry's. Willie Bailey, a local attorney, cooks up a mess of frogs' legs and heaps them on plates in front of us—Malcolm spins the records, runs back and forth among the tables, tells us he's not sure if he should be a politician, a music promoter or a preacher, but he is sure that he wants a Ferrari!

Recently legalized riverboat gambling was approved by popular vote (by an extremely narrow margin, about 140 votes) in Washington County, so everyone in Perry's Flowing Fountain—a florid wall mural justifies the bar's name (Perry's day job is as an undertaker)—was celebrating, hoping that this might be the crack in the door to sparking the local economy. Malcolm says Greenville has a forty percent unemployment rate. The religious fundamentalists—mostly white, some black—voted against gambling. The last time it was voted on, gambling was defeated by about the same margin it passed by today. There are 40,000 residents in Greenville, approximately 12,500 voted. Perry's reminds me of a West Side bar in Chicago, like the old Alex Club on Roosevelt Road—a friendly bar in a rough neighborhood—I tend to like any place in which a 250-pound woman named Peaches hangs out.

4/1 Tupelo—Writing this sitting on the porch swing of Elvis Presley's birthplace on the east side of Tupelo. This morning left Greenville and drove up 49 out of Indianola—the Delta is like another planet, flat and fertile, beautiful, tiny towns dotting the landscape. Stopped at Parchman, the Mississippi State Prison, drove in gates—Bukka White, Sonny Boy Williamson, among others, did time here—18,000 acres—stand of trees behind and to the west of the prison—That's where you run for, try to get to Rosedale and the big river—

In former times, as recently as the '40s, it was on the fifth Sunday of months that have more than four Sabbath days that visitors were allowed at Parchman. This was when the Midnight Special train brought the prisoners' relatives to the farm. The train arrived at dawn and left at dusk. The famous song, "The Midnight Special," originated with the prisoners: "Here comes your woman, a pardon in her hand/gonna say to the boss, I want my man/Let the Midnight Special shine its light on me"—I first heard this song on a record by Big Bill Broonzy, or else it was Big Bill himself singing on Studs Terkel's radio show in Chicago when I was a kid. In the '60s or '70s there was a TV show that featured rock 'n' roll performers called *The Midnight Special*—I wonder how many viewers or participants had any idea of where the name came from—

Drove to Tutwiler and stopped in a Quik-Stop, found a young black guy named Cleveland who agreed to show us where Sonny Boy is buried—"out in the country"—We found it; on gravestone of ALECK MILLER BETTER KNOWN AS WILLIE "SONNY BOY" WILLIAMSON BORN MAR. 11, 1908 DIED JUNE 23, 1965 are twelve harmonicas left in tribute to one of the great harp players—also on the gravestone are two unopened cans of Miller beer, four guitar picks (one of Lonnie Pitchford's, a blues player we later ran into in Clarksdale), a string of Mardi Gras beads, several seashells, seven stones and 93 cents in change—I left a lucky nickel.

I keep thinking about the conversation with Malcolm Walls in Perry's Flowing Fountain Lounge—how gambling might make a dent in the unemployment problem—but the prevailing opinion seemed to be how the '90s are a watershed time in terms of the racial scene, like the '60s were—this because most every so-called change has more or less failed. What's left to try?

In Tutwiler we pass the Mad Dog Disco—Iron Mike bought the local paper in the Quik-Stop, the *Tutwiler Clarion-Messenger*, which includes an editorial expressing outrage over a door-to-door daytime prostitution scam—women offering to do "housework" while the lady of the house is out—Also: "Any resident who has had occasion to drive through town at night has probably made fun of what might just appear to be an extraordinary show of poor taste in exterior decor when they see such things as a red umbrella over a bare light bulb."

On to Clarksdale, birthplace of Sam Cooke, Ike Turner, John Lee Hooker and so many other musicians—At the Stackhouse record shop we meet Julie O'Neal, sister of Jim O'Neal, blues archivist and proprietor of the store. Jim O'Neal's record company, Rooster, is an outstanding blues label. We do a quick tour of the Delta Blues Museum, located in the town library, a monument to the art form. Muddy Waters bequeathed his entire record collection to the museum, we're told.

Our last stop in the Delta is Grenada, birthplace of Magic Sam Maghett, West Side Chicago blues guitarist, hero of my youth—I used to see Sam perform at the Alex Club and emulated on my own guitars his thumb-picking style (which he modeled after Wes Montgomery)—

Met Dr. Edgar Grissom in Tupelo, a friend of John Evans. Grissom is a trim, athletic-looking middle-aged man originally from Cleveland, Mississippi, in the Delta—very bright and a literary man of the first order. Over catfish at Malone's Steak & Fish he relates a probably apocryphal story regarding the famous tornado that ripped up Tupelo in 1936 or 1937—the twister blew bodies of numerous black men into the gum trees, messed them up so badly they were virtually unidentifiable—The cops located a neighborhood prostitute with whom most of the men had consorted to identify them by their penises—Oh, that's so-and-so, she said; and that's so-and-so; and that one was just passin' through. Ed and his buddies, Dick and Chet, both from Jackson, are off to Alabama tomorrow on a camping trip.

4/2 Meridian—From Tupelo we went to Choctaw County, near Ackerman, to visit Iron Mike's Uncle Oren and Aunt Emma Lou. Oren made decent money farming cotton—his house is decorated with photographs of various cotton bolls, a domestic tribute to King Cotton. Oren is 71, is in good shape, sharp-minded and loquacious. He tells us over hamburgers and soup about his and Emma Lou's years working in automobile plants in Flint, Michigan, after the war; about his years in the Army, service as a tank commander with rank of sergeant— "I met Patton, you know, he was a general"—Oren's one of twelve brothers, all born in nearby Eupora, where Mike lived until he was six before moving with his parents to Birmingham, Alabama. Oren spends most of his time now trapping, fox and beaver—

Oren asks us where we're headed and we tell him Meridian via Neshoba County. We intend to drive through Philadelphia, near where the three civil rights workers—Schwerner, Chaney and Goodman—were killed by members of the Ku Klux Klan in 1964. Oren tells us that he and his brother Rex saw the boys' car burning on the side of the road soon after they were shot and killed—he says news of the murders reached him almost immediately, so he and Rex went out there to the scene—he tells us the exact spot where it occurred. Ackerman is about a half hour from there—How could he and Rex have heard the news and then gotten there so fast? He also tells us that Byron de la Beckwith, the white supremacist who murdered Medgar Evers, sat at the same kitchen table we're sitting at now—Beckwith was a farm implement salesman, with whom Oren dealt. Oren says Beckwith showed him the variety of weapons he carried with him in his car—handguns, a 30-06 rifle, grenades.

"Beckwith was a deadeye shot, too," Oren tells us. "He killed Evers, all right. He did it."

We drive from Ackerman—where we stop briefly at Swindle's Farm Supply and Grocery—Rex's store—but Rex isn't there. To Noxapater, where we detour to see Nanih Waiya, the 1,000 year old "mother mound" of the Choctaw nation. The mound was the center of the village. In 1828, Chief Greenwood Leflore called a national assembly at the mound site to make peace with the white civilization, as the sign near the mound informs us. We climb up on top of the mound and look out across the pasture below to the tree line. The field is dotted with mini-mounds full of fire ants. "Them ants is vicious," said Oren. "They can kill a calf."

We drive on to the spot on Mississippi Highway 49 across from Burnside State Park, where Oren told us he and Rex watched the civil rights workers' car burn. If I remember correctly, it took the FBI and local law enforcement three days to find the car. By that time every man, woman and child resident in Neshoba and Choctaw counties had probably seen it. Oren said he knew the bodies had been buried in a levee wall while it was under construction.

Next stop is Philadelphia, hometown of football star Marcus Dupree, who was written about so poignantly by Willie Morris. A sign at the city limits reads: "Welcome to Philadelphia, Our Fair City"—double entendre, referring to the annual Neshoba County Fair. (I record this without malice, irony notwithstanding.) The killers of Schwerner, Chaney and Goodman were taken to the Neshoba County courthouse, located in Philadelphia. It's a cold, windy day, the sky cloudy as Mike and I walk around the town center. (Next to the hotel is a tanning parlor.) The murders and the burning of the Mt. Nebo Baptist Church near here are events still fresh in people's minds. "They told those civil rights fellas to leave town," Oren said, "and they didn't go, so they killed 'em. Was some serious people in Philadelphia." "It still smarts," says Mike.

On to Meridian, birthplace of Jimmie Rodgers, the Singing Brakemen. Iron Mike looks in the Meridian telephone directory and asks me, "What do you think is the first listing in the Yellow Pages?" I give up. "Abortion Alternatives," he says. "Guess what's second?" I don't know. "Abortion Services."

4/3 Meridian/Bovina—In Meridian we head to the Jimmie Rodgers Museum in Highland Park. Dixie Boys Field baseball diamond, signs on the outfield fences—Duck laying eggs next to museum entrance undisturbed—I recall that Jimmie Rodgers died of TB in the Taft Hotel in New York, May 26, 1933. The Taft was the scene of a wild nightmare drunk of mine in 1965 with my old pal Kent Newell, a St. Louis boy who later went crazy and joined the Ku Klux Klan before he was killed in a single-car wreck on a rural California road. Jimmie's home in Meridian was destroyed by a tornado (the same year that strange fruit decorated the gum trees in Tupelo?)—he named his house in Kerrville, Texas, the "Blue Yodeler's Paradise"—Later Mike and I visit JR's grave in the Oak Grove Cemetery in Bonita, next to the Oak Grove Baptist Church, a peaceful, tree-surrounded spot.

At Rosehill Cemetery, we find the graves of a Gypsy King and Queen, Emil and Kelly Mitchell—EMIL MITCHELL DIED OCTOBER 16, 1942 AGED 85 YEARS KING OF THE GYPSIES it says on the gravestone. Kelly died at 47 in 1915. Other gypsies in the plot are SLATCHO MITCHELL AS MIKE WILSON, also died in 1942 (Mike Wilson was the alias he used in the everyday work world); and FLORA MITCHELL JAN. 8, 1930 AGED 70 YEARS SISTER OF THE KING. A tiny stone has engraved on it: TO MA MIA TOMBILENA RICERONA

Driving out of Meridian, I remember Eddie Dixon, a New York rock musician and actor (he had a small role in the film version of *Wild at Heart*), telling me about Ma Shumate's whorehouse outside Meridian, where all of the women supposedly weighed at least 250 pounds—Ma Shumate, Mel Evans tells me later in Jackson (Mel having grown up in Meridian), is still alive but retired.

I'm glad to have paid tribute to Jimmie Rodgers. When my kids were small, I always used to sing his tune "Treasure Untold" to them at bedtime. He was a true crossover artist, accepted by country, blues and rock 'n' roll people alike. He's in the Rock and Roll Hall of Fame, where he belongs. JR kept a cot in the recording studio while he made his last sides, resting between takes—dead at 35.

Meridian doesn't have much happening these days—a quiet, Christian town without much industry, no decent hotels, a dumpy downtown—though Weidmann's restaurant, which has been there since 1870, is still pretty good. I don't mind leaving—even Jimmie Rodgers left as soon as he made some money.

We cruise past Forest, birthplace of Arthur "Big Boy" Crudup, Elvis's early idol—Elvis's first record was of Crudup's tune "That's All Right, Mama"—on to Bovina, near Vicksburg, to see Earl Wayne Simmons, a black folk artist—not unlike Simon Rodia, who built the Watts towers in L.A.—who has constructed a domicile called EARLS ART SHOP, a kind of deranged magical kingdom, a warped Pee Wee's Playhouse, where he lives and works. Earl is a medium-sized man in his late thirties, a sweet guy who says his neighbors think he's crazy. The toy house sags on a little hill and has many tiny rooms filled with found art objects, crudely hand-crafted toys, jukeboxes, signs of all kinds, dolls—too many items to mention. He has built a little restaurant-juke joint in it—when we arrived, three local guys were waiting around for Earl to let them in to play the jukebox. Earl Simmons is a primitive visionary artist with a *plan*—a naif worth supporting. This is his address and telephone number—maybe some New York or Los Angeles patrons of the arts will help him out: EARLS ART SHOP, 6444 Warriors Trail, Vicksburg, MS 39180; tel.(601) 636-5264.

Written on the men's room wall of the Texaco station in Bovina: Next rest area in 82 Ford Blue Van—2 or more Welcome—She 23 140 LB white—never had gay kid—black or white any time after 10 PM—No Diseases.

4/4 Jackson—At the home of John and Mel Evans and their kids, Austin, 11, and Saramel, 14, their two dogs, Sam and Dave, and cat, Ruth. Tonight a barbecue, then tomorrow back to New Orleans, the end of this roadtrip.

Race, as ever, is the issue here. In Mississippi, there's no way around it, the subject does not go away. Racism is the curse of the place and it is crippling. In Choctaw County, where Iron Mike's Uncle Oren and Aunt Emma Lou live, every activity invites comments regarding "niggers."

Mike told me that a friend of his in New Orleans named Warren Pepe, a Creole, who once owned the French Quarter Cleaners on Dumaine Street, used to say, "The things we do here in New Orleans, the way white people and black people mix—you just can't get away with that everywhere." The question, of course, is why not?

A person in Jackson jokingly referred to us as "Negrophiles." Swindle commented, "The difference between generations is that his father would have called us nigger lovers."

Before going to bed on my last night in Mississippi for awhile, I was reading Bill James's new baseball book and came across this quote from Jules Tygiel's landmark study of integration in the major leagues, *Baseball's Great Experiment*. ". . . during spring training, 1955 . . . one afternoon in Tampa . . . after being removed from a game, [pitcher Brooks Lawrence] and catcher Ed Bailey [who were teammates on the

Cincinnati Reds] entered the stands to watch the remainder of the contest. A rope separated the black and white sections and while Bailey sat on the white side, Lawrence sat next to him on the black. 'Boy, this is stupid,' exclaimed Bailey, a Tennesseean. 'I'm gonna change this.' The catcher removed the rope and, according to Lawrence, no one ever reattached it."

So be it.

INTRODUCTION TO *TEXAS STORIES* (1995)

"THIS LOOKS LIKE A LUCKY SPOT, sweetheart," Sailor Ripley says to his girlfriend, Lula Pace Fortune, in *Wild at Heart*, as they cruise in her white '75 Bonneville convertible into Big Tuna, Texas. It turns out to be a load shy of lucky for the pair, and especially unfortunate for Sailor, who ends up spending ten years in the Texas State Penitentiary at Huntsville for attempted robbery with a deadly weapon. Spook Strickland, one of the meaner boys Sailor meets at Huntsville (described in my novel, *Sailor's Holiday*), tells him that God's message is that nobody *deserves* to live, that staying alive is an option not available to everyone, which is why people like Spook exist, to destroy the least worthy among them. Sailor asks Spook Strickland why God had created billions of people in the first place, and why He continues to produce more, a question that provokes Spook to laughter. After settling down, Spook explains to Sailor that most human beings are provided for target practice, then shows him the words tattooed on his right arm: ORDER AT THE BORDER OF HELL.

When I was a kid in Tampa, Florida, I once heard somebody say, "Nothin' good ever happens in Texas." I believe this was said upon hearing the news that a mad gunman named Charles Whitman had just shot and killed sixteen people and wounded a number of others from a tower on the campus of the University of Texas at Austin, before the cops put him down permanently. I know the implied admonition of that statement occurred to me when I learned that John F. Kennedy had been drilled in Dallas. Sure, terrible things happen in other places; Texas doesn't have a monopoly on violent or irrational behavior, but few areas seem to take such inordinate pride in bloody legends.

One of my favorite periods of Texas history is the time of the War

Between the States, when Brownsville was seized from the Union forces by Colonel Rip Ford, a former captain of the Texas Rangers. Ford commanded a renegade army composed of young boys and men too old to have been conscripted into either the Union or Confederate forces. The self-appointed colonel organized his minions using the canard that the federals were about to flood South Texas with Negro troops. Ford falsely claimed association with the Confederate Army, which operated out of Matamoros, across the Mexican border, but they distrusted him; with good reason, as it turned out, because as the war was winding down and defeat for the Confederacy seemed certain, Ford attempted to make a deal with the U.S. government whereby Texas would rejoin the Union and his ragamuffin brigade would then join federal troops in a war on Mexico.

Fighting along the border was as ferocious and bloody as any in the rest of the country at that time. Ford's brigands managed to drive the Union boys into Mexico, where the U.S. was allied with the Juaristas in an effort to overthrow the Imperialists. Local border warlords—the Yellow Flags and the Red Flags—vied with bands of Kickapoo and Apache Indians for territory, as well as clashing with mercenary raiders such as Ford's bunch. Richard King and Mifflin Kenedy, Yankee businessmen who established the King Ranch in South Texas, had come down to profit in the steamboat trade. Rip Ford aided their betrayal of the Union by facilitating the rechartering of their boats under Mexican registry, which allowed them to transport cotton to the thousands of European ships waiting off Matamoros.

Just across the border on the Mexican side, at the end of what is now Texas Highway 4, lay the small town of Boca del Rio, or, as the Europeans named it, Bagdad. Bagdad was a wide-open place where any kind of deal went down. People from all over came to get rich quick: whores, spies, gamblers, con men, army deserters swarmed in. Wages were high and life was cheap; there was no law. Bagdad was like Tangier when it was an international port. Mosquitoes, constant sand-filled winds and murderous deviltry kept tension high. Almost immediately after the war ended, a hurricane destroyed Bagdad, cleansing it from the face of the earth.

It's this kind of past that Texans of my acquaintance seem to relish. Some of the contributors to this anthology, like Cormac McCarthy and Larry McMurtry (on occasion)—and some Texas writers who aren't included, such as Larry L. King and James Crumley—are also decidedly unsqueamish when it comes to Lone Star lore of blood and gore. One or two wax rhapsodic but they're Yankees or worse—Jack Kerouac was from Massachusetts and Jan Morris is British. Don DeLillo's brilliant reinvention of the myth of Lee Harvey Oswald (who was from New Orleans, more or less) gets Texas where it hurts; and Langston Hughes sings the blues about how badly Texas can hurt back, and keep on hurtin'.

I believe it was that venerable Texan J. Frank Dobie who paraphrased a Native American Coyote myth informing us that Coyote divided animal life into three categories: animals to be eaten, animals to aid in capturing food, and animals that would eat him. Man, Coyote taught, belongs in the third category. My guess is the man to whom Coyote was referring was a Texan.

BLACK WINGS HAD HIS ANGEL: A BRIEF MEMOIR OF ELLIOTT CHAZE

from *OXFORD AMERICAN* (2000)

As FOUNDING EDITOR of Black Lizard Books the one novel I wanted most to publish in the series, which ran from 1984–1989, was *Black Wings Has My Angel* by Elliott Chaze. It was brought to my attention as the quintessential Gold Medal paperback original by Edward Gorman and Max Collins, both of whom had written admiringly about it. When I read it, I was floored. *Black Wings* was an astonishingly well-written, literary novel that just happened to be about (or roundabout) a crime. It was a perfect fit for what publisher Don Ellis and I were doing at Black Lizard, publishing books that were psychologically provocative, uniquely on-the-edge and—more often than not—*over* the edge. Our authors—viz. Jim Thompson, Charles Willeford, Jim Nisbet, et al—were uncompromising, cruel, crazy, sexy and daring. Chaze's novel, published originally in 1954 and since then available only in French as *Il gèle en enfer*, was to be a kind of crowning achievement for Black Lizard. Unfortunately, before we could publish it, the company was sold and the editors who inherited the series deemed *Black Wings* unworthy of publication, eventually returning the rights to the author.

When I learned of their decision, I was disappointed, not only because I did not agree with their assessment of the novel's value, but because I had worked hard over several years to convince Chaze to allow us to reprint the book. I believe I first called Elliott in 1985. I told him about the Black Lizard series, our philosophy, our high regard for this particular novel of his, and of course all he wanted to know was how much could we pay him. I told him, he made a nasty noise, and hung up. I wrote him once or twice after this initial, disappointing communication, endeavoring to stay in touch in case he one day changed his mind and allowed us to publish the book for the small advance we could afford.

I told many people about *Black Wings*, one of whom, the movie producer Monty Montgomery, paid Elliott a visit at his home in Hattiesburg, Mississippi. Monty told Elliott he would like to consider making a film of the novel, but Chaze said he'd already sold the film rights to a French director/actor named Jean-Pierre Mocky, ending that conversation. (Mocky did, in fact, make a movie out of it, not a very good one. The story deserves another chance.) Monty told me that Chaze had been borderline polite to him, cordial but crusty.

It so happened that a year or so later, I was in the neighborhood (New Orleans), so I drove up to see Elliott myself. He and his wife lived in a small bungalow with a narrow porch out front near the railroad tracks. I knew Chaze had worked for many years as a reporter for the Associated Press, in Louisiana and Colorado, and then in Hattiesburg. He'd written a number of novels beside *Black Wings*, "literary" novels as well as a short series about a crime-detecting newsman named Kiel St. James. I'd found and read a few of these and the only one I thought had anything to recommend it was *Tiger in the Honeysuckle*, a "straight" story dealing with racism. *Tiger* was all right, but nothing else Chaze wrote came anywhere close to what he had accomplished on all levels in *Black Wings*.

Elliott welcomed me warily, saying right off that in his opinion New Orleans was a cesspool of filth and degeneracy and that it literally stank. Why would I want to spend any time there? he asked rhetorically. Once inside the little house—his wife, Mary, he explained, was sick and locked in her bedroom—he took me into his study, sat down at his desk and pointed to a gun-in-holster hanging on a nail in the wall just above it.

"After my prostate surgery," Elliott said, "I was in so much pain, I came in here and took that pistol—" he stood up, removed the gun from its holster and sat down again—"and put it in my mouth, like this." Chaze put the tip of the business end to his lips, held it there for a few moments, then held it out away from him before resting his hand on the desk. "I decided to wait until the next day before I killed myself, to see if the pain slacked off any. It did, and even more the day after and the day after that. So, for better or worse, mostly worse, I'm still around."

Elliott was a fairly large man, seventy-two years old when I met him. He was cranky, bitter about having been mostly ignored as a serious writer but making weak attempts throughout our visit to pretend that he didn't really care. He cared, all right; and his cynical facade faded the more we spoke. He insisted on making us roast beef sandwiches on white bread with mayonnaise and the crusts cut off. Chaze drank milk. When I told him I preferred to drink something else, he gave me a glass of sink water. We sat in the blue kitchen of his wooden bungalow and ate lunch.

Later we sat on the front porch and he praised his magnolias that he pampered and were growing all around us. I raised the subject of Black Lizard publishing *Black Wings Has My Angel* and he said he didn't see why the hell not, but couldn't we raise the ante a bit? I told him I'd talk to the boss about it and that's how we left the matter. Chaze stood on the porch and watched me drive away. I had to make a U-turn at the corner and double back over the railroad tracks because the street dead-ended without warning. As I passed his house he yelled at me, "I could have told you to go the other way!" "Then why didn't you?" I shouted back. He smiled for the first time since I'd been there.

When I got back to California I convinced Don Ellis to goose the advance a little, and we made a contract for the novel. Two and a half years later I was back in New Orleans, picked up the paper one morning and read Elliott's obituary. He had died without seeing his best book put back into print in his own country. I felt badly for him and silently cursed the publisher who didn't realize what a little gem he had tossed away, thereby refusing Elliott the real pleasure he would have enjoyed at being "rediscovered" by a readership I'm certain is still out there.

It's well worth checking out old paperback bins in used bookstores to find a copy of *Black Wings Has My Angel.* Once you've got the gem in your hands, look it over carefully; it still sparkles.

THE STRANGEST ONE OF ALL

from *EL PAÍS* AND *SPEAK* (1997)

THE FIRST TIME I met William Burroughs was in 1975 at The Bunker, his windowless dwelling on the Bowery in New York City. Number 222, I believe, was the address, directly across the street from the Lighthouse Mission. It was from the Lighthouse Mission that I was instructed to call him from the pay phone so that he or his assistant could come down to the street level entrance and unlock the accordion gate in order that I might enter William's inner sanctum. The Bunker was simply but tastefully furnished. I remember his telling me that at one time the space had been the boys locker room of the neighborhood YMCA. Two or three of the stand-up urinals were still in place in the area partitioned off for use as a bathroom. Given William's particular affection for young men, what could have been more perfect?

I saw Burroughs again in the fall of that year in Boulder, Colorado, to which he had come to teach at the Jack Kerouac School of Disembodied Poetics. In 1981, Burroughs moved to Lawrence, Kansas, not very far from his Ladue, Missouri, birthplace, where he lived until his death in a modest wooden house on Learnard Street. I visited him several times during his residence in Lawrence, but it was in 1991, when my son, Buck, who was then sixteen years old, accompanied me, that was surely the most memorable visit.

Buck and I, accompanied by our friend Jimbo Carothers, a legendary retired baseball player from Kansas, spent a few hours with William on a hot August afternoon. Burroughs was then seventy-seven, and on our way over to his house I told Buck, who had no idea who William was, a bit of Burroughs's history. I informed Buck that he was a famous writer, a Harvard graduate, who had lived in Mexico, Morocco, England, France, New Orleans, Texas and New York, among other places, worked as an exterminator and private detective, was heir to a family fortune and had been for many years—despite his frequent public denials—a remittance man, during much of which time he had been a drug addict (mainly heroin), had shot and killed by accident his wife while playing William Tell in Mexico City, had embraced and then rejected Scientology, had written several ground-breaking works of futuristic, satirical literary fiction, was now a painter of some merit, had acted in a few feature films, and had been for most of his life a confirmed pederast.

"What's that?" asked Buck. "What's a pederast?"

"A homosexual," I said.

"Oh. Okay," said Buck.

William, who had recently seen his novel *Naked Lunch* made into a film, asked me what I thought of the film version of my novel, *Wild at Heart*, also a recent production, and showed us one of the "mugwumps" used in *Naked Lunch* that he had chained to a chair in his painting studio. We had tea and he showed me the manuscript of a book he was working on about dreams. William steered the conversation to firearms, and pulled up his right pantleg to reveal an ankle holster fitted with a small caliber revolver strapped to his skinny red- and blue-veined leg.

"I'm always armed," he said, in his nasal whine. "In fact, I'm going out later to a place I have by a lake to shoot. If you like, you boys can come along."

Jimbo Carothers, who had driven us to Burroughs's house, explained that we had an early dinner engagement, so we would have to take a raincheck on the shooting party.

William got up to get something in another room, and while he was out of earshot, Jimbo whispered to me, "I've done many crazy things in my time, but shooting guns with William Burroughs is not going to be one of them."

William came back with a large jar. He sat next to Buck on a small couch and showed it to him.

"Look at this," William said, "a brown recluse spider. Found him crawling along the window sill in the bedroom."

Buck took the bottle and looked at the large spider.

"A bite from this spider will make a hole in a person's leg the size of a saucer," said William.

He got up and took a book off a shelf, sat down again next to Buck and opened the book.

"Here's some pictures of spider bites. The brown recluse does the most damage," Burroughs said, smiling.

The graphic photographs of epidermal craters caused by arachnids clearly delighted him.

Later, William instructed Buck in the use of a blow-dart gun from New Guinea that he kept by his fireplace. He told Buck that the tips of the darts they were shooting at a target nailed to the back of the front door were dipped before hunting into a powerful poison that immobilized within a few seconds any beast so pierced.

"The hunter," Burroughs explained, "then takes a machete to the fallen prey and decapitates it."

Again, William smiled.

In the car on our way to Jimbo's house, Buck seemed particularly thoughtful and quiet. I asked him if he had enjoyed his visit with Burroughs.

"Yeah, sure," he said. "You know, Pop, you've introduced me to a lot of strange people, but I think that William Burroughs is the strangest one of all."

THE FACE OF THE HERO

from *EL PAÍS* (1995)

"CONSIDER THE UNITED STATES," wrote Roland Barthes, "where everything is transformed into images: only images exist and are consumed." For his entire life O.J. Simpson, the former professional football player turned actor currently on trial for the murder of his ex-wife and a male friend of hers, has worn a mask. Born and raised in the poor Potrero Hill neighborhood of San Francisco, as a boy Orenthal James was already an actor. He had to act tough to get along on the streets; either that or be a target. Once he realized that he could run faster than most boys his age and older, O.J. became a moving target, hard to catch; this ability helped to keep him alive. He exploited his talent and became a football star, a role that came easy to him. Simpson assumed the face of the hero when he was still a teenager. Now the photographs attempt to revise his visage, to reconstruct these features into the mask of a killer. "The mask is the difficult region of photography," Barthes said. "Once I feel observed by the lens, everything changes: I constitute myself in the process of 'posing' . . . I transform myself." My guess is that O.J. Simpson has forgotten what his real face looks like. His struggle now is not only to save his face, but to regain it.

Simpson declared in court that he is "100% innocent" of the charges that he brutally slit the throats of Nicole Brown and Ronald Goldman. Whoever did this—severely beat and cut the deliveryman and then almost entirely severed the woman's head from her body—was not caught in the act wearing the bloody ski mask. ("I transform myself.") The act we are catching now, in the courtroom, is storyboarded by the "star" attorneys as carefully as Alfred Hitchcock conceived *Psycho*. O.J. Simpson is the most famous person ever to stand trial in the United States for a capital crime. That it is taking place in Los Angeles and not "on location" makes this a media dream; since they are already there, there are no travel expenses to threaten the production budget. The judge is allowing the trial to be televised. Everyone involved is happy about this, despite 15,000 letters to Judge Ito protesting the public broadcast. The Japanese cannot make enough cameras to take all of the pictures. ("Only images exist and are consumed.") Everybody needs postcards of the hanging—as if looking into the mirror were not horrifying enough.

The lawyers sign autographs on the street and in the supermarkets. "I do it," said the chief prosecuting attorney, Marcia Clarke, who seems to be a decent enough person, "but I don't know why." ("I constitute myself in the process of 'posing.' ") O.J. Simpson's legal costs will surpass three million dollars. ("I am 100% innocent.") His face has become the mask of the martyr. Instant books appear, deconstructing his image and hers, Nicole's. The beautiful blonde's first female sex partner says Simpson was an abusive husband. Acquaintances of O.J.'s go on television to tell us about the hero's cocaine habit. The newspapers and magazines ceaselessly caress the practically decapitated body of the blonde in the negligee displayed artlessly on the California sidewalk. Click. Like Jayne Mansfield, her platinum scalp sheared off on a southern highway. Click. ("Only images exist.") Home movies appear during dinnertime: Simpson's best pal consorting with porno actresses; O.J. enjoying his kids; Nicole's family showing her baby pictures. When he played football, Simpson wore a facemask; all you could see were his eyes, lizardy, darting, reading the landscape while he ran to avoid almost certain violence. Sitting in the courtroom, his eyes are empty, energy drained; like sitting in a lockerroom after a game, muddy, exhausted, the world a blur.

In the last three days I received the following news: the fifteen year old daughter of a friend of mine was raped and murdered, shot in the head, on a Saturday afternoon while she was walking through a schoolyard on her way to a girlfriend's house. A friend's son and his girlfriend, both twenty years old, were waiting at a bus stop late at night when an eighteen year old male stuck a gun in their faces, forced the boy to lie down on the sidewalk, then kidnapped the girl. He drove her in a car to a deserted area, beat and raped her, then kicked her out into the street and drove away. A sixty-two year old friend of mine, an Hispanic man, was campaigning before the election for a seat on the city council. He was running against the incumbent, a black woman, and was going door-to-door in a predominantly black neighborhood when he was set upon by a group of thugs, all black, who beat him to a pulp.

("Consider the United States, where . . . only images exist.")

Draw the line between fact and fiction. Can you tell the difference? I'm a writer, I can't. In Yuba City, California, six hundred miles north of where O.J. Simpson is being tried for two murders, two severed hands were found in a K-Mart shopping cart. The grisly discovery was made by a clerk collecting carts in the store's parking lot. The hands are being treated as evidence in a crime, but it will take a forensics expert to determine for sure that the body parts found are, in fact, human, and whether homicide is indicated.

What was the look on the face of the clerk when he saw the hands? There is nothing heroic about finding hands in a shopping cart. The clerk's face is not the face of a hero, or is it?

O.J. and the attorneys pose for the camera. ("I transform myself.") We watch them, without removing our masks, soundlessly, dwelling as we do in this difficult region.

FUZZY SANDWICHES OR THERE IS NO SPEED LIMIT ON THE LOST HIGHWAY: REFLECTIONS ON DAVID LYNCH

from *PREMIÈRE* (2002)

WHEN DAVID LYNCH, who had directed the film version of my novel *Wild at Heart*, and also had directed my two plays, "Tricks" and "Blackout" for a television production entitled *Hotel Room*, came to me and asked me to write with him the screenplay for a new film, I could hardly say no. After all, *Wild at Heart* had won the Palme d'Or at the Cannes Film Festival and propelled the book onto best-seller lists all over the world. Besides, we were good friends by now. The problem was that I was busily engaged writing a novel and was scheduled to leave for a trip to Spain in two weeks. How could we get a screenplay done *right now*, as Dave said. In fact, he insisted. So I put aside the novel manuscript and agreed to work hard for two weeks and see what we came up with. If it seemed to be working after my return from Spain, if we both felt good about the project, then we would continue and work straight through until we had it finished.

David had optioned for film my novel *Night People*, and we had talked for a year or more about how that could be done, but nothing happened. (He told me his daughter, Jennifer, wanted to play the role of one of the two lesbian serial killers.) He fell in love with a couple of sentences in the book in particular, one of which was when one woman says to another, "We're just a couple of Apaches ridin' wild on the lost highway." What did it mean? he wanted to know. What was the *deeper* meaning of the phrase "lost highway?" He had an idea for a story. What if one day a person woke up and he was another person? An entirely different person from the person he had been the day before. Okay, I said, that's Kafka, *The Metamorphosis*. But we did not want this person to turn into an insect. So that's what we had to start with: a title, *Lost Highway*; a sentence from close to the end of the book *Night People* ("You and me, mister, we can really out-ugly the sumbitches, can't we?"); the notion of irrefutable change; and a vision Dave had about someone receiving videotapes of his life from an unknown source, something he had thought of following the wrap of the shooting of *Twin Peaks: Fire Walk with Me*. Now all we had to do was make a coherent story out of this.

A few years ago, when David, the producer Monty Montgomery, my friend Vinnie Deserio and I were sitting around talking about another story, Dave, in an effort to explain to me an effect he was after, said, "You know that feeling you get when you've just gotten back from the dry cleaners a pair of slacks, dacron slacks, and you reach your hand in a pocket and you feel those *fuzzy sandwiches* with your fingers? Well, that's the feeling I'm looking for." I just nodded and replied, "Okay, Dave, I know *exactly* what you mean."

I kept this incident in mind while he and I sat across from one another and puzzled out the scenario for *Lost Highway*, which I like to call *Orpheus and Eurydice Meet Double Indemnity*. We made it work—at least for each other—and I love the result, fuzzy sandwiches and all. That being said, it's important to understand that David and I work similarly, very hard, long hours, with times out only for coffee—in Dave's case, *lots* of coffee. Working with Dave is, for me, a great treat, because I know that as the director he's going to add an extra dimension to whatever we come up with on the page. Visually, it will take one giant step beyond. This gives me the confidence to let everything loose, a great privilege for a writer.

Both Lynch and I believe that films are, or should be, as dreams. When you enter the theater the "real" world is shut out. Now you are in the thrall of the filmmakers, you *must* surrender and allow the film's images to wash over you, to drown in them for two hours or so. And David is relentless in his use of imagery. *Lost Highway*, like *Blue Velvet* or *Eraserhead*, especially, is filled with unforgettable images. And we are set in a place, a city, a landscape, that is neither here nor there, a timeless form, presented within a non-linear structure—a Möbius strip, curling back and under, running parallel to itself before again becoming connected, only there's a kind of coda—but, that's how it goes with psychogenic fugues. Figure it out for yourself, you'll feel better later; and if you don't figure it out, you'll feel even *better*, trust us. Trust is what it's all about with filmmakers like David Lynch, one of the very, very few true visionaries in the history of cinema.

Vinnie Deserio once said that the reason Dave and I work so well together is that he takes the ordinary and makes it seem extraordinary, and I take the extraordinary and make it seem ordinary. Maybe so, it sounds good, anyway. But there are no easy explanations for what occurs in *Lost Highway* or *Eraserhead*, nor should there be. When you go on a journey with David Lynch it's a trip you've never been on before—and may never want to take again—but it's unforgettable. Time to fasten your seat belt, as Bette Davis so memorably instructed (words by Joseph Mankiewicz) in *All About Eve*, because there is no speed limit on the lost highway.

from BORDERTOWN (1998)

Cookie Cruz met Tico Mariposa on the Santa Fe bridge between El Paso and Juárez. She was returning from her job at the Camino Real Hotel, where she worked as a maid. Cookie lived with her mother, Rosa, in Juárez, despite the fact that she possessed a green card and could have lived in the U.S.A. Tico was born and raised in El Paso. He worked on and off as a groom at Sunland and Juárez racetracks, but had fallen in with a bad crowd that hung out at the Club Colorada in Juárez. He became a crack dealer and user. Tico was a handsome boy of twenty-two when he hit on Cookie, who was a year younger. They walked together into Mexico and that was the last anyone in El Paso ever saw of her. Tico Mariposa took Cookie Cruz with him to his room above the Buena Suerte bar on the corner of Avenue 16 de Septiembre and Pancho Villa. She was tired after working all day and not eager to make dinner for her mother and herself, so Cookie took a hit when Tico offered her one. She passed out at some point and when she woke up Tico was raping her. Cookie screamed so Tico popped her in the chops with his right fist, then smack on the nose with his left. She was bleeding and crying when Tico turned her over and tried to stick it in her ass. Cookie crawled forward, grabbed a small lamp without a shade and raked it backwards across Tico's face, shattering the bulb. He released her and Cookie jumped up. She was too dizzy from the drug to stand. Cookie fell over and looked at Tico. He was lying on his left side with pieces of the light bulb sticking out of his right eye. Cookie couldn't move from the corner where she had fallen. Her face was streaked with blood and tears. She wanted to close her eyes but they were frozen open. Tico rose to his knees and slowly picked the pieces of glass out of his face. He reached down and picked up a gun and pointed it at Cookie Cruz. She thought about Rose, her mother, waiting for her in the little yellow house on Calle Mejia, the house her mother would never leave. Cookie had fantasized since she was fifteen about going to Nueva York and sitting in the sun on the edge of the fountain in front of the Plaza Hotel, which she'd seen a photograph of in a magazine. Cookie imagined herself standing naked in the Plaza fountain under a warm sun, and she smiled, her eyes closed, as Tico pulled the trigger.

• • •

CHUY REYES AND ESPERANZA MARTINEZ are running through the desert, Chuy carrying the child. Night has fallen hard and they're cold despite the fact that they are sweating profusely. The boy is whimpering now, exhausted from crying. "Mama," he squeaks. Esperanza stops and slips to the ground.

"Come on," says Chuy, "get up. I can't carry you, too." He keeps going. Esperanza rises slowly, reluctantly. She can hear the little boy up ahead, crying louder now. Esperanza walks on. Chuy and the child, Omar, are out of sight. It's dark. Chuy shouts, there's a loud noise, someone falling, Omar screaming. Esperanza runs toward the noise. She trips over a cactus, cuts her hands on the ground. The boy is still screaming, out of control. There are several dull, thudding sounds, all in a row, then silence.

"Chuy?" Esperanza cries. "Chuy, what happened?" She gets up and makes her way slowly forward until she sees him standing in thin moonlight, empty-handed.

"Chuy, where is Omar?"

Chuy kicks at a dark object, moving it toward Esperanza.

"There he is," he says. "I think he's dead."

"Oh, Chuy, no." Esperanza kneels and turns the small, broken body so that she can see his face. "Why did you do this?" she asks.

"He was so heavy," says Chuy, "and the fuckin' kid wouldn't shut up."

"Now what do we have?" Esperanza says. "We have nothing."

"We can always get another one. Come on, help me make a hole."

Chuy begins to kick at the dirt with the heel of his right boot.

• • •

FRIDAY NIGHT IN NUEVO LAREDO 4:45 A.M.

AT BOYSTOWN the girls and women (minimum age: eighteen, though I spoke to one girl who admitted to being seventeen, a miniature beauty with a beguiling schoolgirl's grin) are lined up inside the cuartos, some standing in the doorway actively soliciting, others lying on their beds, a few with TVs on, most (either standing or in recline) reading comic books. Several are stunningly beautiful, Aztec or Mayan princesses in their late teens or very early twenties, a few as lovely as Dolores Del Rio but born into exceedingly mean circumstances, country girls who charge ten dollars for a combination blow job and lay. The women in clubs are the elite—they speak English, are better taken care of, and charge fifty dollars for the same. All of them are examined twice weekly by the Boystown doctor, on Sundays and Fridays. The girls in the cribs pay ten dollars a week rent for their primitive little boxes. Some are sparsely furnished, usually with a photo or two of their tiny son or daughter who is back home in Monterrey or San Luís Potosí, a few Catholic trinkets, a mirror. Others are almost or entirely devoid of any decorative aspect, lit by a harsh overhead bulb, the walls gray, only a thin blanket or sheet on the bed, a plastic bucket of water in a corner.

• • •

ALL OF THESE PUTAS are carefully made up, most overly so—as such they look like typical American high school girls in certain big cities and suburbs today, where the style is to be painted up like a Mexican whore. The women must make their tricks wear condoms, but for a couple of bucks extra nobody in charge will know the difference until they show up HIV positive. A few forlorn-looking Indian girls, very short, stout, stand unblinking and stiff in front of their rooms like dull ceramic dolls on a shelf, rarely dusted and ignored compared to their flashier competition. In some doorways two or three of the younger girls, maybe from the same town, sit together, joking, coming on to the parade of shopping dicks, never forgetting why they're there. The girls are easy to talk to, most—even the older women—still somehow sweet and innocent. Fucking and sucking is their business, that's all, nothing emotional in that. The policía stationed near the entrance in a cuarto of their own protect the women and make sure each vehicle of visiting gringos pays twenty dollars to enter the compound.

• • •

DAVID PAYS SEVERAL of the cuarto girls ten dollars apiece to pose for him in their rooms. Some of the girls refuse to have their picture taken because of fear their relatives in Chicago or L.A. might see them, or their mothers, always their mothers, and be caused embarrassment; one woman keeps insisting she'd rather "fuckee and suckee" me rather than let David take her picture, but she finally relents and allows him in, leaving her door open. Other girls insist on closing the door so it appears that she is turning a regular trick. A heavily made-up, very cute young girl—she's nineteen—named Jacqueline offers to jack me off for free, which shocks our companion, Alejo, a Laredo taxi driver, who says he's never before heard one of these girls make such a proposal. Jacqueline says maybe once she gets me inside and aroused I'll change my mind and fuck her. David photographs Jacqueline and her amiga, Angelita, together in Jacqueline's cuarto with me in attendance. They are lively, quizzical, especially Jacqueline, who is full of good humor in comparison to the rest, who are dead behind their lovely, painted eyes.

I prefer the cheaper girls in their cuartos to the more expensive women in the clubs—there is less guile in them, they seem less hard, their sadness more palpable. Maybe I'm deluded or just wishful, but they are decidedly tender in the tropical Mexican Laredo night.

BORDERTOWN

is a place to make money,
spectacles to
attract tourists,
a sopa picante with
a touch
of evil

****

Man knifed on Juarez
sidestreet,
stiff after
two days,
his stink
not even noticeable
or defined among the
general stench
by Club Colorada
A miniature Yolanda all
mouth and eyes
shimmering in
a doorway

****

Bordertown is the city of spooks,
of greedy ghosts
and unapproachable
visions

****

Dirt streets of
deep southwest,
pariah dogs groan
in the fabulous dust
and heat,
flies laying eggs
on chickens
and hanging
pigs

******

The only certainty is
at the cemeteries, the
only grip
on life to visit and
revisit
the acknowledged dead
The living dead pay homage
to each other's fate,
a place to
finally meet
and be restful

Impossible to be at
peace
in this crush,
this pesthole
life built
on the refuse of
El Norte

*****

Whores in the broken
light like
giant parrots,
birds ready
to peck your eyes
and pick your pockets
At the same time
become dreamy
Aztec princesses muy sincero
y las romanticas
de sus suenos

*****

The ramshackle countryside
devours the border sun,
thin wind
tickles scabrous brush
as border patrol run down
rats scurrying
from the rotten
stinking sinking
ship
like piñatas falling
off the back
of a speeding
truck

*****

Here's where the road
ends,
in the ground or at water's edge—
Boca Chica, the girl's
mouth,
the gates
of hell
or heaven
swung
wide,
waiting to
receive you,
the same in death
as in life,
forever.

I WISH I'D MADE IT UP

I WISH I'D MADE IT UP:
A NOTE TO THE READER

ON A SUMMER'S DAY IN 1957, I was sitting on top of the backrest of a bench next to a ballfield at Green Briar Park in Chicago when for some reason I no longer can remember I thought about how old I would be in the year 2000. The answer was fifty-three, a figure virtually beyond imagining insofar as the possibility of my ever attaining such an age. The millennial year itself likewise eluded serious speculation—at ten I had difficulty contemplating much beyond the very moment. I was shaken from this reverie of the incomprehensible by a kid shouting at me, "Hey, Gif, you're up!"

I am now fully two years older than the fifty-three that seemed so unrealistic as well as unrealizable that afternoon in Green Briar Park forty-four and a half years ago. Turning thirty, or forty, or fifty, did not disturb me. My Uncle Buck, who will be ninety-one this coming May, told me several years ago that according to his research anyone who dies before the age of 120 has died a premature death. About a year ago, he revised this plateau of minimal longevity to 130.

Perhaps he's right. At ninety, Uncle Buck works steadily as a civil engineer and architect, drawing plans for houses and offices, keeping almost as busy as ever. He took off for ten days in November and went fishing out of Progréso, on the Yucatan coast, with a guide only slightly younger than himself. No old men of the sea, Buck reported that they were extremely successful, catching fish every day with nary a mishap.

There's more to the above: the year before, my uncle was in Progréso when he met the guide and arranged to go out fishing with him the next morning. That night he broke his leg and had to be hospitalized. The guide had no telephone, so Buck could not contact him. After one week in the hospital in Progréso, my uncle, using a pair of hand-hewn crutches furnished for him by the husband of one of the nurses in a hospital without doctors, got himself to the closest big town, Mérida, where he literally hopped on a plane back to Tampa, Florida, where he lives. It took quite a while for his leg to heal, but after it did, he returned to Progréso. One morning, about a year later, Buck showed up at the fishing guide's house. "I'm ready to go," Uncle Buck said to the man when he answered the door. The guide stared at my uncle for a few moments, remembered, then said, "Let me get my hat."

It was in the same year, 1957, that I considered the phenomenon of turning fifty, that I began writing stories. My first effort, titled "All in Vain," was about two brothers who fought on opposite sides during the War Between the States. It was about seven pages long, printed on yellow legal paper. My mother threw it out in a cleaning frenzy some years later, so I don't have it for reference, but I do recall that at the end the two boys shot each other and they both died.

I've always considered the short story the most difficult form in which to write. I've written novels, essays, plays, screenplays, poems, songs, even an opera libretto, but the short story has always been my favorite, most challenging mode of composition. It seems to me that the story about my uncle and his fishing guide in Mexico is about as perfect a story as there can ever be. I wish I'd made it up. The ones in this book are the best I've been able to make up so far.

—Christmas 2001

THE CINÉ

from
Post Road
(2002)

ON A CLOUDY OCTOBER SATURDAY IN 1953, when Roy was seven years old, his father took him to see a movie at the Ciné theater on Bukovina Avenue in Chicago, where they lived. Roy's father drove them in his powder-blue Cadillac, bumping over cobblestones and streetcar tracks, until he parked the car half a block away from the theater.

Roy was wearing a brown and white checked wool sweater, khaki trousers and saddle shoes. His father wore a double-breasted blue suit with a white silk tie. They held hands as they walked toward the Ciné. The air was becoming colder every day now, Roy noticed, and he was eager to get inside the theater, to be away from the wind. The Ciné sign had a red background over which the letters curved vertically in yellow neon. They snaked into one another like reticulate pythons threaded through branches of a thick-trunked Cambodian bo tree. The marquee advertised the movie they were going to see, *King of the Khyber Rifles*, starring Tyrone Power as King, a half-caste British officer commanding Indian cavalry riding against Afghan and other insurgents. "Tyrone Cupcake," Roy's father called him, but Roy did not know why.

Roy and his father entered the Ciné lobby and headed for the concession stand, where Roy's father bought Roy buttered popcorn, a Holloway All-Day sucker and a Dad's root beer. Inside the cinema, they chose seats fairly close to the screen on the right-hand side. The audience was composed mostly of kids, many of whom ran up and down the aisles even during the show, shouting and laughing, falling and spilling popcorn and drinks.

The movie began soon after Roy and his father were in their seats, and as Tyrone Power was reviewing his mounted troops, Roy's father whispered to his son, "The Afghans were making money off the opium trade even back then."

"What's opium, Dad?" asked Roy.

"Hop made from poppies. The Afghans grow and sell them to dope dealers in other countries. Opium makes people very sick."

"Do people eat it?"

"They can, but mostly they smoke it and dream."

"Do they have bad dreams?"

"Probably bad and good. Users get ga-ga on the pipe. Once somebody's hooked on O, he's finished as a man."

"What about women? Do they smoke it, too?"

"Sure, son. Only Orientals, though, that I know of. Sailors in Shanghai, Hong Kong, Zamboanga, get on the stem and never make it back to civilization."

"Where's Zamboanga?"

"On Mindanao, in the Philippine Islands."

"Is that a long way from India and Afghanistan?"

"Every place out there is a long way from everywhere else."

"Can't the Khyber Rifles stop the Afghans?"

"Tyrone Cupcake'll kick 'em in the pants if they don't."

Roy and his father watched Tyrone Power wrangle his minions for about twenty minutes before Roy's father whispered in Roy's ear again.

"Son, I've got to take care of something. I'll be back in a little while. Before the movie's over. Here's a dollar," he said, sticking a bill into Roy's hand, "just in case you want more popcorn."

"Dad," said Roy, "don't you want to see what happens?"

"You'll tell me later. Enjoy the movie, son. Wait for me here."

Before Roy could say anything else, his father was gone.

The movie ended and Roy's father had not returned. Roy remained in his seat while the lights were on. He had eaten the popcorn and drunk his root beer but he had not yet unwrapped the Holloway All-Day sucker. People left the theater and other people came in and took their seats. The movie began again.

Roy had to pee badly but he did not want to leave his seat in case his father came back while he was in the men's room. Roy held it until he could not any longer and then allowed a ribbon of urine to trickle down his left pantsleg into his sock and onto the floor. The chair on his left, where his father had been sitting, was empty, and an old lady seated on his right did not seem to notice that Roy had urinated. The odor was covered up by the smells of popcorn, candy and cigarettes.

Roy sat in his wet trousers and soaked left sock and shoe, watching again as Captain King exhorted his Khyber Rifles to perform heroically. This time after the film was finished Roy got up and walked out with the rest of the audience. He stood under the theater marquee and waited for his father. It felt good to Roy to be out of the close, smoky cinema now. The sky was dark, just past dusk, and the people filing into the Ciné were mostly couples on Saturday night dates.

Roy was getting hungry. He took out the Holloway All-Day, unwrapped it and took a lick. A uniformed policeman came and stood near him. Roy was not tempted to say anything about his situation to the beat cop because he remembered his father saying to him more than once, "The police are not your friends." The police officer looked once at Roy, smiled at him, then moved away.

Roy's mother was in Cincinnati, visiting her sister, Roy's Aunt Theresa. Roy decided to walk to where his father had parked, to see if his powder-blue Cadillac was still there. Maybe his father had gone wherever he had gone on foot, or taken a taxi. A black and gold-trimmed Studebaker Hawk was parked where Roy's father's car had been.

Roy returned to the Ciné. The policeman who had smiled at him was standing again in front of the theater. Roy passed by without looking at the cop, licking his Holloway All-Day. His left pantsleg felt crusty but almost dry and his sock still felt soggy. The cold wind made Roy shiver and he rubbed his arms. A car horn honked. Roy turned and saw the powder-blue Caddy stopped in the street. His father was waving at him out the driver's side window.

Roy walked to and around the front of the car, opened the passenger side door and climbed in, pulling the heavy metal door closed. Roy's father started driving. Roy looked out the window at the cop standing in front of the Ciné: one of his hands rested on the butt of his holstered pistol and the other fingered grooves on the handle of his billy club as his eyes swept the street.

"Sorry I'm late, son," Roy's father said, "Took me a little longer than I thought it would. Happens sometimes. How was the movie? Did Ty Cupcake take care of business?"

THE WINNER

from *American Falls* (2002)

My mother and I spent Christmas and New Year's of 1957 in Chicago. By this time, being ten years old and having experienced portions of the northern winter on several occasions, I was prepared for the worst. On our way to Chicago on the long drive from Florida, I excitedly anticipated playing in deep snow and skating on icy ponds. It turned out to be a mild winter, however, very unusual for Chicago in that by Christmas Day there had been no snow.

"The first snowfall is always around Thanksgiving," said Pops, my grandfather. "This year, you didn't need a coat. It's been the longest Indian summer ever."

I didn't mind being able to play outside with the kids who lived on Pops's street, but I couldn't hide my disappointment in not seeing snow, something we certainly did not get in Key West. The neighborhood boys and girls were friendly enough, though I felt like an outsider, even though I'd known some of them from previous visits for as many as three years.

By New Year's Eve it still had not snowed and my mother and I were due to leave on the second of January. I complained to her about this and she said, "Baby, sometimes you just can't win."

I was invited on New Year's Day to the birthday party of a boy I didn't know very well, Jimmy Kelly, a policeman's son who lived in an apartment in a three-flat at the end of the block. Johnny and Billy Duffy, who lived next door to Pops, persuaded me to come with them. Johnny was my age, Billy one year younger; they were good pals of Kelly's and assured me Kelly and his parents wouldn't mind if I came along. Just to make sure, the Duffy brothers' mother called Jimmy Kelly's mother and she said they'd be happy to have me.

Since the invitation had come at practically the last minute and all of the toy stores were closed because of the holiday, I didn't have a proper present to bring for Jimmy Kelly. My mother put some candy in a bag, wrapped Christmas paper around it, tied on a red ribbon and handed it to me.

"This will be okay," she said. "Just be polite to his parents and thank them for inviting you."

"They didn't invite me," I told her, "Johnny and Billy did. Mrs. Duffy called Kelly's mother."

"Thank them anyway. Have a good time."

At Kelly's house, kids of all ages were running around, screaming and yelling, playing tag, knocking over lamps and tables, driving the family's two black cocker spaniels, Mick and Mack, crazy. The dogs were running with and being trampled by the marauding children. Officer Kelly, in uniform with his gunbelt on, sat in a chair by the front door drinking beer out of a brown bottle. He was a large man, overweight, almost bald. He didn't seem to be at all disturbed by the chaos.

Mrs. Kelly took my gift and the Duffy brothers' gift for Jimmy, said, "Thanks, boys, go on in," and disappeared into the kitchen.

Johnny and Billy and I got going with the others and after a while Mrs. Kelly appeared with a birthday cake and ice cream. The cake had twelve candles on it, eleven for Jimmy's age and one for good luck. Jimmy was a big fat kid and blew all of the candles out in one try with ease. We each ate a piece of chocolate cake with a scoop of vanilla ice cream, then Jimmy opened his gifts. He immediately swallowed most of the candy my mother had put into the bag.

Mrs. Kelly presided over the playing of several games, following each of which she presented the winner with a prize. I won most of these games, and with each successive victory I became increasingly embarrassed. Since I was essentially a stranger, not really a friend of the birthday boy's, the other kids, including Johnny and Billy Duffy, grew somewhat hostile toward me. I felt badly about this, and after winning a third or fourth game decided that was enough—even if I could win another game. I would lose on purpose so as not to further antagonize anyone else.

The next contest, however, was to be the last, and the winner was to receive the grand prize, a brand new professional model football autographed by Bobby Layne, quarterback of the champion Detroit Lions.

Officer Kelly, Mrs. Kelly told us, had been given this ball personally by Bobby Layne, whom he had met while providing security for him when the Lions came to Chicago to play the Bears.

The final event was not a game but a raffle. Each child picked a small, folded piece of paper out of Officer Kelly's police hat. A number had been written on every piece of paper by Mrs. Kelly. Officer Kelly had already decided what the winning number would be and himself would announce it following the children's choices.

I took a number and waited, seated on the floor with the other kids, not even bothering to see what number I had chosen. Officer Kelly stood up, holding the football in one huge hand, and looked at the kids, each of whom, except for me, waited eagerly to hear the magic number which they were desperately hoping would be the one they had plucked out of the policeman's hat. Even Jimmy had taken a number.

"Sixteen," said Officer Kelly.

Several of the kids groaned loudly, and they all looked at one another to see who had won the football. None of them had it. Then their heads turned in my direction. There were fifteen other children at the party and all thirty of their eyes burned into mine. Officer and Mrs. Kelly joined them. I imagined Mick and Mack, the cocker spaniels, staring at me, too, their tongues hanging out, waiting to bite me should I admit to holding the precious number sixteen.

I unfolded my piece of paper and there it was: 16. I looked up directly into the empty pale green and yellow eyes of Officer Kelly. I handed him the little piece of paper and he scrutinized it, as if inspecting it for forgery. The kids looked at him, hoping against hope that there had been a mistake, that somehow nobody, especially me, had chosen the winning number.

Officer Kelly raised his eyes from the piece of paper and stared again at me.

"Your father is a Jew, isn't he?" Officer Kelly said.

I didn't answer. Officer Kelly turned to his wife and asked, "Didn't you tell me his old man is a Jew?"

"His mother's a Catholic," said Mrs. Kelly. "Her people are from County Kerry."

"I don't want the football," I said, and stood up. "Jimmy should have it, it's his birthday."

Jimmy got up and grabbed the ball out of his father's hand.

"Let's go play!" he shouted, and ran out the door.

The kids all ran out after him.

I looked at Mrs. Kelly. "Thanks," I said, and started to walk out of the apartment.

"You're forgetting your prizes," said Mrs. Kelly, "the toys you won."

"It's okay," I said.

"Happy New Year!" Mrs. Kelly shouted after me.

When I got home my mother asked if it had been a good party.

"I guess," I said.

She could tell there was something wrong but she didn't push me. That was one good thing about my mother, she knew when to leave me alone. It was getting dark and she went to draw the drapes.

"Oh, baby," she said, "come look out the window. It's snowing."

THE PETERSON FIRE

IT WAS SNOWING the night the Peterson house burned down. Bud Peterson was seventeen then, two years older than me. Bud got out alive because his room was on the ground floor in the rear of the house. His two sisters and their parents slept upstairs, above the living room, which was where the fire started. An ember jumped from the fireplace and ignited the carpet. Bud's parents and his ten- and twelve-year-old sisters could not get down the staircase. When they tried to go back up, they were trapped and burned alive. There was nothing Bud Peterson could have done to save any of them. He was lucky, a fireman said, to have survived by crawling out his bedroom window.

I didn't see the house until the next afternoon. Snow flurries mixed with the ashes. Most of the structure was gone, only part of the first floor remained, and the chimney. I was surprised to see Bud Peterson standing in the street with his pals, staring at the ruins. Bud was a tall, thin boy, with almost colorless hair. He wore a Navy pea coat but no hat. Black ash was swirling around and some of it had fallen on his head. Nobody was saying much. There were about twenty of us, kids from the neighborhood, standing on the sidewalk or in the street, looking at what was left of the Peterson house.

I had walked over by myself after school to see it. Big Frank had told me about the fire in Cap's that morning when we were buying Bismarcks. Frank's brother, Otto, was a fireman. Frank said Otto had awakened him at five-thirty and asked if Frank knew Bud Peterson. Frank told him he did and Otto said, "His house burned down last night. Everybody but him is dead."

I heard somebody laugh. A couple of Bud's friends were whispering to each other and trying not to laugh but one of them couldn't help himself. I looked at Peterson but he didn't seem to mind. I remembered that he was a little goofy, maybe not too bright, but a good guy. He always seemed like one of those kids who just went along with the gang, who never really stood out. A bigger kid I didn't know came up to Bud and patted him on the left shoulder, then said something I couldn't hear. Peterson smiled a little and nodded his head. Snow started to come down harder. I put up the hood of my coat. We all just kept looking at the burned-down house.

A black and white drove up and we moved aside. It stopped and a cop got out and said a few words to Bud Peterson. Bud got into the back seat of the squad car with the cop and the car drove away. The sky was getting dark pretty fast and the crowd broke up.

One of Bud's sisters, Irma, the one who was twelve, had a dog, a brown and black mutt. I couldn't remember its name. Nobody had said anything about Irma's dog, if it got out alive or not. I used to see her walking that dog when I was coming home from baseball or football practice.

Bud Peterson went to live with a relative. Once in a while, in the first few weeks after the fire, I would see him back in the neighborhood, hanging out with the guys, then I didn't see him anymore. Somebody said he'd moved away from Chicago.

One morning, more than thirty years later, I was sitting at a bar in Paris drinking a coffee when, for no particular reason, I thought about standing in front of the Peterson house that afternoon and wondering: If it had been snowing hard enough the night before, could the snow have put out the fire? Then I remembered the name of Irma Peterson's dog.

(previously unpublished)

MY LAST MARTINI

from
American Falls
(2002)

THE BAR OF the Hotel Luneau in Paris is a popular meeting place, especially in the late afternoon and early evening. There is a rather ordinary walnut bar with eight stools and brass footrest, but the charming features of the place are the seven maroon leather banquettes that form a half-circle facing the bar, and the three Marie Antoinette chandeliers with dim plum bulbs that convey the impression of a first-class cruise ship's lounge. The atmosphere is, therefore, both convivial and intimate. Patrons sit alone, reading, smoking, or merely gazing around; occasionally there are groups of three or four, but most common are the couples: The Luneau bar is a favorite rendezvous of lovers.

It was there that I was recently told a remarkable story by a complete stranger, a woman I had never seen before nor expect to see again, except by chance. I had met my friend Sharif, as I do most every Wednesday evening at about six-thirty when we're both in town. Sharif is a businessman in his mid-sixties, his businesses being oil and real estate. He keeps apartments in Paris and Houston, and a house in Algiers that is, apparently, quite palatial. I can't say for certain since I've never been to Algiers, though Sharif has invited me a dozen times to visit. Sharif thinks I don't accept his invitations because I'm afraid the fundamentalist terrorists might slit my throat. Seeing as how I am a white, beardless male, I cannot discount this as a possibility, but the real truth is that I just plain hate to travel.

On this particular evening, Sharif had an early dinner date with another friend, so we spent perhaps forty-five minutes together, during which time we each consumed two martinis and a plate of olives. I believe our conversation concerned the American government's policy of limiting individual companies' investment in Iranian oil to twenty million dollars, and the benefits this has bestowed upon other countries; and the upcoming Prix de l'Arc de Triomphe. Sharif thought the Americans' approach to Iran impossibly parochial, and predicted that Hélissio would take the Arc. I could not dispute him on the oil issue, but I felt that Peintre Célèbre, the American horse, stood a hell of a chance.

After Sharif had gone, I sat quietly, surveying the scene, savoring the dregs of my second martini. Two martinis don't ordinarily affect me other than to provide a feeling of false elation that I treasure for the thirty or so minutes it lasts. I rarely exceed my usual limit of two, however; an excess of elation, I've found, puts the world around me in a light so unflattering that I've been tempted once or twice to make an attempt at extinguishing it. For some reason, when the waiter came by to collect the tab, I astonished myself by ordering a third. The waiter nodded and headed back to the bar.

"Do you mind if I join you?" The voice came from an occupant of the booth to my left.

I looked over and saw an attractive dark-haired woman in her mid-thirties. She was holding a half-filled martini glass in her right hand.

"I heard you order a martini," she said, "and I thought you might be someone I could talk to."

By the time she'd finished this sentence, the woman had slid out of her booth and taken the place of Sharif in mine.

"By all means," I responded.

I studied her as closely as was possible in the muted light. She was even better looking than I first thought. She wore her chestnut hair up, with modest bangs. Her eyes were the same color as her hair. Only her teeth were imperfect, deeply stained by tobacco. She did not, however, light a cigarette while we were together. The waiter arrived with my martini.

"Would you like another?" I asked.

"Thank you, I would."

I passed this information along to the waiter and he went away. I was impressed that she did not feel the need to guzzle the remainder of the drink she kept in her hand, at which I inadvertently glanced.

"You're a martini man," she said, "you know they're not to be rushed."

I settled back and watched her take a sip. The toothpick and olive were still in the glass. She didn't say anything else until after the waiter had come and gone again, leaving a fresh martini in front of her. She smiled at me. Her teeth were almost red. Now she downed the last of the martini she'd brought with her, punctuating it by sliding the impaled olive off the toothpick using only the tip of her tongue. In the peculiar light of the Luneau bar, the hue of her tongue matched that of her teeth. She chewed the olive with her eyes closed, then dropped the toothpick back into the glass.

When she'd finished off the olive, she reopened her eyes and said, "Two is my limit. Martinis, that is, not olives."

She pointed with a black fingernail to the drink awaiting her.

"This," she said, with a puma's smile, "will be my third."

I nodded at the glass in front of me.

"Mine, too."

She picked hers up and held it out toward me. I did likewise.

"Santé," she said.

"Santé," I repeated.

We sipped. Remarkably, mine was still very cold.

"Are you Italian?" I asked, though we were speaking French.

"My mother is from Roma."

"And your father?"

"From the country. But he was not pure Italian. He was half-Polish."

"Dead?"

"Yes."

"I'm sure you favor your mother."

She smiled again but quickly cut it off.

"Look," she said, "you must think I'm a bit forward, if not crazy. But I want you to know, I'm not a working girl."

"It wouldn't matter to me if you were, since I'm not at present in the market."

"So. I said I thought you were someone I could talk to. I hope you are, because I have a story I'd like to tell."

"I'm in no particular hurry," I said. "It's a slow night."

"Good. My grandmother, my father's mother, had eight children, six boys and two girls. My father was the third oldest. When she married, she was sixteen years old, a virgin. She lived in a small village in Tuscany. The man to whom she was given in marriage by her parents could not make love. This, of course, she had not known before the marriage."

"Was it annulled?"

"No, impossible. In my grandmother's village, a marriage was forever."

She took a long sip of her martini. I did the same with mine.

"My grandmother was very upset by this, since she wanted to have many children."

"I can barely imagine," I said.

"She made her husband, who was a farmer, ask his Polish worker, who lived in a room underneath the house, below ground, to make love to her. It was this Pole who was the father of my father and his five brothers and two sisters."

"Who knew beside your grandmother and her husband and the Pole?"

"Nobody, until many years later. The Pole would take a broomstick and poke the end of the handle against the ceiling of his underground room to let my grandmother know when he wanted to make love to her."

I swallowed half of what was left of my martini.

"What a remarkable circumstance," I said.

"My father found out when he was twenty-two years old, after my grandmother's husband had died."

"Your grandmother told him?"

"Yes. It was accidental, perhaps. He had done something she didn't like and she cursed him, calling him a dumb Polish bastard. Of course she'd cursed him many times before, but she'd never called him a dumb Polish bastard, and he asked her why she'd said that particular thing."

"And she confessed."

"Yes, it all came out. She cried bitterly and told my father how she had hated both her husband and his Polish worker. She did it to have a family, but finally one night when the Pole banged his broom handle against her floor, she refused to answer. The next morning, when her husband was ready to work, the Pole was gone. He disappeared and nobody in the family ever saw him again."

"How did this news affect your father and the others?"

"My father left for Roma the same day. He rarely saw his mother after that. It was my mother who took me and my sister and brother to see our grandmother. My father was a terrible womanizer, going from girl to girl always. My mother was quite an unhappy woman."

"But she stayed with your father."

"Until two years before he died. Then he was living with another woman."

Both of us finished our drinks. The woman suddenly leaned over and kissed me full on the lips, a cold martini kiss.

"I'm glad I was right," she said.

"About?"

"Your being a good listener. Often when I have the need to talk, it's difficult to find someone, and I've no use for the church."

She withdrew from the booth, stood for a moment looking at me, then walked away. The waiter came over.

"Another martini, sir?" he asked.

"No," I said, pointing to my empty glass, "this one was definitely my last."

THE TUNISIAN NOTEBOOK

from
American Falls
(2002)

AUTHOR'S PREFACE

In April of 1914, the Swiss painters August Macke, Paul Klee and Louis René Moilliet embarked on a journey to North Africa to "capture the Mediterranean light." The trip lasted about two weeks, during which time they traveled from Marseilles to Tunis—St. Germain, to Sidi-bou-Said, to Carthage, to Hammament, to Kairouan, and back to Tunis. Klee kept and later published his Diary of Trip to Tunisia, *which, according to Moilliet, Klee had endeavored to keep in a formal, literary style, resulting in the description of certain incidents being exaggerated or manufactured in keeping with Klee's vision of how events should properly have proceeded.*

That same year, shortly after the outbreak of World War I, Macke was killed in action. It was not until 1979, sixty-five years after the Tunisian excursion, that this imaginary notebook, containing August Macke's own diary of the trip, was discovered. It provides an interesting contrast to Klee's perceptions, as well as being a valuable and illuminating document in its own right.

> *"Every people has its own manner of feeling, of telling lies, of producing art. . . . One way of lying drives me to the next one."*
>
> —*AUGUST MACKE*
>
> *"One always has to spoil a picture a little bit, in order to finish it."*
>
> —*EUGÈNE DELACROIX*

Sunday, April 5, noon, Marseilles.
Arrived in Marseilles early this morning after travelling by ship from Hilterfingen to Thun, then by train to Bern, where I changed to the

Southern Express. Throughout the journey I have been thinking of Elisabeth, and wish now I had insisted she accompany me, despite Louis and Paul. Never again. At least there is the consolation of her having already seen Tunisia, but I cannot help feeling it would be better were we together.

Perhaps my mood will change once I have met up with Louis and Paul. They may be here now. I look forward to seeing Moilliet—after all, it is because of an invitation from his friend Jaeggi, the good doctor from Bern, now of Tunis, that this trip has come about. With Klee it's different; we don't always get along, not only personally but professionally. He doesn't like my poking fun at "theory." Klee is already a fine artist but he's so premeditated about everything. In deference to Louis I'll do my best not to antagonize Klee, at least so long as he doesn't begin touting Kandinsky to me! Will try to keep painterly discussion to a minimum, stick to the example of Cézanne and Delaunay.

Hot, tired, hungry—the usual condition. Downstairs for refreshment.

April 5, 11 P.M.

Marseilles is a miracle of color! After eating I walked around the town, admiring the flowers, boats in the harbor, the clean, distinct whites, blues, yellows, greens and reds. A healthy breeze came up, which diminished my fatigue. Noticed a tall, striking woman with an unusual hairdo—amber curls piled high and spilling over her forehead—and followed her. She met some people outside of an arena where a bullfight was about to begin. As I'd never witnessed a bullfight I followed them in. The admission was cheap, a couple of francs.

The arrangement of shapes and contrasts in the crowd was spectacular, and far more interesting to watch than the spectacle itself. The bull was not killed but so poked and battered about that by the time the devils had done with the game it might have been kinder to murder the beast and spare it the misery of recovery, if indeed recovery were possible.

The bull began a thick, brown hue, with almost yellow horns, and became progressively darker during the ordeal. By the finish his hide was grayish-black, the horns sandy white. I forced myself to watch it all. I completely forgot the tall woman with the red-yellow curls. It became difficult to control myself, but somehow I managed to keep from being sick.

Afterwards walked along the quais and stopped at a sidewalk table on the Vieux Port. Sat over a vermouth until I felt sufficiently recovered, then ordered a big meal, which I was just finishing when Moilliet and Klee peeked over the hedge that surrounded the restaurant and spotted me.

I was glad to see them, and felt increasingly better as I described for them the woman with the odd hairdo and the bullfight. Louis remarked that Jaeggi had quite an eye for the ladies. Klee added that he thought it only appropriate that it should have been a woman to have led me to a scene of slaughter. Louis laughed and I reminded them that the bull, in France, anyway, was allowed to survive. "You look healthy enough!" Klee said, and suggested that we go to the music hall, which we did.

Paul seemed especially to enjoy a comedy routine wherein a young man impersonated a Tyrolian girl, but neither Louis nor I were much taken by it. The performers seemed less than enthusiastic, their movements wooden and artificial, and so, too, the impression that remains, the colors somber and dim.

Walking back to the hotel I mentioned this to the others, pointing to a pair of violet birds perched on the lip of a bluish-gray rainspout. "Immortal moments meant to be captured."

But I was speaking more for the benefit of Klee than Moilliet. Louis understands. It was he who paid me the greatest compliment, last December, when we first met to discuss this venture. "Until I met you," Moilliet said, "I painted the way a man looks out the window."

Monday, April 6, 10 P.M., aboard the Carthage, the Mediterranean Sea. We spent the morning exploring Marseilles. Klee was moved enough by the sights to consider staying on but Louis—"The Count," Klee calls him—regaled us with promises of greater treasures in the days ahead. Klee said the colors around Marseilles were "new." I disagreed politely—"They're only new to you because you've never seen them before." Louis got the joke but not Paul. Sometimes I think he is too serious to ever become a really great painter.

Boarded the Carthage at midday. A clean, freshly painted barque. A nice sail out of the harbor, but once in the Gulf of Lions each of us was forced, one by one, to take seasick pills. Klee's didn't work—he got them from Gabriele Münter—so I gave him some of mine and soon he was holding up all right.

Klee knows I don't think much of him sometimes—though I don't dislike him. He's jealous of my "success." What success? I asked Louis. Because Kohler likes my paintings and gives me something for them? Paul is dedicated, he'll have his day, perhaps more than one, and it will be bigger than either Moilliet's or mine, I fear, knowing the public taste. He is by far the toughest of us three.

My unreasonable prejudice against Klee begins with his pipe. He is a pipe-smoker, and I have, in my twenty-six years, yet to meet a pipe-smoker I didn't find to be a bore. Often a mean bore, the worst kind, the ones who insist on boring the hell out of you even after they've realized you're not in the least interested in what they're saying. Not that Klee is one of those—not yet anyway.

At dinner Louis and Paul ate like pigs, but I outdid them.

The seas are a steady six feet, the boat rolls, but not uncomfortably. Standing on deck tonight I could feel the sun waiting to come out.

Tuesday, April 7, 10:30 P.M., Tunis.

Klee is an early riser. By the time I came out on deck this morning he had breakfasted and begun sketching. "That's Sardinia," he told me, pointing toward the coastline.

I found Moilliet in the dining room. While we ate he told me how even as a child—they'd been schoolmates—Klee had been extraordinarily self-centered. Louis says Paul went forward and sat around with the third-class passengers for awhile. He likes to pretend he is one of them so that they will not react to him differently than they do to each other. This way, says Klee, he'll be able to capture their true expressions in his memory. He collects children's drawings, and saved many of those from his own childhood. Louis says Paul believes they hold the key to the future.

I don't mean to be going on all the time complaining about Klee and his attitudes. Perhaps there is something about him that I envy—his physical energy, or his confidence. Elisabeth is always joking about what she considers my laziness, but she only half-jokes. She must be serious or she wouldn't mention it so often. She remarks about it to guests. "Whatever will become of him when he grows old?" What she means by that I'm not certain. Perhaps I won't grow old.

It will be interesting to see what Klee accomplishes here. Actually, I don't think he is half as adventuresome as I am, or even Moilliet. But he has an astonishing ability to relate objects and images historically. This evening at dinner he quoted Delacroix on North Africa—"every man I see is a Cato or a Brutus"—the Greco-Roman world incarnate. Paul is more well-read than I. But reading is more tiring than anything!

We spotted the African coast late in the day, at what seemed the pinnacle of the afternoon heat. It was white-green. Not until Sidi-bou-Said did we discern a land-shape, a hill covered with white dots—houses in regular up-and-down rows.

The boat navigated a narrow inlet which led to a long canal. It was white-hot and dead feeling, the water unmoving, though we could clearly see the Arabs along the shore in turbans and robes. We stood at the rail to try and catch a bit of wind, but the boat moved terribly slowly and the air was terrifically hot and sticky.

Klee commented ecstatically about the picturesqueness of the shoreline, and talked excitedly about the prospect of painting the Arab faces. I am not quite sure how to regard these remarks of his. It's as if he's just another philistine standing before an exquisite view, saying, "Beautiful, beautiful, beautiful," which reaction is the cheapest kind of traditional expression. But I know he's not. The manner of reacting varies not only with race but with personality. The Egyptians, the Chinese, the men of the Gothic age, Memling, Snyders, Cézanne, Mozart. The type of reaction varies as the human condition varies. Today it is impossible for an artist to work as a Renaissance or a Pompeiian artist worked. Most important is the conclusion: A Cézanne still life is as real as the wall on which it stands.

Dr. Jaeggi and his family—wife, daughter—met our boat and took us into Tunis, all of us squashed into their little yellow automobile. Jaeggi is a wonderful fellow, my age, very agreeable, just as Moilliet said he was. Louis likened him to Dr. Gachet, Van Gogh's doctor friend at Auvers. The Arabs call him "Father Jaeggi," and act like fawning children around him. He is an obstetrician. In Bern he was, at an extremely early age, a prominent surgeon. I meant to ask Louis—or Jaeggi himself—why he came to Tunisia. I must remember to do so tomorrow. His wife and daughter are lovely—the girl has a dancing face.

Jaeggi took us to his house in St. Germain—he keeps an office in Tunis, at No. 2 Bab-el-Allouch, his card says—where we rested and recovered from the intense heat under large fans, and then had a superb meal prepared by Frau Jaeggi and the servant Ahmed, a lithe, chocolate fellow with a brilliant smile. Jaeggi says that he, Ahmed, is a genuine artist, a good one.

After dinner Jaeggi drove me into the city to the Hôtel de France—the others are staying at the house—and saw that I was properly settled before leaving me. On the way in the car he told me how pleased he was that we—through Moilliet—had accepted his invitation, and that I, too, was welcome to stay in St. Germain. I thanked him and explained that, unlike Louis and Paul, I had a patron, and could afford the luxury of a hotel, adding that it would be less work for Ahmed and Frau Jaeggi. He said I was welcome to change my mind at any time.

The night air is sweet and warm. Tunisia is already a pleasant surprise.

Wednesday, April 8, midnight, St. Germain.

Louis and Paul arrived early this morning with Jaeggi, in his car. I hadn't had breakfast as yet so they accompanied me to a café near the marketplace. While I ate they shopped at nearby stalls—the souks.

Jaeggi sat and had a coffee, telling me he's never bothered to get a license, here or in Bern. A driver's license, that is. He says he's never been reprimanded for not having one, not even when stopped by the police for some reason. They see his identification as a doctor and make their apologies for having delayed him. Why bother with a driver's permit when a medical certificate will do? Jaeggi's an extraordinary man.

Tunisia is a real world, he told me, not an artificial one like Europe, with its parks and gardens. "Paint what you see," he said, "it's enough." If by "real" he means no derby hats or Paris styles he is correct.

Moilliet came over to tell us of a funeral procession. We could hear the wailing and moaning and then a cart drawn by six scrawny mules clattered slowly past the café, a blue and gold coffin strapped onto it. Louis followed after it, fascinated. Ever since old Gobat's death he has been exceedingly passionate about funerals.

The rest of us went along and watched as the burial was accomplished in a little field just beyond the market. Klee kept his smile fixed just so. He thinks Louis is a bit of a fool and that I am too set in my ways. He's right, but so what?

After a short tour courtesy of Dr. Jaeggi, he went to his office and I decided to explore the native quarter on my own, enlisting the aid of a policeman who observed me buying charcoals and paints. I asked him if he could guide me to the more interesting spots, the whorehouses, drug dens, etc. Who should know better than a police officer where to go?

For not very much money he agreed to show me around and, presumably, abandoned his official duties for the remainder of the afternoon. Klee refused to go along, though I hadn't asked him to come with me. He seemed upset and wanted to make his disapproval known, but I didn't pay him much attention. He and Moilliet went off to explore some mosques.

Abdoul, the policeman, earned his francs, showing me, in fact, more than I could absorb in an afternoon. I made dozens of sketches, several of the prostitutes in a house on Rue Rouge, lounging on divans in negligees, their necks strung with pearls, smoking and joking with one another. They were very familiar with Abdoul, as I'd guessed they'd be. I gave them each a sketch of themselves and they seemed quite taken by them. I promised to return soon, without my drawing materials, and they all laughed. To my surprise they appeared to be very bright girls.

There is so much here to attract the eye! Ornate, arched gates, bazaars, the market, terraces with awnings, tents, domes of mosques, mules, camels, and these beautiful, brown-skinned people.

In the evening drove with Jaeggi out to St. Germain for dinner. He would like Klee and me to paint the interior of his studio. We agreed to do so. I am staying the night, much to the apparent displeasure of the housemaid, a heavy, sweaty girl from Aargau, who did a poor job of preparing my bed. I mentioned this to Louis a few moments ago in the hall. "There's one thing the Aargau girl does know how to do," he said, "to draw a bath! That she does perfectly."

Thursday, April 9, 11 P.M., Tunis.

After breakfast Jaeggi drove Klee and me into town, left us at the hotel, and continued on to his surgery. Paul insisted that I accompany him to the harbor to paint. I made a number of small paintings, but was so bothered by the coal dust in my eyes and in the watercolors that I was forced to stop. Klee worked on despite the conditions, and in the face of taunts by crew members of a French torpedo boat tied up nearby, who cursed us in broken German.

I ate lunch alone in the same café as yesterday and then wandered on my own until I found the tomb of a Marabu, a Moslem saint. My policeman told me yesterday they were everywhere because Arab saints were always buried on the spot where they died. There are many in Tunis and, apparently, in and around Sidi-bou-Said. I did a painting of the entranceway, without interference from dust, sailors, or fellow artists!

Met Louis and Paul for supper and afterwards went with them to a concert Arabe. They are real tourists, as obvious as though they wore large red badges emblazoned with the word itself. Moilliet, because of his naiveté, is the easier to accept, but Klee looks down on the natives. His condescending conversation is insufferable. There is nothing barbaric about belly dancing. The women and their glistening skin adorned with multifarious decorations form a symmetry that is a kinetic delight. Tunisia is not a prudish country. Paul pretends he is undisturbed by this kind of performance; Louis exults. I am someplace in between.

Friday, April 10, 9 P.M., Tunis.

Made sixty sketches today! A truly inspired one for me. I share Klee's respect for the images of childhood and children's works of art. To produce true art one must experience a rebirth, as does nature with each fresh season. One must tap the flow of nature in order to be able to create art in a musical, Mozartian manner.

The day was filled with such a lively, pristine, childlike light that I had no thoughts of eating. Upon arising I dressed quickly, gathered up my paints and pencils and the paper I brought from Switzerland, and hurried out into the street without bothering about washing. By noon I'd done two dozen drawings and felt fresh as ever.

I stopped in the market to buy some fruit but instead fell into conversation with an Italian photographer who showed me a portfolio of amazing pictures. I bought fifteen of them, portraits of women in many imaginative positions, which I showed around the dinner table this evening at the house of Captain Lecoq. Lecoq is a friend of Jaeggi's, a French officer who is quite popular with the Arabs since he has taken their side against the government in Paris. He says after ten years in Tunis he feels more like an Arab than a Frenchman—Lecoq is not an ordinary official, he is quite outgoing. He practically licked the photographs and made some appropriately wicked remarks concerning the poses. After dinner he asked me if I'd yet visited any of the houses in the Quarter. When I told him I had, but only to make drawings, he looked at me strangely. Then I told him I was in the company of a policeman.

Lecoq laughed and said the policeman must have been very amused. "The behavior of foreigners never ceases to amaze."

Saturday, April 11, 11:45 P.M., St. Germain.
Spent a couple of hours in and around the market this morning looking for something to bring Elisabeth. I bought her several uniquely detailed pieces of embroidery and an amber necklace—a Mohammedan rosary—with a stone seal from Achat inlaid with mysterious signs, and a pair of yellow slippers for myself. Wrote her a letter, the first since our arrival, and a short one at that. There are too many things to do and see to spend one's time writing letters.

Jaeggi called for me at the hotel about three, and we drove out to St. Germain. Sat on the terrace drinking wine and talking with Jaeggi—a pleasant afternoon. He is actually a bit younger than I, a renowned surgeon, and yet he insists on calling me the "accomplished" one.

Jaeggi told me the story of Lecoq's infatuation with a thirteen-year-old Arab girl. Apparently she came to him every day for six months until her father found out about it. Because Lecoq gave the girl money now and then the mother begged her husband not to do anything—and of course as an officer of the French garrison Lecoq commands substantial political power. But the father went berserk and attacked Lecoq with a knife. Lecoq shot him dead. Immediately thereafter he was given a holiday leave, which he spent in France. He returned to Tunis a month later, by which time both the girl and her mother had disappeared.

Klee came in from working on the beach. Louis was sketching the sunset from the balcony. Jaeggi suggested we decorate Easter eggs for the holiday tomorrow, which we did. Ahmed brought them in and helped make the designs. His eggs were far more intricately fashioned than any of ours, supporting Jaeggi's judgment of his talent.

After another generous and well-prepared dinner, Klee and I set to the dining room wall. Klee contented himself with a few doodles in the corners, while I marked out a six-foot square in the middle in which I depicted a market scene—a small black donkey laden with baskets of oranges, flanked by two red-tarbooshed Arab drivers. Jaeggi seemed more than a little pleased with our work.

Moilliet opened a bottle of brandy for the occasion, and insisted we finish it before retiring. Curiously, I don't feel at all drunk, only fatigued from the constant heat, which I doubt I could ever get used to.

Easter Sunday, April 12, 4 P.M., Tunis.
A poor day for me. Holidays are not the time to be away from home. I fear I miss Elisabeth and my sons too much. Tried to rouse myself from the doldrums at Jaeggi's, drew a picture of his daughter and gave it to her—her parents will frame it and hang it in her room—but was unsuccessful. I dare not write home while I am in this condition.

I joined feebly in the hunt for the eggs. Klee was upset that the colors came off on our fingers, but nobody else seemed to mind.

Jaeggi drove me into Tunis and deposited me at the hotel so that I could rest without being disturbed before our journey tomorrow to Hammamet. There is a measurable amount of moisture in the air.

Tuesday, April 14, 10:30 P.M., Hammamet.
Slept all day yesterday, therefore no entry in the notebook. Had to postpone our travel plans until today. It must have been a slight case of influenza that brought on my melancholia.

Louis and Paul were in good spirits throughout the trip. They seemed to have been inspired by the dawn departure. The ancient locomotive wound slowly through stretches of desert broken occasionally by pathetic patches of forest. Moilliet (with his bottle of brandy—he is not without one these days) and Klee were enraptured by the—to me—sparse scenery.

Outside Hammamet station we spent half an hour watching a camel, instructed by a veiled young woman, draw water from a well by walking back and forth pulling a rope attached to a bucket. A time-tested method. Klee would have remained there forever had Louis and I not threatened to go on without him. Paul worships the primitive.

Spent the day with watercolors in the main cemetery. Unlike in Tunis, here we are free to explore them. Fabulous cactuses tower over us. From a distance they resemble the great dusty buildings of an abandoned city. I set up my things on a small hill from which I could observe the crooked coastline and benefit from a gentle but steady breeze.

Found lodging in a rooming house run by a tough old dame who claims she's French, from Nice, but she's an Arab. Smokes black tobacco. Her fingers are deeply stained. For dinner she offered us cow liver, so we went to a café instead: The food there was not very appealing either, but we had a light meal while being "entertained" by a blind nasal singer accompanied by a young boy on a drum.

After dinner we followed the noise of a band to a little street fair, where we watched a fakir let a cobra bite him on the nose and another devour live scorpions.

Louis and I finished off his brandy, the melancholic's companion.

Wednesday, April 15, just past midnight, Kairouan.
Quite a trip today. This morning trekked to Bir-bou-rekba from Hammamet, earning curious stares from robed Arabs along the road. Passersby spat greetings to us, nodding and smiling. Three European gentlemen on foot, wearing suits and straw hats, packing gear on their backs—surely as ridiculous a sight as they've ever seen. It was Louis who insisted we walk, to "gain the feel" of the province.

It was actually quite a short distance, perhaps two kilometers, to the Bir-bou-rekba station, where we boarded a train to Kalaa-Srira. There we stopped for lunch at a dusty café run by a black Arab madman in a torn red djilaba. Dozens of wild chickens ran amongst the tables searching for drops of food in the dust. Moilliet was undisturbed by the situation—he smiled and sipped his brandy. Klee and I attempted to order, but the proprietor chased insanely around after the chickens, shouting threats on the life of his neighbor, to whom the fowl belonged.

Soon all of the customers were laughing and taunting the restaurant owner. I took the remnants of a meal from an abandoned nearby table and scattered the bits on the ground, causing a crazed clucking, screeching, dust-swirling stampede. The chickens were now hopping onto the tables and chairs and the poor proprietor was beside himself.

He yelled at me to stop encouraging the beasts, to please not throw them breadcrumbs. I responded indignantly—"But sir, I wouldn't dare to feed them breadcrumbs, I'm giving them cheese!"

After that the unfortunate man gave up. All we managed to pry from his kitchen was some weak coffee, for which we reluctantly paid three francs. At that moment our train entered the station and we embarked for Kairouan. After a brief stopover in Acouda, which from the train appeared as a raging storm of flies and dust, we arrived in Kairouan in mid-afternoon.

Found a French hotel in the center of town—the Marseilles—ate, drank, slept until evening. No work. Tonight attended a marriage feast—the daughter of the hotel proprietor and a local, apparently well-to-do businessman. A magnificent outdoor banquet: roasted lamb, chicken, dozens of unfamiliar delicacies. We ate and drank everything that was offered. Klee was ecstatic—for the first time on the trip he looked completely relaxed.

Thursday, April 16, 8 P.M., Tunis.
The Tunisian sky in the moment before dawn is mysteriously affecting. Watching it brighten, my feeling of personal insignificance increased. Reds, blues, yellows folded over and under one another, orange clouds, merged and parted in a living collage. Finally, light, pure light, orchestrated by camel groans and dispersing shadows, a gray-pink cat without a tail stretching and rolling over in the dust.

Made a series of paintings in the morning, a herdsman in red fez and brown robe, two heavily draped women on the road to the city, date trees, domed roofs, a leopard-faced boy in the town square. This afternoon we hired a guide, who showed us through the local mosques. He expressed interest in learning German, so I taught him the words for white, black, shit, piss, fuck, eat and how much. A sufficient vocabulary in any language.

Arrived back in Tunis at dusk. Louis joined the Jaeggis at Lecoq's, Klee went off to spend some time alone, and I took a long bath at the hotel, after which I found Paul at the Chianti restaurant and stuffed myself with pasta al pesto. Paul is planning to leave for home on Sunday. He thinks Louis intends to stay on for a few days past that. I would like to stay longer also, and will speak to Moilliet about it tomorrow.

Friday, April 17, 11 P.M., Tunis.
Sketched until noon in the marketplace. Thus far I've made more than thirty watercolors and dozens of drawings. Wrote a short letter—only the second since I've been gone—to Elisabeth, telling her I will be bringing some colossal things back with me. I must travel more often to exotic places! I seem able to see everything so clearly, to understand the people by an expression, a tilt of the head. Because of my unfamiliarity with them, things become more distinct.

We took an afternoon trip back to Kalaa-Srira to see a mosque Klee heard about last night. Had tea and bread at the madman's café—no chickens! He must have poisoned them all. The mosque was less than spectacular, a rather ordinary facade and whitewashed interior, and we were there at the wrong hour—and apparently the wrong season—to witness the angles of light that distinguished it. Moilliet and I were bored, the waste of an afternoon.

On the way to Tunis we wrestled in the train compartment—Louis and I, that is. Klee is outraged by this kind of behavior. He says the Arabs will think less of us if we act improperly, i.e., "un-European." Any manner of physical spontaneity disgusts him. I can't take too much of Klee—and he considers me facile, I know. It's just as well we don't have much time left together.

Had dinner alone in a café near the hotel, and read the first European newspaper I've seen since coming to Tunisia. My interest in that world has drastically diminished. If it weren't for the unsanitary conditions, I think I should like to stay on in North Africa indefinitely.

Saturday, April 18, after midnight, Tunis.

Just returned from a marvelous evening at Jaeggi's, where we all got drunk and made passes at everyone's wives. Louis passed around my famous Italian photographs, which were universally admired—especially by the ladies—and that got everything started. Jaeggi's other dinner guests—there were sixteen in all—had been invited, in view of our impending departure, for a farewell celebration.

I'm afraid I'm too drunk to write very much or very well. When one officer's wife asked me where I'd bought the pictures—which she called "French cards"—I told her to please take for herself her favorite one. I thought my offer would be humorously rejected, but the lady surprised me by choosing one of my own favorites and depositing it in her purse!

The rest of the day was rather dull; I remember very little other than that it rained steadily for the first time, putting the natives in a good mood.

Sunday, April 19, 6 P.M., Tunis.

Back from seeing Klee off, third class on a rusty tub. He pretends to be happy when he's miserable, a compulsion with which I have no sympathy. The day has been taken up with farewell conversations and the gathering together of belongings. Moilliet and I will leave tomorrow for Thun via Palermo and Rome. The Jaeggis are wonderful people. They have been glad to see us, and now they're glad to see us go, which is how it should be.

Time to eat, and afterwards, perhaps a stroll in the little rain.

SAILOR AND LULA

"You need a man to go to hell with."

—Tuesday Weld
in *Wild in the Country*

from
WILD AT HEART
(1990)

WILD AT HEART

SAILOR AND LULA lay on the bed in the Cape Fear Hotel listening to the ceiling fan creak. From their window they could see the river as it entered the Atlantic Ocean and watch the fishing boats navigate the narrow channel. It was late June but there was a mild wind that kept them "not uncomfortable," as Lula liked to say.

Lula's mother, Marietta Pace Fortune, had forbidden her to see Sailor Ripley ever again, but Lula had no intention of following that order. After all, Lula reasoned, Sailor had paid his debt to society, if that's what it was. She couldn't really understand how going to prison for killing someone who had been trying to kill him could be considered payment of a debt to society.

Society, such as it was, thought Lula, was certainly no worse off with Bob Ray Lemon eliminated from it. In her mind, Sailor had performed a service beneficial in the short as well as the long run to mankind and should have received some greater reward than two years in the Pee Dee River work camp for second-degree manslaughter. Something like an all-expenses-paid trip for Sailor with the companion of his choice—Lula, of course—to New Orleans or Hilton Head for a couple of weeks. A top hotel and a rental car, like a snazzy new Chrysler LeBaron convertible. That would have made sense. Instead, poor Sailor has to clear brush from the side of the road, dodge snakes and eat bad fried food for two years. Because Sailor was a shade more sudden than that creep Bob Ray Lemon he gets punished for it. The world is really wild at heart and weird on top, Lula thought. Anyway, Sailor was out now and he was still the best kisser she'd ever known, and what Mrs. Marietta Pace Fortune didn't find out about wasn't about to hurt her, was it?

"Speakin' of findin' out?" Lula said to Sailor. "Did I write to you about my findin' Grandaddy's letters in the attic bureau?"

Sailor sat up on his elbows. "Were we speakin'?" he said. "And no."

Lula clucked her tongue twice. "I was thinkin' we'd been but I been wrong before. Sometimes I get like that now. I think somethin' and then later think I've said it out loud to someone?"

"I really did miss your mind while I was out at Pee Dee, honey," said Sailor. "The rest of you, too, of course. But the way your head works is God's own private mystery. Now what about some letters?"

Lula sat up and fixed a pillow behind her back. Her long black hair, which she usually wore tied back and partly wrapped like a racehorse's tail, fanned out behind her on the powder blue pillowcase like a raven's wings. Her large grey eyes fascinated Sailor. When he was on the road gang he had thought about Lula's eyes, swum in them as if they were great cool, grey lakes with small violet islands in the middle. They kept him sane.

"I always wondered about my grandaddy. About why Mama never chose to speak about her daddy? All I ever knew was that he was livin' with his mama when he died."

"My daddy was livin' with his mama when he died," said Sailor. "Did you know that?"

Lula shook her head. "I surely did not," she said. "What were the circumstances?"

"He was broke, as usual," Sailor said. "My mama was already dead by then from the lung cancer."

"What brand did she smoke?" asked Lula.

"Camels. Same as me."

Lula half rolled her big grey eyes. "My mama smokes Marlboros now," she said. "Used to be she smoked Kools? I stole 'em from her beginnin' in about sixth grade. When I got old enough to buy my own I bought those. Now I've just about settled on Mores, as you probably noticed? They're longer."

"My daddy was lookin' for work and got run over by a gravel truck on the Dixie Guano Road off Seventy-four," said Sailor. "Cops said he was drunk—daddy, not the truck driver—but I figure they just wanted to bury the case. I was fourteen at the time."

"Gee, Sailor, I'm sorry, honey. I never would have guessed it."

"It's okay. I hardly used to see him anyway. I didn't have much parental guiding. The public defender kept sayin' that at my parole hearin'."

"Well, anyway," said Lula, "turns out my mama's daddy embezzled some money from the bank he was clerkin' in? And got caught. He did it to help out his brother who had TB and was a wreck and couldn't work. Grandaddy got four years in Statesville and his brother died. He wrote Grandmama a letter almost every day, tellin' her how much he loved her? But she divorced him while he was in the pen and never talked about him to anyone again. She just refused to suffer his name. But she kept all his letters! Can you believe it? I read every one of 'em, and I tell you that man loved that woman. It must have broke him apart when she refused to stand by him. Once a Pace woman makes up her mind there's no discussin' it."

Sailor lit a Camel and handed it to Lula. She took it, inhaled hard, blew the smoke out and half rolled her eyes again.

"I'd stand by you, Sailor," Lula said. "If you were an embezzler."

"Hell, peanut," Sailor said, "you stuck with me after I'd planted Bob Ray Lemon. A man can't ask for more than that."

Lula pulled Sailor over to her and kissed him soft on the mouth. "You move me, Sailor, you really do," she said. "You mark me the deepest."

Sailor pulled down the sheet, exposing Lula's breasts. "You're perfect for me, too," he said.

"You remind me of my daddy, you know?" said Lula. "Mama told me he liked skinny women whose breasts were just a bit too big for their bodies. He had a long nose, too, like yours. Did I ever tell you how he died?"

"No, sugar, you didn't that I recall."

"He got lead-poisoned from cleanin' the old paint off our house without usin' a mask. Mama said his brain just fell apart in pieces. Started he couldn't remember things? Got real violent? Finally in the middle of one night he poured kerosene over himself and lit a match. Near burned down the house with me and Mama asleep upstairs. We got out just in time. It was a year before I met you."

Sailor took the cigarette out of Lula's hand and put it into the ashtray by the bed. He put his hands on her small, nicely muscled shoulders and kneaded them.

"How'd you get such good shoulders?" Sailor asked.

"Swimmin', I guess," said Lula. "Even as a child I loved to swim."

Sailor pulled Lula to him and kissed her throat.

"You got such a pretty, long neck, like a swan," he said.

"Grandmama Pace had a long, smooth white neck," said Lula. "It was like on a statue it was so white? I like the sun too much to be white like that."

Sailor and Lula made love, and afterward, while Sailor slept, Lula stood at the window and smoked one of Sailor's Camels while she stared at the tail of the Cape Fear River. It was a little spooky, she thought, to be at the absolute end of a body of water. Lula looked over at Sailor stretched out on his back on the bed. It was odd that a boy like Sailor didn't have any tattoos, she thought. His type usually had a bunch. Sailor snorted in his sleep and turned onto his side, showing Lula his long, narrow back and flat butt. She took one more puff and threw the cigarette out the window into the river.

UNCLE POOCH

"Five years ago?" Lula said. "When I was fifteen? Mama told me that when I started thinkin' about sex I should talk to her before I did anything about it."

"But honey," said Sailor, "I thought you told me your Uncle Pooch raped you when you were thirteen."

Lula nodded. She was standing in the bathroom of their room at the Cape Fear Hotel fooling with her hair in front of the mirror. Sailor could see her through the doorway from where he lay on the bed.

"That's true," Lula said. "Uncle Pooch wasn't really an uncle. Not a blood uncle, I mean. He was a business partner of my daddy's? And my mama never knew nothin' about me and him for damn sure. His real name was somethin' kind of European, like Pucinski. But everyone just called him Pooch. He came around the house sometimes when Daddy was away. I always figured he was sweet on Mama so when he cornered me one afternoon I was surprised more than a little."

"How'd it happen, peanut?" Sailor asked. "He just pull out the old toad and let it croak?"

Lula brushed away her bangs and frowned. She took a cigarette from the pack on the sink and lit it, then let it dangle from her lips while she teased her hair.

"You're terrible crude sometimes, Sailor, you know?" Lula said.

"I can't hardly understand you when you talk with one of them Mores in your mouth," said Sailor.

Lula took a long slow drag on her More and set it down on the edge of the sink.

"I said you can be too crude sometimes. I don't think I care for it."

"Sorry, sugar," Sailor said. "Go on and tell me how old Pooch done the deed."

"Well, Mama was at the Busy Bee havin' her hair dyed? And I was alone in the house. Uncle Pooch come in the side door through the porch, you know? Where I was makin' a jelly and banana sandwich? I remember I had my hair in curlers 'cause I was goin' that night with Vicky and Cherry Ann, the DeSoto sisters, to see Van Halen at the Charlotte Coliseum. Uncle Pooch must have known nobody but me was home 'cause he come right in and put both his hands on my butt and sorta shoved me up against the counter."

"Didn't he say somethin'?" said Sailor.

Lula shook her head and started brushing the teases out of her hair. She picked up her cigarette, took a puff and threw it into the toilet. The hot end had burned a brown stain on the porcelain of the sink and Lula licked the tip of her right index finger and rubbed it but the stain wouldn't come off.

"Not really," she said. "Least not so I recall now."

Lula flushed the toilet and watched the More come apart as it swirled down the hole.

"What'd he do next?" asked Sailor.

"Stuck his hand down my blouse in front."

"What'd you do?"

"Spilled the jelly on the floor. I remember thinkin' then that Mama'd be upset if she saw it. I bent down to wipe it up and that got Uncle Pooch's hand out of my shirt. He let me clean up the jelly and throw the dirty napkin I used in the trash before doin' anything else."

"Were you scared?" Sailor asked.

"I don't know," said Lula. "I mean, it was Uncle Pooch. I'd known him since I was seven? I kind of didn't believe it was really happenin'."

"So how'd he finally nail you? Right there in the kitchen?"

"No, he picked me up. He was short but powerful. With hairy arms? He had a sort of Errol Flynn mustache, kind of a few narrow hairs on the rim of his upper lip. Anyway, he carried me into the maid's dayroom, which nobody used since Mama lost Abilene a couple years before when she run off to marry Sally Wilby's driver Harlan and went to live down in Tupelo? We did it there on Abilene's old bed."

"'We' did it?" said Sailor. "What do you mean? Didn't he force you?"

"Well, sure," said Lula. "But he was super gentle, you know? I mean he raped me and all, but I guess there's all different kinds of rapes. I didn't exactly want him to do it but I suppose once it started it didn't seem all that terrible."

"Did it feel good?"

Lula put down her hairbrush and looked in at Sailor. He was lying there naked and he had an erection.

"Does my tellin' you about this get you off?" she said. "Is that why you want to hear it?"

Sailor laughed. "I can't help it happenin', sweetheart. Did he do it more than once?"

"No, it was over pretty quick. I didn't feel much. I'd broke my own cherry by accident when I was twelve? When I came down hard on a water ski at Lake Lanier in Flowery Branch, Georgia. So there wasn't any blood or nothin'. Uncle Pooch just stood and pulled up his trousers and left me there. I stayed in Abilene's bed till I heard him drive off. That was the bad part, lyin' there listenin' to him leave."

"What'd you do then?"

"Went back in the kitchen and finished makin' my sandwich, I guess. I probably took a pee in between or somethin'."

"And you never told nobody about it?"

"Just you," Lula said. "Uncle Pooch never acted strange or different after. And he never did anything else to me. I always got a nice present from him at Christmas, like a coat or jewelry? He died in a car crash three years later while he was holidayin' in Myrtle Beach. They still got way too much traffic there for my taste."

Sailor stretched an arm toward Lula. "Come on over to me," he said.

Lula went and sat on the edge of the bed. Sailor's erection had reduced itself by half and she took it in her left hand.

"You don't have to do nothin' for me, baby," said Sailor. "I'm okay."

Lula smoothed back her hair with her right hand.

"Damn it, Sailor," she said, "it's not always you I'm thinkin' of."

Lula sat still for a minute and then she began to cry. Sailor sat up and held her in his arms and rocked her and didn't say anything until she stopped.

DIXIE PEACH

SAILOR AND LULA sat at a corner table next to the window in the Forget-Me-Not Cafe sipping their drinks. Lula had an iced tea with three sugars and Sailor had a High Life, which he drank straight from the bottle. They'd both ordered fried oysters and cole slaw and were enjoying the view. There was a nail paring of a moon and the sky was dark grey with streaks of red and yellow and beneath it the black ocean lay flat on its back.

"That water reminds me of Buddy Favre's bathtub," said Sailor.

"How's that?" Lula asked.

"My daddy's duck-huntin' partner, Buddy Favre, used to take a bath ever' evenin'. Buddy was a stumpy guy with a mustache and goatee and kinda slanty eyes so he looked like a devil but he was a regular guy. He was a truck mechanic, worked on big rigs, eighteen-wheelers, and he got awful filthy doin' it. So nights when he got home he soaked himself in a tub full of Twenty Mule Team Borax and the water turned a kind of thick grey and black, like the way the ocean looks tonight. My daddy would go over to Buddy's and sit in a chair in the bathroom and sip I. W. Harper while Buddy bathed, and sometimes he took me with him. Buddy smoked a joint ever' night while he was in the tub. He'd offer it to Daddy but he stuck to the whisky. Buddy said the reefer come from Panama and that he was gonna end up there one day."

"Did he?"

"I don't know, honey. I lost track of him after Daddy died, but Buddy was a pretty determined type of man, so I imagine he'll make it eventually if he ain't already."

"Where'd you get high first, Sailor? You remember?"

Sailor took a long swig of his High Life. "Sure do. I was fifteen and Bobby Tebbetts and Gene Toy—my half-Chinaman friend I told you about?—we was drivin' Bobby's '55 Packard Caribbean to Ciudad

Juarez so we could get laid. Bobby'd been down there before when he'd been visitin' some family in El Paso, and he and a cousin of his went over to Juarez and got their peckers wet for the first time. Gene Toy and I got Bobby to talkin' about it one night and we just decided on the spot to get up and go get it done."

"That's an awful long way to go," said Lula, "just to get some pussy."

"We was only—let's see, I was fifteen and Tebbetts was seventeen and a half and Gene Toy was sixteen. I had my first taste on that trip. At that age you still got a lot of energy."

"You still got plenty energy for me, baby. When's the first time you done it with a girl who wasn't hookin'?"

"Maybe two, three months after Juarez," said Sailor. "I was visitin' my cousin, Junior Train, in Savannah, and we were at some kid's house whose parents were out of town. I remember there were kids swimmin' in a indoor pool and some of 'em was standin' around in the yard or the kitchen drinkin' beer. A girl come up to me that was real tall, taller than me, and she had a real creamy complexion but there was a interestin' star-shaped scar on her nose."

"Was it big?"

"No. About thumbnail size, like a tattoo almost."

"So she come up to you?"

"Yeah." Sailor laughed. "She asked me who I was with and I said nobody, just Junior. She asked me did I want a beer and I held up the one I was holdin'. She asked me did I live in Savannah and I said no, I was visitin' family."

"She know them?"

"No. She looked right at me and run her tongue over her lips and put her hand on my arm. Her name was Irma."

"What'd you say to her then?"

"Told her my name. Then she said somethin' like, 'It's so noisy down here. Why don't we go upstairs so we can hear ourselves?' She turned around and led the way. When she got almost to the top step I stuck my hand between her legs from behind."

"Oh, baby," said Lula. "What a bad boy you are!"

Sailor laughed. "That's just what she said. I went to kiss her but she broke off laughin' and ran down the hallway. I found her lyin' on a bed in a room. She was a wild chick. She was wearin' bright orange pants with kind of Spanish-lookin' lacy black stripes down the sides. You know, them kind that doesn't go all the way down your leg?"

"You mean like Capri pants?" said Lula.

"I guess. She just rolled over onto her stomach and stuck her ass up in the air. I slid my hand between her legs again and she closed her thighs on it."

"You're excitin' me, honey. What'd she do?"

"Her face was half pushed into the pillow, and she looked back over her shoulder at me and said, 'I won't suck you. Don't ask me to suck you.'"

"Poor baby," said Lula. "She don't know what she missed. What color hair she have?"

"Sorta brown, blond, I guess. But dig this, sweetie. Then she turns over, peels off them orange pants, and spreads her legs real wide and says to me, 'Take a bite of peach.'"

Lula howled. "Jesus, honey! You more than sorta got what you come for."

The waitress brought their oysters and slaw.

"Y'all want somethin' more to drink?" she asked.

Sailor swallowed the last of his High Life and handed the bottle to the waitress.

"Why not?" he said.

THE REST OF THE WORLD

"I'LL DROP MAMA A POSTCARD from somewhere," said Lula. "I mean, I don't want her to worry no more than necessary."

"What do you mean by necessary?" said Sailor. "She's prob'ly already called the cops, my parole officer, her p.i. boyfriend—What's his name? Jimmy Fatgut or somethin'?"

"Farragut. Johnnie Farragut. I suppose so. She knew I was bound to see you soon as you was sprung, but I don't figure she counted on us takin' off together like this."

Sailor was at the wheel of Lula's white '75 Bonneville convertible. He kept it steady at sixty with the top up to avoid attracting attention. They were twenty miles north of Hattiesburg, headed for Biloxi, where they planned to spend the night.

"I guess this means you're breakin' parole, then?" said Lula.

"You guess," Sailor said. "My parole was broke two hundred miles back when we burnt Portagee County."

"What'll it be like in California, Sailor, do you think? I hear it don't rain much there."

"Considerin' we make it, you mean."

"We got through two and a half states already without no problem."

Sailor laughed. "Reminds me of a story I heard at Pee Dee about a guy had been workin' derrick on the Atchafalaya. He hooked up with a prostitute in New Iberia and they robbed a armored car together, killed the driver and the guard, got away with it. The woman done the shootin', too. She planned the whole thing, she told this guy, only she was followin' a plan laid out by her boyfriend who was doin' a stretch for armed robbery up at Angola.

"They were headed for Colorado and had gone north through Arkansas and then over through Oklahoma and were around Enid when who bushwhacks 'em but the boyfriend from Angola. He'd gone over the wall, went lookin' for his old squeeze, and learned about the armored-car robbery. It'd made all the papers because it was so darin' and ingenious. It couldn't have been nobody but her, he figured, 'cause of the way it'd been pulled off, and he'd told her the best route to take to Colorado where the cash could be hid out in a old mine he knew about. He never counted on her attemptin' to pull this gig on her own, of course. It was the score he'd reckoned on makin', maybe usin' her, when he got out of Angola. Anyway, he caught up with 'em before the feds did, and blew 'em both away."

"Nice story, honey," said Lula. "What on earth made you think of it?"

"They'd made it through two and a half states, too, before the road ended."

"What happened to the hardcase from Angola?"

"He got caught by the FBI in Denver and sent back to Louisiana to finish his time on the robbery beef. He's supposed to've stashed the armored-car loot in the Colorado mine. The bodies ain't never turned up."

"Maybe they're buried in the mine, too," said Lula.

"Could be. I heard this from a guy'd done time in Angola. You hear lots of stories in the slam, babe, ain't many of which float. But I buy this one."

Lula lit up a cigarette.

"That don't smell like a More," said Sailor.

"It ain't," said Lula. "I picked me up a pack of Vantages before we left the Cape?"

"They sure do stink."

"Yeah, I guess, but they ain't supposed to be so bad for you."

"You ain't gonna begin worryin' about what's bad for you at this hour, are you, sugar? I mean, here you are crossin' state lines with a A-number-one certified murderer."

"Manslaughterer, honey, not murderer. Don't exaggerate."

"Okay, manslaughterer who's broke his parole and got in mind nothin' but immoral purposes far's you're concerned."

"Thank the Lord. Well, you ain't let me down yet, Sailor. That's more'n I can say for the rest of the world?"

Sailor laughed and shot the Pontiac up to seventy.

"You please me, too, peanut," he said.

SPEED TO BURN

" 'I DON'T LOCOMOTE NO MORE.' "

"What's that?" said Sailor. "You don't what?"

"I'm just readin' here? In the *Times-Picayune*?" said Lula. "About Little Eva, who sung that song 'The Locomotion' that was a hit before we was even born?"

"Still a good one," Sailor said. "What's it say?"

" 'Little Eva's doin' a brand-new dance now,' " Lula read. " 'I don't locomote no more,' said Eva Boyd as she wiped the counter at Hanzies Grill, a soul food restaurant in Kingston, N.C. It's been twenty-five years since Boyd, as teen-aged Little Eva, hit the top of the charts with 'The Locomotion.' 'I ain't into singin' over chicken,' the forty-three-year-old Boyd said in a recent interview. She still sings with a gospel group from her church and is considerin' makin' a record. 'She sounds beautiful,' said waitress Loraine Jackson."

"Good to know she ain't quit singin'," said Sailor. "It's a gift."

Sailor and Lula were sitting on a bench by the Mississippi watching the barges and freighters glide by. It was late evening but the sky was plum colored, soft and light.

"I don't think we should hang around too long in N.O.," Sailor said. "This is likely the first place they'll come lookin'."

Lula folded the newspaper and put it down next to her on the bench. "I don't see what Mama can do about us," she said. "Seems to me unless she has me kidnapped, there's no way I'm goin' back without you. And you'd just get popped for violatin' parole if you do. So, there ain't much choice now."

"You know Dimwit Taylor, guy hangs around front of Fatty's Dollar-Saver?"

"Sure. He don't have no teeth and's always smilin' so ugly and sayin', 'Man ain't lonesome long's he got a dog.' Only he ain't got no dog?"

"The one."

"What about him?"

"You ever sit down and talk with him?"

"Not hardly. Always looks like he just crawled out of a pit. Smells it, too."

"He used to be a ballplayer, professional, mostly on barnstormin' teams around the South. Told me once in Alabama, like forty years ago, he was playin' in a game against a black team from Birmin'ham had an amazin' young center fielder could grab anythin' hit his way. There wasn't no outfield fence at the field they was playin' at, so nobody on Dimwit's team could put the ball over this kid's head. He'd just spin, run out from under his cap and take it out of the air like a piece of dust. After the game, Dimwit talks to the boy, turns out he's only fifteen years old."

"What's this got to do with us bein' on the run?"

"That's just it," said Sailor. "Dimwit asked the kid how'd he know just where to head soon's the ball's hit, so he'd snatch it before it touched the ground. And the kid said, 'I got the range and the speed to change.' Dimwit said the kid had it exactly right, and he made it to the big leagues, too."

"So you figure you got the range, huh?"

Sailor laughed. "I do, peanut. I just got to trust myself, is all. And I got speed to burn."

Lula pushed herself right up against Sailor and rested her head on his chest.

"I like how you talk, Sailor. And you know what? I believe you, I really, really do."

TALK PRETTY TO ME

"KNOW WHAT I like best, honey?" said Lula, as Sailor guided the Bonneville out of Lafayette toward Lake Charles.

"What's that, peanut?"

"When you talk pretty to me."

Sailor laughed. "That's easy enough. I mean, it don't come hard. Back at Pee Dee all I had to do to cheer myself up was think about you. Your big grey eyes, of course, but mostly your skinny legs."

"You think my legs is too skinny?"

"For some, maybe, but not for me they ain't."

"A girl ain't perfect, you know, except in them magazines."

"I been makin' do."

"Can't see where it's harmed you none."

"I ain't complainin', sweetheart, you know that."

"I think most men, if not all, is missin' an element, anyways."

"What's that mean?"

"Men got a kind of automatic shutoff valve in their head? Like, you're talkin' to one and just gettin' to the part where you're gonna say what you really been wantin' to say, and then you say it and you look at him and he ain't even heard it. Not like it's too complicated or somethin', just he ain't about to really listen. One might lie sometime and tell ya he knows just what you mean, but I ain't buyin'. 'Cause later you say somethin' else he woulda got if he'd understood you in the first place, only he don't, and you know you been talkin' for no good reason. It's frustratin'."

"You think I been lyin' to you, Lula?"

Lula stayed quiet for a full minute, listening to the heavy hum of the V-8.

"Lula? You there?"

"Yeah, I'm here."

"You upset with me?"

"No, Sailor, darlin', I ain't upset. Just it's shockin' sometimes when what you think turns out to not be what you think at all."

"It's why I don't think no more'n necessary."

"You know, I had this awful, long dream last night? Tell me what you think of it. I'm out walkin' and I come to this field. This is all in bright color? And there's all these bodies of dead horses and dead children lyin' all around. I'm sad, but I'm not really sad. It's like I know they're all gone to a better place. Then a old woman comes up to me and tells me I got to bleed the bodies so they can be made into mummies. She shows me how to make a cut at the sides of the mouths of the corpses to drain 'em. Then I'm supposed to carry the bodies over a bridge across a real beautiful river into an old barn.

"Everything's really peaceful and lovely where I am, with green grass and big trees at the edge of the field. I'm not sure I got the strength to drag the bodies of the horses all that way. I'm frightened but I'm ready to do it anyway. And I'm sorta cryin' but not really sad? I can't explain the feelin' exactly. So I walk to the rear of this huge grey horse. I go around to his mouth and start to cut him. As soon as I touch him with the knife he wakes up and attacks me. The horse is furious. He gets up and chases me across the bridge and into and through the old barn. Then I woke up. You were sleepin' hard. And I just laid there and thought about how even if you love someone it isn't always possible to have it change your life."

"I don't know what your dream means, sweetheart," said Sailor, "but once I heard my mama ask my daddy if he loved her. They were yellin' at each other, like usual, and he told her the only thing he ever loved was the movie *Bad Men of Missouri*, which he said he seen sixteen times."

"What I mean about men," said Lula.

OLD NOISE

"You didn't raise a fool, Marietta. Lula got too much Pace in her to throw her life away on trash. My guess is she's havin' herself a time, is all."

Marietta and Dalceda Delahoussaye were sitting on the side porch of Marietta's house drinking Martini & Rossi sweet vermouth over crushed ice with a lemon slice. Dalceda had been best friends with Marietta for close to thirty years, ever since they boarded together at Miss Cook's School in Beaufort. They'd never lived further apart in that period than a ten-minute walk.

"Remember Vernon Landis? The man owned a Hispano-Suiza he kept in Royce Womble's garage all those years before he sold it for twenty-five thousand dollars to the movie company in Wilmington? His wife, Althea, ran off with a wholesale butcher from Hayti, Missouri. The man gave her a diamond ring big enough to stuff a turkey and guess what? She was back with Vernon in six weeks."

"Dal? Just *what*, you tell me, has Althea Landis's inability to control herself have to do with my baby Lula's bein' stole by this awful demented man?"

"Marietta! Sailor Ripley prob'ly ain't no more or less demented than anyone we know."

"Oh, Dal, he's lowlife. He's what we been avoidin' all our lives, and now my only child's at his mercy."

"You always been one to panic, Marietta. When Enos Dodge didn't ask you right off to go with him to the Beau Regard Country Club cotillion in 1959, you panicked. Threatened to kill yourself or accept an invitation from Biff Bethune. And what happened? Enos Dodge'd been in Fayetteville with his daddy and asked you soon as he got back two days later. This ain't a moment to panic, lovey. You're gonna have to quit spittin' and ride it on out."

"You're always such a comfort to me, Dal."

"I give you what you need, is all. A talkin'-to."

"What I need is Lula safe at home."

"Safe? Safe? Ain't that a stitch! Ain't nobody nowhere never been safe a second of their life."

Dalceda drained the last drop of vermouth from her glass.

"You got any more of this red vinegar in the house?" she asked.

Marietta rose and went into the pantry and came out carrying a sealed bottle. She unscrewed the cap and poured Dalceda a drink and freshened her own before sitting back down.

"And what about you?" said Dalceda.

"What about me?"

"When's the last time you been out with a man? Let alone been to bed with one."

Marietta clucked her tongue twice before answering.

"I plain ain't interested," she said, and took a long sip from her glass.

Dalceda laughed. "What was it you used to tell me about how Clyde carried on when you and him made love? About his gruntin' that come from way down inside sounded so ancient? Old noise, you called it. Told me you felt like you was bein' devoured by a unstoppable beast, and it was the most thrillin' thing ever happened to you."

"Dal, I swear I hate talkin' to you. You remember too much."

"Hate hearin' the truth is what it is. You're just shit scared Lula feels the same way about Sailor as you did with Clyde."

"Oh, Dal, how could she? I mean, do you think she does? This Sailor ain't nothin' like Clyde."

"How do you know, Marietta? You ever tried the boy on for size?"

Dalceda laughed. Marietta drank.

"And Mr. Dogface Farragut comes mopin' and sniffin' around you regular," said Dalceda. "You could start with him. Or how about that old gangster, Marcello 'Crazy Eyes' Santos, used to proposition you when you was married to Clyde?"

Marietta snorted. "He stopped askin' after Clyde died. My bein' too available musta thrown him off the scent."

"That's most certainly the case with Louis Delahoussaye the Third," said Dalceda. "I don't think he's asked for it more'n twice in six months for a grand total of a not so grand eight and one-half minutes."

"Dal? You think I oughta keep dyein' my hair or let it go white?"

"Marietta, what I think is we both need another drink."

THE MIDDLE OF THINGS

In San Antonio, Lula said, "You know about the Alamo?"

"Talked about it in school, I remember," said Sailor. "And I seen the old John Wayne movie where mostly nothin' happens till the Mexicans overrun the place."

Sailor and Lula were in La Estrella Negra eating birria con arroz y frijoles and drinking Tecate with wedges of lime.

"Guess it's a pretty big deal here," said Lula. "Noticed drivin' in how ever'thing's named after it. Alamo Road, Alamo Street, Alamo Square, Alamo Buildin', Hotel Alamo. They ain't forgettin' it in a hurry."

"Pretty place, though, San Antone," said Sailor.

"So what we gonna do, hon? About money, I mean."

"I ain't worried. Figure we'll stop somewhere between here and El Paso and find some work."

"When you was a boy?"

"Uh huh."

"What'd you think about doin' when you grew up?"

"Pilot. Always wanted to be a airline pilot."

"Like for TWA or Delta, you mean?"

"Yeah. Thought that'd be cool, you know, wearin' a captain's hat and takin' them big birds up over the ocean. Hang out with stews in Rome and L.A."

"Why didn't you do it?"

Sailor laughed. "Never really got the chance, did I? Wasn't nobody about to help me toward it, you know? Not bein' much of a student, always gettin' in trouble one way or another, I kinda lost sight of it."

"You coulda joined the air force, learned to fly."

"Tried once. They didn't want me 'cause of my record. Too many scrapes. I never even been in a plane."

"Shoot, Sail, we oughta take a long flight when we got some money to waste. Fly to Paris."

"I'd go for that."

As soon as they'd finished eating, Sailor said, "Let's keep movin', Lula. Big towns is where they'll look."

Sailor drove with Lula curled up on the seat next to him. Patsy Cline was on the radio, singing "I Fall to Pieces."

"I wish I'd been born when Patsy Cline was singin'," said Lula.

"What's the difference?" Sailor asked. "You can still listen to her records."

"I coulda seen her maybe. She got the biggest voice? Like if Aretha Franklin woulda been a country singer all those years ago. That's what I always wanted to do, Sailor, be a singer. I ever tell you that?"

"Not that I recall."

"When I was little, eight or nine? Mama took me to Charlotte and put me in a talent show. It was at a big movie theater, and there was all these kids lined up on the stage. Each of us had to perform when our name was called. Kids tap-danced, played instruments or sang, mostly. One boy did magic tricks. Another boy juggled balls and stood on his head while he whistled 'Dixie' or somethin'."

"What'd you do?"

"Sang 'Stand By Your Man,' the Tammy Wynette tune? Mama thought it'd be extra cute, havin' me sing such a grown-up number."

"How'd it go?"

"Not too bad. Course I couldn't hit most of the high notes, and all the other kids on stage was talkin' and makin' noises durin' my turn."

"You win?"

"No. Some boy played 'Stars Fell on Alabama' on a harmonica did."

"Why'd you quit singin'?"

"Mama decided I didn't have no talent. Said she didn't wanta waste no more money on lessons. This was when I was thirteen? Prob'ly she was right. No sense playin' at it. You got a voice like Patsy's, you ain't got no hesitation about where you're headed."

"Ain't easy when you're kinda in the middle of things," said Sailor.

"Like us, you mean," said Lula. "That's where we are, and I don't mean in the middle of southwest Texas."

"There's worse places."

"If you say so, honey."

"Trust me on it."

"I do trust you, Sailor. Like I ain't never trusted nobody before. It's scary sometimes. You ain't got much maybe or might in you."

Sailor laughed, and put his arm over Lula, brushing her cheek with his hand.

"Maybe and might are my little brothers," he said. "I gotta set 'em a good example, is all."

"It ain't really them worries me, it's those cousins, never and ever, make me shake."

"We'll be all right, peanut, long as we got room to move."

Lula clucked her tongue twice.

"Know what?" she said.

"Uh?"

"I don't know that I completely enjoy you callin' me peanut so much."

Sailor laughed. "Why's that?"

"Puts me so far down on the food chain?"

Sailor looked at her.

"Really, Sail. I know how you mean it to be sweet, but I was thinkin' how everything can eat a peanut and a peanut don't eat nothin'. Makes me sound so tiny, is all."

"How you want, honey," he said.

WELCOME TO BIG TUNA

BIG TUNA, TEXAS, POP. 305, sits 125 miles west of Biarritz, 125 miles east of Iraaq, and 100 miles north of the Mexican border on the south fork of the Esperanza trickle. Sailor cruised the Bonneville through the streets of Big Tuna, eyeballing the place.

"This looks like a lucky spot, sweetheart," he said. "Whattaya think?"

"Not bad," said Lula. "Long as you're not large on cool breezes. Must be a hundred and ten and it ain't even noon yet."

"Hundred twelve, to be exact. What it said on the Iguana County Bank buildin' back there. And that's prob'ly two degrees or more shy of the actual temp. Chamber of commerce don't like to discourage visitors, so they set it low."

"I can understand that, Sail. After all, there's a big difference between a hundred twelve and a hundred fourteen."

Sailor circled back and stopped the car in front of the Iguana Hotel, a two-story, whitewashed wooden building with the Texas state flag draped over the single porch above the entrance.

"This'll do," he said.

The second-floor room Sailor and Lula rented was simple: double bed, dresser, mirror, chair, sink, toilet, bathtub (no shower), electric fan, window overlooking the street.

"Not bad for eleven dollars a day," said Sailor.

"No radio or TV," said Lula. She stripped off the spread, tossed it in a corner and sat down on the bed. "And no AC."

"Fan works."

"Now what?"

"Let's go down to the drugstore and get a sandwich. Find out about where to look for work."

"Sailor?"

"Yeah?"

"This ain't exactly my most thrillin' notion of startin' a new life."

They ordered bologna and American cheese on white with Cokes at the counter of Bottomley's Drug.

"Pretty empty today," Sailor said to the waitress, whose plastic name tag had KATY printed on it.

"Ever'body's over to the funeral," Katy said. "This is kind of a sad day around here."

"We just got into town," said Lula. "What happened?"

"Buzz Dokes, who run a farm here for twenty years, died somethin' horrible. Only forty-four."

"How'd he go?" asked Sailor.

"Bumblebees got him. Buzz was on his tractor Monday mornin' when a swarm of bees lit on his head and knocked him off his seat. He fell underneath the mower and the blades chopped him up in four unequal parts. Run over a bee mound and they just rose up and attacked him. Poor Buzz. Tractor trampled him and kept goin', went through a fence and smacked into the side of a Messican's house. Took it clean off the foundation."

"That's about the most unpleasant incident I heard of lately," said Lula.

"There's always some strange thing or other happenin' in Big Tuna," Katy said. "I've lived here all my life, forty-one years, except for two years in Beaumont, and I could put together some book about this town. It wouldn't all be pretty, I tell you. But it's a sight better than bein' in a place like Beaumont, where people come down the street you don't know 'em and never will. I like bein' in a place where I know who I'm gonna see every day. What are you kids doin' here?"

"Lookin' for work," said Sailor.

"Any kind in particular?"

"I'm pretty fair with cars, trucks. Never done no ranchin', though, or farmin'."

"You might talk to Red Lynch. He's got a garage just two blocks up the street here, 'cross from the high school. Called Red's. He might have somethin', seein' as how the boys he usually hires don't last too long before they take off for Dallas or Houston. Not enough goin' on to keep 'em here. Red oughta be back from Buzz's funeral in a half hour or so."

"Thanks, Katy, I'll check it out. Tell me, why's this town named Big Tuna? There ain't no body of water around here woulda ever had no tuna in it."

Katy laughed. "That's for sure. All we got's wells and what falls from the sky, which ain't been a whole heck of a lot lately. The Esperanza's dry half the year. No, it's named after an oilman, Earl 'Big Tuna' Bink, who bought up most of Iguana County back in the twenties. Used to be called

Esperanza Spring, only there ain't no spring, just like there ain't no tuna. Bink'd go off on fishin' trips to California, Hawaii and Australia and such, and have these big mounted fish shipped back here to his ranch. He died when I was ten. The whole county went to his funeral. Ever'body called him Big Tuna. There's a oil portrait of him hangin' in the Iguana County Bank, which he owned. Where you-all from?"

"Florida," said Sailor. "Orlando, Florida."

"Boy, my grandkids'd sure love to go to that Disney World. You been there plenty, I guess."

"Lots of times."

Lula sucked on the straw in her Coke and stared at Sailor. He turned and smiled at her, then went back to making conversation with Katy. Lula suddenly felt sick to her stomach.

"I'm gonna go back up to the room and lie down, Sailor," she said. "This heat makes me tired."

"Okay, honey, I'll see you later."

"Bye," Lula said to Katy.

"Have a nice *siesta,* dear," said Katy.

Outside everything looked cooked, like the white of a fried egg, with brown edges. Lula walked very slowly the half block to the Iguana Hotel and barely made it up the stairs into the room before she threw up.

NIGHT AND DAY AT THE IGUANA HOTEL

"HOW DO YOU GET SIXTEEN HAITIANS into a Dixie cup?" said Sparky.

"How?" asked Lula.

"Tell 'em it floats."

Sailor, Lula, Sparky and Buddy were sitting in the lobby of the Iguana Hotel at ten P.M., sharing Sparky's fifth of Ezra Brooks and shooting the shit.

"Sparky's big on Florida jokes," said Buddy.

"You need a active sense of humor to survive in the Big Tuna," said Sparky.

Bobby Peru walked in and came over.

"Hey, everybody," he said.

"Sailor, Lula, this here's the man himself," said Buddy. "Bobby, this is Sailor and Lula, the most recent strandees, economic variety."

Bobby nodded to Lula and offered a hand to Sailor.

"Bobby Peru, just like the country."

Sparky and Buddy laughed.

"Accordin' to Red and Rex," said Buddy, "Bobby's the most excitin' item to hit Big Tuna since the '86 cyclone sheared the roof off the high school."

"Only in town two months and there ain't a young thing around don't know how that cobra tattoo works, right, Bob?" Sparky said.

Bobby laughed. He had a lopsided grin that exposed only three brownish front teeth on the upper right side of his mouth. He had dark, wavy hair and a small, thin nose that bent slightly left. His eyebrows were long and tapered and looked as if they'd been drawn on. What frightened Lula about Bobby Peru were his eyes: flat black, they reflected no light. They were like heavy shades, she thought, that prevented people from seeing inside. Lula guessed that he was about the same age as Sparky and Buddy, but Bobby was the kind of person who would look the same when he was forty-five as he did when he was twenty.

"You from Texas, Mr. Peru?" Lula asked.

Bobby pulled up a chair and poured himself a shot glass full of whisky.

"I'm from all over," he said. "Born in Tulsa, raised in Arkansas, Illinois, Indiana, lived in Oregon, South Dakota, Virginia. Got people in Pasadena, California, who I was headin' to see when my Dodge busted a rod. Still meanin' to get out there."

"You was in the marines, huh?" said Sailor, noticing a USMC tattoo on Bobby's right hand.

Bobby looked down at his hand, flexed it.

"Four years," he said.

"Bobby was at Cao Ben," said Sparky.

"What's Cao Ben?" asked Lula.

"How old are you?" Buddy asked her.

"Twenty."

"Bunch of civilians got killed," said Bobby. "March 1968. We torched a village and the government made a big deal out of it. Politicians tryin' to get attention. Put the commandin' officer on trial for murder. Only problem was, there weren't no such persons as civilians in that war."

"Lotta women and kids and old people died at Cao Ben," said Buddy.

Bobby sipped the whisky and closed his eyes for several seconds before reopening them and looking at Buddy.

"You was on a ship, pardner. Hard to make contact with the people when you're off floatin' in the Gulf of Tonkin. It weren't simple."

"Saw Perdita this afternoon," said Sparky. "Came by Red's lookin' for you."

"Had some business over by Iraaq," said Bobby. "I'm just about to go check on her now."

He stood up and set the shot glass on his chair.

"Good meetin' you," Bobby said to Sailor and Lula. "*Adiós*, boys."

He walked out.

After Bobby was gone, Lula said, "Somethin' in that man scares me."

"Bobby's got a way," said Buddy.

"Can't shake that institution odor," Sparky said, and poured himself another shot.

Lula put a hand on Sailor's leg.

"Darlin', I still ain't feelin' so well," she said. "I'm goin' to bed."

"I'll come along," said Sailor.

They said good night to Sparky and Buddy and went upstairs.

In the room, Sailor said, "Man, that barf smell don't fade fast."

"I'll get some white vinegar to rub on it tomorrow, honey, take care of it."

Lula went into the bathroom and stayed there for a long time. When she came out, Sailor asked if there was anything he could do for her.

"No, I don't think so, Sail. I just need to lie down."

Lula listened to Sailor brush his teeth, then urinate into the toilet and flush it.

"Sailor?" she said as he climbed into bed. "You know what?"

"I know you ain't particularly pleased bein' here."

"Not that. Might be I'm pregnant."

Sailor rolled over and looked into Lula's eyes.

"It's okay by me, peanut."

"Well, nothin' personal, but I ain't so sure it's okay by me."

Sailor lay down on his back.

"Really, Sailor, it ain't nothin' against you. I love you."

"Love you, too."

"I know. Just I'm sorta uncomfortable about the way some things is goin', and this don't help soothe me."

Sailor got out of bed and went over by the window. He sat down in the chair and looked out. Bobby Peru and a Mexican woman with black hair longer than Lula's were parked across the street in a maroon 1971 Eldorado convertible with the top down. Sailor watched as the woman pulled a knife out of her purse and tried to stick Bobby with it. He took the knife away from her and tossed it. She got out of the car and ran. Bobby fired up the Eldo and drove after her.

"I know this ain't easy, Lula," Sailor said, "but I ain't gonna let things get no worse, I promise."

FRIENDS

"NICE OF YOU TO DROP BY," said Perdita.

Bobby let the screen door bang shut behind him as he came in.

"Told you I would."

Perdita sat down on the couch, shook a Marlboro from the pack on the coffee table and lit it with a red Bic. Bobby roamed around the living room. The taps on the heels and toes of his boots clacked loudly against the hardwood floor.

"You still riled?" asked Bobby.

Perdita laughed. "You still screwin' sixteen-year-olds in the ass?"

Bobby smiled and kept circling.

"Ain't never had no teenaged girl pull a blade on me."

"Wish I'd cut you up good."

"Heard from Tony?"

"Juana called. They're stayin' another week."

Bobby stopped walking and stared at a family photograph on the wall.

"Stayin' a few extra days in the cow town, huh? This you?"

Perdita turned her head and looked, then turned back.

"Yes."

"How old were you? Twelve?"

"Almost. Eleven and a half. Ten years ago in Corpus."

"Mm, mm. What a tasty thing you musta been."

"Nobody was tastin'."

"Shame."

Bobby turned around and leaned down and put his face next to Perdita's from behind.

"The cobra's waitin' to strike, *chica*," he said.

Perdita crossed her legs and smoked. Bobby lowered his hands into the front of her blouse and cupped her small breasts. Perdita pretended not to care. He rubbed her nipples with the tips of his fingers, making them become rigid. She burned the back of his left wrist with her cigarette.

Bobby jumped back, then grabbed Perdita's hair and pulled her over the couch onto the floor. Neither of them spoke. She tried to stand up but Bobby kept his right foot on her chest while he blew on the back of his wounded wrist. Perdita shoved his leg to one side and rolled away. She stood up and spit at him.

Bobby grinned. "I knew we could be friends again," he said.

BOBBY'S BAD DAY

"TAKE ONE OF THESE," Bobby Peru said, handing a plastic-wrapped package to Sailor.

"What is it?"

"Panty hose. Work better'n stockin's. Pull one of the legs down over your face and let the other leg trail behind your head."

They were in the Eldorado, about two blocks away from the Ramos Feed Store in Iraaq. Perdita was at the wheel, Bobby was next to her and Sailor rode in back. The top was up.

"Here's the pistol," said Bobby, taking the Smith and Wesson out of his belt and passing it to Sailor. "Remember, soon as we get inside you keep that bad boy up where those hicks can see it. Once they notice the Ithaca and the Smith, they'll know we ain't foolin' with 'em."

Perdita tossed her cigarette out the window and immediately took out another and lit it with the dashboard lighter.

"Comin' up on it now, Bobby," she said.

Bobby slipped the panty hose over his head and adjusted it. His face looked crooked, distorted and flat, the lips pancaked across the lower half and his hair plastered down over his forehead like broken teeth on a comb.

"Come on!" Bobby stage-whispered, his head snapping toward Sailor like a striking asp's. "Get that mask on!"

Sailor ripped open the package and pulled a nylon leg over his head, stretching the calf part to fit.

Perdita pulled up in front of the store. The street was deserted.

"Keep it revved, Chiquita. We won't be long," Bobby said.

It was two o'clock in the afternoon and the sun took up the entire sky. As Sailor got out of the car, he felt the intense heat of the day for the first time. Until that moment, he'd been numb. Sailor had passed the preceding hours in a kind of trance, unaware of the temperature or anything other than the time. Fourteen hours, Bobby had said, that's when they'd go in. They'd be out at fourteen-oh-three and thirty seconds, he promised, with something in the neighborhood of five thousand dollars.

Bobby went in first, carrying a black canvas Sundog shoulder bag in his left hand. He raised the sawed-off shotgun with his right and in a firm voice said to the two men behind the counter, "Move into the back room, both of you. Now!"

They moved. Both in their mid-fifties, portly, with wire-rim glasses and crown-bald heads, the men looked like brothers.

"Stay here," Bobby told Sailor as he followed them. "Keep an eye on the door. If anyone comes in, herd 'em on back, quick."

Sailor held the Smith up high, where Bobby could see it if he looked. Behind him, Sailor could hear Bobby instructing one of the men to open the safe. Neither of the men, so far as Sailor could tell, had said a word.

An Iguana County deputy sheriff cruised up in a patrol car and parked it on an angle in front of the idling Eldo. The deputy got out of his car and walked over to the driver's side of the Cadillac. He looked at Perdita through his aviator-style reflector Ray-Bans, smiled, and placed both of his hands on the rag top.

"Waitin' for somebody, miss?" he said.

"*Mi esposo,*" said Perdita. "He's in the feed store picking up some supplies."

"You'd best be careful of that cigarette, ma'am. It's about to burn down between your fingers."

Perdita stubbed out her Marlboro in the ashtray.

"*Gracias*, officer."

Bobby came out of the store in a hurry, still wearing the panty hose on his head, carrying the shoulder bag and the shotgun. Perdita jammed the gearshift into reverse and peeled out, knocking the deputy down. She floored the Eldo for fifty yards, braked hard, yanked it into drive and spun a mean yo-yo, fishtailing viciously but managing to keep the car under control. Perdita hit the accelerator again as hard as she could and never looked back.

The deputy came up on one knee with his revolver clasped in both hands. He fired his first shot into Bobby's right thigh and his second into Bobby's left hip. The shock of the initial slug caused Bobby to drop the bag. The impact of the second forced Bobby's right hand to twist sideways so that both barrels of the shotgun wedged under his chin. The Ithaca went off, blowing Bobby backwards through the RAMOS on the plate-glass window of the feed store.

Sailor had been right behind Bobby until he saw Perdita hightail it. As soon as he spotted the deputy, Sailor hit the ground, losing the Smith as he fell. He put his hands over his hosieried head and kept his face in the dirt until the deputy ordered him to stand up.

LETTER FROM LULA

Sailor Ripley
 # 461208
Walls Unit
Huntsville, Texas 77340

Dearest Sailor Darling,

The first thing youll want to know is Im keeping the baby. Mama wasnt for it in the beginning but I think shes looking forward to it. Im gonna name it Pace no matter if its a boy or a girl. Pace Ripley sounds good dont it? Its kind of hard to believe that Pace will be ten years old when you get out.

What else can I tell you? Im feeling fine its not so terrible being with mama cause shes calmed down a lot. I think our running off that way scared her plenty and she has more respect for me now. She doesnt even speak poorly of you no more at least not so often. I explained to her how you was worried about us not having money and the idea of a baby and all and how of course it was no excuse for committing an armed robbery but there it is.

I hope its not too horrible for you inside the walls again I know how much you hate being confined. Is it different in a Texas prison than it was at Pee Dee? I bet it aint as pretty. The doctor here says I got to stay at home while Im pregnant. Theres something wrong with the way Im carrying the baby but if I keep still and dont smoke and eat right which mama and her friend Dalceda Delahoussaye are seeing to he says I should be just fine. It sure is hard not to smoke. I miss my Mores!!! I feel like Im kind of in prison too but I know in six months itll be over and Ill have a son or daughter to show for it. Our child!!

I hope you know it hurts me to not be able to visit you all I can do is write letters which is OK I like writing. Did you know that Johnnie Farragut is a writer? Mama told me he showed her some stories and things he wrote and that she liked them. She says he has an interesting imagination.

Did Perdita Durango ever get caught? Ill bet shes in Mexico now or somewhere out of the authorities reach. I have to confess it dont bother me one little bit about Bobby Peru being shot dead. He was one of them types you could feel it was coming and he killed his share as we know. Remember once I called him a black angel well hes not in heaven Ill guarantee. If he is then I never want to go there!!!

It was excellent of you to give yourself up the way you did and not try to shoot it out youd be dead too and never have got to see your child Pace. I hope this name is all right with you Sailor if its not tell me and Ill think it over some more but I love it and certainly hope you do.

Im going to take a nap now. Your probably thinking about how I was always sleeping at the end there in the Iguana Hotel and now I still am but the doctor says sometimes being pregnant makes the mother be that way and Im one of them. I love you Sailor. I dont know how much or what it means though I miss you an awful bunch sometimes I know your thinking about me cause I can feel it. I miss your not being around to call me peanut nobody else ever called me that.

Like I said I have to rest again. Its not really so simple to write like this at least not like it was before when you was at Pee Dee cause that was for only two years not ten. Time dont really fly honey does it?

Love,
your Lula

LETTER FROM SAILOR

Lula P. Fortune
127 Reeves Avenue
Bay St. Clement, N.C. 28352

Dear Lula,

It is fine with me about the baby as you already know. And Pace being your family name and all is just right. What about a middle name if it is a boy after my grandaddy Roscoe? He would be proud I know though he is long passed. Pace Roscoe Ripley does not sound so bad do you think? If it is a girl instead choose whatever name you want for a middle I do not care. Leaving it be is OK without a middle or you might want to put in your mother Marietta. Anyway is good. Just you stay healthy.

Your right this place is not so pretty as Pee Dee. Not pretty at all. There are boys inside these walls meaner than Peru you can bet. There is a Death House. I am getting along. The only thing is not thinking about the future. Your right there 10 years is not 2. The baby will be 10 but I will be 33. There is always a chance of early parole though the rap back home and the fact I busted parole there probably cancels that. I am not there idea of a good risk.

I really got no idea what happened to Perdita. She disappeared as you figured. She is a strange person and I did not know her well. Tell your mama I am dreadful sorry about each and everything that has happened and the last thing ever in my mind is to see you harmed. You are her daughter but I would like to marry you if you would consent while I am inside. This can be arranged because I asked. The preacher would do it but I know you cannot leave home. Maybe after you have the baby you would come here.

Write often peanut. I am in the laundry at 5. There are car magazines and TV. Other than that is mail.

I love you. It is hard to end this letter. If I stop writing your gone. There is not a lot more to say though. Vaya con dios mi amor.

Sailor

from
SAILOR'S HOLIDAY
(1991)

PLAN B

"MOST GATORS GO FOR GARS. Not often one tackles somethin' much larger, like a human."

"Bob Lee knows more about alligators than anyone, almost," said Beany. "Least more about 'em than anyone I ever knew, not that I ever knew anybody before cared."

Lula, Beany, and Bob Lee were sitting at the dining room table in the Boyle house in Metairie. Lula and Pace had flown in late in the afternoon, and they had just finished dinner. Pace and Lance were upstairs in Lance's room watching TV, and Madonna Kim, the baby, was asleep.

"It sounds fascinatin', Bob Lee," Lula said, fiddling with the spoon next to her coffee cup. "How'd you get started on gators?"

"Grew up around 'em in Chacahoula, where my daddy's folks're from. I spent considerable time there as a boy. We lived in Raceland, and my mama's people come from Crozier and Bayou Cane, near Houma. Later I worked for Wildlife Management at Barataria. Started workin' on my own mix after a biology professor from Texas A&M came by askin' questions. Told me a man could make a fortune if he figured out how to keep crocs from devourin' folks live on the Nile River in Africa, for instance, and in India and Malaysia. Crocs and gators react about the same to stimuli. Secret to it's in their secretions, called pheromones. They got glands near the tail, emit scents for matin' purposes. Other ones around their throat mark territory. Beasts use the sense of smell to communicate."

"Lula and I've known a few pussy-sniffin' beasts ourselves," said Beany, making them all laugh.

"If that's true, Lula," said Bob Lee, "then you know what I'm talkin' about. Same thing goes for these reptiles."

"What do y'all call your product?"

" 'Gator Gone.' Got it trademarked for worldwide distribution now. Warehouse is in Algiers and the office is on Gentilly, near the Fair Grounds. Come around some time. Right now, though, I gotta go make some phone calls, you ladies don't mind."

"We got lots to talk about," Beany said. "You go on."

Bob Lee got up and went out of the room.

"He's a swell man, Beany. You're fortunate to have him."

"Only man I ever met didn't mind my bony ass!"

They laughed.

"And he don't beg me to give him head all the time, neither. Not that I ever cared particularly one way or the other about it, but it's a change. Only thing is the name, Beany Boyle. Sounds like a hobo stew."

"You look like you-all're doin' just fine."

"Pace sure is a sharpie. Image of his daddy."

"Ain't he? Breaks my heart, too."

"You and Sailor ain't in touch, I take it."

Lula shook her short black hair like a nervous filly in the starting gate.

"Haven't heard from him since he got out of prison over six months ago. We met that one time for about fifteen minutes at the Trailways, and then he just walked off in the night. Guess it was too much to expect we could work anything out. And I think seein' Pace scared Sailor, made those ten years I never went to visit him jump up in his face. I don't know, Beany, it's hard to figure out how I feel for real. And Mama don't make thinkin' for myself any easier."

"Marietta's a vicious cunt, Lula, face it. She ain't got a life and she's afraid you'll get one. That's why she freaked when you and Sailor run off. I'm surprised she let you come here, knowin' how she hates me."

"She don't hate you, Beany, and she ain't really vicious. Also I'm twenty-nine and a half years old now. She can't exactly tell me what I can or can't do."

"Don't stop her from manipulatin' you every chance. So what's the plan?"

"Thought maybe you could work on one with me. I need help and I know it."

Beany reached across the table and held Lula's hand.

"I'm with you, Lula, same as always. We'll figure out somethin'."

The baby began to cry. Beany smiled, squeezed Lula's hand and stood up.

"There's my Madonna Kim," she said. "Another complainin' female. Let's go get her in on this."

SAVING GRACE

ELMER DÉSESPÉRÉ PUT HIS RAILROAD ENGINEER'S CAP over his stringy yellow-white hair and went out. At the foot of the stairs of his rooming house he stopped and took a packet of Red Man chewing tobacco from the back pocket of his Ben Davis overalls, scooped a wad with the thumb and index finger of his right hand and planted it between his teeth and cheek in the left side of his mouth. Elmer replaced the packet in his pocket and strolled down Claiborne toward Canal Street. The night air felt thick and greasy, and the sidewalk was crawling with people sweating, laughing, fighting, drinking. Police cars, their revolving red and blue lights flashing, prowled up and down both sides of the road. Trucks rumbled like stampeding dinosaurs on the overhead highway, expelling a nauseating stream of diesel mist.

Elmer loved it all. He loved being in the city of New Orleans, away from the farm forever, away from his daddy, Hershel Burt, and his older brother, Emile; though they'd never bother a soul again, since Elmer had destroyed the both of them as surely as they had destroyed his mama, Alma Ann. He had chopped his daddy and brother into a total of exactly one hundred pieces and buried one piece per acre on the land Hershel Burt owned in Evangeline Parish by the Bayou Nezpique. After doing what he had to, Elmer had walked clear to Mamou and visited Alma Ann's grave, told her she could rest easy, then hitchhiked into N.O.

Alma Ann had died ten years ago, when Elmer was nine, on November 22nd, the birthday of her favorite singer, Hoagy Carmichael. Alma Ann's greatest pleasure in life, she had told Elmer, was listening to the collection of Hoagy Carmichael 78s her daddy, Bugle Lugubre, had left her. Her favorite tunes had been "Old Man Harlem," "Ole Buttermilk Sky," and Bugle's own favorite, "Memphis in June." But after Alma Ann was worked to death by Hershel Burt and Emile, Hershel Burt had busted up all the records and dumped the pieces in the Crooked Creek

Reservoir. Now Elmer had buried Hershel Burt just like he'd buried Bugle Lugubre's Hoagy Carmichael records. It made Elmer happy to think that the records could be replaced and that Hoagy Carmichael would live on forever through them. Alma Ann would live on as well, by virtue of Hoagy's music and Elmer's memory, but Hershel Burt and Emile were wiped away clean as bugs off a windshield in a downpour.

The only thing Elmer needed now was a friend. He'd taken the two-thousand-four-hundred-eighty-eight dollars his daddy had kept in Alma Ann's cloisonné button box, so Elmer figured he had enough money for quite a little while to come. Walking along Claiborne, watching the people carry on, Elmer felt as if he were a visitor to an insane asylum, the only one with a pass to the outside. When he reached Canal, Elmer turned down toward the river. He was looking for a tattoo parlor to have his mama's name written over his heart. A friend would know immediately what kind of person Elmer was, he thought, as soon as he saw ALMA ANN burned into Elmer's left breast. The friend would understand the depth of Elmer's loyalty and sincerity and never betray or leave him, this Elmer knew.

The pain was gone, too. The constant headache Elmer had suffered for so many years had vanished as he'd knelt next to Alma Ann's grave in Mamou. She soothed her truest son in death as she had in life. Jesus was bunk, Elmer had decided. He'd prayed to Jesus after Alma Ann had gone, but he had not been delivered. There had been no saving grace for Elmer until he'd destroyed the two marauding angels and pacified himself in the name of Alma Ann. It was he who shone, not Jesus. Jesus was dead and he, Elmer, was alive. He would carry Alma Ann's name on his body and his friend would understand and love him for it.

"Say, ma'am," Elmer said to a middle-aged woman headed in the opposite direction, "there a place near here a sober man can buy himself a expert tattoo?"

"I suppose there must be," she said, "farther along closer to the port."

"Alma Ann blesses you, ma'am," said Elmer, walking on, spitting tobacco juice on the sidewalk.

The woman stared after him and was surprised to see that he was barefoot.

BROTHERS

ELMER'S ROOM WAS TEN FEET BY TEN FEET. There were two windows, both of which were half-boarded over and nailed shut; a sink; a single bed; one cane armchair; a small dresser with a mirror attached; and a writing table with a green-shaded eagle-shaped lamp on it. The one closet was empty because Elmer had no clothes other than the ones he wore. He had been meaning to buy some new pants and shirts, but he kept forgetting. Elmer foreswore shoes; they interfered with the electrical power he absorbed from the earth through his feet. In one corner was a pile about two feet high of canned food, mostly Campbell's Pork and Beans and Denison's Chili. On the dresser were two half-gallon plastic containers of spring water and a Swiss Army knife that contained all of the necessary eating utensils plus a can opener. There was no garbage in the room, no empty cans or bottles. Elmer disliked refuse; as soon as he had finished with something, he got rid of it, depositing it in a container on the street.

Pace slept on the bed. Elmer sat in the cane armchair, twirling his hat on the toes of his left foot and looking at the illustrations in his favorite book, *The Five Chinese Brothers*. His mother, Alma Ann, had read this story to him countless times and Elmer knew every word of it by heart. This was fortunate, because Elmer could not read. He'd tried, both in the two years he'd attended school and with Alma Ann, but for some reason he found it impossible to recognize the letters of the alphabet in combination with each other. Elmer had no difficulty identifying them individually, but set up together the way they were in books and newspapers and on signs and other things confused him. He had taken *The Five Chinese Brothers* with him from the farm and he looked at the pictures in it while reciting the story to himself several times a day. Elmer was anxious to show the book to his friend, but he would wait until he was certain Pace was really his friend. Alma Ann had told Elmer that sharing something, even a book, was the greatest gift one human being could bestow upon another. It was very important, she said, to have complete and utter faith in the sharer, to know that he or she would share in return. Elmer was not yet sure of this friend, since he had never had one other than Alma Ann, though he hoped that he and Pace would become perfect companions.

The five Chinese brothers were identical to one another, and they lived with their mother. They had no father. One brother could swallow the sea; another had an iron neck; another could stretch his legs an unlimited distance; another could not be burned; and another could hold his breath forever. Elmer recited the story softly to himself as he looked at the pictures, twirling his engineer's cap for a few minutes on one foot, then switching it to the other. The Chinese brother who could swallow the sea went fishing one morning with a little boy who had begged to accompany him. The Chinese brother allowed the boy to come along on the condition that he obey the brother's orders promptly. The boy promised to do so. At the shore, the Chinese brother swallowed the sea and gathered some fish while holding the water in his mouth. The boy ran out and picked up as many interesting objects that had been buried under the sea as he could. The Chinese brother signaled for his companion to return but the boy did not pay attention to him, continuing to hunt for treasures. The Chinese brother motioned frantically for him to come back, but his little friend did not respond. Finally the Chinese brother knew he would burst unless he released the sea, so he let it go and the boy disappeared. At this point in the story, Alma Ann had always stopped to tell Elmer that this boy had proven not to be the Chinese brother's perfect friend.

The Chinese brother was arrested and condemned to have his head severed. On the day of the execution he asked the judge if he could be allowed to go home briefly and say goodbye to his mother. The judge said, "It is only fair," and the Chinese brother who could swallow the sea went home. The brother who returned was the brother with an iron neck. All of the people in the town gathered in the square to see the sentence carried out, but when the executioner brought down his sword, it bent, and the Chinese brother's head remained on his shoulders. The crowd became angry and decided that he should be drowned. On the day of his execution the Chinese brother asked the judge if he could go home and bid his mother farewell, which the judge allowed. The brother who returned was the one who was capable of stretching his legs. When he was thrown overboard in the middle of the ocean, he rested his feet on the bottom and kept his head above water. The people again became angry and decided that he should be burned.

On the day of the execution, the Chinese brother asked the judge for permission to go home to say goodbye to his mother. The judge said, "It is only fair." The brother who returned was the one who could not catch on fire. He was tied to a stake and surrounded by stacks of wood that caught fire when lit, but the Chinese brother remained unscathed. The people became so infuriated that they decided he should be smothered to death. On the day of his execution, the Chinese brother requested that he be allowed to go home to see his mother. The judge said, "It is only fair," and of course the brother who returned was the one who could hold his breath indefinitely. He was shoveled into a brick oven filled with whipped cream and the door was locked tight until the next morning. When the door was opened and the Chinese brother emerged unharmed, the judge declared that since they had attempted to execute him four different ways, all to no avail, then he must be innocent, and ordered the Chinese brother released, a decision supported by the people. He then went home to his mother with whom he and his brothers lived happily ever after.

Elmer knew that he and Alma Ann could have lived happily ever after had she not been worked to death by Hershel Burt and Emile, who would have also worked him to death had Elmer not executed them. He hoped with all of his might that this boy Pace would be worthy of his friendship and not be like the boy who accompanied the Chinese brother to the sea. Elmer put down *The Five Chinese Brothers* and looked at Pace. The boy's eyes were open. Elmer stopped twirling his foot.

"You gonna let me go home to my mama?" Pace asked.

Elmer remembered what the judge had said to the Chinese brothers. "It's only fair," he said.

Pace sat up. "Can I go right now?"

"Problem is," said Elmer, "I don't know I can trust you yet."

"Trust me how?"

"To come back."

Pace stared at Elmer's pale blue eyes.

"You're crazy, mister," he said.

"Alma Ann said I weren't, and she knows better'n you."

Pace looked around the room.

"Guess the door's locked, huh?"

Elmer nodded. "I don't guess."

"So I'm a prisoner."

Elmer started twirling his cap on his right foot.

"You'n me is gonna be perfect friends."

"Holy Jesus," said Pace.

Elmer shook his head. "Jesus is bunk."

THE CUBAN EMERALD

"You partial at all to hummin'birds?" asked Elmer.

"What you mean, 'partial'?" said Pace.

Elmer Désespéré sat in the cane chair twirling his engineer's cap on the toes of his city-dirt-blackened right foot.

"Mean, do you like 'em."

Pace rested on his elbows, dangling his legs over the edge of the narrow bed.

"Ain't seen many, but I suppose. They just birds."

Elmer bared his mossy teeth. "One time Alma Ann and me spotted a Cuban Emerald," he said, and shifted the cap to his equally soiled left foot. "Alma Ann had her a bird book said that kinda hummin'bird don't naturally get no further north'n South Florida. But we seen it hoverin' over a red lily at Solange Creek. Alma Ann said it musta been brought up by someone to Louisiana 'cause it was too far for it to've strayed."

"What color was it?"

"Green, mostly, like a emerald, and gold."

"You ever seen a emerald?"

"No, but they's green, I guess, which is why the bird's called that."

"What's Cuban about it?"

Elmer frowned and let the hat fall off his foot.

"This'n's special, Alma Ann said. Ain't no other bird like it over the world."

"My mama and me had us a bird, but it died."

Elmer's eyes opened wide. "What kind?"

"Parakeet. It was blue with a white patch on the head. His name was Pablo."

"How'd he die?"

Pace shrugged. "We just found him one mornin' lyin' on his side on the floor of his cage. I took him out and looked in his mouth."

"Why'd you do that?"

"What the doctor always does to me when I'm sick, so I done it to Pablo."

"See anythin'?"

"Not real much. Pulled out his tongue with my mama's eyebrow tweezer. It was pink."

"You bury him?"

"Uh-uh. Mama wrapped Pablo in a ripped-up dishtowel and put him in the freezer."

"Why'd she do that?"

"We was gonna burn him later, but we forgot. Mama says throwin' a body on a fire's the only way to purify it and set free the soul. The kind of Indians they got in India do it, Mama says. But we just forgot Pablo was in the freezer till a bunch of time later when Mama was cleanin' it out and found the dishtowel all iced up. She run hot water over it and unrolled it and there was Pablo, blue as always."

"What'd she do?"

"Stuffed him down the disposal and ground him up."

Elmer whistled through his green teeth. "Don't guess that done heck for his soul."

Pace lay back on the bed and crossed his arms over his chest.

"I reckon his soul had pretty well froze solid by then," he said.

"If I ever had a Cuban Emerald died on me, I wouldn't burn it, or stuff it in no disposal, neither. I'd eat it."

Pace closed his eyes. "The beak, too? Bird beaks is awful sharp."

"Yes, I believe I would. I'd swallow it beak and all, so my insides'd glow emerald green."

"Don't know how I ever coulda thought you was crazy, Elmer. I apologize."

Elmer nodded. " 'Preciate it."

NIGHT IN THE CITY

"My daddy murdered a man once," Pace said. "I heard my grandmama talkin' about it with her friend Johnnie, who's a private investigator and carries a gun. Mama thinks I don't know Sailor really killed Bob Ray Lemon, but I do. He'll get you, too, soon as he finds out what's happened and where I am, which'll be any minute. Him or Crazy Eyes Santos, Grandmama's other man friend, who's a big gangster and kills people all the time. Won't bother him a bit to twist your puny chicken head clean off the neck. You'd best just let me go and run for it, or you'll be fish scum, you'll see."

Elmer Désespéré was beginning to realize his mistake. He had grabbed an unworthy boy, someone not suited to be his perfect friend, and he was in a fix over what to do about it.

"I done murdered two men," said Elmer, who was sitting in the cane armchair across from where Pace sat on the floor next to the bed. Elmer had tied Pace's hands together behind his back after the boy had attempted to put out Elmer's eyes with the fork part of the Swiss Army knife. "And prob'ly I'll have to murder a mess more before I'm through, includin' you, it looks like."

"Let me go and you won't have to kill me. I won't tell anyone where you live. You don't let me go, they'll find us and kill you sure. Least right now you got a choice."

Elmer stood up. "I got to go out, get some fresh water. I'll figure out later what I'm gonna do, when I talk to Alma Ann. She'll guide my hand."

Elmer took hold of Pace, dragged him into the empty closet and shut the door.

"I wouldn't be surprised she instructs me to twist your puny chicken head," Elmer shouted. "Clean off the neck!"

He went out into the street and headed for the Circle K convenience store. This child was a puzzlement, Elmer thought. He would have to be more careful of who he snatched next. Follow him for a while, maybe, see if he acted right. This one weren't no good at all and likely never would be. Can't trust a pretty face, ain't that the truth!

Elmer had been thinking so hard about Pace that he did not realize he'd turned the wrong way off Claiborne. Somehow he had wandered onto a street called St. Claude and he was lost. It was very late at night and Elmer missed Alma Ann. He wished she were here and he was tucked into bed with her reading to him. He saw some men gathered up ahead at the corner and he walked toward them. Before Elmer had gone halfway, he noticed that three men were walking toward him, so he stopped where he was and waited, figuring if the direction he needed to go in was behind him then he wouldn't need to cover the same ground. The three men, all of whom were black and no older, perhaps even younger, than Elmer, surrounded and stared at him.

"Come you ain't got no shoes on?" asked one.

"Don't make no connection otherwise," said Elmer.

"Feet's black as us," said another of the men.

"You heard of the Jungle lovers?" the third man asked.

Elmer shook his head no.

"We them," said the first man. "And this our street."

"You a farm boy?" asked the second.

Elmer nodded. "From by Mamou," he said. "Road forks close the sign say, 'If It Swim I Got It.'"

"Where that?"

"Evangeline Parish."

The three men, each of whom was wearing at least one gold rope around his neck, began moving around Elmer, circling him, glancing at one another. Elmer stood absolutely still, unsure of what to do.

"You got any money, hog caller?" said one of the men.

"No," said Elmer.

The man behind Elmer pulled out a Buck knife with a six-inch blade, reached his right arm around Elmer and slit his throat completely across, making certain the cut was deep enough to sever the jugular. Elmer dropped to his knees and stuck all four fingers of his left hand into the wound. He sat there, resting back on his heels, blood cascading down the front of his overalls and on the sidewalk, for what seemed to him like a very long time. Elmer looked up into the dark eyes of one of the men and tried to speak. He was asking the man to tell Alma Ann he was sorry to have failed her, but the man did not try to listen. Instead, he took out a small handgun, stuck its snub nose all the way into Elmer's mouth and pulled the trigger.

OUT OF THIS WORLD

GUADALUPE DELPARAISO HAD LIVED at the same address all of her life, which was seven months more than eighty-six years. She had never married, and had outlived each of her sixteen siblings—nine brothers, seven sisters—as well as many of her nephews and nieces, and even several of their children. Guadalupe lived alone in the downstairs portion of the house her father, Nuncio DelParaiso, and his brother, Negruzco, had built on Claiborne Avenue across the street from Our Lady of the Holy Phantoms church in New Orleans. The neighborhood had undergone numerous vicissitudes since Nuncio and Negruzco had settled there. At one time the area had been home to some of the Crescent City's most prominent citizens, but now Our Lady of the Holy Phantoms, where the DelParaiso family had worshiped for forty years, and where Guadalupe and her sisters and brothers had attended school, was closed down, and the street was littered with transient hotels, beer and shot bars, pool halls, and the drunks, junkies and whores who populated and patronized these establishments.

Guadalupe rented the upstairs rooms in her house by the week. She made sure to get the money in advance and kept a chart on the wall in her kitchen listing the dates the rent was due for each room. Guadalupe would rent to singles only, and not to women or blacks under the age of fifty. She had not left the house in four years, depending on her bachelor nephew, Fortunato Rivera, her sister Romana's youngest son, who was now fifty-two years old, to bring her groceries and other supplies twice a week. She paid Fortunato for what he brought her on Wednesdays and Sundays, and gave him a shopping list for the next delivery. Guadalupe had not been sick since the scarlet fever epidemic of 1906. The doctor who attended her at that time told her mother, Blanca, and Nuncio, that Guadalupe's heart had been severely damaged by the fever and that he did not expect her to live beyond thirty. It was Guadalupe's oldest sister, Parsimonia, however, who succumbed to a weak heart at the age of twenty-nine. As the years passed, Guadalupe only became stronger in both body and mind.

Guadalupe was making up her list for Fortunato, who would be coming the next day, Wednesday, when she heard a pounding noise, like the stamping of feet, coming from the room above the kitchen. She had rented the room almost a week before to a soft-spoken, polite but bedraggled-looking young man who, she believed, worked for the railroad. The young man had seen the ROOM FOR RENT sign in the front window and had taken what had once been her brothers Rubio, Martin, and Danilo's room immediately. He paid Guadalupe a month's advance because, he told her, it looked like the kind of a place his mama, Alma Ann, would have been pleased to occupy. Guadalupe had not seen the young man since the day he'd rented it.

This pounding disturbed Guadalupe; she could not concentrate on her grocery list. She went into the pantry, picked up her broom, brought it back with her to the kitchen and bumped the end of the handle several times against the ceiling.

"You stop!" she shouted. "No noise in Nuncio's house or you get out!"

The pounding did not stop, so Guadalupe put down the broom, left her part of the house and walked slowly up the stairs. She stopped at the door to the young railroad worker's room and listened. She could not hear the pounding as distinctly from the hallway as she could in her kitchen, but she heard it and knocked as hard as she could on the door with her left fist.

"You stop! You stop or leave Nuncio and Blanca's house!"

The pounding continued and Guadalupe removed her keychain from the right front pocket of her faded rose-colored chenille robe and unlocked the door. The single overhead sixty-watt bulb was burning, but there was nobody in the room. The noise was coming from the closet, so she opened it. A body hurtled past Guadalupe so fast she did not see who or what it was, and by the time she turned around, it was gone. Guadalupe had been tremendously startled; suddenly she felt faint, and staggered to the cane armchair. She sat down and attempted to calm herself, but she was frightened, thinking that the shadow that had rushed out of the room had been the ghost of her severely disturbed brother Morboso, the one who had hanged himself in that closet. It had been Parsimonia who discovered Morboso swinging there, and it was this incident, Nuncio and Blanca believed, that had damaged Parsimonia's heart and led to her premature death. The ghost of Morboso DelParaiso was loose, Guadalupe thought. Perhaps he had driven away the young railroad man, or even murdered him as he had the pretty young nun, Sister Panacea, whose body Nuncio and Negruzco and Father Vito had secretly buried after midnight on October 21, 1928, in the garden of Our Lady of the Phantoms. Guadalupe rested and remembered, seeing again what she could not prevent herself from seeing.

Pace ran down the stairs and managed to turn the big gold knob on the front door by holding it between the bottom of his chin and his neck. He ran a block down the street before he stopped in front of an old Indian-looking guy who was leaning against the side of a building sipping from a short dog in a brown paper bag.

"Untie me, mister!" Pace shouted at him. "Get my hands loose, please!"

The Indian's eyes were blurry and he seemed confused.

"A crazy man kidnapped me and tied me up!" Pace yelled. "I just ran away! Help me out, willya?"

The Indian held out his half-pint of wine, as if he didn't know what to do with it if he assisted Pace.

"Put your bottle down on the ground and undo this here knot," said Pace, turning around and showing the Indian his hands.

The old guy bent over and carefully deposited his sack on the sidewalk, then straightened up and tugged on Pace's hands until they were freed.

"Thanks a lot, mister," said Pace, tossing away the strip of bedsheet Elmer had used to bind him. He reached down and picked up the Indian's short dog and handed it to him. "Don't know if God loves ya," Pace shouted, "but I do!"

Pace ran along Claiborne until he saw a police car parked at the curb. He went over to the car and stuck his head in the open window on the passenger side.

"Evenin', officer," Pace said to the policeman sitting behind the steering wheel. "I'm Pace Roscoe Ripley, the boy got kidnapped in the park the other day? Are you lookin' for me?"

• • •

THE OVERCOAT

FEDERAL BUREAU OF INVESTIGATION agents Sandy Sandusky and Morton Martin stopped into the Lakeshore Tap, a tavern on Lincoln Avenue about a mile from Wrigley Field. In another hour or so, when the Cubs game ended, the place would be packed; at the moment, the two agents were the only customers. They sat on adjoining stools, ordered drafts of Old Style, and drained half of their beers before Sandusky said, "Is there a field office in North Dakota?"

"Where in North Dakota?" asked Martin.

"Anywhere."

"Why do you ask?"

"Because that's where we're going to be transferred to unless we can nail whoever ordered the hit on Mona Costatroppo, that's why."

Both men took another swig of beer.

"We know it was Santos," Martin said.

"The man hasn't had a rap pinned on him once. Never done time, Morty, never had a speeding ticket."

"If we can locate the shooter, we got a chance."

"He's in the sports book at Caesar's Palace right now, a hooker on each arm, betting trifectas at Santa Anita with the fee."

"So what do we do, Sandy?"

"Buy bigger overcoats."

Sandusky swallowed the last of his draft and climbed down from his stool.

"Order me one more, Morty. I'll call the office."

Sandusky came back five minutes later, a big grin on his ruddy face, and slapped Morton Martin on the back.

"Give us a couple shots of Chivas," Sandusky said to the bartender.

"What's up?" asked Martin. "Santos turn himself in?"

"Not quite, but Detroit picked up the hammer."

"No kiddin'. I thought you told me he was in Vegas juggling bimbos."

"Where I'd be."

The bartender brought two Scotches and Sandusky slapped down a ten.

"Keep the change," he said. "Looks like I won't need a new overcoat, after all."

Sandusky handed a glass to Morton Martin, tapped it with his own, and said, "To Tyrone Hardaway, a.k.a. Master Slick, resident of Chandler Heights, Detroit, Michigan, product of the Detroit public school system, who just couldn't keep his mouth shut or the blood money in his pocket for more than twenty-five minutes."

Sandusky and Martin knocked down the Chivas.

"Apparently, this Hardaway was letting all of his homeboys know what a big man he was, working for the guineas. He was buying gold chains, leather jackets and primo drugs for everyone in the neighborhood while bragging about the fresh job he'd done in Chicago for the famous Mr. Crazy Eyes. Somebody snitched on him, of course, and the Bureau brought him in no more than an hour ago. They say he told them that Santos's people forced him to whack the broad; otherwise, Tyrone said, the organization was going to move him off his turf and let another gang handle the crack trade."

"I know J. Edgar Hoover always said there was no such thing as organized crime in this country, but I'd bet Tyrone is telling the truth."

Sandusky laughed, and motioned to the bartender. After both men had refills, Sandusky held up his glass and admired its amber contents.

"To the truth!" he said.

EVIDENCE

AFTER AN UNUSUALLY LATE SUPPER, Bob Lee excused himself and said he had to go back to the office to take care of the paperwork he'd ignored during the excitement of the last few days, and Beany took Lance and Madonna Kim upstairs to put them to bed, leaving Lula, Pace, and Sailor at the dining-room table. Lula had told Beany not to worry about the dirty dishes, she'd heated up more of the Community coffee Sailor had taken such a liking to, and poured them each another cup. During the time Lula had gone into the kitchen for the coffee and come back, Pace had put his head down on the table and dozed off. Lula sat next to Sailor and together they watched their son sleep.

"Well, peanut, I'd like to believe we got us a fightin' chance."

"You'd best believe it, Sail. Look at that little boy breathin' there. If he ain't worth the effort won't never nothin' will be. Pace and us both just come through the worst scare we've ever had, and I guess to hell we've had a few in our short lives. It's one thing your gettin' yourself in deep shit with bad actors like Bob Ray Lemon in North Carolina and Bobby Peru in Texas, but now you got a fast-growin' son needs you. Reverend Willie Thursday back home in Bay St. Clement says a boy without a father's a lost soul sailin' on a ghost ship through the sea of life."

"It ain't my intention to let you and Pace down, and I won't be playin' no chump's game again, neither. Speakin' of the past, though, I seen Perdita Durango."

"Here in New Orleans?"

Sailor nodded. "Didn't figure on tellin' you this, but someone took a potshot at me in the shoppin' center by the Gator Gone office the other day. I'm pretty sure it was Perdita. I made Bob Lee swear he wouldn't say nothin' about it."

"But, Sail, why would she want to shoot you?"

"Maybe she thinks I'm out to get her for runnin' out on me and Peru. I'm the only one could I.D. her for the caper. I also spotted her on the street last week when I was leavin' Hattiesburg. She was with the same blue BMW squealed away from the shootin' in the shoppin' center."

"Sweet Jesus, honey. What're we gonna do about this?"

"Don't panic, peanut. I'll just have to keep the eyes in the back of my head open. Prob'ly Perdita was aimin' to warn, not kill, makin' sure I knew it was her had the drop on me. I wouldn't say nothin' to the cops, anyway."

"Sail, this unpredictable scary behavior don't almost improve my peace of mind."

"I know it, but you're my baby Lula, and at least we're in it together again. You, me, and Pace, that is. Reverend Willie Thursday won't be preachin' no ghost ship sermon concernin' our son."

Lula leaned over and kissed Sailor below his left ear.

"I love you, Sailor Ripley. I always figured we'd find our way."

Sailor grinned and put his left arm around Lula, pulling her closer to him.

"Peanut, it was just inevitable."

from SULTANS OF AFRICA (1991)

SULTANS OF AFRICA

"THE BEST THING you can hope for in this life is that the rest of the world'll forget all about ya."

Coot Veal shifted his shotgun from right to left and checked the fake Rolex on his right wrist. Buford Dufour had bought the watch for forty bucks in Bangkok when he was in the air force and sold it later to Coot for fifty.

"Half past four," he said. " 'Bout time to give it up, I'd say."

Pace Ripley pulled a brown leather-coated flask from the left hip pocket of his army surplus field jacket, unscrewed and flipped open the top and took a swift swig of Black Bush that he'd filched from his daddy's bottle.

"Want 'ny?" he asked Coot, holding out the flask.

"Naw. I'll get mine shortly."

Pace recapped the flask and put it back in his pocket.

"What you mean, Coot, hopin' you get forgot?"

Coot Veal, who was fifty-eight years old and had never been farther away from South Louisiana than Houston, Texas, to the west; Mobile, Alabama, to the east; and Monroe, Louisiana, to the north; who never had married or lived with a woman other than his mother, Culebra Suazo Veal, who had died when Coot was forty-nine; grinned at the fifteen-year-old boy, his friend Sailor Ripley's son, and then laughed.

"Mean it's not in a man's interest to let anyone interfere with or interrupt what's there for him to do."

Coot pulled out a pistol from his hip holster and held it up.

"This here's a single-shot Thompson Contender loaded with .223

rounds. Not the biggest gun in the world, not the best, either, but it suits me. Read about a Seminole brought down a panther with one in the Everglades."

Coot replaced the pistol in its holster.

"Zanzibar slavers over a century ago called the gun the Sultan of Africa. The world's still ruled by weapons, Pace. They're what separates the operators from the pretenders."

Pace looked out over the marsh. He and Coot hadn't had a fair crack at a duck all day. Water had somehow leaked into his high rubber boots and soaked his woollen socks.

"Okay, Coot," he said, "let's hit it. Gettin' skunked like this is insultin'."

THE MIDDLE YEARS

"THAT YOU, Sail?" Lula shouted.

Sailor Ripley let the screen door slam shut behind him.

"No," he said. "It's Manuel Noriega."

Lula came into the front room from the kitchen and saw Sailor slump down into the oversized, foam-filled purple chair that Beany and Bob Lee Boyle had given them last Christmas.

"Who'd you say? Barry Manilow?"

"No. Manuel Noriega, the deposed president of Panama."

"Uh-uh, you ain't him. You got too good a complexion."

Lula went over and kissed Sailor on the top of his head.

"Long day, huh, Sail?"

"You know it, peanut. Gator Gone's goin' great guns since the envir'mentalists got that new reptile protection law passed. Ever' fisherman in the state of Louisiana needs it now. You up to fetchin' me a cold Dixie?"

"*No hay problema, esposo,*" Lula said, heading toward the kitchen. "Bet even Bob Lee never figured his gator repellent'd go this good."

"Yep. That one ol' formula 'bout to make him a rich man. He's talkin' about settin' up a Gator Gone Foundation that'll make funds available to poor folks been victims of gator and croc attacks who're in need of ongoin' medical treatment."

Lula returned with the beer and handed it to Sailor, who drank half of it right away.

"Thanks, honey," he said. "Sure build up a thirst overseein' that shippin' department. You know we're gonna build us our own warehouse in Gretna?"

Lula sat down on the zebra-striped hideaway.

"First I heard. Beany ain't said nothin' about it."

"Yeah, the Algiers location can't hold us, and besides, makes more sense to own than rent."

"Best thing we coulda done is settle here, Sail. New Orleans give us a whole bunch more opportunity than we ever coulda got back in North Carolina."

Sailor took another swig of Dixie.

"Not the least of which is bein' a thousand miles away from your mama. We never woulda had a chance in Bay St. Clement, peanut. Not with Marietta on my case."

"She's calmed down now, darlin', since she seen how swell a daddy you been to Pace. Also your workin' so hard for Bob Lee and everythin'."

"Wouldn'ta made it this far is all I know."

The telephone on the front hall table rang. Lula got up and answered it.

"Ripley home. Hi, Beany. Uh huh, Sail too. God don't make men the way He used to, like Mama says. Madonna Kim got over her cold yet? Uh huh. Suppose I might could. Lemme ask God's almost-best piece of work."

Lula tucked the receiver into her breast and turned toward Sailor.

"Honey? Beany'd like me to 'comp'ny her to Raquel Lou Dinkins's house for about a hour? See her brand new baby, Farrah Sue. You-all be able to survive without me that long?"

Sailor tipped the bottle and drained the last bit of beer, then nodded.

"Hell, yes. Me'n Pace'll get us a pizza or somethin'. Where is that boy, anyway?"

"Went huntin' this mornin' with Coot Veal, your buddy married his mama."

Lula put the phone back to her mouth and left ear.

"Want me to drive?" she asked Beany. "Uh huh. See ya in a minute."

Lula hung up, picked up her purse and car keys from the table, went over to Sailor and kissed him again on the top of his head.

"Sweetheart, you know what?" she said.

"What's that?"

"You losin' some hair right about there."

"Where?"

"Kinda in the middle toward the back."

Sailor felt around on his head with the fingers of his right hand.

"I can't feel nothin' missin', Lula. Anyway, it can't be. Nobody in my fam'ly went bald. Not my daddy or his daddy or my mama's daddy."

"None of 'em lived long enough to go bald, darlin'. Don't worry about it, just a small patch is all. I gotta go."

Sailor jumped up and dropped the beer bottle on the floor.

"Goddammit, Lula! You just gonna run out and leave me after tellin' me I'm goin' bald?"

"Bye! Back soon!"

Sailor watched Lula go out the front door, heard her open and close the door of her new Toyota Cressida station wagon and start the engine. He went over to the hall mirror and leaned his head forward while attempting to look up into the glass, but he couldn't see the top of his head. He turned sideways, tilted his head toward the mirror and rolled his eyes all the way over, but that didn't work, either. The front door slammed and Pace came in.

"What you doin', Daddy?" he said. "And where's Mama goin'? What're you all twisted around for?"

Sailor bent forward toward the mirror again, angling off slightly to the right.

"Take a look, son. Am I losin' my hair?"

Pace stared at Sailor, then shook his head slowly.

"More likely you're losin' your mind, Daddy. We gettin' a pizza for supper?"

RATTLERS

THE RATTLER BROTHERS, Smokey Joe and Lefty Grove, nonidentical sixteen year old twins who were named by their daddy, Tyrus Raymond Rattler, after the two men his daddy, Pie Traynor Rattler, considered to have been the two best pitchers in major league history, tooled through Gulfport along Old Pass Christian Road in their Jimmy, trading swigs off a fifth of J. W. Dant. They were headed back to New Orleans from Biloxi, where they had gone to pay their respects to the memory of Jefferson Davis on his birthday. Smokey Joe and Lefty Grove had taken advantage of the school holiday to visit Beauvoir, the last home of the Confederate president. The federal holiday officially honored the birth of the Reverend Martin Luther King, Jr., who happened to have been born on the same day as Jeff Davis, a convenience appreciated by the Rattlers.

Their mother, Mary Full-of-Grace, had been institutionalized for the past six years in Miss Napoleon's Paradise for the Lord's Disturbed Daughters in Oktibbeha County, Mississippi, and the Rattler boys had considered visiting her but decided the drive was too far for the short time they had. Besides, Lefty Grove reasoned, she wouldn't recognize them for who they were. The last time they'd gone up with their daddy, six months before, she'd called them the apostles James and John, sons of Zebedee. Sometime during the twins' seventh year, Mary-Full-of-Grace became convinced that she was in fact the Holy Virgin, mother of Jesus. She'd insisted that the people about her were not who they pretended to be and that every man she encountered desired to sleep with her. Tyrus Raymond took her to several doctors during the following two years, but her condition worsened, resulting finally in the diagnosis of a breakdown of a schizoid personality, with the recommendation that she be institutionalized as a hopeless case.

"What you think about Mama?" Lefty Grove asked Smokey Joe, who was behind the wheel.

"What you mean, what I think?" said Smokey Joe, reaching out his right hand for the bottle.

"Mean, you got a notion she ever gonna recover her mind?"

"Ain't 'xactly likely, how Daddy claims."

Smokey Joe took a quick swallow of Dant and handed the fifth back to his brother.

"You finish it, Lef'. I be dam see the road."

"Want me to drive? I feel good."

"Feelin' good and drivin' good ain't the same. I'll handle her home."

Lefty Grove put his red and yellow L.A. Gear high tops up on the dashboard and sucked on the bottle.

" 'Bout Ripley?" said Smokey Joe. "Figure to trust him?"

"You mean on the deal, or just keep his mouth shut?"

"Either."

"Need a third, Smoke, you know? Pace a good boy."

"Mama's boy, you mean."

"Least he got him a almost sane one."

Smokey Joe snorted. "What you mean, almost sane?"

"Like Daddy said when he come home after deliverin' Mama to Miss Napoleon's, 'Ain't one of the Lord's daughters got a firm grip on life.' He put a extra pint of fear in their blood, makes 'em more uneasy than men."

"Daddy ain't naturally wrong."

"Uh-uh," said Lefty Grove. "He's a Rattler, by God."

AFTER HOURS

SAILOR FLOPPED DOWN into the Niagara, levered the footrest chest high, fingered the space command and flipped on the new RCA 24-inch he'd bought at Shongaloo's Entertainment Center right after his recent raise from Gator Gone. He dotted the i across cable country until it hit channel 62, when the sound of CCR's "Bad Moon Risin'" stopped him. It was past one o'clock in the morning. Pace was asleep upstairs and Lula was at Beany's, baking cakes for the Church of Reason, Redemption and Resistance to God's Detractors fundraiser. Sailor ticked the volume up a couple of notches. Suddenly the music faded out and a man's face in close-up came on the screen. The man was about forty years old, he had blond, crew-cut hair, a big nose that looked like it had been sloppily puttied on, and a dark brown goatee.

"Howdy, folks!" said the man, his duckegg-blue eyes blazing out of the set like laser beams. "I'm Sparky!"

The camera pulled back to reveal Sparky standing in front of an old-fashioned drugstore display case. Behind the counter and just to the side of Sparky's left shoulder was another man of the same approximate age but four inches taller. This man had thick, bushy black hair with a severe widow's peak and a discernibly penciled-in mustache under a long, sharply pointed nose.

"This asparagus-shaped fella behind me's my partner, Buddy," Sparky said, and Buddy nodded. "We'd like to welcome you-all to Sparky and Buddy's House of Santería, the store that has everything can make that special ceremony just right."

The words SPARKY & BUDDY'S HOUSE OF SANTERIA 1617 EARL LONG CAUSEWAY WAGGAMAN, LOUISIANA flashed on the screen in giant red letters superimposed over the two men. The letters stopped flashing and Sailor sat up and took a closer look. Blood root suspended from the ceiling and dozens of jars filled with herbs, votive candles in a variety of colors, and various unidentifiable objects lined the rows of shelves behind Sparky and Buddy. Sparky raised his arms like Richard Nixon used to, the fingers of each hand formed in a V.

"We've got the needs for the deeds, ladies and gentlemen. We've got the voodoo for you! Oh, yes! We've got the voodoo, hoodoo, Bonpo tonic, Druid fluid, Satan-ratin', Rosicrucian solution, Upper Nile stylin', Lower Nile bile'n Amon-Ra hexes, Tao of all sexes, White Goddess juice'll kick Kundalini loose, the Chung-Wa potion'n ev'ry santería notion!"

Sparky lowered his arms, walked forward past the camera eye, then returned carrying two twisting snakes in each hand.

"Get a load of the size of these rattles, Pentecostals!" he shouted, raising his right arm, the one draped with a pair of diamondbacks. "And ladies, check out these elegant coachwhips!" Sparky raised his left arm to show them off. "Hey, Buddy! Tell the good folks what else we got!"

Sparky walked off-camera again and Buddy leaned forward over the counter, pointing to the floor with his right hand.

"Take a good look here, people," he said, and the camera eye dipped down, closing in on a one-hundred-ten-pound brindled pit bull stretched out on the floor, his head resting between his front paws, a seeing-eye harness strapped to his barrel chest. Next to his enormous head was a black water bowl with the name ELVIS stenciled on it in raised white letters. "We got a good selection of man's best friends, too."

Sparky's legs came back into view and the camera panned back up.

"Mullahs, mullahs, mullahs!" Sparky intoned. "You got trouble with the Christian Militia? Come on down! And hey, troops! Them mullahs makin' you a cardiac case? Those Ayatollah rollers got you grittin' your bicuspids? You-all come on down, too! We are a hundred and five percent bona fide non-sectarian here at Sparky and Buddy's!"

Again the giant red letters spelling out SPARKY & BUDDY'S HOUSE OF SANTERIA 1617 EARL LONG CAUSEWAY WAGGAMAN, LOUISIANA flashed on the screen.

"Right, Buddy?" Sparky said, and the flashing letters blinked off.

"Affirmative, Sparky!"

"And, Buddy, we got a special I ain't even told my mama about! This week only we discountin' mojos. Mojos for luck, love, recedin' hairlines, bald spots, money honey and—my own favorite, works like a charm—irregularity. This one's guaranteed to get you goin' and flowin'!"

Sailor watched as from behind the counter Buddy lifted up two wine glasses filled to the brim with amber liquid. He handed one to Sparky and together they raised the glasses high.

"Well, Buddy, as our old pal Manuel used to say in Tampa many years ago, *salud* and happy days! This is the four-hundred-sixty-sixth appearance we've made for Sparky and Buddy's House of Santería. Remember, we're at 1617 Earl Long Causeway, in the community of Waggaman, servicin' all of south Louisiana. Y'all come on down!"

"Bad Moon Risin' " started up again and the giant red letters reappeared for several seconds before the station segued into the video of L.L. Cool J's "Big Ole Butt." Sailor pressed the OFF button on his space command. He sat still for a minute, then lifted his left arm and with his fingers explored the crown area of his head where Lula had told him his hair was thinning. He got up and went over to the hall table, picked up the pencil and pad next to the telephone and wrote down Sparky and Buddy's address.

BACK TO BUDDHALAND

SMOKEY JOE PULLED the Jimmy up to the premium pump at the self-serve Conoco in Meridian and cut the engine.

"Be right back," he said to Lefty Grove, as he got out and headed for the pay-in-advance window.

As he approached the pay window, Smokey Joe could see that there was a problem. A medium-sized black man in his thirties, with long, slanted, razor-shaped sideburns, wearing a camel hair sportcoat, was arguing with the Vietnamese kid behind the bulletproof pane.

"Pay for cigarettes!" said the Vietnamese kid, nodding his head quickly, causing his lank, black forelock of hair to flop forward almost to the tip of his nose.

"I paid you for 'em, motherfucker!" the black man shouted. "You already got my money!"

"No, no! Pay now! You pay for cigarettes!"

Standing off to one side, about eight feet from the man, was a young black woman wearing a beige skirt that ended mid-thigh of her extraordinarily skinny legs, and a short brown jacket that she held tightly around her shivering body despite the intense heat.

"Pay him or let's go!" she shouted. "I ain't wastin' street time on no cigarettes!"

"Keep the damn cigarettes, then, chump monkey!" the man yelled at the kid, throwing a pack of Winstons at the window. The pack bounced off and fell on the ground. "And go back to Buddhaland! Leave America to us Americans!"

The man turned away from the window and saw Smokey Joe approaching.

"Hey, man," he said, "you familiar with this area?"

"Why?" asked Smokey Joe.

"My wife and me got a problem with our car, see, and we need—"

"Sorry," Smokey Joe said, "I don't have any money to give away today."

"No, man, I don't want no money. All we need is a ride. We got to get our car towed."

"Call a tow truck."

"That's the problem, see, we don't know our way around here and we got to get the car fixed."

There was a large sign next to the garage door in the station that said MECHANIC ON DUTY 24 HOURS. Smokey Joe pointed to it.

"There's a mechanic right here," he told the man.

"Wouldn't let no chump monkey from Buddhaland touch it!"

"Come on!" shouted the woman, her thin naked knees shaking. "Turn loose, Chester. It ain't happenin'!"

Smokey Joe saw the man's eyebrows twitch and his face contort, twisting up on the left side, his nostrils flaring. The man hesitated for a moment and Smokey Joe braced himself, thinking that the man might attack him. But the man turned his back to Smokey Joe and followed the woman into the coffee shop of a motel next door.

"Ten bucks premium," Smokey Joe said to the kid, sliding a bill on the metal plate beneath the window.

As Smokey Joe pumped the gas, a well-dressed, overweight, middle-aged black woman, who had just finished fueling her late-model Toyota sedan, said, "Shouldn't be treatin' nobody like that. Ain't no way to be treatin' people here. This ain't no Asia."

She got into her car and drove away. One of the Vietnamese attendants, dressed in a clean, crisp blue uniform, walked out of the garage and over to Smokey Joe.

"This is bad neighborhood," he said, shaking his head. He took the fuel hose from Smokey Joe, who had drained his ten dollars' worth, and replaced it on the pump.

Smokey Joe slid behind the steering wheel of the Jimmy and started it up.

"You hear any of that?" he asked Lefty Grove.

Lefty Grove nodded and said, "Even gettin' gas nowadays reminds me of what Ray L. Menninger, the veterinarian-taxidermist, who Daddy said was the most honest man in Iguana County, Texas, used to say: 'With me, one way or the other, you get your dog back.' "

• • •

THE PARADISE

NELL BLAINE NAPOLEON had moved into The Paradise eighty-two years ago, when she was four and a half years old. Her father, Colonel St. Jude Napoleon, a career army man, and her mother, Fanny Rose Bravo, had designed and had the twenty-six-room Paradise house built for them, and they had both lived and died there. Nell was their only child. By the age of twelve, Nell had decided to devote her life to the well-being of others. She was initially and forever inspired by a local black woman called Sister Domino, who spent each day administering to the sick and needy. Sister Domino allowed the young Nell to accompany her on her rounds of mercy, and taught her basic nursing skills, which Sister Domino had acquired at the Louise French Academy in Baltimore, where she had lived for eighteen years before returning to her Mississippi birthplace. Sister Domino's ambition had been to assist Dr Albert Schweitzer at Lambarene, in Africa, and she read everything she could about him and his work, constantly telling Nell what a great man Schweitzer was and how there could be no higher aspiration in life than to work to alleviate the suffering of those persons less fortunate than themselves. The "Veritable Myriad" Sister Domino called the world's population.

Nell's parents never attempted to dissuade their daughter from her passion, or to turn her away from Sister Domino. Both St. Jude Napoleon and Fanny Rose Bravo were great believers in self-determination, and if this was the path Nell chose to follow, it was her business and no one else's. Their feeling was that there were certainly worse directions a life could take, and they let her be. The only time Nell had unwillingly had to separate herself from Sister Domino was the period during which she was required by her parents to attend Madame Petunia's School for Young Women in Oriole, between the ages of fourteen and seventeen. During her holidays, however, Nell would be back at Sister Domino's side, going from home to home among the poorest residents of Oktibbhea, Lowndes, Choctaw, Webster, Clay, Chickasaw, and Monroe counties. Following graduation from Madame Petunia's, Nell never wavered, dedicating herself fully to Sister Domino's work, which became her vocation also.

After her parents were killed by a falling tree that had been struck by a double bolt of ground lightning during a late-August electrical storm, Nell, who was then twenty-four, inherited The Paradise and invited Sister Domino to live there with her, which offer Sister Domino accepted. Eventually, Sister Domino and Miss Napoleon, as Nell came to be called, succeeded in converting the house into a combination hospital and retreat for those individuals incapable of dealing on a mutually acceptable basis with the outside world. Sister Domino's mandate, however, held that those residents of The Paradise be *serious* Christians. No blasphemy was tolerated and no waffling of faith. This policy, though, extended only to The Paradise; those persons she and Nell treated outside the house were not required to adhere to Christian tenets, the Lord's beneficence being available to the Veritable Myriad.

Sister Domino never did get to the Congo to assist Dr. Schweitzer, though Nell offered to pay her way. There was always too much work to be done at home, Sister Domino said, and when news of Dr. Schweitzer's death reached her, Sister Domino merely knelt, recited a brief, silent prayer, arose and continued scraping the back of a woman whose skin was inflamed and encrusted by eczema. Sister Domino died three years later, leaving Nell to carry on alone. As the years passed, however, Nell limited her ministrations to women, preferring their company to that of men, whom, Nell concluded, tended toward selfishness in their philosophy, which displeased her. Once made, Nell's decision was irreversible, and her devotion was further refined by her increasing acceptance of nonviolent, mentally disturbed women. A decade after Sister Domino's death, Nell officially registered her home with the county as Miss

Napoleon's Paradise for the Lord's Disturbed Daughters. A large oil portrait of Sister Domino, painted from memory by Nell, hung on the wall opposite the front door so that the first sight anyone had upon entering was that of Miss Napoleon's own patron saint.

Mary Full-of-Grace Crowley Rattler fit in perfectly at The Paradise. As the mother of Jesus Christ, it was simply a matter of being acknowledged as such that contented her. At no time during her stay had Mary Full-of-Grace caused Miss Napoleon the slightest difficulty, not even when another woman, Boadicea Booker, who also believed she was the mother of the Christ child, lived at The Paradise. Boadicea had died within three months of her coming, so it was possible, Miss Napoleon believed, that Mary Full-of-Grace had no knowledge of her existence. When Tyrus Raymond Rattler and his sons came to visit Mary Full-of-Grace, Miss Napoleon was pleased to welcome them, as they were unfailingly polite and well-behaved. Even when Lefty Grove and Smokey Joe were small children, Miss Napoleon noticed, they had minded their father precisely and comported themselves properly in the presence of their mother. Therefore, when Mary Full-of-Grace's sons and another boy appeared on the front porch of The Paradise one windy afternoon, Miss Napoleon welcomed them inside.

"Afternoon, L.G.," she said. "Afternoon, S.J. Your mother will be pleased to see you. And who is this young gentleman?"

"Hello, Miss Napoleon," said Lefty Grove. "This is our friend, Pace Ripley."

Pace set down the sack he'd been carrying and nodded to the old woman, who was barely more than four feet tall. Pace figured her weight at about seventy-five pounds. His daddy could lift her off the ground with one hand, he figured, dangle her by her ankles with his arm stretched straight out.

"Hello, ma'am," Pace said. "Beautiful place you got here."

"My parents, Colonel St. Jude and Fanny Rose Bravo, built it and left it in my care so that I might care for others. You boys can go right up, if you like. Mary Full-of-Grace is in her room. She never leaves it until dark."

"Thank you, Miss Napoleon," said Smokey Joe. "We 'preciate all you done for Mama."

"The Lord prevails and I provide," said Miss Napoleon, as the Rattler brothers, followed by Pace, who carried the sack, filed up the stairs.

Mary Full-of-Grace was sitting perfectly still in a high-backed wing chair next to the windows when the boys entered her room. Her long, silver-blue hair hung in two braids, one on either side of her V-shaped head. She wore a white, gauzy robe with a golden sash tied at the waist. Pace noticed that she had almost no nose, only two air holes, and hugely dilated brown eyes. She kept her long, thin hands folded in her lap. Her fingers looked to Pace as if they were made of tissue paper.

"Hello, Mama," said Lefty Grove, who kissed her forehead.

"Hello, Mama," said Smokey Joe, who followed suit.

The brief, soft touch of their lips left dark marks on her skin.

"This boy here's our associate, Pace Ripley," Lefty Grove said.

"Hello, Mrs. Rattler," said Pace, trying to smile.

Both brothers looked quickly and hard at Pace.

"This here's the mother of Baby Jesus," said Smokey Joe.

Mary Full-of-Grace stared out the window to her left.

"My son is soon in Galilee," she said. "I keep the vigil."

Smokey Joe motioned to Pace and Pace slid the sack containing most of the money from the robbery under the light maple four-poster bed.

"Well, Mama, we don't mean to disturb you none," said Lefty Grove. "We'll just come back by and by."

Smokey Joe headed out the door and Pace followed.

"By and by," said Mary Full-of-Grace. "He will be by, by and by." She continued to stare out the window.

"So long, Mama," said Lefty Grove, closing the door behind him.

They did not see Miss Napoleon on their way out but Pace spotted the portrait of Sister Domino.

"Who's that?" he asked, walking over to take a closer look. "And what does this mean?" he said, reading the words carved into the bottom of the frame. "God's Gift to the Veritable Myriad."

"Must be was Miss Napoleon's mammy," said Smokey Joe. "What the hell you think?"

Pace trailed the Rattlers out of The Paradise, wondering about those words carved into the frame. A hunchbacked old woman was coming carefully up the steps of the porch, holding a large, blue plastic fly swatter.

"Suck cock!" she spat at them. "Suck cock! Suck cock! Suck cock!"

RIOT AT ROCK HILL

"YOU WON'T REGRET GOIN', Bunny. Reverend Plenty puts on a show and a half."

"I'm lookin' forward to it, Lula. Been needin' to get away from the laundromat anyway. More'n even a two-armed woman can handle there."

Lula and Bunny Thorn were riding in Lula's rented T-bird from Charlotte to Rock Hill to witness Reverend Goodin Plenty's first-ever sermon in South Carolina. His Church of Reason, Redemption and Resistance to God's Detractors had been running ads in every newspaper within two-hundred-fifty miles of Rock Hill for a month.

"How's your sex life, Lula? You don't mind my askin'."

Lula laughed, looked quickly at Bunny, then back at the road.

"Well, okay, I guess," she said, and with her right hand shook a More from an opened pack on the seat next to her, stuck it between her lips and punched in the dashboard lighter. "How's yours?"

"Lousy, you don't mind my complainin'. Guys'll do it once with a one-armed woman, just for a kick, 'cause it's kinda unusual, you know. That's it, though. They don't come lookin' for seconds. I been wed to a rubberized dick for a year now. Least it don't quit till my arm give out. I'm considerin' joinin' some women's group just to meet some queer gals. Maybe they won't mind a two-hundred-twenty-pound washerwoman with one musclebound arm. And I almost lost it, too, tryin' to unjam a Speed Queen the other day."

The lighter popped out and Lula lit her cigarette, took a couple of powerful puffs and laughed again.

"Bunny, you're somethin' fresh, I tell you. Sailor'd love you to death."

"Yeah? Think I oughta come visit, stay at your house? Maybe get Sailor to give me a workout or two?"

Lula coughed hard and tossed the More out the window.

"Just jokin', hon'. Tried to get Beany to ask Bob Lee if he'd do it, but she didn't go for the idea. And she's my cousin! Guess I'll have to stick with Big Bill."

The parking lot at the Rock Hill church site was full by the time Lula and Bunny arrived, so Lula parked the T-bird across the road. Since groundbreaking for the church building had not yet commenced, a giant tent had been set up and filled with folding chairs. Lula and Bunny managed to find two together at the rear. The tent was filled to capacity by the time Reverend Goodin Plenty, dressed in a tan Palm Beach suit with a black handkerchief flared out of the breast pocket, walked in and strode down the center aisle, hopped up on the platform, grabbed a microphone and faced the audience.

"My goodness!" Goodin Plenty said as he smiled broadly and sized up the crowd. "Ain't this just somethin' spectacular! My, my! Not a empty seat in the Lord's house tonight. Ain't it grand to be alive and holdin' His hand!"

"Yes, sir, Reverend!" someone shouted.

"Tell us about it, Reverend!" said another.

Reverend Plenty smoothed back his full head of prematurely white hair with both hands, making the microphone squeal, then raised up his arms as if he were a football referee signaling that a touchdown had been scored.

"I am gonna give you somethin' tonight, people! The Church of Reason, Redemption and Resistance to God's Detractors is here in the great state of South Carolina, first to secede from the Union, to stay!"

"Maybe so," shouted a tall, skinny, bald-headed man wearing a blue-white Hawaiian shirt with red and yellow flowers on it, who jumped up from the front row, "but you ain't!"

The skinny man held out a Ruger Redhawk .44 revolver with a seven-and one-half-inch scoped barrel and pointed it straight at the Reverend's chest.

"This is for Marie!" the man yelled, as he held the gun with both hands and pulled the trigger, releasing a hardball round directly into Goodin Plenty's left temple as he attempted to dodge the bullet. The shell exploded inside the Reverend's brain and tore away half of the right side of his head as it passed through.

A riot broke out and Lula and Bunny got down on their knees and crawled out of the tent through a side flap. As soon as they were outside, they stood up and ran for the car.

"Holy shit!" said Bunny, as Lula cranked the engine and sped away. "That was better than the Hagler-Hearns fight! Only thing, it didn't last as long."

Lula put the pedal down and drove as fast as she dared.

"Uh-uh-uh," Bunny uttered. "That Marie must be some serious piece of ass!"

SHAKE, RATTLE & ROLL

WENDELL SHAKE WATCHED the Jimmy's oversized tires crawl through the mud ruts toward his farmhouse. He lifted the 30-06 semi-automatic rifle to his right shoulder and sighted down the four-power Tasco scope. At his feet, propped on end under the window, was a loaded eleven-and-three-quarter inch, forty-pound draw Ninja pistol crossbow with a die cast aluminum body and contoured grips. Wendell had come home to Mississippi and the Shake family farm two months before, after the fifth severed head had been found in a garbage can in the Bronx. That was the last of them, Wendell decided, one for each borough of New York City, to show the Jews, Catholics, and coloreds what he thought of their so-called civilization. Armageddon was about to commence, Wendell believed, and he was an operative of the avant-garde. It was his Great Day in the Morning, as he liked to call it, at last, after forty-eight years of silent suffering, witnessing the slaughter of the innocents. Now, however, the rest of the avenging angels were poised to strike, and the message Wendell had delivered was being read and discussed. Perhaps, Wendell thought, as he watched the Rattler brothers and Pace disembark from their vehicle, he was about to receive an acknowledgment of his effort.

"This place been abandoned for years," Lefty Grove said to Pace, as the three boys walked up the path to the house. "Daddy and us used it lots of times when we come up to visit Mama. Been about three, four months since we been here, I guess. Right, Smoke?"

" 'Bout that, Lef. You remember this gate bein' wired shut like this?"

Smokey Joe placed his left hand on the post and vaulted himself up in the air.

Before Smokey Joe had cleared the top rail, a bullet smacked into the center of his forehead, knocking him backward, so that his legs looped over the front of the rail by the backs of his knees, leaving the upper half of his body dangling upside down on the opposite side.

Lefty Grove and Pace both hit the ground and covered their heads. They heard the screen door of the house open and slam shut, footsteps coming down the porch steps and then on the path toward them. Neither of the boys dared to move. The footsteps stopped at the gate.

"Charity, gentlemen," said Wendell Shake, "ain't got nothin' to do with mercy. Even in a foreign land."

Lefty Grove raised his head and saw a middle-aged man about six feet tall and two-hundred pounds, wearing a red and gray flannel shirt, red suspenders, black pants and low-cut, steel-toed, brown work shoes. His hair was almost completely gray, with dark patches at the front, worn very long, touching his shoulders. It was difficult to see the man's face because of his heavy red beard and the way his head was pressed down close to the rifle. The man's eye sockets seemed devoid of white.

"Suppose you say somethin'," Wendell said to Lefty Grove, "and they ain't the right words?"

Wendell rested the rifle barrel on Smokey Joe's right knee, keeping the business end directed at Lefty Grove's head.

"Could be there'd be repercussions."

Pace looked up and saw Wendell standing at the gate. A light rain was falling.

"Both you boys stand up," Wendell ordered, and they obeyed.

Wendell flipped Smokey Joe's legs up with the barrel, causing the corpse's head to hit the ground before the rest of it pretzeled over. Lefty Grove and Pace got to their feet.

"Come in, gentlemen," said Wendell, unfastening and opening the gate to admit them.

Wendell marched the boys up the steps into the house, where he motioned with the gun to a wooden bench against a wall of the front room.

"Sit yourselves down there, gentlemen, and tell me what's brought you this far."

Pace sat down and Lefty Grove remained standing.

"Look, mister," said Lefty Grove, and Wendell shot him through the heart.

The last Rattler brother collapsed on the floor next to Pace's feet, made one slight lurch after he was down, then lay perfectly still. Pace closed his eyes.

"Didn't exactly sit, did he?" said Wendell, looking down at Lefty Grove's body, then up at Pace. "That's a rhetorical question, son. You needn't answer. Open your eyes."

Pace looked at the man. Wendell Shake had mud puddles where his eyes ought to have been, and he was grinning, exposing gums that matched his suspenders and a dozen crowded, yellow teeth.

"We'll wait together, son," Wendell said. "There are terrible things soon to be revealed, and man craves company. That's but one flaw in the design. Do you love the Lord, boy?"

Pace said nothing.

"Please answer."

"I do, sir," said Pace. "I surely do love the Lord."

"Then the Lord loves you."

Wendell pulled up a goose-neck rocker and sat down, resting his 30-06 across his knees. He began to sing.

"I'm goin' to take a trip in that old gospel ship, I'm goin' far beyond the sky. I'm gonna shout and sing, till the heavens ring, when I kiss this world goodbye."

Pace saw the pistol crossbow lying on the floor beneath a window on the other side of the room.

PURE MISERY

"YOU DON'T HAVE TO BE AFRAID to talk to me, boy," Wendell Shake said to Pace. "Got somethin' to say, say it."

"I ain't," said Pace.

"This world's an awful cruel place, son. Worst place I ever been."

"You remind me of a person I met once, named Elmer Désespéré," said Pace, "hailed from Mamou. He weren't so crazy for it, neither."

"There's a few of us is sensitive to more'n the weather. Where's this Elmer now?"

"He was killed on the street in New Orleans."

"Mighta guessed. It's the good go young, like they say. But there'll be one Great Day in the Mornin' before it's finished, I guarantee."

"Sir?"

"Yes, son?"

"What is it exactly gripes you, you don't mind my askin'."

Wendell grinned. "Ain't worth explainin'. Best repeat what Samuel Johnson said: 'Depend upon it that if a man talks of his misfortunes there is something in them that is not disagreeable to him; for where there is nothing but pure misery there never is any recourse to the mention of it.' "

Pace stared at Wendell, who sat stroking his red beard.

Wendell stood up and said, "Time to tend the garden. You'll stay put, won't ya?"

Pace nodded and watched Wendell walk out of the room. As soon as the madman was out of sight, he scrambled to his feet, ran over to the pistol crossbow and picked it up. Pace heard Wendell relieving himself in what he assumed was the toilet. He crouched under the window and waited. When Wendell reentered the room, Pace pressed the trigger that released a black dart into his captor's left eye. Wendell fell down and Pace dropped the crossbow and ran out of the house, headed on foot the four miles to Miss Napoleon's Paradise.

Wendell Shake carried no identification of any kind, and when his body was found, along with those of the Rattler brothers, the only item discovered in his pockets by police was a personal ad torn from a newspaper.

> If any open-minded, good-humored men of any race wish to write, I'm here and waiting. BF doing a 60-year term for something that just came out bad.
>
> Lamarra Chaney # 1213 P-17
> Women's Correctional Facility
> Box 30014, Draper, UT 84020

from CONSUELO'S KISS (1991)

CONSUELO'S KISS

CONSUELO WHYNOT LICKED IDLY at her wild cherry-flavored Tootsie Pop while she watched highway patrolmen and firefighters pull bodies from the wreckage. The Amtrak Crescent, on its way from New Orleans to New York, had collided with a tractor-trailer rig in Meridian, hard by the Torch Truckstop, where Consuelo had stopped in to buy a sweet. The eight train cars had accordioned on impact and the semi, which had been carrying a half-ton load of Big Chief Sweet 'n' Sour Cajun-Q Potato Chips, simply exploded.

"The train's whistle was blowin' the whole time and, Lord, it sounded like a bomb had went off when they hit," said Patti Fay McNair, a waitress at the Torch, to a rubbernecker who'd asked if she'd seen what happened.

Consuelo Whynot, who was sixteen years old and a dead ringer for the actress Tuesday Weld at the same age, stared dispassionately at the carnage. The truck driver, a man named Oh-Boy Wilson from Guntown, near Tupelo, had been burned so badly over every inch of his body that the firemen just let him smolder on the spot where he'd landed after the explosion. His crumpled, crispy corpse reminded Consuelo of the first time she'd tried to make Roman Meal toast in the broiler pan of her cousin Vashti Dale's Vulcan the summer before last at the beach cottage in Ocean Springs. She never could figure out if she and Vashti Dale were once or twice removed. That was a result, Consuelo decided, of her unremarkable education. Venus Tishomingo would fix that, too, though, and the thought almost made Consuelo smile.

Four hospital types dressed in white and wearing plastic gloves slid

Oh-Boy Wilson into a green body bag, zipped it up, tossed it into a van, and headed over to the wrecked Crescent, which had passenger parts sticking out of broken windows and crushed feet, hands, and heads visible beneath the overturned cars. Consuelo didn't think there'd be anything more very interesting to see, so she turned away and walked back to the truckstop.

"You goin' north?" she asked a man coming out of the diner.

The man looked at the petite young thing wearing a red-and-white polkadot poorboy that was stretched tightly over her apple-sized breasts, black jean cutoffs, yellow hair chopped down around her head like somebody had given it the once-over with a broken-bladed lawn mower, red tongue still lazily lapping at the Tootsie Pop, and said, "How old're you?"

"I been pregnant," Consuelo lied, "if that's what you mean."

The man grinned. He had a three-day beard, one slow blue-green eye and a baby beer gut. Consuelo pegged him at thirty.

"West," he said, "to Jackson. You can come, you want."

She followed him to a black Duster with mags, bright orange racing stripes, Moon eyes and a pale blue 43 painted on each side. She got in.

"My name's Wesley Nisbet," he said, and started the car. The ignition sounded like thunder at three A.M. "What's yours?"

"Consuelo Whynot."

Wesley laughed. "Your people the ones own Whynot, Mississippi? Town twenty miles east of here by the Alabama line?"

"Sixteen, be exact. You musta passed Geography."

Wesley whistled softly and idled the Duster toward Interstate 20.

"Where you headed, Consuelo?"

"Oxford."

"You got a boyfriend there?"

"Better. I'm goin' to see the woman of my dreams."

Wesley checked the traffic, then knifed into the highway and went from zero to sixty in under eight without fishtailing.

"This a 273?" Consuelo asked.

"Dropped in a 383 last week. You into ladies, huh?"

"One. What's the '43' for?"

"Number my idol, Richard Petty, ran with. Lots a man can do for ya a chick can't."

Consuelo bit down hard on the outer layer of her Tootsie Pop and sank her big teeth deep into the soft, dark brown core. She sucked on it for a minute, then opened her mouth and drooled down the front of her polkadot poorboy. Wesley wolfed a look at Consuelo, grinned, and gunned the Duster past ninety before feathering back down to a steady seventy-five.

"You ain't met Venus," she said.

THE AGE OF REASON

"YOUR FOLKS KNOW where you're goin'?" asked Wesley Nisbet, as he guided his Duster into the Bienville National Forest.

Consuelo had not looked at Wesley since she'd gotten into the car. She didn't feel like talking, either, but she knew it was part of the price for the ride.

"They ain't known where I'm goin' ever since I been able to reason."

"How long you figure that is?"

"More'n seven years, I guess. Since I was nine, when me'n Venus got brought together in the divine plan."

Wesley slapped his half-leather-gloved right hand hard on top of the sissy wheel.

"Goddam! You mean that woman been havin' her way with you all this time? Hell, that's sexual abuse of a child. How is it your folks didn't get this Venus put away before now?"

"They couldn't prove nothin', so they sent me away to the Mamie Franklin Institute in Birmin'ham. I escaped twice, once when I was eleven and got caught quick, and then two years ago I stayed gone three whole months."

"Where'd you go?"

"Venus and me was shacked up in the swampy woods outside Increase. Didn't have no money, only guns, ammo and fishin' tackle. We ate good, too. Venus is about pure-blood Chickasaw. She can live off the land without askin'."

"How'd you get found out?"

Consuelo snorted. "Simon and Sapphire—those are my parents—hired about a hundred and one detectives. Still took 'em ninety days. Venus found us a pretty fair hideout that time."

"What's she doin' in Oxford?"

"Got her a full scholarship to study the writin's of William Faulkner, the greatest writer the state of Mississippi ever provided the world. Venus is also a writer, a poet. She says I got the makin's, too."

"You write poetry?"

"Not yet, but Venus says I got the *soul* of a poet, and without that there's no way to begin. It'll come."

"You ever read any books by this fella she's studyin'?"

Consuelo shook her head no. "Venus says it ain't important. 'Course I could, I want."

Wesley kept his ungloved left hand on the steering wheel and placed his right on Consuelo's naked left thigh. She didn't flinch, so Wesley slid his leather-covered palm up toward her crotch.

"You wouldn't know what to do with my clit if I set it up for you on the dashboard like a plastic Jesus."

Wesley's right hand froze at the edge of her cutoffs. He kept it there for another fifteen or twenty seconds, then removed it and grabbed the gear-shift knob, squeezing it hard.

"You're some kinda wise little teaser, ain't you?" he said.

Consuelo turned her head and stared at Wesley's right profile. He had a scar on the side of his nose in the shape of an anchor.

"How'd you get that scar?" asked Consuelo. "Bet you was doin' such a bad job the bitch just clamped her legs closed on it."

Wesley Nisbet grinned and took the Duster up a notch.

"I'm likin' this more and more we go along," he said.

RED BIRD

SAILOR AND LULA SAT in a tan Naugahyde booth in Rebel Billy's Truck-stop off 55 near Bogue Chitto, eating bowls of chili and drinking Barq's. Sailor was reading the *Clarion-Ledger* he'd bought from a box out front.

"Guess we been real lucky with Pace, peanut," he said.

Lula looked over the red lumps on her tablespoon at the top of Sailor's head and noticed that the bald spot on his crown was growing larger. Sailor was supersensitive about losing his hair. Whenever Lula said anything about it, like suggesting he get a weave or try Monoxidil, he got upset, so she ignored the urge to reiterate her feelings regarding the situation.

"Why you say that, sweetheart? I mean, you're right and all, but what made you think of it?"

Lula stuck the spoon into her mouth.

"Item here in the Jackson paper. Headline says, 'Sorrow Ends in Death,' and underneath that, 'Boy, 12, Hangs Self after Killing Red Bird.' Story's out of San Antonio."

Lula retracted the spoon. "Nothin' good happens in Texas, I'm convinced."

"Here it is: 'Conscience-stricken after he had shot and killed a red bird, Wyatt Toomey, twelve years old, hanged himself here last night. The body was found by his sister. A signed note addressed to his parents told the motive for the act.' This is what he wrote: 'I killed myself on account of me shooting a red bird. Goodby mother and daddy. I'll see you some day.' "

"Jesus, Sail, that's a terrible story."

Sailor folded the newspaper to another page.

"Hard to know what a kid's really thinkin'," he said. "Pace had himself a few scrapes, of course, but he got clean, thank the Lord."

"Thanks to you, too, Sail. You been a fine daddy. Want you to know I appreciate it."

Sailor smiled, blew Lula a kiss and leaned back in his corner of the booth and lit up a Camel.

"Hope you don't mind my smokin', peanut. I may be a good daddy but I ain't always such a clean liver."

A waitress came over carrying a pot of coffee.

"Need refills?" she asked.

Sailor covered his cup with his left palm.

"I'm peaceful," he said. "Peanut?"

Lula nodded. "Don't mind a drop."

"Folks don't drink so much coffee they used to," said the waitress, as she poured. "Don't smoke, neither."

The waitress carried a good one-hundred-eighty-five pounds on her five-feet two-inches. She was about forty-five, Sailor guessed, and she reeked of alcohol. Sailor figured her for a nighttime cheap gin drinker. Five minutes after she was in her trailer door after work, he imagined, she'd be kicked back in her Barcalounger watching the news, four fingers of Gilbey's over a couple of cubes in a half-frosted chimney in one hand and five inches of menthol in the other.

"My wife's tryin' to quit," he said.

"I got thirty years worth of tar and nicotine in me," said the waitress, "too late to stop. Anyway, I like it. This health thing's gone just about far as it can now, I reckon. What with AIDS and the Big C, not to mention heart disease and drug-related crimes, might as well let yourself go a little and get some pleasure out of life. My son, Orwell, he's twenty-two now, was born deaf and with a withered-up left arm? He won't eat nothin' but raw vegetables, no meat or dairy. Runs three miles ev'ry damn mornin' before seven, then goes to work at the telephone office. In bed by nine-thirty each night. You'd think Orwell'd want to cut loose, 'specially after the cards he been dealt, but he figures he might could live forever he don't smoke or drink liquor and sticks to eatin' greens. What for? That ain't livin', it's runnin' spooked. Can't stand to see it, but half the world's in the coward's way at present. You folks take care now. Highway's full of God's worst mistakes."

She left the check on the table.

"Gimme a drag on that Camel, willya, Sail?"

He handed his cigarette to Lula and watched her suck in Winston-Salem's contribution to the good life.

"Feel better?" Sailor asked, as she exhaled and handed it back to him.

Lula nodded. "It's terrible, but I do love tobacco. Must be it's in our blood, comin' from North Carolina."

" 'Member that woman kept a vigil out front of the Lorraine Motel in Memphis for three years, place where Martin Luther King got shot? She was protestin' it bein' made into a civil rights museum, 'stead of a medical clinic or shelter for the homeless."

"Kinda do, honey. What happened to her?"

"Cops dragged her away, finally. Don't know where she went after."

"Why you askin' now, Sailor? That was a long time back."

"Oh, I'm thinkin' it might be interestin', long as we're in Memphis, go look at the Lorraine, maybe see the spot James Earl Ray aimed from. I mean, it's our history."

"Think James Earl Ray ever shot a bird when he was a boy?"

"He did," said Sailor, "don't guess it bothered his mind none."

PICKUP

"I HAVE A COLLECT CALL for Venus Tishomingo from Consuelo Whynot. Is this Venus Tishomingo?"

"Yes, it is."

"Will you accept the charges?"

"Yes, I certainly will."

"Go ahead, please."

The operator cut out.

"Hi, Venus, I'm on my way."

"Where you, Suelo, sweets?"

"Next to a A&W in Jackson. Just hitched a ride here from a weird dude in a nasty short. No boy wants to believe a girl ain't simply dyin' to lick the lint off his nuts."

"He make a attempt?"

"Not directly. Told him you was my dream woman and I didn't need no further stimulation."

"Sapphire and Simon know you split?"

"Don't think yet. Was a big train wreck in Meridian, I was there. Fireman on the scene said it's the worst in Miss'ippi hist'ry. Rescue squad'll be pullin' people's parts out of that mess for hours. Prob'ly be findin' pieces in the woods around for days."

"I know, it's on the news here. How long you gonna be?"

"Depends on when I can get a lift. I'm gonna have me a root beer and a burger and catch another ride."

"What happened to the hotrod boy?"

"Made him leave me off. He'd been trouble I woulda asked him to take me up to Oxford. Figure I'll make it in by midnight, I'm lucky."

"Okay, precious. I'll be waitin' up. You call again, there's a problem."

"I will, Venus. Love you dearly."

"My heart's thumpin', baby. Be careful, you hear?"

They both hung up and Consuelo left the phone booth, which was on the side of the road, and walked up to the window of the drive-in.

"Cheeseburger and a large root beer, please," she ordered from the fat man behind the glass.

"Ever'thin' on it?" he asked.

"No pickles."

"Three dollars," said the fat man, as he slid a bag through the space in the window.

Consuelo dug a five dollar bill out of her shorts, handed it to him, and he gave her back two dollars, which she folded in half and stuffed into her right front pocket.

"Y'all hurry back," the man said, his gooey, small hazel eyes fixed on her breasts.

Consuelo smiled at him, tossed her blond chop and pulled back her shapely little shoulders and expanded her chest.

"Maybe," she said.

The A&W was only a few hundred yards from the on-ramp to the Interstate, and Consuelo sipped at her root beer as she headed toward it. She took out the cheeseburger, dropped the bag on the ground and ate it as she walked. Next to the on-ramp was a Sun Oil station, and Consuelo spotted Wesley Nisbet's Duster, the hood raised, parked at a gas pump with Wesley bent into it, eyeballing the engine. She hoped he wouldn't see her. She also noticed a road-smudged white Cadillac Sedan de Ville with a man and a woman in it, about to pull away from the pump opposite the one occupied by Wesley's vehicle. Consuelo wolfed down the rest of her burger, wiped her right hand on her black jean cutoffs and stuck out her thumb as the Sedan de Ville rolled her way. The car stopped next to Consuelo and the front passenger window went down.

"Where you goin'?" Lula asked.

"Oxford," said Consuelo. "I'm a student at Ole Miss and I got to get there tonight so's I can make my classes in the mornin'."

"Guess we can take you far's Batesville," said Sailor, leaning over against Lula. "You'll have to catch a ride east from there on route 6."

"Good enough," Consuelo said, and opened the right rear door and climbed in, careful not to spill her root beer.

Sailor accelerated and guided the heavy machine onto 55 North and had it up to sixty-five in twelve seconds. Wesley Nisbet watched the white Cad disappear and snickered. He gently closed the Duster's hood and slid behind the steering wheel. He wouldn't have a problem keeping a tail on that whale, Wesley thought.

"What river's this?" Consuelo asked, as the Sedan de Ville crossed a bridge just before the fairgrounds.

"The Pearl, I believe," said Sailor. "Where you-all from?"

"Alabama," said Consuelo. "I been home on vacation 'cause my grandmama died."

"Sorry to hear it, honey," said Lula, who was turned around in her seat studying the girl.

"Yeah, we was real close, me and my grandmama."

"You didn't take no suitcase with you, huh?" Sailor asked.

"No," Consuelo said, "I only been gone a few days. Don't need much in this close weather."

Lula examined Consuelo, watching her sip her drink, then turned back toward the front. She looked over at Sailor and saw the half-grin on his face.

"You let me know the AC's too strong for you, Miss," said Sailor. "Wouldn't want you to get a chill in that outfit."

"Thanks, I'm fine," Consuelo said. "And my name's Venus."

PROFESSIONALS

VENUS TISHOMINGO WAS SIX FEET even and weighed a solid one-hundred-seventy-five pounds. Her hands were each the size of an infielder's glove, and she wore a 12-D shoe. Her hair was chestnut brown and very thick, and hung down loose past her waist. She wore at least one ring on every finger other than her thumbs. They were cheap, colorful rings she'd bought in pawn shops in Memphis. Her eyes were clear, almost colorless stones set deep in her skull. Most people had a difficult time staring into them for very long before becoming uncomfortable and having to look away. At first glance, Venus's eyes resembled pristine pebbles in a gentle, smooth-flowing stream, but then they came alive and darted toward whomever's eyes met hers. She sat in her one-bedroom cottage in a gooseneck rocking chair, wearing only a well-faded pair of Wrangler blue jeans, reading the *Oxford Eagle*, waiting for Consuelo to arrive or call. An item datelined Jackson caught her eye.

"Pearl Buford, of Mockingbird, accused of trying to sell two of her grandchildren in an adoption scam, has pleaded innocent to charges in federal court here. Buford, 34, who told authorities she used to baby-sit professionally, also pleaded innocent to six counts of mail fraud involving solicitation of offers for the children. She is currently unemployed. Her daughter, Fannie Dawn Taylor, 16, a dropout after finishing 8th grade at Mockingbird Junior High, pleaded innocent to one count of mail fraud."

Venus had it in mind to adopt a child that she and Consuelo could raise together. Maybe more than one. It was too bad, Venus thought, that Pearl Buford hadn't contacted her about taking on Fannie Dawn's kids.

Venus massaged her left breast with her right hand, tickling the nipple with the second and third fingers until it stood out taut and long as it would go. She had large breasts that were extremely sensitive to touch, and Consuelo knew perfectly how to suck on and fondle them. Venus dropped the newspaper and slid her left hand down inside the front of her jeans and rubbed her clit. She closed her eyes and thought about a photograph of a cat woman she'd seen in a book in the Ole Miss library that afternoon. It wasn't really a cat woman but two negatives printed simultaneously, one atop the other, of a cat and a woman, so that the face was half-human, half-feline, with long white whiskers, weird red bolts for eyes and perfect black Kewpie doll lips. Venus came quickly, bucking sharply twice before relaxing and slumping down in the chair. She removed her left hand and let it drape over the arm of the rocker. Her right hand rested in her lap. Venus was almost asleep when Consuelo knocked on the door.

Venus jumped up and opened it. Consuelo threw herself forward onto her naked chest.

"I'm starved, Venie," Consuelo said. "I need your lovin'."

"Got it comin', baby," said Venus, stroking Consuelo's wheat-light hair with a large brown hand.

Venus heard a car engine idling, looked over Consuelo's left shoulder out the door and saw the black Duster in front of the house.

"Who's that?" she asked.

"Wesley Nisbet, the one I told you about. He's a pest, but he give me a lift here. Followed the ride I caught outta Jackson, picked me up again in Batesville."

"He truly dangerous?"

"Maybe, like most."

"He figurin' you're gonna invite him in?"

Consuelo swung her right leg backward and the door slammed shut.

"Just another mule kickin' in his stall," she said.

When Wesley saw the door close, he shifted the Duster into first and eased his pantherlike machine away. He drove into town, parked on the northwest side of the square in front of a restaurant-bar named The Mansion, got out of the car and went inside.

"J. W. Dant, double," Wesley said to the bartender, as he hopped up on a stool. "One cube, splash water."

A toad-faced man with a greasy strand of gray-yellow hair falling over his forehead sat on the stool to Wesley's left. The man was wearing a wrinkled burgundy blazer with large silver buttons over a wrinkled, dirty white shirt and a wide, green, food-stained tie. He wobbled as he extended his right hand toward Wesley.

"Five Horse Johnson," the man said. "You?"

"That a clever way of tellin' me you got a short dick or's it your name?"

The man laughed once, very loudly, and wiped his right hand on his coat.

"Nickname I got as a boy. Had me a baby five HP outboard on a dinghy, used to go fishin' in Sardis Lake. Can't hardly remember my so-called Christian one, though the G-D gov'ment reminds me once a year. Hit me up for the G-D tax on my soul, they do. Strip a couple pounds a year. Forty-five G-damn years old. Amazed there's any flesh left to cover the nerves. You ain't from Oxford."

"No, ain't."

"Then you prob'ly don't know the local def'nition of the term 'relative humidity.' "

Wesley picked up his drink, which the bartender had just set in front of him, and took a sip.

"What's it?"

"Relative humidity is the trickle of sweat runs down the crack of your sister-in-law's back while you're fuckin' her in the ass."

Five Horse Johnson grinned liplessly, exposing six slimy orange teeth, then fell sideways off his stool to the floor. Wesley finished his whisky and put two dollars on the bar.

"This do it?" he asked the bartender, who nodded.

Wesley unseated himself and stepped over Five Horse Johnson, who was either dead or asleep or in some indeterminate state between the two.

"Professional man, I'll guess."

"Lawyer," said the bartender.

"I known others," Wesley said, and walked out.

from
BAD DAY FOR THE LEOPARD MAN
(1992)

BAD DAY FOR THE LEOPARD MAN

THE LEOPARD MAN's name was Philip Reãl. He was called the Leopard Man behind his back by others in the movie business because of the gothic nature of the films he'd directed and written during the past two decades. Val Lewton, a producer at RKO in the 1940s, had made a series of low-budget horror pictures, including one titled *The Leopard Man*. In a review of Phil Reãl's startling first feature, *Mumblemouth*, made when Reãl was twenty-three, the Los Angeles *Times* critic had compared the look and feel of the film—heavy shadows and deep suggestions of off-camera hideous goings-on—to Lewton's black-and-white B's that most film historians considered classics of the genre. At the time, it was construed as a compliment, but as the years wore on, and Reãl repeated himself with such efforts as *Death Comes Easy*, *Face of the Phantom*, *The Slow Torture and Sexual Re-education of Señor Rafferty* and others, culminating in the universally maligned *Dog Parts*, which featured a denouement wherein two Pit Bulls brutally dismember a pregnant Collie bitch and devour her fetus, Phil Reãl had become unbankable and persona non grata in Hollywood.

He had gone to Europe, living first for two years in France, then for three in Italy, where he directed and acted in a cheapie called *Il Verme* ("The Worm"), a soft-core pornographic version of the myth of Cadmus, before returning to L.A. Since his return, he had been living alone in a house in the Hollywood hills, working on an original screenplay called *The Cry of the Mute*, based on his own experiences in the industry.

Phil let the telephone ring three times before he picked up.

"Happy birthday, darlin'! How's it feel to be fat and fifty?"

"My birthday was yesterday, Flower, and I'm forty-eight. But thanks, anyway."

"Sorry, sugar. Least you know I'm thinkin' about you."

"I thought you were in Kenya, with Westphal."

"Picture wrapped a month ago, Philly. Where you been keepin' yourself?"

"Right here by my lonesome. I stopped reading the trades and I do my own cooking."

Flower laughed. "You still writin' on that *Moot* script, huh?"

"The word is *Mute*, Flower, and yes, I am. What do you have in the works?"

"Well, you do know me'n Jason got divorced?"

"No, I missed that."

"Yeah, he's livin' with Rita Manoa-noa now, the top whore outta Tahiti that was brought over by Runt Gold to be in the remake of Captain Cook's Revenge that never got made? Final decree came through just after I got to Africa. Let me tell you, Philly, they don't call it the dark continent for nothin'. People there're the blackest I ever seen anywhere, includin' Alabama."

"Africa wasn't called the dark continent because of the color of the skin of most of its inhabitants, Flower. It's because it was one of the last places the Europeans got to. 'Dark' referred to unexplored and unknown."

"Phil, you always know about everything."

"That's why I'm such a popular guy."

"Oh, sugar, everyone thinks you're the smartest man in Hollywood."

"As Daffy Duck said, 'Ridicule is the cure of genius.' "

"Anyway, I'm seein' Clark now."

"Westphal? What happened to Suki?"

"He thrown her out before Africa. She's suin' him now, of course. But they weren't never married so he says she can't get much. Clark made her sign a paper while they was livin' together said she couldn't make no claims on him. He done it with all his women."

"I think Clark may be just a tad brighter than I am."

"He sure has more money, Philly, that's the truth. Not as much hair, though."

"He can buy some."

"Don't need to, now the natural look is in. Thinnin' hair is a sign of maturity, you know."

"Spell maturity for me, Flower."

She laughed. "Sugar, ten years ago when I came to California from Mobile, I had me a choice between practicin' spellin' or keepin' my lips over my teeth when I give head. Can't have it both ways in this town.

"Look, I gotta run," Flower said. "Clark's takin' me down to his place in darkest Mexico tonight, the house he bought from Jack Falcon, the famous old director who died last year?"

"I know who Jack Falcon was, Flower."

"Oh, of course you do. Prob'ly you and him went boar huntin' together and everything."

"As a matter of fact, I think I still have my boar rifle around here somewhere."

"I got to go shop now, honey. Happy birthday, even though it's the wrong day. I'll call you when I'm back from Mexico. You still hangin' at Martoni's?"

"Once in a while."

"We'll meet for drinks. Bye!"

Flower hung up, so Phil did, too. He suddenly flashed on the bathtub scene in *Señor Rafferty*, where Flower Reynolds, as the crazed transsexual Shortina Fuse, wearing only a pair of red panties, tosses the sulfuric acid into Rafferty's face. The camera remains fixed on Flower's red triangle while she laughs and Rafferty screams, holding until the final fade. It was Flower's laugh people remembered later, not Rafferty's screams. She had a great laugh. Phil had always regretted not having used it in *Dog Parts*.

ARTIFICIAL LIGHT

PHIL HAD AN 11:30 with Arnie Pope at Five Star. The meeting had been set up for him by Bobby Durso, who, during Phil's European hiatus, had become a powerful agent despite his lack of affiliation with an established agency. Bobby operated on his own and specialized in handling writers. Actors, he'd decided, were—with few exceptions—essentially undependable and insecure; dysfunctional people, his shrink called them. Writers, Bobby found, were the hardest-working, most clearly focused and dedicated individuals he'd ever known.

Bobby had been Phil Real's A.D. on *Death Comes Easy,* then gone back to UCLA, where he'd earned a degree in American history, worked as a bartender for a couple of years, gotten married and begun his present career by representing his wife, Alice, who wrote screenplays. The first script of Alice's that Bobby Durso sold, *Goodbye To Everyone*, wound up grossing over two hundred million for Paramount, and the sequel, *Hello To Nobody*, did equally well. Since then, every producer in town found time to talk to, if not openly court him.

Bobby was not intending to represent Phil Real, however. At least not in any official capacity. The meet with Arnie Pope had been arranged as a favor, and that's where Bobby wanted to leave it. He hadn't even read Phil's screenplay, if he had one yet, or allowed Phil to describe the story. Phil, Bobby knew, would want to direct the picture himself, and there was no way a studio would allow that. Bobby dealt exclusively with the majors, he didn't touch the independents, and he'd explained his position to Phil, who said that he understood completely.

Arnie Pope was Bobby's brother-in-law—Alice was Arnie's sister—he and Bobby got along all right, and when Bobby asked him to take a meeting with the Leopard Man, no strings attached, he said okay. After all, Arnie figured, the man was a kind of legend in the business, and it could be interesting. Arnie told his assistant, Greta, to reschedule his shiatsu for 11:45.

Phil appeared in Arnie Pope's outer office at 11:29. He did not bring the screenplay with him. Greta buzzed Arnie, who asked her to show in Mr. Real.

"This is a real pleasure, Mr. Real," said Arnie, as he stood up and leaned across his desk to shake hands.

"Phil, please."

"Arnie. Sit."

They both sat down.

"This is really great," Arnie said. "I can still remember the first time I saw *Face of the Phantom*. At the Riviera in Chicago, when I was fourteen. Scared the piss out of me. My girlfriend wouldn't even look at the screen. Kept her head buried in my right shoulder the whole time."

Arnie rubbed his right shoulder with his left hand. Phil noticed Arnie's diamond pinkie ring.

"It was great, great," said Arnie.

Arnie smiled and Phil nodded.

"So, what's this Bobby says you've got? Have to tell you, though, that since the Germans bought Five Star, all we've been able to push through are one-namers."

Phil looked puzzled.

"You know: Rheinhold, Dirk, those guys. Muscle men. Put a title underneath, like *Death Driver*, all that's necessary. So, it's 11:31:35. Tell me."

"This is a special picture."

"They're all special, Phil." Arnie again looked quickly at his watch. "Got a title?"

"The Cry of the Mute."

"A mute's someone can't talk, right?"

Phil nodded. "The title is meant to be ironic."

"Ironic, yeah, sure. I got it. So, what happens?"

"It's about a writer-director who was at one time very successful, when he was young, and then his career slipped away from him. He drinks, takes drugs, he travels, and finally returns to make one last picture. Nobody believes in him anymore except for a girl, a woman, who began her acting career in his early films. She's become a big star and gets him a deal, based on her agreement to play the female lead."

"Good. I was waiting for the girl. What does she do?"

"Sells tickets."

"I know. I mean in the story. She helps the guy get back on his feet, cleans him up, marries him, what? Where's the big play come in?"

"He shows he can still pull it off. The picture's both a critical and box office success."

"What about him and her? In the end?"

Phil shook his head. "They don't get together. She marries someone else."

Arnie Pope looked at his watch and stood up.

"When Nick Ray made *In a Lonely Place* he had Bogart," Arnie said.

"Gloria Grahame made the picture work," said Phil.

"Phil," Arnie stuck out his hand as he came around the desk, "I gotta be Japanese in five minutes. Less. Have Bobby send me the script. I promise I'll read it."

Phil stood and let Arnie pinch the fingers of his right hand. Greta appeared.

"Almost time, Arnie," she said.

"Greta," said Arnie, "when Phil's script arrives, read it right away."

Arnie turned and looked directly into Phil's eyes.

"I'll never forget *Face of the Phantom*, Phil. Never. It's a classic."

Arnie nodded and grinned. "Janet Coveleski," he said. "That was her name."

"Whose name, Arnie?" asked Phil.

"The girl I took to see your picture at the Riviera."

Arnie walked out of his office, followed closely by Greta. Phil stood without moving for twenty seconds. He remembered the last frame of *Phantom*, where the man who has never slept with his eyes closed finally closes them, knowing he'll never wake up. Phil closed his eyes.

WRANGLER'S PARADISE

NOBODY IN HOLLYWOOD has a past that matters. What counts is what someone is doing right now or might be doing tomorrow. The film business is open to anyone, and that was the great thing about it, Phil thought, as he drove home from Five Star. A person could be a multiple murderer escapee from prison or a lunatic asylum but if he or she had a bright idea that was considered do-able, and the proper pieces fell together in the right hands at the right time, that person, certifiably depraved or otherwise, could have a three-picture deal in less than the lifetime of a Florida snake doctor.

If one of them is a hit, the escapee could be running a studio within a few months, and as long as the people kept buying tickets the studio lawyers would do everything they could to keep the authorities at bay. A big enough flop, though, and the *wunderkind* would no doubt be back doing laps inside a padded cell before it went to video. Phil loved the strangeness of it, he really did. Hollywood was a wrangler's paradise: the cattle either got to market or they didn't. Rustled, died of thirst, train derailed, didn't matter. No excuses, no prisoners. That was the law of the bottom line.

Driving along La Brea, Phil decided to stop at Pink's. He parked his leased Mustang convertible around the corner on Melrose, got out and joined the line at the outdoor counter. When his turn came, he ordered a double cheeseburger with chili and a black cherry Israeli soda. As he waited for the food, Phil looked across the street. A middle-aged bum had disrobed and begun doing jumping jacks on the sidewalk, his long hair and beard flopping around. Pedestrians passed on either side of him. A swarthy man came out of the convenience store on the corner and walked swiftly toward the naked bum. The swarthy man, who wore a thick black mustache and a square of hair in the center of his chin, pulled a small-caliber revolver from a pocket, pushed the nose of it into the bum's left ear and pulled the trigger. The bum fell down and blood gushed from his head. The swarthy man ran back toward the convenience store.

Phil picked up his cheeseburger and soda, paid the Mexican girl who'd served him, walked to his car, got in and drove away. The bum had looked familiar, Phil thought. He made a mental note to check the newspaper the next day for the story, to see if the bum had been someone he'd known in the old days.

• • •

CAT PEOPLE

ORETTA "KITTY KAT" CROSS, black female, twenty-five, black hair with two dyed red braids, black eyes—the left with a slight strabismus, or cast—five-five, one hundred ten pounds, no tattoos, rode shotgun.

"Don't see why we had to do this, Kitty Kat. Now we up for kidnappin', too."

Archie Chunk, white male, twenty-eight, sandy-brown hair cut short, blue eyes, five-nine, one hundred sixty pounds, broken nose, two-inch horizontal scar middle of forehead, fire-breathing dragon tattoo right biceps, anchor tattoo with snake entwined back of left hand, squirmed around in the back seat of the Cadillac. He kept turning to look out the rear window.

"You prefer we be walkin'?" said Kitty Kat. "The woman be right there. Nobody chasin' us, Arch. Relax."

Archie twisted toward her. "How I gonna relax you shot the dude?"

Kitty Kat vaulted into the back seat, shoved Archie over so that she could sit directly behind Lula, shifted the Colt Python she was holding into her left hand, unzipped Archie's trousers with her right, took out his penis and started jacking him off.

"You stay on 23 to West Pointe à la Hache," Kitty Kat said to Lula, sticking the barrel point into the soft spot at the back of Lula's head, holding it there for several seconds, "then I tell you what to do."

Archie let his head roll back and closed his eyes as Kitty Kat caressed him. She put her thick lips to his left ear and purred like a cat, making a soft, rumbling growl in the back of her throat. Archie's penis, at first touch tiny and flaccid, soon swelled to its full four-and-one-quarter inches and filled with blood so that it resembled a Montecristo Rojo. Kitty Kat growled louder and increased the speed and intensity of her caress. A few seconds later, Archie came, splattering the back of the front seat and dribbling onto his pants. Kitty Kat released her hold on him, reached over and pulled the gold and black leaf-patterned scarf off Lula's neck and used it to wipe up Archie's emission.

"Feelin' better now, peach?" asked Kitty Kat, cleaning her hand with Lula's scarf, then tossing it on the floor.

"Some," Archie said. "Wish I could do for you."

"It okay, I ain' nervous. Seen on *Geraldo* bunch of bitches called theyselfs non-orgastic, or somethin'. They same as me. Ain' like havin the AIDS or cancer. Bet this old bitch she come easy. Hey, old bitch, you come easy, I bet."

Lula had not said a word since Archie and Kitty Kat had jumped into the car and the woman had put a gun to her head and commanded her to drive fast. She tried to respond but could not.

"Bitch!" shouted Kitty Kat. "Ask you nice does you come!"

Lula nodded. "Yes," she said softly, "I do."

"Easy? It easy comin'?"

"Not always."

Kitty Kat poked the tip of Archie's shrunken penis with the barrel of her Python.

"Zip up, peach," she said. "There ladies present."

BALL LIGHTNING

LULA LOOKED AROUND the room. Tacked to the walls were pictures severed neatly from magazines, books, calendars and newspapers of different types of lightning. There was one of a rainstorm with a single vertical bolt of cloud-to-ground lightning in a purple sky and a bright pink spot atop the bolt that marked its exit spot; a flame-like ribbon of ball lightning looping through a bloody backdrop; triple ground lightning over Las Vegas that looked like a flaming match head waved over a black bat wing; lightning striking behind a ridge line, its meandering main stem resembling the Mississippi River; an anvil-shaped, violet-tinted storm cloud disclosing a scorpionlike excretion onto a barren landscape; double ground lightning with the secondary channel striking more than five miles away from the primary route; slow-moving air discharge lightning outlining the state of Florida; and double bolts from a monstrous magenta thunderhead.

She sat on a nude, high-backed wooden chair, the only chair in the room, which she guessed to be about fifteen feet by fifteen feet. It was devoid of any other furniture. There were three windows, one in each wall other than the one containing a door, which was closed and, Lula presumed, locked. She was unbound but sat still, waiting for her abductors, to whom she had not spoken excepting the brief exchange with the woman in the car. Lula thought about opening one of the windows and running away, but she was not young anymore, she certainly could not run very fast or very far, and she did not want to antagonize the two captors, who, it seemed to Lula, were unpredictable types. She needed a cigarette. Her Mores were in her purse, which she had last seen on the floor under the front seat of the Cadillac. The door opened.

"You like the pictures, lady?" asked Archie Chunk, walking in. "I love lightnin'. Back in Broken Claw, where I was born and mostly raised—that's in Oklahoma—is the best electrical storms. Come August, I'd stand in the field behind my granny's house and pray for the lightnin' to hit me. Never did, though, even when I held up a five iron."

"Can I have a cigarette?" asked Lula.

Archie took a pack of Marlboros and a book of matches from the breast pocket of his Madras shirt, shook one out to Lula and lit it for her before doing the same for himself.

"Kitty Kat and me don't mean to keep you in suspense," he said, replacing his cigarettes and matches in the same pocket, "but you're a sorta unplanned-on part of the deal, you know? We gotta do one of three things: let you go, kill you, or ransom you. Them're the options."

The black woman came into the room. She was holding a thick, foot-long clear plastic dildo in her right hand and the Colt Python in her left. She walked over to Lula and showed her the dildo, the head of which was smeared generously with some kind of salve.

"You ever use one of these?" Kitty Kat asked.

Lula shook her head no.

"Here," Kitty Kat said to Archie, handing him the gun.

He took it and Kitty Kat hiked her skirt up over her naked crotch, bent her knees slightly as she spread her legs wide enough to admit the instrument into her vagina, then manipulated the dildo with both hands, inserting it slowly, a half inch at a time, until most of it was inside her. Kitty Kat stood directly in front of Lula while she pumped the toy into and partway out of herself. She began to sweat heavily, even though the temperature in the room was only fifty-three degrees. Lula felt the Marlboro burning down between the first and second fingers of her left hand, so she dropped it onto the floor. Archie Chunk stood by, intently watching Kitty Kat work out.

"Master! Master!" cried Kitty Kat. "Master, make me! Make me, master!" she shouted, plunging the dildo deeper and harder.

Suddenly she stopped and extracted it, breathing hard, her legs quivering. Kitty Kat held the wet tool out to Archie.

"Gimme the gun now," she said, and they exchanged weapons.

Kitty Kat inserted the barrel of the Python into her cunt and massaged herself.

"Got to be gentle with this," said Kitty Kat. "Torn myself before."

Lula remained motionless. Archie Chunk held the slimy stick in his left fist and grinned.

"Wish I could pull the trigger," Kitty Kat whined. "Wish Kitty Kat push it up pussy, pull trigger. Pull pussy trigger. Open pussy, up pussy, pull trigger."

Kitty Kat Cross swayed, shuddered, her mouth open, made a gagging sound and held the stainless blue steel cylinder tight to the left side of her cunt. She trembled and whinnied, then her contractions slowly tapered off until they ceased entirely. Kitty Kat withdrew the Python's nose and stood up straight. She held the gun to her mouth and ran her tongue along the barrel, first one side, then the other, licking it clean.

"Close as Kitty Kat get," she said.

KITTY KAT TALKS

"I TELL YOU how people like me an' Archie Chunk come up, maybe you get the picture. My mama worked as a aide in a nursin' home, cleanin' after old folks' dirt. Had me an' my two brothers to care for herself after our daddy disappeared. Mama out cleanin' up piss, shit, vomit, wipin' drool off they half-dead faces, proppin' 'em in they wheelchairs for next to no money an' no benefits. She was too proud to take the welfare, she wanted to work. Wouldn't let the state take her kids for no foster homes. She was for keepin' the fam'ly together, even when Daddy gone.

"Mama made us go to school long as we'd mind. We lived in a closed-down motel without no runnin' water or heat. Had us a wood stove but no ice box. Mama got up four ev'ry mornin' fix our clothes, breakfast. She an' me sleep together in one bed, Yusef an' Malcolm in another. We walk with Mama five miles each mornin' in rain an' dark to school. I get sick an' tired walkin' in rain an' dark.

"When Yusef break his arm, fall through a hole in the floor, Mama had to pay cash to fix it, but after his cast come off he never had no pin put in keep the shape, like he suppose to, 'cause Mama ain't had enough money. His arm bent wrong and dangle weird.

"I was twelve a drug dealer hung out around the motel got me pregnant. After I had the baby, I leave it with Mama and go. Malcolm, he drown. Mama, Yusef and my baby, girl name Serpentina, burn to death when the motel catch fire one night.

"Ain't was no diff'rent for Archie. Black or white don't make no diff'rence you down so far. He be on the street since he six, chil' alcoholic. Stealin' all he know, or lettin' some ol' sick fool pinch his peepee fo' a meal at Mickey D.

"I know you scared, lady. Maybe this work out. It don't, least you know there tougher roads than one you been on."

FODDER

WHILE SAILOR, PACE AND PHIL crouched in hiding around the entrance to Judge Perez Park, and Rhoda waited in Lula's Crown Victoria station wagon that was parked on Tupelo Street, Archie Chunk was at the wheel of Sailor's Sedan de Ville. Kitty Kat Cross sat in the front passenger seat with the visor down and the interior light on, applying her makeup.

"Man, I in love with this car, Arch," she said. "Got so many nifty convenience, must was design by women."

"I'm glad we didn't kill that old lady," said Archie. "She reminds me of my grandma some."

"Could I'd gone either way with it," Kitty Kat said, as she wielded her blue eyeliner. "Was kinda nice to seen again where my mama worked, though."

"It was the right thing. Never pays to murder folks remind you of loved ones. Now we got fresh plates on the Cad here, and we gonna stop up in Slaughter, get the Barnwell boys to slap on a new paint job, be all set. What color you like it, Kat?"

"This kind classy car, oughta be some type red."

"Sounds good to me."

"You sure you can trust these Barnwells, huh?"

"Oh yeah. Jimmy Dean and Sal Mineo Barnwell been doin' this since they got out of prison, four, five years ago."

"What beef they go down for?"

"Animal cruelty. They was sellin' videos of Rottweilers in leather armor rippin' apart a captured pig. Fish and Wildlife agents busted 'em at a warehouse out in East Feliciana Parish, confiscated four beauty Rotts."

"Shit!" cried Kitty Kat, bending over and looking around the floor. "Dropped my applicator."

Kitty Kat crawled down and wedged her slender body between the seat and the dashboard.

"Hey, Kat, be careful."

"There it is," she said, reaching for the swab.

The car hit a pothole and Kitty Kat fell forward. She attempted to brace herself with her right hand and accidentally depressed Archie's right foot, which was on the accelerator pedal. The black Cadillac swerved out of control directly into the path of an oncoming Mack semi loaded with several hundred 110-pound bags of Dr. Fagin's Organic Fish Fodder.

LETTER TO DAL

Dalceda Delahoussaye
809 Ashmead Drive
Bay St. Clement, N.C. 28352

Dearest Dal,

You are the only person in the world other than maybe Beany who ever really understood me so your the one I need to write this letter to. Thank the Lord Dal your still alive even though you been smoking since before I was born. Mama loved you more than anyone Dal including me probably. I know what a terrible loss it was for you when Mama died and so I feel its OK to tell you not only what has happened here but what Im thinking now about things.

The bad news is Sailor was killed in a wreck. I had to stop just now a minute to catch my breath sometimes it happens I lose control of my breathing and I kind of panic though not so much as I used to when I was a girl. This is Monday when Im writing so last Thursday Sailor was driving home from Bridge City where Gator Gone got there new storage facility and as he was headed on the Huey P. Long Bridge a dumb boy in a Apache pickup cut in front of Sailor from the shoulder and Sailor swerved his car to avoid him but couldnt straighten out in time before he hit the road divider. After smacking into it the car turned over and a transport truck carrying a dozen new Mitsubishi jeeps plowed him half way toward the Old Spanish Trail. Sail probably was already dead by then or knocked out for sure and didnt feel anything else at least its what I hope. The Cadillac with Sailor inside was crushed like it had been squeezd into a metal cube at the junk yard. There was no fire and believe it or not Sailors face was almost unmarked just his body was mashed in a 100 places.

There it is Dal I cant hardly believe it. Pace and me decided to cremate Sailor and we got his ashes here in a box we didnt want no funeral. I got to tell you Dal I feel kind of dead myself. I read once in Readers Digest I think about how often if two people been together a real long time and one of them dies the other dies soon after. Im only 62 and Mama lived into her 80s and youll most probably hit a 100 but I feel like how am I supposed to go on now? I know Mama would say look how she done after Daddy burned himself up so many years ago and didnt she have a long and useful life but you know me Dal and as much as Mama wanted me to be I am not really like her not in the way of strength. I am not exactly a serious religious person either I know that ever since I left the Church of Reason Redemption and Resistance to Gods Detractors. What do I have left Dal I mean it.

Pace is the greatest comfort of course. He and Rhoda tried there for a bit to tie the knot again but as Pace says once the string come unraveled you got to get you a new piece so its off for good. After his boss the movie director was killed in that plane crash Pace went to New York with Rhoda and then to LA to get his possessions and now he dont want to leave me alone so hes at the house. I told him hes 42 just about and I dont want him to end up like Sailors former hunting buddy Coot Veal what never left his mama and didnt make a real life. Pace is different from Coot of course since he been so many places around the world almost but itd be easy for him to stop his life on my account I can tell and I dont want that. He is a Ripley though as well as a Fortune and there aint too much good can be accomplished by arguing, I guess I should feel lucky in that regard to have such a good son and I do but you understand what Im saying.

Thats really about it I dont mean to go on you had plenty enough sorrows through your own life not to need mine. Just I felt you should know what happened to Sailor the way it did. I suppose Ill figure out what happens next for me Dal but if I dont it aint but the end of my world nobody elses. It aint either that Im feeling sorry for myself its different. I suppose since Sailor and me come back together thirty some years ago I never even give a thought to our being apart ever again and its the biggest kind of shock to face this knowing Sailor aint in prison this time hes dead and thats the end of that tune like hed say. I cant play no other tune Dal I wont. Remember how the Reverend Willie Thursday used to say a boy without a father is just a lost soul sailing on a ghost ship through the sea of life? Well Im one now a lost soul that is without my man. Sailor Ripley was my man Dal he was the one and Im so glad we found each other the world being as big as it is it was a miracle Im certain. We was never out of love Dal all this time since I was 16 aint that something? I been a fortunate woman I know but I cant believe its over and truth is I guess I might never.

Love you,
Lula

from PERDITA DURANGO (1991)

FAST FORWARD

PERDITA MET MANNY FLYNN in the San Antonio airport restaurant and bar. He was gobbling chicken fajitas and she was smoking a cigarette, an empty glass in front of her on the table, which was next to his.

"You wanna 'nother one?" Manny asked.

Perdita looked at him. Fat but neat. He wiped his thin lavender lips with a napkin. A waitress came over.

"Sweetheart, bring me another Bud and give that girl there whatever she wants."

"Wish somebody'd make me an offer like that," said the waitress. "What'll it be, honey?"

Perdita took a long drag on her Marlboro, blew out the smoke and killed it in an ashtray.

"Coke," she said.

"Diet?"

"Not hardly."

The waitress looked hard at Perdita for a moment, then wrote on Manny Flynn's check.

"One Bud, one Coke," she said, and hurried away.

Manny forked down the last bite of fajita, wiped his mouth again with the napkin, stood up and redeposited himself at Perdita's table.

"You live in San Antone?" he asked.

"Not really."

"You sure do have beautiful black hair. See my reflection in it just about."

Perdita withdrew another Marlboro from the pack on the table and lit it with a pink and black zebra-striped Bic.

"You catchin' or waitin' on one?" asked Manny.

"One what?"

"A plane. You headin' out somewhere?"

"My flight's been cancelled."

"Where you lookin' to go?"

"Nowhere now. About yourself?"

"Phoenix. Four-day computer convention. I sell software. By the way my name is Manny Flynn. Half Jewish, half Irish. What's yours?"

The waitress brought their drinks, set them down quickly on the table without looking at Perdita, and left.

"Perdita Durango. Half Tex, half Mex."

Manny laughed, picked up his beer and drank straight from the bottle. "Pretty name for a pretty Miss. It *is* Miss, isn't it?"

Perdita looked directly into Manny Flynn's eyes and said, "You want me to come to Phoenix with you? You pay my way, buy my meals, bring me back. I'll keep your dick hard for four days. While you're at the convention, I'll do some business, too. Plenty of guys at the hotel, right? Fifty bucks a pop for showin' tit and milkin' the cow. Quick and clean. You take half off each trick. How about it?"

Manny put the bottle back down on the table, then picked it up again and took a swig. Perdita turned away and puffed on her cigarette.

"I gotta go," Manny said. He threw several bills on the table. "That'll cover mine and yours."

He stood and picked up a briefcase and walked away. The waitress came over.

"I'm goin' off duty now," she said to Perdita. "You finished here?"

Perdita looked at her. The waitress was about forty-five, tall and skinny with bad teeth and phony red hair that was all kinked up so that it resembled a Brillo pad. She wore one ring, a black cameo with an ivory scorpion on the third finger of her right hand. Perdita wondered what her tattoos looked like.

"Just about," said Perdita.

The waitress scooped up Manny Flynn's money. Perdita nodded at it.

"Gentleman said for you to keep the change."

"Obliged," said the waitress.

Perdita sat and smoked her Marlboro until the ash was down almost to the filter.

"Dumb cocksucker," she said, and dropped the butt into the Coke.

LOCAL COLOR

PERDITA STOPPED the Cherokee at the entrance to the Rancho Negrita Infante. She cut the engine and got out, leaving the driver's door open. A few feet from the jeep she squatted, coiled her skirt around her and urinated on the sand. Romeo watched Perdita from the passenger seat and grinned.

"Always liked it that you don't never wear panties," he said, as Perdita climbed back in.

"Easier that way," she said. "Used to I wore 'em, but one day I just left 'em off. Now I don't think I own a pair."

Perdita started the Jeep up and proceeded toward the complex. She liked this drive, the dust and white sun. It was like being on another planet.

"You know I never asked you," Perdita said, "about how the ranch was named."

"Story is some local woman got pregnant by a black American soldier, and when the child was born it was black, too, a baby girl. So some of the villagers—they're called *'Los Zarrapastrosos,'* the ragged ones—took the baby and killed her and buried the body out this way in an unmarked grave."

"Why'd they do that?"

Romeo shrugged. "Ashamed, I guess. Surprised they didn't kill the mother also and bury them together."

Perdita wiped the sweat from above her upper lip and pulled the hair out of her eyes.

"Jesus but I hate that kind of ignorant shit," she said.

• • •

BAD ROAD

AS ROMEO DROVE, Estelle Satisfy thought about her mother, Glory Ann Blue Satisfy, and wondered whether she'd ever see her again. Glory Ann had been born and raised in Divine Water, Oklahoma, a place she dearly loved and wished she'd never left. The house on Worth Avenue in Dallas, where Estelle had grown up, never pleased Glory Ann, nor did Dallas. Glory Ann never stopped complaining about the city. "When I wake up in the mornin'," she'd say to Estelle, "I like to know who I'm goin' to see that day. There's too many surprises here in the Big D."

Glory Ann weighed three hundred pounds now. Her husband, Estelle's daddy, Ernest Tubb Satisfy, who'd been named after the famous singer, stood five-feet four and weighed one-hundred-ninety-five. He drove a 7-Up delivery truck and smoked Larks but took only three puffs of each one before putting it out. Ernest Tubb claimed the Larks lost their taste after the first two drags. He took the third one, he said, just to keep proving it to himself.

Estelle remembered her dog, Gopher, who died after he ate an entire extra large anchovy and onion pizza when she was in the seventh grade. Ernest Tubb buried Gopher under the plum tree in the backyard and Estelle still placed flowers on the grave every year on the anniversary of Gopher's death, April fifth. Estelle thought about these and other things that had happened in her life as the Cherokee bounced down a bad road to only the devil knew where.

Romeo, if that really is his name, looks like the devil, thought Estelle. And that Perdita woman looks weird and dangerous, too. I just hope they're not going to kill us, not before I've even got my cherry popped. That'd be a slap and a half, for sure, after all I've done to preserve my chastity. I should have left it to Stubby Marble. Grace Jane says the Marble boys, Eugene and Stubby, do it better than anyone, and I guess to hell she knows. Stubby kept after me the better part of a month before he gave up. Duane now, he acts like he don't care. I don't know, maybe he don't. I wish I knew what's goin' on here, really. I'm just a college girl with a lot of potential in the field of commercial art who ain't never even got laid yet. I know life ain't fair or even supposed to be, but this is somethin' different.

Duane pretended to be asleep. He kept his head down and tried hard not to think, but he couldn't help it, the thoughts just kept on coming. This wasn't the end of a good time, it was the beginning of a bad one. If Estelle hadn't insisted on goin' out for a beer, Duane thought, we'd be in our hotel room now and maybe she'd be lettin' me. Be a shame to die havin' been with only one girl, and her just Grace Jane Bobble, who the Marbles nicknamed "The Wide Missouri" not for no good reason. This gal Perdita is a picture, though. Reminds me of that poisonous snake from South America in the reptile and amphibian book we used in biology, one with the triangle-pointed, yellow-red face and orange ice eyes. She's the type'll bite and once the teeth are sunk you'd have to chop off the head with a hatchet to pry loose.

Duane opened his eyes and looked at Estelle. She had her eyes shut and was biting her lower lip and crying. Duane felt like crying, too, but he didn't. He wouldn't stop himself if he started, but no tears came. Maybe I can figure a way out of this, Duane thought. Estelle would be grateful, I bet, and let me do it. I wonder who done it to her other than the Marbles. They said she was some sweet meat. This life's sure got question marks scattered around like dogshit in a empty lot, the way Daddy says. I guess I ain't been steppin' careful enough.

HEROES

"TELL YOU WHO my heroes are, Duane. That way you get a better idea of who I am."

Romeo and Duane were sitting in chairs on the porch of the main house at Rancho Negrita Infante. Estrellita, as Romeo insisted Estelle be called, was asleep in a locked bedroom. It was almost midnight.

"I on purpose am leavin' your legs free, Duane. Sorry about your hands, though. You tell me if the wire's too tight."

"No, it ain't."

"Bueno, bueno. We got to keep the blood circulatin'. So here's my list: James Ruppert, George Banks, Howard Unruh, Pat Sherrill, Charles Whitman, R. Gene Simmons, Sr., James Oliver Huberty, and Joseph Wesbecker. Know every name by heart. Recognize any?"

"Don't think so."

"Not even Whitman?"

Duane shook his head no.

Romeo laughed. "Guess you don't do so good in history class."

"Got a B."

"Maybe they didn't cover this part yet. Here's what these men done. Ruppert killed eleven people, eight of 'em kids, at a Easter Sunday dinner in Ohio. Banks took out twelve, includin' five kids, in Pennsylvania. Unruh shot thirteen people in twelve minutes in Camden, New Jersey. He was somethin' else, too. Said, 'I'd've killed a thousand if I'd had enough bullets.'

"Sherrill murdered fourteen at a post office in Oklahoma. Simmons, Senior, got fourteen, too, all family members, in Arkansas. Buried a dozen under his house. Huberty slaughtered twenty-one at a McDonald's in San Diego, I believe. Wesbecker shot seven and wounded a bunch in a printing plant in Kentucky. And Whitman, of course, cut down sixteen from the tower on the campus of the University of Texas in Austin. Surprised you ain't heard of him."

"When did he do it?"

"About 1966, around in there."

"Before my time."

"Hell, boy, so was Hitler, and you can't tell me you ain't heard of him!"

"I heard of him."

"How about Attila the Hun? You heard of him?"

"I guess so. He was some kind of Turk or somethin'."

"Well, I don't include those guys had armies or other people doin' their killin' for 'em. I just rate the ones take it into their own hands. Also, I don't count the serial murderers, the ones done it over a long, drawn out period of time. It's only the ones just all of a sudden know they can't take no shit no longer and just explode on the world! There's more than those I mentioned but those are right off the top of my head. This kind of thing is a particular study of mine."

Perdita came out on the porch and rubbed her left thigh against Duane's right arm. She put her left hand into his thick blond hair and rubbed it around.

"You been tellin' the boy a bedtime story, Romeo?" she said.

"Just fillin' in a few holes in Duane's education."

Perdita smiled. "I got one or two need fillin', too. You two intellectuals feel like helpin' a lady out?"

IL AFFARE

ROMEO LISTENED to the train whistles in the distance. They sounded like wheezes from an organ with a mouse running across the keys. He sat in the driver's seat of the Cherokee, smoking, the windows rolled down, waiting for his cousin, Reggie San Pedro Sula, and Marcello "Crazy Eyes" Santos. It was almost two o'clock in the morning. The crescent moon lit the desert landscape partially, giving it the feel of a bombsite, twenty years after, the only residents rodents, insects and reptiles.

The deal sounded strange, thought Romeo, but if Santos was involved it would, of necessity, be very profitable. Reggie had worked for Santos before, several times, usually as a shooter. He'd do the job, pick up his money and go back to the islands. The money lasted quite a while in Caribe, but sooner or later he'd need another jolt, and as long as Santos survived there would be work for Reginald San Pedro Sula. Romeo was agreeable to the meet, although this was a slightly unusual procedure in a couple of ways. First, Reggie rarely was involved at the top of a deal; and two, Santos seldom ventured out of his hometown of New Orleans. But Romeo was prepared to listen. He knew when and how to be patient.

Romeo heard the car coming. He tossed away his cigarette and waited, listening for half a minute as the engine noise grew louder. The long, black car pulled off the highway across from Romeo and came to a dusty stop. The motor idled and Reggie got out of the back seat, closed the door behind him, and walked over to Romeo.

"Hola, primo," Reggie said. *"Qué tal?"*

"You tell me," said Romeo, as they shook hands.

Reggie was very tall, at least four or five inches over six feet, and heavyset. He was about fifty years old, his skin was the color of milk chocolate, and he wore a lavender leisure suit. His bald head reflected the moonlight. It was odd, Romeo thought, for Reggie not to be wearing a porkpie rain hat. In fact, Romeo could not recall a time he'd seen Reggie without a hat, other than when he went to sleep, since he'd lost most of his hair.

"I think I let the man, Señor Santos, tell you himself," said Reggie. "It's a good deal, a fair arrangement, you'll see."

Reggie smiled broadly, revealing his numerous gold teeth.

"There must be some danger in it, though," said Romeo, "for him to get you off the island."

Reggie gave a brief laugh. "There is usually some danger involved, is there not?" he said. "Though the man needs me for another matter, for where we are heading from here."

"I see. And how is everyone back home? Danny Mestiza wrote to me that Rocky James got a double sawbuck in the joint."

"Oh, yes, but he's out now again. I think for good. There was some irregularity but Señor Santos was able to clear it up for him. Halcyan an' Rigoberto is fine an' healthy. The money you sent helped out very good. I talk very strong about you to Señor Santos so he would consider you for this job."

"What is the job?"

"You come to the car an' he tell it himself. Remember you don't call him "Crazy Eyes." He don't like it when he see it in the newspaper, how they do just to annoy him."

Romeo climbed down, walked across the road and got into the back seat of the Mercedes-Benz limousine. Reggie closed the door and stood outside. A soft light was on inside the car. Marcello Santos had a drink in his right hand, three fingers of his favorite single malt Scotch whisky, Glenmorangie. He was wearing a dark gray suit with a blue shirt and a red tie; a pair of black Cole-Haan loafers, with tassels, and red, blue and yellow argyle socks; two-dollar drugstore sunglasses with bright yellow frames; and a large gold or diamond ring on each finger of both hands, excluding his thumbs, one of which was missing. He had a brownish-black, curly toupee glued to his head; some mucilage had trickled onto his forehead and dried there. Santos was sixty-eight years old and had ruled organized crime in the southern and southwestern United States for a quarter-century without ever having been convicted of either a felony or a misdemeanor.

"*Buona notte*, Mr. Dolorosa. Romeo," said Santos, extending his left hand, the one minus a thumb, as would the Pope or a princess. "Good to see you again."

Romeo squeezed the fingers.

"It is always my pleasure," he said.

"This is somewhat of an unusual place to meet, I know, Romeo, but as we are on our way to another meeting, and I hate to fly, I thought it would be the most expedient. I'm glad you could come."

"It's no problem, Marcello, in any case."

"*Bene*. Your cousin, Reginald, speaks well of you, you know. He tells me you take care of your family and friends back on the island. It's commendable of you."

"I do what I can."

Santos nodded and sipped his Scotch whisky.

"Would you like a drink, Romeo?"

"No, thank you. I am driving, and it's very late."

"Yes, all right. Here is my proposal. It is very simple. There will be a truck here at this spot forty-eight hours from now, a refrigerated truck, accompanied by a car. The truck will be loaded with human placentas to be used in the cosmetics industry. They are blended in skin creams that some people think can keep them looking young. Maybe it does, maybe not. I don't know. This load must be delivered as soon as possible to a private laboratory in Los Angeles. I would like you to drive the truck there for me. That way I know the shipment will be in good hands. The driver of the truck will turn it over to you, should you decide to do this, and leave in the accompanying automobile. All you have to do is deliver it to the address in Los Angeles that this man will give you. I have ten thousand dollars for you now, in old bills, fifties and hundreds. When you arrive safely in LA, your cousin, Reggie, will be there to give you another ten thousand dollars, also in old bills, and in similar denominations."

"Why don't you just have Reggie drive the truck?"

"I need him with me for a situation between now and when the delivery must be made. He'll fly to California as soon as this other business is finished. Can you do this?"

Romeo nodded. "Certainly, Marcello. I am glad to help you however I can."

Santos took off the cheap yellow sunglasses and looked at Romeo. His eyes were grayish-green with large red pupils that jumped and shimmied like flames. Crazy eyes. Despite himself, Romeo shivered.

"*Bene! Molto bene!*" said Santos, patting Romeo on the knee with the four fingers on his left hand. He put the sunglasses back on and drank the remainder of his whisky.

Santos flipped open a panel in the floor and took out a package and held it out to Romeo.

"*Buona fortuna, amico mio,*" said Santos. "Remember always that God and I, we both are with you."

Romeo accepted the package.

"I won't forget," he said.

GHOULS

ESTRELLITA WATCHED Perdita smoke. Perdita kept both hands on the steering wheel of the Cherokee and controlled the cigarette with her lips and teeth. She puffed on the Marlboro while it was between her lips and held it in her teeth when she exhaled. Perdita's long, loose black hair rested on the shoulders of her magenta tee shirt. She was wearing black cotton trousers and huaraches. Hidden by her hair were large silver hoop earrings, to each of which was attached a thin strip of red ribbon. Romeo had told her that a piece of red or brown material worn on the body neutralized the power of one's enemies, drained it from them like a grounding wire pulling electricity into the earth.

"How long you been smoking?" Estrellita asked.

Perdita did not respond. She did not really dislike Estrellita; she cared nothing about her.

"I only tried it twice," said Estrellita. "The first was in the summer before high school. I was with Thelma Acker at her house when her parents were gone. Her mother had an opened pack of Pall Malls in a kitchen drawer, so we smoked one. Only about half of one, really. I took about three puffs and coughed like crazy every time. Then around a month ago at a Sig Chi party I tried a Sherman. You ever have one of those? They're black. Kind of sweet tastin', too. Didn't care for it, either, though I didn't cough so much as with the Pall Mall."

Perdita took a final drag on her Marlboro and put it out in the ashtray.

"I know I'm just talkin' about nothin', and that you hate me," said Estrellita, "but I'm so scared I don't know what to do. I always talk a lot when I'm nervous. Do you talk a lot when you're nervous? Are you ever nervous? Are you ever gonna talk to me?"

Perdita looked quickly at Estrellita, then back at the road.

"You're gonna murder us, too, eventually," Estrellita said. "Isn't that right? Duane isn't very smart, really. I hope you know that. I mean, he's okay so far as pullin' on his pants one leg at a time, but he can't understand you people."

Perdita grinned slightly. "Do you?" she asked.

"I think you and Romeo are incredibly deranged individuals with no morals. You're the most evil creatures on the planet. I know you'll kill me soon so I'm sayin' it. My only hope is in the next life, which is what my Aunt Crystal Rae Satisfy always says. Now I know she's been absolutely correct all this time, that it's literal truth. There's too much ugliness on this earth, seein' how it's crawlin' with soulless ghouls."

"What's a ghoul?" said Perdita.

"What you and Romeo are. The worst kind of evil person. A person who'd violate a corpse."

Estrellita bit her lower lip but didn't cry.

"Whoever gave you the notion you was God's perfect child?" Perdita said. "Does Romeo call you Santa Estrellita when you go down on him? He always likes the religious angle. Tell you straight, Miss Satisfy, honey, you're right. It was up to just me, you'd be buried by now out in that desert along with them others. Your blond pussy's what's keepin' you alive, so you'd best make use of it for all it's worth. Girls like you got a kind of sickness, the only way to cure it is to kill it. Always talkin' about love and what's good, that shit, when you're same as me, just no particular piece of trash."

"You really think that? That we're the same kind of person?"

"Ain't seen no evidence to doubt it."

"Well, you're plenty wrong, I don't mind tellin' you. God may create people equal, but after that they're on their own."

Perdita laughed. She shook another Marlboro from the pack on the dash, stuck it between her lips and punched in the lighter. She kept her eyes on the jittery red taillights of the truck.

"A person don't never know who they are till someone knows better tells 'em," said Perdita. "A person won't listen might never know, they never stop to hear. Romeo's good at figurin' out people."

The lighter popped out and Perdita took it and lit her cigarette.

"He's a kind of fake, 'course," she said, "but he's got a unlimited way of seein' things. He's got the power to make people believe him."

"He's horrible," said Estrellita. "You're both so horrible I bet God don't even believe it."

Perdita laughed as she spit out the smoke.

"God don't take everything so serious, *gringa*. You see pretty soon how much He cares about you."

SALAMANDERS

PERDITA DIDN'T LIKE what was happening. She was pleased to be going to Los Angeles, but she knew already that it was over between her and Romeo. She wouldn't say anything yet, just let the deal go down and pick her spot to split. Maybe take care of this Estrellita bitch before then.

"What's on your indecent little mind tonight, honey?" asked Romeo. "You been awful quiet lately."

Romeo and Perdita were at the Round-up Drive-in in Yuma, waiting at the take-away counter for their order. They'd left Duane and Estrellita tied up together back in the motel room.

"Nothin' much, tell the truth. Just appreciatin' the beautiful evenin'."

Cars and trucks zoomed by on the street in front of the drive-in. The air was sickly warm and sticky and stank of burnt oil. A grayish haze hung like a soiled sheet across the sky. The breeze kicked at a corner of it now and again, wrinkling the gray just long enough to permit a peek at the twinkling platinum dots decorating the furious fuchsia. A tall, lean, cowboy-looking guy in his late twenties walked up to the take-out window.

"How you people doin' tonight?" he said.

"Not bad," said Romeo. "Yourself?"

The cowboy took off his black Stetson, reached into it and took out a half-empty pack of unfiltered Luckies. He offered it to Romeo and Perdita, both of whom declined, then shook one between his lips, flipped the pack back in and replaced the hat over his thick, tangled dark-brown hair.

"Can't complain," he said, and pulled a book of matches from the left breast pocket of his maroon pearl buttoned shirt and lit the cigarette. He bent down a little and looked in the window.

"Hey, Betsy!" he called. "How about a couple double-cheeseburgers and a side of chili and slaw."

"Be a few minutes, Cal," a woman shouted from within. "You want any fries with that?"

"Why not?" said Cal. "I'll take whatever you got to give, Betsy."

The woman laughed and yelled back, "Oh, hush! You know that bar talk don't cut it with me."

Cal smiled and straightened up. He stood off to the side of the window away from Romeo and Perdita and puffed on the Lucky Strike.

"So what's doin' in Yuma these days?" asked Romeo.

Cal looked at him and said, "That your Cherokee there, with the Texas plates?"

"That's right."

"You all from Texas, then?"

"Right again."

"Passin' through, I suppose."

"You got it."

"Headed for California, I bet. LA."

"You're on the money tonight, cowboy."

Cal laughed, took a last drag, and tossed away the butt.

"Not a whole lot to keep people here, I don't guess," he said. "It ain't the most excitin' city in the world."

"Nothin' wrong with peace and quiet, that's what you want."

"Ain't much of that here, either. Heat gets people mean, fries their brains and makes 'em dangerous. Tough on every livin' thing except salamanders."

"Salamanders?" said Perdita.

"Yeah," said Cal, "you know, them lizards can withstand fire."

An eighteen-wheeler downshifted and belched as it passed by, spewing a brown cloud of diesel smoke over the drive-in. Perdita coughed and turned away.

"Here's your order, sir," Betsy said to Romeo from the window, shoving it through. "Be $17.25."

Betsy was a middle-aged Asian woman with badly bleached blond hair.

Romeo put a twenty down on the counter, picked up the bag, and said, "Change is yours."

"'Preciate it and come back now. Yours is comin' up, handsome," she said to Cal.

"I ain't goin' nowhere."

"No kiddin'," she said, and laughed.

"You folks take care now," Cal said to Romeo and Perdita.

"Do our best," said Romeo. "You, too."

Driving back to the motel, Perdita said, "You get a good look at that gal back there?"

"You mean Betsy?"

"Woman had the worst hair, Jesus. Never saw no Oriental person with blond hair before."

"Plenty more surprises where we're headed, Perdita. Just you wait. I got big plans for us."

She turned and stared at Romeo. He was grinning, confident, full of himself.

"Don't make me no promises you can't keep," Perdita said. "There ain't nothin' worse for a woman than a man punks out on her. That happens, no tellin' what she'll do."

"I'll keep this in mind, sweet thing," said Romeo, nodding and grinning, "I surely will."

HISTORY LESSON

"E. T. Satisfy, is it? Hometown, Dallas."

"Right the first time."

The clerk looked up from the registration card across the desk and down at Ernest Tubb.

"How you mean to pay for this?"

"Cash," said Ernest Tubb, handing the clerk a hundred dollar bill.

The clerk took it, examined both sides, went into another room for a minute, then came back and gave Ernest Tubb his change plus a receipt and a room key.

"You got 237. Upstairs and around to the right. Ice and soda pop machines by the staircase. Need more you holler."

"I'm obliged."

In the room the first thing he did was phone home.

"Glory Ann? It's me, Ernest Tubb."

"Just where in Judas's country are you?" she asked. "I been worried crazy!"

"Easy, woman. I'm at the Holiday on Madre Island. Got a lead in Larry Lee County that Estelle and Duane Orel mighta come down here. College kids on break partyin' both sides of the border. Heard about two were kidnapped a week ago. Might be them. I'm headed for Mextown soon's I hang up."

"Kidnapped! Save Jesus! Rita Louise Samples is here with me now, and Marfa Acker's comin' back later. They been my cross and crutch since you disappeared on me."

"I ain't disappeared. I told you, I'm huntin' for Estelle."

"If I lose you, too, don't know what I'll do."

"You ain't lost nothin', Glory, includin' weight. You stickin' to that lima bean diet Dr. Breaux put you on?"

"Ernest Tubb, be serious! Who can think about dietin' at a time like this?"

"I am serious, Glory Ann. You keep eatin' like a herd of javelinas cut loose in a Arby's and you'll flat explode! Rita Louise and Marfa be scrapin' your guts off the kitchen walls and collectin' 'em in a box to bury. You keep clear of them coffeecakes, hear?"

Glory Ann began to cry.

"Oh, Ernest Tubb, you're just a mean tiny man."

"Lima beans, Glory Ann, Lima beans," he said, and hung up.

Ernest Tubb backed his Continental out of the parking space, drove to the motel lot exit and turned right. He was thinking about the last time he and Glory Ann had made love. She'd insisted on being on top and just about squashed him. He'd felt like he imagined those people in their cars felt when that freeway fell on them during the big quake in California.

It was several seconds before Ernest Tubb realized that he'd turned his Mark IV in the wrong direction on a one-way thoroughfare. By the time he saw the nose of the White Freightliner and heard the horn blast it was too late for him to do anything about it.

"Oh, Glory!" Ernest Tubb said, and then he was history.

BACK AT THE NURSERY

"YOU UNDERSTAND what has to be done?"

"I do."

"You have no problem about it?"

Reggie hesitated, then shook his head no.

"Good."

Santos poured more Glenmorangie into his glass, swirled the brown liquid around and stared down into it.

"You and your cousin have been close friends, have you not?"

"We were raised together as boys, but then Romeo and his mother left Caribe. Since then we are in touch."

Santos took off his yellow-framed sunglasses and set them on the table. He rubbed his eyes with his abbreviated left hand, then smoothed back his hair. He looked at Reginald San Pedro Sula, who wanted to turn away from the two small darting animals imprisoned in Marcello's face, but Reggie steeled himself and did not flinch. Santos's eyes were the color of Christmas trees on fire.

"It's not that there is anything personal in this," Santos said, "but Romeo has done some terrible things, things so terrible that not even the Mexican authorities can allow him to operate there any longer. I have sent some people in to take care of the situation in Zopilote. From now on we will handle the business. It was necessary to remove your cousin from the area in order to effect the change. In the meantime, he does us the favor of transporting other goods for us, for which he is fairly compensated. After the delivery is secured, you will pay him the remainder of what we have agreed, and then you will kill him."

Santos lifted his glass with the fingers and opposing digit of his right hand and drank most of the Scotch in it.

"After Romeo is dead, of course," he said, "the money is no good to him, so you will take it as payment for doing me this favor."

"That is most generous of you," said Reggie.

Santos closed his eyes and shook his head.

"Not generous, Reggie—just. There is a difference."

He reopened his eyes and put his sunglasses back on. Reggie relaxed, taking off his powder-blue porkpie hat and wiping the sweat from his bald head with a lime-green handkerchief.

"Deception is merely a tool of resourcefulness," said Santos. "Have you ever heard of Captain Philippe Legorjus?"

"I don't believe so, sir."

"Well, he is the commander of France's elite anti-terrorist forces. Not long ago he was sent by his government to New Caledonia, which is in the South Pacific, to quell an uprising by the Kanak rebels on the island of Ouvea. New Caledonia is part of the French Overseas Territories, and so it was necessary to protect the French citizens who live there. It is also the place from which the French conduct their nuclear tests.

"In any case, Captain Legorjus was kidnapped by the rebels, along with twenty-two others. The leader of the Kanak Socialist National Liberation Front, I believe it was called, was something of a religious fanatic, and had been trained for guerilla warfare in Libya by Khadafy.

This man vowed to maintain a state of permanent insecurity in the French South Pacific Territory if the separatists' demands for independence were not met. A familiar story. I remember a newspaper photograph of him, wearing a hood and holding a rifle, the pockets of his field jacket stuffed with cartridges. He threatened to kill a white person a day so long as the French government occupied Noumea, the capital of New Caledonia.

"While the Kanak leader carried on making speeches to the press, Legorjus organized the hostages and not only led them to freedom but took control of the separatist stronghold, disarmed the rebel soldiers, and captured their leader, enabling several hundred French naval infantrymen to swarm in and restore order. Upon his return to Paris, Legorjus was accorded a parade down the Champs d'Elysées and declared a national hero."

Santos paused and looked at Reggie, who smiled and said, "He must be a brave man, this captain."

Santos nodded. "Brave and cunning, Reggie. I make a point of studying these kinds of extraordinary men. There is much to be learned from their behavior. My firm belief is that life must be lived according to a man's own terms, or else it is probably not worth living."

"I am sure you are right, Mr. Santos."

Marcello licked the stub on his left hand where his thumb had been.

"I know you will do a good job for me," he said, walking over to the window and looking out at the sky.

"Ah, *si sta facendo scuro*," Santos said. "It's getting dark. You know, Reggie, I am almost seventy years old, and despite all I know, there is still nothing I can do about that."

59° AND RAINING IN TUPELO

TATTOOED ON THE BICEP of Shorty's left arm were the words ONE LIFE ONE WIFE and tattooed on his right bicep was the name CHERRY ANN.

"That her?" Perdita asked him.

"Who?" said Shorty.

"Cherry Ann your wife's name?"

"Was."

"She change it?"

Shorty laughed and shook his head no.

"Changed wives," he said.

"Kinda puts the lie to your other arm, don't it?"

Shorty yawned and closed his eyes. He opened them and picked up his glass and took a long swallow of Pearl.

"Ain't nothin' stays similar, sweetheart, let alone the same. Or ain't you figured that out yet?"

Perdita Durango and Shorty Dee were sitting on adjacent stools at the bar of Dottie's Tupelo Lounge. It was eight-thirty on Friday night, December thirtieth. Oklahoma State was playing Wyoming in the Sea World Holiday Bowl football game on the television set above the bar.

"Know what I like to watch more than anything else?" Shorty said.

"Not knowin' you any better than I do, which is not at all practically," said Perdita, "I'd be afraid to ask."

"Punt returns."

"That so."

"Yeah. Some people it's triples. Me it's punt returns. I like any kind of runbacks: kickoffs, interceptions, fumbles. But there's somethin' special about a little jack-rabbit of a guy takin' a tall ball and turnin' on his jets."

Shorty took another sip of beer.

"You been in town long?" he asked.

"Few days."

"How's it goin' so far?"

"Been rainin' since I got here. Weather always like this?"

"Time of year it is. Fifty-nine and rainin' sounds about right for Christmas."

"What else Tupelo got to offer?"

"Other than bein' the birthplace of Elvis Presley, you mean?"

Perdita laughed. She swept back her long, straight black hair with one hand and picked up her glass with the other.

"Didn't know about Elvis bein' born in Miss'ippi," she said, and took a sip of beer.

"Where you from?" asked Shorty.

"Here and there. Texas, mostly."

"Brings you this way?"

"Lookin' for somethin', I guess."

Shorty offered his right hand.

"Shorty Dee. Glad to be of service if I can."

She squeezed his fingers.

"Perdita Durango. Pleased to meet you, Shorty. You still married?"

Shorty laughed. "Thought we was beginnin' a conversation here."

Perdita smiled. "How about buyin' me a new beer?"

"Now you're talkin', honey," he said, signaling for another round. "Got any more potentially embarrassin' questions you want to get out of the way?"

"You rich?"

The bartender set two more bottles on the bar in front of them.

Shorty laughed again. "Nigger rich, maybe," he said.

"Bein' nigger rich is all right, I guess," said Perdita, "long as a body got enough friends is rich for damn sure."

They picked up the fresh bottles of beer and tapped them together.

"There you go," said Shorty.

Perdita smiled. "Here I go," she said.

OUT OF TIME

"Words, as is well known,
are the great foes of reality."

—Joseph Conrad
Under Western Eyes

from LANDSCAPE WITH TRAVELER:

THE PILLOW BOOK OF FRANCIS REEVES (1980)

I DON'T KNOW THAT THIS WILL BE OF VERY GREAT INTEREST

I DON'T KNOW that this will be of very great interest to anyone, but it seems such a perfect place to begin. I'm on a bouncing bus going back to New York after a weekend on Fire Island, which was quite pleasant in spite of my misgivings beforehand. The bus service is the best thing that's happened in years for going to F.I. It picks you up at various convenient places around New York, gives you a free drink—fifty cents each for seconds and thirds—and a package of toasted almonds, and takes you right to the ferry. Plus they allow dogs (sans carriers).

Before, I had to cab it to the station, take a train (with dog in carrier), then another cab to the ferry—and usually had to stand all the way on the train—all of which usually cost well over the bus price besides being a rather unpleasant trip being bustled about by Long Island commuters, feisty conductors, hot trains (the buses are air conditioned), etc., ad infinitum. But then some enterprising fellow got the idea of chartering buses, and the Bus-A-Long was born.

At first, so I'm told, it was strictly a gay affair, with orgies all the way back to New York in the back part of the bus. Dick Cornelia swears that the first time he took the bus a giggling voice was heard to say, "Don't come in the air conditioner, Mary—it'll go all over the bus!" *Se non è vero, è ben trovato.* Now, however, it's quite integrated and proper.

But I was rather sad on the trip out just from looking at all the people—the handsome young men so secure in their youth and beauty, and the old ones looking at them, envying them, desiring them perhaps, remembering probably when they too were young and sure that (if they ever thought about it at all) they always would be.

As they looked at them there seemed also to be a certain pity in their eyes that these kids had such a bitter lesson to learn in front of them—a certain sad tolerance of their arrogant flaunting of their invulnerable youth and good looks. Fair cheeks and fine bodies, etc.

There is also a great deal of projection in all this on my part, I'm sure, though I don't really have those feelings about growing old. Still, to most "active" (as opposed to old tranquil me!) homosexuals youth is the pinnacle, so I doubt I was too far wrong in my musings. And they all seemed so awfully lonely, young and old alike—as opposed to being alone (like me). And as I thought that, it occurred to me that they might be thinking the same thing when they looked at me.

Sad, too, to look at the beautiful young men and have their beauty almost totally canceled out by their theatrically effeminate mannerisms. They were all smoking like Bette Davis, calling each other "Dahling" like Tallulah, holding their eye-lids half-shut like Dietrich—etc., etc., but even that wasn't consistent. It alternated with limp-wristed slaps and playful shoves and high-pitched squeals of "Oh, *Mary*, you bitch, you're really *such* a camp!" and the inevitable sidelong glances to make sure it was not lost on the spectators. But they mostly got drunk and/or tired and finally calmed down.

It was nice at last to leave the bus and sit on the open top deck of the little "ferry" (I had to laugh the first time I went to Fire Island, remembering the ferries on the Mississippi, to see these little sixty or so foot boats) with spray hitting you in the face and to forget the bus trip.

Mostly it was a quiet and very nice (therefore) weekend. I "had" to go to one big loud cocktail party, but only for a half hour or so, and refused both nights to go to the bars. The moon was full so Zagg (my dog) and I took long walks along the beach all by ourselves and it was beautiful enough to bring tears to one's eyes. Nothing like "nature" to clear the head! I don't mean necessarily *visible* nature, to which I am fairly indifferent, but rather the hiss of cosmic silence, or the natural sounds and smells of air and water and sand squeaking under your bare heels, and the expansion that only solitude in the open produces—preferably the virgin, uninhabited open, but in this case the illusion was made convincing by the moonlit dark and by keeping one's eyes toward the ocean until one was in a sufficient trance of self-communication to see nothing.

I was amused to be flagrantly flirted with by a most handsome young man for whom everyone was on the make but me. He had come by with several friends the night before (friends of his) at about midnight to pick up my host and go to the bars. He kept insisting that I come with them, at which knowing looks passed among the others. But I stuck to my guns and went for a walk (and to bed) alone, much, apparently, to the others' consternation and amazement. Though I can't say that I wasn't at least a little tempted.

However, it's good to be going home, as always. Why *do* I always weaken and accept these invitations?

I CAN RECALL MY FIRST ORGASM QUITE CLEARLY

I CAN RECALL my first orgasm—at six or seven—quite clearly. I had just seen the movie *Lost Horizon*, and that night in bed I pretended I was flying an airplane over the Himalayas, searching for Shangri-La. Actually, I was Nelson Eddy searching for it! As I moved in the bed my penis rubbed against the sheet, and it felt so good that I kept rocking and dipping the plane. As I got more and more excited I imagined I saw it and started shouting "Shangri-La, Shangri-La, Shangri-Laaaaa!" until my penis exploded, as did my imaginary airplane against the mountains.

At about age eight or nine, I pondered that ejaculation (for which I naturally longed) might possibly be more a matter of suction than of age. Being one day alone in the house and having no friend handy to provide the suction, I turned to the vacuum cleaner hose. I carefully determined that it contained no grinding, cutting, or biting mechanism, inserted my poor little penis, and switched the motor on—an altogether hair-raising, terrifying experience as my tiny organ was violently whipped back and forth in the suction. I admitted defeat and set myself to wait a few years.

There was also that unforgettable time, when we were twelve, when my friend Timmy, as full of self-importance, I daresay, as he has ever been, took Rick and me out to his uncle's farm to initiate us into the ecstasy of fucking a cow. We were an odd triumverate, the school's two star jocks and I, but the relationship was one of three equals and not at all one that hindsight might have expected. But to that Saturday—we rose early and biked the ten or twelve miles out to the farm to rouse his cousin. He brought a box ("the" box, I guess) and we went to look for a suitable cow, Rick and I, the awestruck innocents, trailing behind the two masters. Having secured the beast to a fence and placed the box just right, Timmy mounted it, dropped his jeans to his ankles, and, with Rick close in on one side and me on the other to observe (the cousin was at the cow's head), inserted his ready prick into the flabby and rather filthy slit and started ramming.

It was as though his cock pushed a button in the wrong place. Immediately a huge flood of liquid shit poured out of the cow over Timmy's belly, cock, and legs, filling his dropped jeans and overflowing to the ground. Timmy's face, Timmy's face! Rick and I collapsed in laughter, as did the cousin when he saw. Timmy reddened for every possible reason—except where he was brown—but mainly fury.

The three of us stripped, picked Timmy up, and threw ourselves into the nearby creek. Our ardor was cooled, but soon revived, and we soothed it in the more usual way, which even the cousin, I believe, preferred to the cow.

AS I WRITE THIS SENTENCE

As I WRITE this sentence, I am forty-eight "going on forty-nine," as it was put in the South of my childhood. If I don't think hard about that from time to time, I am unconscious of my age. I smoke a pack a day, drink socially, eat junk food (usually) for my one daily meal, drink fifteen to twenty cups of coffee a day, go to bed too late, and feel fine, though I catch colds with the greatest of ease. When I was in college, nineteen or twenty, I was taken to a fortune teller of high repute, an ancient black lady who lived in a little dark cabin deep in the woods. The plain wood of the large chair she sat in was burnished with lifetimes of use. Her only name, that anyone knew about, was Mother, and she smelled of wood smoke. She would receive you if you were brought by someone she knew, then would hold your face between her hands and gaze into your eyes for as long as she needed to decide whether she would tell you your future. For her services she would accept nothing but a little tobacco, though if you wanted potions, charms, or spells, you had to pay a moderate sum, and she told you flatly that she had no confidence in such things. Her grandmother had taught her how to concoct them, so she continued the tradition. There was the hiss of silence about her. She looked at me for a long time and said quickly: "Happiness till fifty-five. Then death from your lungs. Not much money. Not much love.

Enough." Then she let go of my face and smiled. I gave her the tobacco I'd brought, thanked her, and left. When I think about what she said, it's the last word that holds my attention. It somehow seems the core of her insights, and though I share with my namesake a horror of interpretation, the word fascinates me. If she had been a simpler woman, I'd accept it at its face value as a dismissal. She was not a simple woman, however. Looking at her face was like seeing the Earth after all life had left it, and looking into her eyes was like looking back through the tunnel of time to the beginning. She was an embodiment with a slight rearrangement of the opening theme of the Quartets. Well anyhow, I have thought much about that word, and I believe she was right. It all is, or will be, enough. I have accepted her lesson and have not asked for more.

• • •

BY THIS TIME THERE WERE THREE OF US

BY THIS TIME there were three of us who wanted out in order to go to New York and become big stars. We made a pact that if any one of us got caught in the bushes with our pants down, he'd be sure to turn in the other two, as the military investigators always asked for other names. It was unlikely that I'd be caught as I wasn't doing anything much but going out with Portia, so it was up to the other two, who were named Don and Dan. Dan it was who eventually got caught and in two weeks he was out. Two weeks later Don was out.

I noticed that I was being followed when I'd leave the base in the evening, but when the guy saw me coming out of a very posh apartment house with a beautiful girl in tow, he'd follow us to a restaurant or bar or concert hall and then go on about his business. A month passed and nothing happened, except that I was always followed.

Then the commander of the photo center sent for me and said he'd had a report about me that had to be checked out. I asked what it might be and he hemmed and hawed embarrassedly and finally came out with it in a very round-about way. I coolly told him it was true and was thereupon whisked out to an interrogation center in Embassy Row, a CIA or CID or something headquarters.

The interrogation was an amusing adventure, in itself, which I enjoyed immensely. It was pure Hollywood, and the agents and I approached our roles in dead seriousness. I was put into a room with a desk, two chairs, and a big, rather oddly placed mirror. I'd seen enough movies to realize that the mirror was not an attempt at interior decoration.

A handsome, well-suited young man entered, sat, and began to ask me stern, vulgarly stated questions like, "Did you ever suck a dick?" I told him politely (with just a hint of firmness) that I would answer no questions until his partner came out from behind the mirror, as I liked to know to whom I was speaking. We both stuck to our guns. "I've got all day," he said with a belligerent patience. "And so," I smiled, "have I."

The other man eventually appeared. He was much like his colleague, but even prettier. The questions began again, but now I objected to their language, telling them that I did not speak in that fashion and supposed, since they seemed reasonably well educated and gentlemanly, that neither did they, and proposed that we use language with which we were all more comfortable (the bus dispatcher in Tucson popped into my head, and I had to suppress a smile).

They sat staring at me for a long moment, and that one little moment put control of the situation into my hands. "Now," I said in my most businesslike manner, "I have indulged in all the more usual 'perversions,' as you call them, except annilingus. I have enjoyed both serial and mutual, simultaneous fellatio, anal intercourse, mutual masturbation, even, at times, the 'Princeton Rub.' These things I have done times past counting and, if I *do* say so, do them very well. Is there anything further you desire to know?" (I would have said, "my good man," except that there were two of them and that expression loses something in the plural. "Good sirs" was a possibility, but I rejected it as too servile.)

My inquisitors looked at each other. I suddenly loved them. One said, "It's time for lunch." Against all regulations, I would suppose, they invited me to lunch with them at a nice little restaurant in Georgetown, where we had a lovely, real conversation, about homosexuality, the law, freedom, "life," love, me. I told them freely that I had, in a sense, "engineered" this whole thing, and why. Facts were facts and rules rules, so they were mated and had to let me have my discharge. There was even a small tender sadness and mutual sympathy acknowledging each other's predicaments—acknowledging each other, in short. Then silence and rumination. We had finished our coffee. "Well," I said at last, gently this time, "shall we go?"

JIM'S EARLY LETTERS WERE TRULY ASTONISHING

JIM'S EARLY LETTERS to me were truly astonishing. Never had I thought it possible so completely to "know" another person without ever having met him, and I was filled with happy expectations when, a few months after Ada had returned to Greece, Jim came to visit me for the first time.

I suppose it's always a bit of a shock finally to meet someone with whom you've been corresponding or of whom you've had intimate knowledge of one sort or another for a considerable period beforehand, and it was, it seemed to me, like that for Jim. Not that I wasn't somewhat nervous and apprehensive as well, but Jim's distance surprised me. At first I actually supposed that he disliked me, but I relaxed and decided this uncomfortable stage would pass.

To be sure there were friends of mine who suspected Jim of "hustling" me, for the airfare to New York at first—he didn't have the money at the moment so I sent it to him—and whatever else he could after that. Jim later told me there were friends of his who assumed I was merely a lecherous old queen trying to get Jim to stay with me so that I could seduce him. Happily, both suspicions proved false, as Jim repaid me soon after returning to the West Coast, and, though I found Jim quite attractive, sex was not my objective.

But this whole homo/hetero bit is just a further extension of what I mean about opening up and living what one feels. It would seem that maybe the division between men and women had gone as far as it could possibly go, so in their need for walls "they" had to divide homosexuals and heterosexuals. It's a pity. There is such beauty in everyone that it seems proper to enjoy it. I remember reading an interview with James Dean years ago, who, when asked—rather rudely, I thought—whether it was true that he was bisexual, said with a smile that he had no intention of going through life with one hand tied behind his back.

This isn't really a plea for total sensualism, but I find that most straight men and women (though not so much as men) are really afraid to look at another person of their own sex and even visually appreciate his beauty. There are, of course, certain socially acceptable outlets for this feeling—for instance, it's perfectly all right for any man to think and to say that this or that movie actor is very handsome, but he has to keep silent if he sees a man even more handsome on the street. According to

Francis Reeves, a happy, healthy, open-minded, curious bisexuality is the natural state of man. Why doesn't the world just relax!

I was aware, as I say, of this distance on Jim's part, and I couldn't understand why things should be any different between us in person than they had been in our correspondence. The feeling did gradually pass, though a certain tentativeness remained, not really disappearing, I felt, until my visit the following year to Jim and Jean's home in San Francisco, where they had moved.

The first time he came to New York, however, we did have some good times. It was a feeling-out period, but our mutual likes conquered any temporary doubts about whether or not we were really even *intellectually* compatible. Jim enjoyed my favorite little restaurants—especially the ropa vieja at a Cuban-Chinese place near my house—and I took him around to the best secondhand bookstores. We did the usual things people do, went to a couple of movies, etc., but mostly we stayed at home in the evenings and talked.

At first we must each have wondered what the other "wanted" from the relationship, though I should think it's fairly obvious we both wanted a friend. (Who can say what a friend is?!) But when I felt a distrust (or dislike) on his part, I'd close up and hold back and just stay neutral, hoping it would reassure him, but realizing at the same time that it might make him feel that I distrusted or disliked him! Straight guys can be as prissy as virgins.

I admit that my knowledge of friendship is mainly theoretical, but I don't feel at all unique in that. I wonder at times if my idea about it isn't too absolute. Nevertheless, I can't change it. Champagne comes from Champagne, goddamnit! On the other hand, I'm not so romantic as to believe that friendship "just happens." I'm sure that, just like marriage, it has to be worked at with a lot of effort and goodwill.

I do think that Jim was expecting me to be somewhat of a teacher for him, an old hand if not a kind of father figure, and was surprised to find me more of a contemporary—albeit a rather "other-worldly" one. And I suppose, too, that I, with my brother-fetish, really hoped he would be that sought-after sibling with whom I could share things without the fear of being importunate, prepossessing, or rejected. I like to think we've each given the other at least some of what we needed. And life continues, does it not?

AN INVITATION

JIM AND I spent a bizarre evening with a couple I'd met when I was working for Sylvia Fowler. For the longest time Jason and Sara had been asking me over to dinner and, for one reason or another, I'd been unable or unwilling to accept their invitation.

After I left Fowler's, Jason went to work there, and whenever I visited the shop I'd see him and he'd ask when I was going to come over for supper and to see his and Sara's paintings. Both he and Sara were artists—though I had no idea what their work was like—and finally, one day I decided it would be really impolite to refuse any longer, and I told Jason I'd come. Jim was staying with me at the time, however, and I told Jason that, but he just said to bring him along, one more wouldn't be any problem. If Jim wanted to come, too, that was fine.

I told Jim I had no idea what to expect, except that both Jason and Sara seemed very nice people, and it would probably be fun. Jim agreed to accompany me, and at the appointed time we arrived at their door.

We rang the bell several times, but there was no answer. I was certain I'd gotten both the address—they lived in a loft on Broome Street—and time correct, and I couldn't imagine where they could be. Jim and I went over a couple of blocks to a bar and I telephoned them, but there was no answer.

Jim thought they might be out at the store buying groceries, and, since it was freezing outside, suggested that we wait awhile in the bar, have a beer, and check back again in a half hour. We had a beer and played a pinball machine—the first time I'd done that since I could remember—and in a half hour I called again.

This time Sara answered. When I told her it was I she sounded very cheerful, and asked what was up. I explained that Jim and I had been there when Jason told us to be and there'd been no answer. That was too bad, Sara said, Jason hadn't mentioned anything to her about our coming. They had been to a local gallery to see a friend's new paintings.

I didn't know quite what to say, so I asked her how they had looked to her. "Not very interesting, I'm afraid," she said. "He's hung up on boxes." Then she asked if I'd like to speak to Jason, and I said yes.

They kept me waiting for at least five minutes before Jason came to the phone. "Sorry, Francis," he said, "Sara forgot all about the dinner. Where are you?"

Well, Sara's forgetting about dinner did not explain Jason's presence at the gallery at the time he was supposed to be home expecting us. We were at a bar a couple of blocks away, I told him.

"We?" Jason said. "Who's 'we'?"

"My friend Jim and I," I said. "My friend who's visiting from California. You said it would be all right to bring him along."

"Oh," said Jason, "of course, of course. Tell you what, Sara and I'll just get ourselves together here and meet you up at the bar. Where did you say it was?"

I told him.

"We'll be there in a jiffy. Hang on and we'll take you out to a really good place for dinner. Bye."

I hung up and told Jim the news. Neither of us cared particularly, but the situation seemed strange, nonetheless. We waited, drank another beer or two, and in about an hour Jason came in alone.

"Sorry about Sara," he said. "She has an awful time of it once a month, and this is the time."

I introduced him to Jim, who by now was wondering just what I'd gotten him into, and I was beyond wondering. It was a bad situation, one I'd endeavor not to repeat, but now there was nothing to do but carry off the evening as best we could.

"Well, where would you like to go?" asked Jason.

I reminded him that he had mentioned on the phone that he knew a good place.

"Oh, Fiorelli's," he said. "We'd never get in there at this hour. Besides, it's full of tourists. Why don't we go to a Mexican place around the corner?"

I said that I didn't know a decent Mexican restaurant existed in New York.

"Well, come on," said Jason, "it's not far."

He led the way. It was getting colder and windier and after four or five blocks I asked Jason just how much farther around the corner was the place.

"I hope it hasn't closed down," he said. "I'm sure it was right here somewhere. I haven't been for a while."

We walked on. I was embarrassed and furious, and I was certain Jim was getting angry, but he didn't say anything, so I kept quiet, too.

"There it is!" Jason said, suddenly, pointing to a dimly lit doorway across the street. We crossed over and of course it was closed.

"Well, that's too bad," said Jason. "It's a really good place. Look," he said quickly, before I could say anything, "let's just go back to my place and fix something up."

"What about Sara?" Jim asked. "I thought she wasn't feeling well."

"Oh, it'll be all right," he said. "She's probably already eaten, and we can make our own dinner. I'm a good cook."

By this time I was frozen and I couldn't argue. We followed Jason back to Broome Street. Once we were upstairs in their loft, while Jim and I huddled around the living-room heater, Jason disappeared into what I assumed was the bedroom to talk to Sara. Pretty soon we could hear loud voices and the door to the living room slammed. It was Sara who came out.

"Would you like some wine?" she asked us, and disappeared into what I assumed was the kitchen.

I looked around. There was a hideous green painting that took up an entire wall and a hideous gray painting that took up another wall. Then a young, bearded guy came into the room bouncing a basketball. He looked at us and bounced the basketball into the kitchen. Sara came out with three glasses filled with red wine on a tray. She offered the tray to each of us, took the third glass for herself, and sat down on the only chair in the room. Jim and I took our coats off and sat down on the floor.

"Don't lean against that wall," she said, "it might still be a little wet."

We moved forward a bit and turned and looked at the wall. It was a dark pink with light bulbs sticking out of it at various angles. I could hear the bearded guy bouncing the basketball in the kitchen.

"Charles!" Sara shouted, and the pounding stopped. "He's a genius," she said. "He could be a great painter but he won't paint anymore, or can't. I don't know. I'm losing patience with him."

"Does he live here, too?" Jim asked.

"He used to. He's here a lot."

Jim and I sipped the wine while Sara prattled on ridiculously about "minimal," "semi-minimal," and "seminally minimal" art. I was truly horrified. More than horrified, I was insulted. Jason did not appear.

After several minutes of this, I arose and announced that we really had to go. I couldn't imagine how Jim was managing to keep his cool. I'm sure it was only out of politeness to me, but he needn't have bothered. I'd never experienced anything like it before.

"Oh, but I want you to see my paintings!" Sara cried.

"Aren't these—" I said, waving at the living-room walls, "yours?"

"Oh, no," she said. "A friend did these as a wedding gift for me and Jason. Mine are in my studio."

Jim didn't—or wouldn't—return my look, and I followed her into another room. *Why* was I doing this?

It was worse than I could have imagined. The canvases—huge, giant stretches of *real*, very expensive canvas—were almost entirely blank. There were only a few very tiny blood-red spots on off-white backgrounds. Most of the dots were located near the bottom of each canvas. There were dozens of them. I was actually frightened that she would ask me what I thought of them.

"What do you think of them?" she asked.

"Yes, well . . . I've never seen anything quite like them," I said.

We stood around for a minute and then Sara covered them over affectionately, and we went out. Jim had his coat on. He handed me mine.

"I hope you'll come over again," said Sara, "when Jason is feeling better."

A DESERT ISLAND LIBRARY

A DESERT ISLAND LIBRARY: If, as is usual, only one book is allowed, then it would be a blank book like the one I'm writing in—the biggest one I could find. To choose a given small number of books already written would likely give one more regrets than pleasure. I would like to have:

The Blue Estuaries.
All of Austen, Forster, Kerouac, and Nabokov.
The Last of the Wine.
Genji.
The Lord of the Rings.
The Silmarillion.
We Think the World of You.
Cavafy.
Byron's letters.

Makriyannis's memoires (but only in Greek).
Balzac.
Proust.
Plato.
Homer.
Nocturnes for the King of Naples.
The Jerusalem Bible.

LETTER TO MARSHALL CLEMENTS

20 March 1971

dear Marshall,

Your letter was beautiful—like a Henry Miller only not so egotistical and bullshit-hungup. The details of your sexual disappointments and eventual arrival at your relationship with Flora (now to be severed you say) are like any number of careful 19th century French novels—that not meant as to deprecate you in any way—but the sadness is the same—only there is just the sadness that comes across, not despondency, which is quite a small miracle—

Why not expand it and really write it up? It would take considerable energy but would make terrific "underground" stuff . . .

It's a remarkable letter and I wish you would write me again your reminiscences, boyhood and otherwise—perhaps you don't realize how interesting it is. It's a completely different life, from a completely different viewpoint than mine, so, naturally, fascinating . . .

Love,

B.

from
PORT TROPIQUE
(1980)

THE FIRST THING was the sky, how wide it was and how many clouds there were in it. There were many clouds and every five minutes one of them would block out the sun for as long as a minute and it would still be hot but without the glare. The sun was very hot, it burned you even if you were already deeply tanned. When your back was turned it came into your shoulder blades and felt like the heat was coming from the inside out.

Beautiful Indian girls passed on the street. It was impossible to guess their ages except that they were very young, between fourteen and twenty. Their wide eyes looked at you for a moment very seriously then turned away suddenly and completely.

Franz sat in the zócalo and walked around the town like it was all a dream. He drank beer and ate onions and peppers in the bars by the market where men fell over dead drunk on their faces on the floor. He bargained for whatever he wanted to buy and didn't buy if he didn't feel the price was as low as he wanted to pay and didn't feel badly later because he hadn't bought something.

It rained furiously for a few minutes every day and late at night the wind shook the birds from the flamboyana trees.

• • •

FRANZ SAT IN the zócalo across from the side of the fountain where the swishes hung out. If there weren't so many babies he would have been convinced the entire country was queer. Every so often one of the pompadours turned toward Franz and said in a loud voice, "Do you like to dance with me?" or "Do you like homosexuals?"

Early evening was the best time for sitting in the zócalo. You could watch the sun fall behind the church and the girls going home or to the shops. All of the girls wore crucifixes of course and Franz thought about fucking them on the cool stone floor of the big church while their bent little mothers and grandmothers genuflected and prayed and agonized.

• • •

NIGHT IN THE TROPICS was supposed to be peaceful. Buzzing insects maybe but cooler and calmer without the white heat and hiss of the day.

Franz was nervous but hoped he looked calm. He was at the old dock where the famous novelist and short story writer had once boxed the famous poet at the insistence of the poet and badly beaten him. They had boxed in the evening and the poet, wearing dark glasses and a hat, had left Port Tropique early the next morning.

The famous poet had been several years older than the famous novelist. Both of them had gone on to write about the place but neither had ever referred publicly to the boxing match, this being much to the credit of the novelist, who was not widely known for his humility. After the poet's death there was delivered to the by that time absurdly famous novelist and short story writer a letter from the poet thanking him for this kindness.

It was only a short time before his own death that the novelist admitted the incident to a reporter from a national publication with the comment that he had taken it easy on the "old man," that he could have "taken him apart" if he'd wanted to, but he'd known it would have "buried" him—the novelist—"even deeper" with the critics. A poet wasn't supposed to know how to fight, anyhow, he said, and the "old fellow" had been no exception.

Franz felt cold and uncomfortable waiting on the pier. He was on time and then he saw the running lights of the small boat coming in. He caught the line and looped it around a cleat. El Serpiente jumped onto the dock and took the suitcase. His face was yellow, one eye glowed red and the other gold. The snake handed the suitcase to a man on the boat whose face Franz could not see and the man went below with it.

There were not many stars out but Franz watched the few there were disappear and reappear. In a few minutes the man whose face he couldn't see came back out and handed the suitcase back to the serpent who gave it to Franz. It was filled now so it was heavy and the snake looked quickly at Franz and without a warning remark told him to be back with it at this place at ten o'clock the next night. He jumped into the boat and Franz threw him the line and the boat moved slowly away.

Franz began immediately back to Calle Cincuenta Ocho. The gun in his left pants pocket was glued by sweat to his leg. He felt like a schoolboy embarrassed by a sudden erection while standing in front of the class, and he closed his hand around it as he walked.

• • •

FRANZ WAS AT THE OLD DOCK at nine fifty-five. At exactly ten o'clock he heard the boat engine. The boat ran dark up next to the pier and idled and someone shone a blinding light in his face.

"Put down the suitcase and walk away twenty paces," a man shouted.

They kept the light in his eyes and from twenty paces he could see nothing. It seemed to take a long time and Franz got worried. He wanted to say something about his being paid but he did not. Instead he stood and fidgeted and fingered the .32 in his right coat pocket and the .38 in his left. It was too hot even at this time of night to be wearing a jacket but he had promised himself to go down wailing if it came to it and he had no other way to pack the iron.

Suddenly the dock went dark again and the boat was moving out. Franz walked quickly back to where he'd left the suitcase. It was lying open and there was money in it. He lit a match and counted it. There was twenty-five hundred on the nose. He stuffed the cash into his pockets and put the guns into the suitcase, locked it up and started walking. He'd passed a few soldiers on the way out but there didn't appear to be anything out of the ordinary. God bless the governor, thought Franz. God bless him a little longer, then perhaps both he and I will get away with our heads and something extra.

• • •

SMOKEY ROBINSON SINGING "Bad Girl" kept going through his head. A Mohawk high steel worker he'd once been on a job with named Luther Two Ax had liked that song and used to repeat the first line of it over and over: "She's not a bad girl because/she made me see/how love could be."

Franz wandered around town that day feeling the new money in his pocket. He stopped twice to drink papaya milkshakes. He already had the runs so it didn't matter what he ate or drank, he had been fairly cavalier about it anyway, and he stood with a papaya drink in his hand humming "Bad Girl" and watching the army troops filter into the city.

So it was true about the battle at Ciudad Domingo. These soldiers looked tired and shabby and la gente spoke muy rápido today, which, unlike their Caribbean cousins, was uncharacteristic.

He gave two pesos to the thing folded up like a crushed spider outside The Habana and sat down at a table close to the street. An Indian boy came in and sat in the chair opposite him at the table and asked if he wanted to buy a flower, holding up a thin-stemmed red paper rose. Franz gave him fifty centavos and the boy ran off without giving him anything.

The waiter with the most gold teeth of any of the waiters in the café and whose station included those tables nearest the street where the tourists were encouraged to sit said that the governor was rumored to be about to depart the country on a diplomatic mission to an unnamed destination. So far as he, the head waiter, could discern, the imminence of the governor's journey, and quite possibly the duration of his absence, was dependent largely on the results of the al fresco political conference currently being concluded in Domingo.

Franz ordered a dish of guava con queso and an espresso and watched the traffic crawl. The headwaiter's English was very good. If the situation in Port Tropique became really impossible he would have no difficulty getting a job in Miami or New York.

• • •

THINGS WERE HEATING UP in the Montejo district. All along the Calle Montejo people were carrying furniture down the stairs of the big houses and loading it into trucks and cars. Well-dressed old ladies clutching elaborately carved and decorated boxes were being assisted down the stairs and into vehicles.

Franz walked up and down the streets of the Section Montejo watching the rich folks panic. He spent the rest of the afternoon this way and an hour or so after it had become dark he stopped at the Café Biarritz for a beer.

He sat at a sidewalk table in order to better observe the continuing exodus and had half finished his beer when the same Indian boy who had approached him earlier in the day at The Habana came up to him and asked him if he wanted to buy a flower. Franz told the boy he had paid him fifty centavos that afternoon for a flower and that he had gone off without giving him one.

The boy, who could not have been more than seven or eight years old, acting in the fashion of the Indians of that region, did not look at

Franz but stood absolutely still staring at the cars stream by, then suddenly put on the table the same artificial rose he had offered Franz at The Habana and walked swiftly away.

• • •

FRANZ HAD A BIT in excess of five thousand dollars now, the second drop having gone off without a hitch. This time the party had been less concerned about exposure and had openly conducted the transfer. Two Chinese had effected the exchange while a white man wearing a black and gold dime store captain's hat and a yellow terry-cloth shirt watched from the boat.

Franz had waited until the Chinese had gone back aboard before picking up his money. As he was folding it into his pockets the man in the captain's hat and terry-cloth shirt shouted, "Viva Raoul!" and laughed sarcastically as the boat pulled away.

Franz fastened the suitcase and stood on the dock watching them go. "Viva la Franz!" he said.

• • •

PANCHO VILLA NEVER TOLD ANYONE his plans. When his troops bedded down for the night Villa would hand his horse over to an orderly, wrap himself in a serápe and walk off into the dark and reappear the next morning from a different direction. Before he went to work for Madero as a Captain, then as a General, when he was still a bandit, Villa would make camp with a companion, then pretend to sleep until he could steal away unnoticed and ride all night in the direction in which he was least likely to be followed.

Franz watched the other passengers board the airplane. He waited until it had taken off and then hired a taxi to drive him to the railroad station in Ciudad Domingo. He bought a ticket to Istmo Delgado de las Palmas in Tampeche and sat down to wait for the train, which, he was informed by the drunken Raoulista stationmaster, was going to be a few hours later than the scheduled two hours behind the arrival listed on the timetable.

Villa would approve of this tactic, thought Franz. From Istmo Delgado he would be able to get a boat to anywhere, and now nobody knew where to find him.

from THE PHANTOM FATHER: A MEMOIR (1997)

A GOOD MAN TO KNOW

I WAS SEVEN YEARS OLD in June of 1954 when my dad and I drove from Miami to New Orleans to visit his friend Albert Thibodeaux. It was a cloudy, humid morning when we rolled into town in my dad's powder blue Cadillac. The river smell mixed with malt from the Jax brewery and the smoke from my dad's chain of Lucky Strikes to give the air an odor of toasted heat. We parked the car by Jackson Square and walked over a block to Tujague's bar to meet Albert. "It feels like it's going to rain," I said to Dad. "It always feels like this in New Orleans," he said.

Albert Thibodeaux was a gambler. In the evenings he presided over cockfight and pit-bull matches across the river in Gretna or Algiers but during the day he hung out at Tujague's on Decatur Street with the railroad men and phony artists from the Quarter. He and my dad knew each other from the old days in Cuba, which I knew nothing about except that they'd both lived at the Nacional in Havana.

According to Nanny, my mother's mother, my dad didn't even speak to me until I was five years old. He apparently didn't consider a child capable of understanding him or a friendship worth cultivating until that age and he may have been correct in his judgment. I certainly never felt deprived as a result of this policy. If my grandmother hadn't told me about it I would have never known the difference.

My dad never really told me about what he did or had done before I was old enough to go around with him. I picked up information as I went, listening to guys like Albert and some of my dad's other friends like Willie Nero in Chicago and Dummy Fish in New York. We supposedly lived in Chicago but my dad had places in Miami, New York, and

Acapulco. We traveled, mostly without my mother, who stayed at the house in Chicago and went to church a lot. Once I asked my dad if we were any particular religion and he said, "Your mother's a Catholic."

Albert was a short, fat man with a handlebar mustache. He looked like a Maxwell Street organ-grinder without the organ or the monkey. He and my dad drank Irish whiskey from ten in the morning until lunchtime, which was around one-thirty, when they sent me down to the Central Grocery on Decatur or to Johnny's on St. Louis Street for muffaletas. I brought back three of them but Albert and Dad didn't eat theirs. They just talked and once in a while Albert went into the back to make a phone call. They got along just fine and about once an hour Albert would ask if I wanted something, like a Barq's or a Delaware Punch, and Dad would rub my shoulder and say to Albert, "He's a real piece of meat, this boy." Then Albert would grin so that his mustache covered the front of his nose and say, "He is, Rudy. You won't want to worry about him."

When Dad and I were in New York one night I heard him talking in a loud voice to Dummy Fish in the lobby of the Waldorf. I was sitting in a big leather chair between a sand-filled ashtray and a potted palm and Dad came over and told me that Dummy would take me upstairs to our room. I should go to sleep, he said, he'd be back late. In the elevator I looked at Dummy and saw that he was sweating. It was December but water ran down from his temples to his chin. "Does my dad have a job?" I asked Dummy. "Sure he does," he said. "Of course. Your dad has to work, just like everybody else." "What is it?" I asked. Dummy wiped the sweat from his face with a white-and-blue checkered handkerchief. "He talks to people," Dummy told me. "Your dad is a great talker."

Dad and Albert talked right past lunchtime and I must have fallen asleep on the bar because when I woke up it was dark out and I was in the backseat of the car. We were driving across the Huey P. Long Bridge and a freight train was running along the tracks over our heads. "How about some Italian oysters, son?" my dad asked. "We'll stop up here in Houma and get some cold beer and dinner." We were cruising in the passing lane in the powder blue Caddy over the big brown river. Through the bridge railings I watched the barge lights twinkle as they inched ahead through the water.

"Albert's a businessman, the best kind." Dad lit a fresh Lucky from an old one and threw the butt out the window. "He's a good man to know, remember that."

THE OLD COUNTRY

MY GRANDFATHER NEVER WORE an overcoat. That was Ezra, my father's father, who had a candy stand under the Addison Street elevated tracks near Wrigley Field. Even in winter, when it was ten below and the wind cut through the station, Ezra never wore more than a heavy sport coat, and sometimes, when Aunt Belle, his second wife, insisted, a woolen scarf wrapped up around his chin. He was six foot two and two hundred pounds, had his upper lip covered by a bushy mustache, and a full head of dark hair until he died at ninety, not missing a day at his stand till six months before.

He never told anyone his business. He ran numbers from the stand and owned an apartment building on the South Side. He outlived three wives and one of his sons, my father. His older son, my uncle Bruno, looked just like him, but Bruno was mean and defensive whereas Ezra was brusque but kind. He always gave me and my friends gum or candy on our way to and from the ballpark, and he liked me to hang around there or at another stand he had for a while at Belmont Avenue, especially on Saturdays so he could show me off to his regular cronies. He'd put me on a box behind the stand and keep one big hand on my shoulder. "This is my *grandson*," he'd say, and wait until he was sure they had looked at me. I was the first and then his only grandson; Uncle Bruno had two girls. "Good *boy!*"

He left it to his sons to make the big money, and they did all right, my dad with the rackets and the liquor store, Uncle Bruno as an auctioneer, but they never had to take care of the old man, he took care of himself.

Ezra spoke broken English; he came to America with his sons (my dad was eight, Bruno fourteen) and a daughter from Vienna in 1918. I always remember him standing under the tracks outside the station in February, cigar stub poked out between mustache and muffler, waiting for me and my dad to pick him up. When we'd pull up along the curb my dad would honk but the old man wouldn't notice. I would always have to run out and get him. I figured Ezra always saw us but waited for me to come for him. It made him feel better if I got out and grabbed his hand and led him to the car.

"Pa, for Chrissakes, why don't you wear an overcoat?" my dad would ask. "It's cold."

The old man wouldn't look over or answer right away. He'd sit with me on his lap as my father pointed the car into the dark.

"What cold?" he'd say after we'd gone a block or two. "In the *old* country was cold."

MRS. KASHFI

My mother has always been a great believer in fortune-tellers, a predilection my dad considered as bizarre as her devotion to the Catholic Church. He refused even to discuss anything having to do with either entity, a policy that seemed only to reinforce my mother's arcane quest. Even now she informs me whenever she's stumbled upon a seer whose prognostications strike her as being particularly apt. I once heard my dad describe her as belonging to "the sisterhood of the Perpetual Pursuit of the Good Word."

My own experience with fortune-tellers is limited to what I observed as a small boy, when I had no choice but to accompany my mother on her frequent pilgrimages to Mrs. Kashfi. Mrs. Kashfi was a tea-leaf reader who lived with her bird in a two-room apartment in a large gray brick building on Hollywood Avenue in Chicago. As soon as we entered the downstairs lobby the stuffiness of the place began to overwhelm me. It was as if Mrs. Kashfi lived in a vault to which no fresh air was admitted. The lobby, elevator, and hallways were suffocating, too hot both in summer, when there was too little ventilation, and in winter, when the building was unbearably overheated. And the whole place stank terribly, as if no food other than boiled cabbage were allowed to be prepared. My mother, who was usually all too aware of these sorts of unappealing aspects, seemed blissfully unaware of them at Mrs. Kashfi's. The oracle was in residence, and that was all that mattered.

The worst olfactory assault, however, came from Mrs. Kashfi's apartment, in the front room where her bird, a blind, practically featherless dinge-yellow parakeet, was kept and whose cage Mrs. Kashfi failed to clean with any regularity. It was in that room, on a lumpy couch with dirt-gray lace doily arm covers, that I was made to wait for my mother while she and Mrs. Kashfi, locked in the inner sanctum of the bedroom, voyaged into the sea of clairvoyance.

The apartment was filled with overstuffed chairs and couches, dressers crowded with bric-a-brac and framed photographs of strangely dressed, stiff and staring figures, relics of the old country, which to me appeared as evidence of extraterrestrial existence. Nothing seemed quite real, as if with a snap of Mrs. Kashfi's sorceress's fingers the entire scene would disappear. Mrs. Kashfi herself was a small, very old woman who was permanently bent slightly forwards so that she appeared about to topple over, causing me to avoid allowing her to hover over me for longer than a moment. She had a large nose and she wore glasses, as well as two or more dark green or brown sweaters at all times, despite the already hellish climate.

I dutifully sat on the couch, listening to the murmurings from beyond the bedroom door, and to the blind bird drop pelletlike feces onto the stained newspaper in its filthy cage. No sound issued from the parakeet's enclosure other than the constant "tup, tup" of its evacuation. Behind the birdcage was a weather-smeared window, covered with eyelet curtains, that looked out on the brick wall of another building.

I stayed put on the couch and waited for my mother's session to end. Each visit lasted about a half hour, at the finish of which Mrs. Kashfi would walk my mother to the doorway, where they'd stand and talk for another ten minutes while I fidgeted in the smelly hall trying to see how long I could hold my breath.

Only once did I have a glimpse of the mundane evidence from which Mrs. Kashfi made her miraculous analysis. At the conclusion of a session my mother came out of the bedroom carrying a teacup, which she told me to look into.

"What does it mean?" I asked.

"Your grandmother is safe and happy," my mother said.

My grandmother, my mother's mother, had recently died, so this news puzzled me. I looked again at the brown bits in the bottom of the china cup. Mrs. Kashfi came over and leaned above me, nodding her big nose with long hairs in the nostrils. I moved away and waited by the door, wondering what my dad would have thought of all this, while my mother stood smiling, staring into the cup.

AN EYE ON THE ALLIGATORS

I KNEW AS THE BOAT pulled in to the dock there were no alligators out there. I got up and stuck my foot against the piling so that it wouldn't scrape the boat, then got out and secured the bowline to the nearest cleat. Mr. Reed was standing on the dock now, helping my mother up out of the boat. Her brown legs came up off the edge weakly, so that Mr. Reed had to lift her to keep her from falling back. The water by the pier was blue black and stank of oil and gas, not like out on the ocean, or in the channel, where we had been that day.

Mr. Reed had told me to watch for the alligators. The best spot to do it from, he said, was up on the bow. So I crawled up through the trapdoor on the bow and watched for the alligators. The river water was clear and green.

"Look around the rocks," Mr. Reed shouted over the engine noise, "the gators like the rocks." So I kept my eye on the rocks, but there were no alligators.

"I don't see any," I shouted. "Maybe we're going too fast and the noise scares them away."

After that Mr. Reed went slower but still there were no alligators. We were out for nearly three hours and I didn't see one.

"It was just a bad day for seeing alligators, son," said Mr. Reed. "Probably because of the rain. They don't like to come up when it's raining."

For some reason I didn't like it when Mr. Reed called me "son." I wasn't his son. Mr. Reed, my mother told me, was a friend of my father's. My dad was not in Florida with us, he was in Chicago doing business while my mother and I rode around in boats and visited alligator farms.

Mr. Reed had one arm around me and one arm around my mother.

"Can we go back tomorrow?" I asked.

My mother laughed. "That's up to Mr. Reed," she said. "We don't want to impose on him too much."

"Sure kid," said Mr. Reed. Then he laughed, too.

I looked up at Mr. Reed, then out at the water. I could see the drops disappearing into their holes on the surface.

THE TROPHY

MY DAD was not much of an athlete. I don't recall his ever playing catch with me or doing anything requiring particular athletic dexterity. I knew he was a kind of tough guy because my mother told me about his knocking other guys down now and again, but he wasn't interested in sports.

He did, however, take me to professional baseball and football games and boxing matches but those were, for him, more like social occasions, opportunities to meet and be greeted by business associates and potential customers. At Marigold Arena or the Chicago Amphitheater Dad spent most of his time talking to people rather than watching the event. He may have gone bowling on occasion but never in my company.

When I was nine I joined a winter bowling league. I was among the youngest bowlers in the league and certainly the youngest on my team. The league met on Saturday mornings at Nortown Bowl on Devon Avenue between Maplewood and Campbell streets. The lanes were on the second floor up a long, decrepit flight of stairs above Crawford's Department Store. I told my dad about it and invited him to come watch me bowl. I wasn't very good, of course, but I took it seriously, as I did all competitive sports, and I steadily improved. I practiced after school a couple of times during the week with older guys who gave me tips on how to improve my bowling skills.

There were kids who practically lived at the bowling alley. Most of them were sixteen or older and had pretty much given up on formal education. The state law in Illinois held that public education was mandatory until the age of sixteen; after that, a kid could do whatever he wanted until he was eighteen, at which time he was required to register for military service. It was the high school dropouts who got drafted right away; but for two years these guys got to sleep late and spend their afternoons and evenings hanging out at the bowling alley, betting on games and gorging themselves on Italian beef sandwiches. At night they would go to Uptown Bowl where the big, often televised professional matches took place.

The announcer for these events was usually Whispering Ray Rayburn, a small, weaselish man who wore a terrible brown toupée and pencil-line mustache. His ability to speak into a microphone at a consistently low but adequately audible decibel level was his claim to fame. Kids, including myself, often imitated Whispering Ray as they toed the mark preparatory to and as they took their three or four step approach before releasing the bowling ball:

"Zabrofsky casually talcs his right hand," a kid would whisper to himself as he stood at the ball rack, "slips three digits into the custom-fit Brunswick Black Beauty, hefts the sixteen pound spheroid" (one of Whispering Ray's favorite words for the ball was "spheroid"), "balances it delicately in the palm of his left hand. Amazing how Zabrofsky handles the ebony orb" ("orb" was another pet name) "almost daintily, as if it were an egg. Now Zabrofsky steps to his spot, feet tight together. He needs this spare to keep pace with the leader, Lars Grotwitz. Zabrofsky studies the five-ten split that confronts him with the kind of concentration Einstein must have mustered to unmuzzle an atom." ("Muster" was also big in Whispering Ray's lexicon.) "Zabrofsky's breathing is all we can hear now. Remember, fans, Big Earl is an asthmatic who depends heavily on the use of an inhaler in order to compete. You can see the impression it makes in the left rear pocket of his dacron slacks. Despite this serious handicap his intensity is impressive. He begins his approach: one, two, three, the ball swings back and as Big Earl slides forward on the fourth step the powerful form smoothly sets his spheroid on its way. Zabrofsky's velvet touch has set the ebony orb hurtling toward the kingpin. At the last instant it veers left as if by remote control, brushes the five as it whizzes past and hips it toward the ten. Ticked almost too softly, the ten wobbles like an habitué dismounting a stool at Johnny Fazio's Tavern," (Johnny Fazio was a sponsor of the local TV broadcasts) "then tumbles into the gutter! Zabrofsky makes the tough spare."

On the last Saturday in February, the league awarded trophies to be presented personally to each team member by Carmen Salvino, a national champion bowler. My team had won its division despite my low pin total. Each team had on its roster at least one novice bowler, leaving it up to the more experienced members to "carry" him, which my team had managed to do. I was grateful to my older teammates for their guidance, patience and encouragement, and thanks to them I was to be awarded a trophy. The only guy on the team who had not been particularly generous toward me was Gilbert Bonito, who worked part-time as a pin-setter. Bonito, not to my displeasure, had left the team two weeks into the league season, after having beaten up his parents with a bowling pin when they gave him a hard time about ditching school. One of the other guys told me Gilbert had been sent to a reformatory in Colorado where they shaved his head and made him milk cows in below-freezing temperatures. "That's tough," my teammate said, "but just think how strong Gilbert's fingers'll be when he gets back."

My dad had not made it to any of the Saturday morning matches, so I called him on Friday night before the last day of the league and told him this would be his final chance to see me bowl, and that Carmen

Salvino would be there giving out trophies. I didn't tell Dad that I'd be receiving a trophy because I wanted him to be surprised. "Salvino," my dad said. "Yeah, I know the guy. Okay, son."

It snowed heavily late Friday night and into Saturday morning. I had to be at Nortown Bowl by nine and flurries were still coming down at five-to when I kicked my way on a shortcut through fresh white drifts in the alley between Rockwell and Maplewood. Dashing up the steep wet steps I worried about Carmen Salvino and my father being able to drive there. I lived a block away, so it was easy for me and most of the other kids to walk over. I hoped the snowplows were out early clearing the roads.

During the games I kept watching for my dad. Toward the end of the last line there was a lot of shouting: Carmen Salvino had arrived. Our team finished up and went over with the other kids to the counter area, behind which hundreds of pairs of used bowling shoes, sizes two to twenty, were kept in cubbyholes similar to mail slots at hotel desks. Carmen Salvino, a tall, hairy-armed man with thick eyebrows and a head of hair the color and consistency of a major oil slick, stood behind the counter in front of the smelly, worn, multi-colored bowling shoes between the Durkee brothers, Dominic and Don, owners of Nortown Bowl.

Dominic and Don Durkee were both about five-foot six and had hair only on the sides of their heads, sparse blue threads around the ears. They were grinning like madmen because the great Carmen Salvino was standing next to them in their establishment. The Durkees' skulls shone bright pink under the rude fluorescent lights. The reflection from the top of Carmen Salvino's head blinded anyone foolish enough to stare at it for more than a couple of seconds.

I was the last kid to be presented a trophy. When Carmen Salvino gave it to me he shook my small, naked hand with his huge, hairy one. I noticed, however, that he had extremely long, slender fingers, like a concert pianist's. "Congrajalayshuns, son," he said to me. Then Carmen Salvino turned to Dominic Durkee and asked, "So, we done now?"

When I walked back home through the alley from Maplewood to Rockwell the snow was still perfectly white and piled high in front of the garages. At home I put my trophy on the top of my dresser. It was the first one I had ever received. The trophy wasn't very big but I really liked the golden figure of a man holding a golden bowling ball, his right arm cocked back. He didn't look at all like Carmen Salvino, or like me, either. He resembled my next door neighbor Jimmy McLaughlin, an older kid who worked as a dishwasher at Kow Kow's Chinese restaurant on the corner of Devon and Rockwell. Jimmy worked all day Saturday, I knew. I decided I'd take the trophy over later and show it to him.

THE AERODYNAMICS OF AN IRISHMAN

THERE WAS A MAN who lived on my block when I was a kid whose name was Rooney Sullavan. He would often come walking down the street while the kids were playing ball in front of my house or Johnny McLaughlin's house. Rooney would always stop and ask if he'd ever shown us how he used to throw the knuckleball back when he pitched for Kankakee in 1930.

"Plenty of times, Rooney," Billy Cunningham would say. "No knuckles about it, right?" Tommy Ryan would say. "No knuckles about it, right!" Rooney Sullavan would say. "Give it here and I'll show you." One of us would reluctantly toss Rooney the ball and we'd step up so he could demonstrate for the fortieth time how he held the ball by his fingertips only, no knuckles about it.

"Don't know how it ever got the name knuckler," Rooney'd say. "I call mine the Rooneyball." Then he'd tell one of us, usually Billy because he had the catcher's glove—the old fat-heeled kind that didn't bend unless somebody stepped on it, a big black mitt that Billy's dad had handed down to him from *his* days at Kankakee or Rock Island or someplace—to get sixty feet away so Rooney could see if he could still "make it wrinkle."

Billy would pace off twelve squares of sidewalk, each square being approximately five feet long, the length of one nine-year-old boy's body stretched head to toe lying flat, squat down, and stick his big black glove out in front of his face. With his right hand he'd cover his crotch in case the pitch got away and short-hopped off the cement where he couldn't block it with the mitt. The knuckleball was unpredictable, not even Rooney could tell what would happen once he let it go.

"It's the air makes it hop," Rooney claimed. His leather jacket creaked as he bent, wound up, rotated his right arm like nobody'd done since Chief Bender, crossed his runny gray eyes, and released the ball from the tips of his fingers. We watched as it sailed straight up at first, then sort of floated on an invisible wave before plunging the last ten feet like a balloon that had been pierced by a dart.

Billy always went down on his knees, the back of his right hand stiffened over his crotch, and stuck out his gloved hand at the slowly whirling Rooneyball. Just before it got to Billy's mitt the ball would give out entirely and sink rapidly, inducing Billy to lean forward in order to catch it, only he couldn't because at the last instant it would take a final, sneaky hop before bouncing surprisingly hard off of Billy's unprotected chest.

"*Just* like I told you," Rooney Sullavan would exclaim. "All it takes is plain old air."

Billy would come up with the ball in his upturned glove, his right hand rubbing the place on his chest where the pitch had hit. "You all right, son?" Rooney would ask, and Billy would nod. "Tough kid," Rooney'd say. "I'd like to stay out with you fellas all day, but I got responsibilities." Rooney would muss up Billy's hair with the hand that held the secret to the Rooneyball and walk away whistling "When Irish Eyes Are Smiling" or "My Wild Irish Rose." Rooney was about forty-five or fifty years old and lived with his mother in a bungalow at the corner. He worked nights for Wanzer Dairy, washing out returned milk bottles.

Tommy Ryan would grab the ball out of Billy's mitt and hold it by the tips of his fingers like Rooney Sullavan did, and Billy would go sit on the stoop in front of the closest house and rub his chest. "No way," Tommy would say, considering the prospect of his ever duplicating Rooney's feat. "There must be something he's not telling us."

THE WEDDING

When my mother married her third husband, I, at the age of eleven, was given the duty, or privilege, of proposing a toast at the banquet following the wedding. My uncle Buck coached me—"Unaccustomed as I am to public speaking," I was to begin.

I kept going over it in my head. "Unaccustomed as I am to public speaking . . ." until the moment arrived and I found myself standing with a glass in my hand saying, "Unaccustomed as I am to public speaking—" I stopped. I couldn't remember what else my uncle had told me to say, so I said, "I want to propose a toast to my new father"—I paused—"and my old mother."

Everybody laughed and applauded. I could hear my uncle's high-pitched twitter. It wasn't what I was supposed to have said, that last part. My mother wasn't old, she was about thirty, and that wasn't what I'd meant by "old." I'd meant she was my same mother, that hadn't changed. No matter how often the father changed the mother did not.

I was afraid I'd insulted her. Everybody laughing was no insurance against that. I didn't want this new father, and a few months later, neither did my mother.

MY MOTHER'S PEOPLE

MY FATHER WAS Jewish, and soon after his funeral my mother was approached by my father's family, who told her that the least she could do was to have me bar mitzvahed. "For Rudolph's sake," Esther, my father's sister, said. "He would have wanted his son to be bar mitzvahed."

She knew as well as I and my mother that Rudolph had not been at all religious. In fact, he had almost been ostracized by his family for marrying my mother, a Catholic. The marriage had not worked out because of family interference, mainly by my mother's mother, who didn't want her twenty-two-year-old daughter (my father was fifteen years older) running around with gangsters.

That part of it was true. My father ran an all-night liquor store on the corner of Chicago and Rush, next door to the Club Alabam, where I used to watch the showgirls rehearse on Saturday afternoons. I often ate breakfast at the small lunch counter in the store, dunking doughnuts with the organ-grinder's monkey. Big redheaded Louise ran the counter and fed me milk shakes while I waited for my dad. The place was a drop joint for stolen goods, dope, whatever somebody wanted to stash for a while. The story was that you could get anything at the store day or night. I used to see my dad giving guys penicillin shots in the basement, and I remember my mother throwing a fit when I was four years old sitting at three in the morning on a bundle of newspapers playing with a gun Bill Moore, a private cop, had given me to look at.

This kind of thing spooked my mother. My dad wore black shirts and gold ties, spoke with "dese" and "dose" and was famous for knocking guys through plate-glass windows. He'd done it twice—once in the newspaper the next day he'd been described as "that well-known man-about-town." Al Capone's brother, who was then using the name White, would come into the store often, as well as movie star Dorothy Lamour, ex-middleweight champ Tony Zale (who had a restaurant across the street—he used to show me the gloves from his matches), and whoever else was in town. We lived on Chestnut Street, next to the lake, in the Seneca Hotel, which was later described to me as containing "the lobby of the men with no last names."

My grandmother's fears were not unfounded. At one point, while my mother and father were vacationing in Hawaii, my dad received a phone call telling him somebody had been shot and that it would be best for them to extend their holiday. That was the first six-month absence of which I was aware. Later my parents spent a few months as the guest of Johnny Reata in Jamaica during another cooling-off period. Reata, my mother told me, had made his money running guns to Trujillo in the Dominican Republic.

While my mother, being a former University of Texas beauty queen, enjoyed the high-life aspects of being married to my father, the hoodlum end of it, plus the great influence her mother had over her, forced her to leave him, and I moved with her to the far North Side of the city. I continued to see my dad regularly until he died, and at no time did he ever so much as point out to me what a synagogue looked like, let alone tell me that he wanted me to be bar mitzvahed.

For some reason my mother allowed herself to be influenced by my aunt Esther and my dad's brother Bruno, both of whom were hypocritical Jews. Neither they, nor my uncle Joel, Esther's husband, who also interceded on my deceased father's behalf, and who once told me, looking me straight in the eye, that deep down inside 95 percent of the Gentiles hate the Jews and could not be trusted—including me, he meant, because of my mother—went to the synagogue except for High Holiday services; social appearances. They were stingy, mean, conniving people who had always been envious of my mother's good looks and power over my father, resenting the fact that my father had ever married her.

What made it so important that I be bar mitzvahed, they told my mother, was that I was the first son in the family. Both Bruno and Esther had had two girls apiece. I was the first one eligible to carry on the family name and tradition. And my father's father, the old man, my grandfather Ezra, who used to run numbers from his candy stand under the Addison Street el, was still alive. For his sake, before he passed away, they whined to my mother, I should be bar mitzvahed.

So my mother was persuaded. Her mother had died a few years before so there was no one to whom she could go for advice. I had to take Hebrew lessons. Three days a week after school I would sit with a little man who smelled of smoked fish, who spoke almost no English, and memorize words I did not understand. I also went to the synagogue each Saturday morning for nearly a year after my father died to say a prayer for him. My father's family insisted that I go, even though I had never been inside a synagogue before in my life. This was necessary, it was a son's duty, they explained, and my mother reluctantly acceded to their wishes. So on Saturdays I stood at the back of the temple, put on a black skullcap and recited a prayer written in English next to the Hebrew on a little pink card.

As the bar mitzvah day came closer I thought more and more about it, about why I was having to do this. Several times I told my mother I wouldn't go to Hebrew lessons anymore. None of it made sense to me, it was stupid, the whole thing was ridiculous. She knew I was right, but she told me to go through with it. "For your father's sake," she said. "My father's dead," I told her. "It doesn't matter to him and it wouldn't matter to him if he were alive."

But she said to finish it, then the debt to the family would be paid. This reasoning escaped me—I didn't see what we owed them in the first place. But I stuck it out, and vowed that it really would be the end of it, that no one would ever make me do anything again.

After the bar mitzvah, which ritual I performed like an automaton, mouthing the lines as if I weren't really there, weren't the one doing it at all, I did not see a member of my father's family—except briefly when my grandfather died—for seven years.

Passing through town those seven years later I went to see my dad's brother. Like my father, Uncle Bruno was a strong-willed, stubborn man. He had done well financially and kept his large brown brick house locked up like a fortress. When he saw me through the front-door window he motioned for me to come around the back way. "Too many bolts to undo in the front," he explained, as he and his wife admitted me through the rear entrance. They expressed their surprise at my being there, they hadn't recognized me right away. I told them I'd just come by to say hello, that was all.

Uncle Bruno insisted that I eat with them, they were just sitting down to dinner, which I did, and tell them what I'd been doing the past few years. I gave them a brief history after which Uncle Bruno asked me if I'd come to see him about a job, or did I need money?

"I don't need any money," I told him, "and I have a job. I'm a writer," I said. My uncle looked annoyed and got up and walked into the living room and sat down. I followed him in and stood by the window. "Why did you come here then, if you don't need any money?" he asked. "Out of curiosity," I said. Bruno lit a cigar. "Curious about what?" he said.

"Do you think things would have been different with me had my father lived?" I asked. "Of course they would," Bruno said. "You would have been a doctor or a lawyer or a pharmacist. Something important."

I knew it bothered Uncle Bruno that I didn't want any money, or anything else, from him. It would have bothered him had I asked for something but at least then he would have had the satisfaction of being right.

"Then I'm glad he died when he did," I said, "before we had any trouble about it."

"Being a Jew means nothing to you, does it?" said Uncle Bruno. "You're one of your mother's people."

I realized I had no reason to be there, that I should never have come. I put on my jacket.

"What did you expect?" I said, and left.

THE KID WHO TORCHED *THE CHARTERHOUSE OF PARMA*

GREEN BRIAR PARK, bounded by Peterson, Washtenaw, Talman, and Glenlake Streets, consisted of a baseball and football field (sans goalposts) encircled by magnificent Dutch elm trees, a concrete outdoor basketball court with chain-net baskets, and a field house.

There were baseball games at GB, as the park was called, every clear day from April until the first snow. We played softball only, not hardball, with a sixteen-inch "Clincher" and no gloves. Balls hit into the overhanging trees were usually playable if caught—if the tree interfered with a player's catching a ball and it dropped to the ground, it was considered a foul ball; if it was caught before hitting the ground, the batter was out.

Kids of all ages played ball at GB, even guys who'd graduated or dropped out of high school. One famous regular was Chuck Syracuse, a crazy kid who'd been thrown out of school at the age of nineteen, in his third year of high school, and spent every day at GB playing softball. At night he drove a cab. He always carried around with him big, important-looking books, like *The Charterhouse of Parma* and *The Brothers Karamazov*. My guess is that Syracuse never attempted to read these books; he just wanted us to think that he did. There was a pile of them on the back floor of his cab, so I imagine every once in a while a customer perused one or two.

One afternoon Syracuse came by in his cab, got out to watch the game for a few minutes—he needed extra money, he said, so that week he was working days, too—and after an inning or so somebody left and Chuck took his place. It was a high-scoring game that went into extra innings, it took a long time to play, and when Syracuse got back to his taxi he discovered that he'd left the meter running. He went berserk and began beating on the roof of the cab. Finally he got in and drove away.

A few days later—during which time Chuck had not shown up at GB—we found out that Syracuse had turned the cab over in an empty lot in another neighborhood and torched it (and, presumably, the books, too), then told the cab company that it had been stolen while he was eating lunch. The company didn't buy his story and investigated the case. When they confronted him with the truth, he told them he'd done it so that he wouldn't be charged the thirty-five bucks run up on the meter while he'd been playing softball at the park.

Since Chuck couldn't pay the three or four grand the company said he owed them for the cab, he did a little time at Joliet. After he got out of the joint Chuck continued to hang out at GB, where he suddenly found himself a famous person. He spent more time answering questions about his insane torch job than playing softball. One day Magic Frank was kidding around and asked Syracuse if he thought he'd handled the situation properly.

"What do you mean?" Chuck asked.

"Do you think it was worth it?" said Frank.

"Well," said Syracuse, thinking it over a bit, "you know I went four for five in the game that day."

THE CHINAMAN

I ALWAYS SPOTTED the Chinaman right off. He would be at the number two table playing nine ball with the Pole. Through the blue haze of Bebop's Pool Hall I could watch him massé the six into the far corner.

My buddy Magic Frank and I were regulars at Bebop's. Almost every day after school we hitched down Howard to Paulina and walked half a block past the Villa Girgenti and up the two flights of rickety stairs next to Talbot's Bar-B-Q. Bebop had once driven a school bus but had been fired for shooting craps with the kids. After that he bought the pool hall and had somebody hand out flyers at the school announcing the opening.

Bebop always wore a crumpled Cubs cap over his long, greasy hair. With his big beaky nose, heavy-lidded eyes, and slow, half-goofy, half-menacing way of speaking, especially to strangers, he resembled the maniacs portrayed in the movies by Timothy Carey. Bebop wasn't supposed to allow kids in the place, but I was the only one in there who followed the Cubs, and since Bebop was a fanatic Cub fan, he liked to have me around to complain about the team with.

The Chinaman always wore a gray fedora and sharkskin suit. Frank and I waited by the Coke machine for him to beat the Pole. The Pole always lost at nine ball. He liked to play one-pocket but none of the regulars would play anything but straight pool or nine ball or rotation. Sometimes the Pole would hit on a tourist for a game of eight ball but even then he'd usually lose, so Frank and I knew it wouldn't be long before we could approach the Chinaman.

When the Chinaman finished off the Pole he racked his cue, stuck the Pole's fin in his pocket, lit a cigarette, and walked to the head. Frank followed him in and put a dollar bill on the shelf under where there had once been a mirror and walked out again and stood by the door. When the Chinaman came out, Frank went back in.

I followed Frank past Bebop's counter down the stairs and into the parking lot next to the Villa Girgenti. We kicked some grimy snow out of the way and squatted down and lit up, then leaned back against the garage door as we smoked.

When we went back into the pool hall Bebop was on the phone, scratching furiously under the back of his Cub cap while threatening to kick somebody's head in, an easy thing to do over the phone. The Chinaman was sitting against the wall watching the Pole lose at eight ball. As we passed him on our way to the number nine table he nodded without moving his eyes.

"He's pretty cool," I said.

"He has to be," said Frank. "He's a Chinaman."

THE FAVORITE

IT WAS MY MOTHER who introduced me to horse racing. She loved going to the track and often took me with her when I was a little boy. In Florida, at Hialeah, I loved to watch the pink flamingos pick their way among the fluttering green and yellow palms; and in Chicago, at Arlington Park or Sportsman's or Maywood, to listen to the heavyset, well-dressed men with diamond pinkie rings and ruler-length Havana cigars as they fussed over my mother, asking if she'd like something to eat or drink or if she wanted them to place a bet for her.

My father rarely, if ever, went to the racetrack. There may have been a bookmaking operation in the basement of his liquor store, but he told me that he didn't bet on anything with more than two legs that couldn't speak English. I doubt seriously if he'd ever heard of Xanthos, one of the two immortal horses of Achilles (the other being Balius) who had the power of speech and prophesied his master's death. If he had, I'm certain it would have served only to disaffect him further.

When I was in high school I became a real devotee of the so-called sport of kings. My friend Big Steve and I would often head for the track as soon as classes let out. Big Steve was a canny and gutsy bettor who won more often than he lost. Such was not the same in my case. I had as many off days as on and I always felt fortunate when I broke even. But there came a day I knew I couldn't lose. I was sixteen and Gun Bow, with Walter Blum up, was running in the feature race at A.P. I was certain there were no other horses in the eighth race that day that could beat Gun Bow, who was destined to be named Horse of the Year, beating out the great Kelso, a four-time winner of the award. The one problem for me was that I was broke at the time, so I had to borrow what I could in order to bet.

Big Steve was generous and loaned me twenty bucks. He was going through one of his periodic phases of gambling abstinence. Steve decided that he'd been gambling too much of late—horses, cards, craps—and he would test his willpower by refusing to bet on Gun Bow, even though he agreed with me that it was as close to a sure thing as there could possibly be. He even offered to drive me to the track and stand by me during the race.

Now, there are sure things and there are *sure* things. Gun Bow belonged in the former category. An example of the latter was the time my friend D.A. and I stopped before the first race to visit his uncle, Ralphie Love, who was working one of the ten-dollar combination windows in the clubhouse. Ralphie was a self-described "semiretired businessman" who formerly had been in the vending machine business. He now worked part-time at the track and spent a lot of time attending sports events. I used to see him regularly at college basketball games in Chicago in the early sixties, especially before the game-fixing, point-shaving scandal hit. The day D.A. and I saw him at the track Ralphie told us he thought the five horse, Count Rose, would be a nice bet in the first race. The jockeys liked him, Ralphie Love said. D.A. and I bet the five to win, he went off at nine to two, and sure enough, just as the pack hit the top of the stretch they parted like the Red Sea and Count Rose came pounding down the middle to win by a comfortable margin. What I didn't know about Gun Bow was whether or not the jockeys liked him.

I borrowed a total of a hundred dollars and Big Steve and I headed out toward Arlington Heights. I intended to bet only the eighth, no other races, so we didn't have to be there until around three o'clock. Post time would be at approximately three-thirty. I'd place my bet, watch them run, cash in, go home. The sun was out, the road uncrowded. As Big Steve and I rolled along in his dusty red Olds a warm feeling of well-being engulfed me. I was so confident that Gun Bow would win in a breeze that I told Big Steve I was going to put the entire C-note on the nose, not across the board as I'd originally planned.

When we were about ten minutes from the track, the sky suddenly clouded over. Then a few drops of rain appeared on the windshield. Thunder rolled, lightning flashed. Seconds later we were inundated by a torrential downpour. Big Steve turned on the windshield wipers full speed but it didn't do much good. It was one of those sudden blinding midwestern summer rainstorms. "Oh no," I said, "I can't believe this." "Don't worry," said Big Steve, "we'll make it on time." "That's not what I'm worried about," I said, "it's Gun Bow. How does he run in the mud?"

I worried the rest of the way to the racetrack. By the time we pulled into the parking lot the rain had slowed to a steady drizzle but I knew the track surface would no longer be fast and I had no idea what effect sloppy footing would have on Gun Bow's performance. Due to the storm we arrived later than we'd figured to and I had to make a dash for the betting window.

I met Big Steve at the rail near the finish line. The rain had stopped entirely. "So," he said, "what did you do?" I showed him the two fifty-dollar win tickets. There were puddles on the track. The starter's bell rang and the horses were off. I recalled the time I'd picked a long shot named Miss Windway out of the paper one morning before Big Steve, his brother Big Lar, and I went out to the track. I knew Miss Windway would win but by the time the seventh race, the one in which she was entered, rolled around, I was busted and had no more money to bet. I was disgusted with myself for having lost everything so quickly that day and didn't even bother to ask Steve or his brother for a loan. Big Steve, however, put six dollars across the board on Miss Windway, Big Lar put two on the nose, and she went off at something like eighty-five to one. Miss Windway won the race by five lengths.

Now, I figured, even though I had to bet more money to win less, it was my turn. Gun Bow wouldn't let me down, he was too good a horse to let a little mud bother him. Walter Blum was a top jock, too; he wouldn't blow a big stakes race like this. As the horses were moving into the far turn a guy behind us shouted, "Do your job, Blum! I brought my gun with me today!" I turned away and looked up at the sky. The sun came out. As the horses reached the stretch an old guy next to me yelled, "Wa Wa Cy! Come on, Wa Wa Cy!" The odds on Wa Wa Cy, I knew, were fifteen to one. I looked at the man. The top of his head was bald and he was pulling hard with both hands at the small amount of hair he had left above his ears. At the wire Gun Bow was in front by three lengths.

On our way home Big Steve asked me what was the matter. Why was I so quiet? I'd won, hadn't I? "Just thinking," I said. In my mind I kept seeing that old guy tearing at his hair. "I don't think I'll ever really be much of a gambler," I told Big Steve. "It's foolish to bet long shots and no fun to bet the favorite." Steve laughed. "You didn't see *me* betting," he said, "did you?" The sky clouded over again and I closed my eyes. Wa Wa Cy, I thought, how could that guy have bet on Wa Wa Cy?

A LONG DAY'S NIGHT IN THE NAKED CITY

My dad had a friend in New York named Edgar Volpe whom I used to visit every so often when I was in town. He died about ten years ago but until then Edgar hung out at the Villa Luna restaurant on Grand Street between Mott and Elizabeth in Little Italy. I could usually find him there in a booth at the back talking to a couple of guys who looked like they were in a hurry. Edgar was a fat man, he weighed about two hundred and fifty pounds and stood maybe five foot eight with his shoes on. He always looked like he had plenty of time to talk.

From what little Edgar told me about his relationship with my dad I gathered that they had collaborated on a few liquor heists during the thirties. Edgar never really opened up to me and there was no reason that he should have. He was always very nice and insisted on buying me lunch at the Villa. One afternoon when I was eating linguini with clam sauce and discussing with Edgar the vicissitudes of the New York Rangers, of whom he was an avid follower, a short, wiry guy came in and over to our table and held out to Edgar an envelope. "It's there," he said. "I'm fuckin' t'rough wid it."

Edgar didn't touch the envelope, motioning with a nod for the man to lay it on the table, which he did. "Siddown, why doncha," said Edgar. "Have some linguini." "Nah, t'anks," said the man. "I got my cab outside. I'm workin'." He shifted from foot to foot and looked quickly around the restaurant. The man was about thirty-five to forty, five-nine or ten. He was wearing sunglasses so I couldn't see his eyes. "So we're t'rough now, right?" he said to Edgar. "Dis makes it." Edgar nodded slowly and gave the man a small half-smile. "If you say so," said Edgar. "I'm always around if you want." The wiry man gave a loud, short laugh. "I hope to fuck I won't," he said. He looked around again and back at Edgar, then at me, then back at Edgar. "So I'm goin'," he said. "And t'anks, Mr. Volpe. T'anks a million." "Anytime," said Edgar.

The man left and Edgar slowly picked up the envelope and put it into his inside jacket pocket. "Funny guy," Edgar said to me. "He was a cop. Then he's moonlightin' one night guardin' some buildin's over onna West Side an' almost gets his eye shot out. Some fancy-lookin' white broad is out stoppin' cars—Mercedes, Cadillacs, Jags, expensive models—an' tellin' the driver she got a flat tire or somethin'. Then as the driver's about to give her a lift, a black guy dressed like a bum comes up behind the broad and drags her into an alley. Naturally, the driver jumps out and chases the attacker. I mean this broad is a doll, dressed to the nines, a real fox, an' the guy thinks he's got somethin', see, so he goes to help her, right? The black guy takes off when he sees the driver comin' and drops the broad. The driver comforts the broad, takes her into his car. Asks her where she wants to go. She puts a gun to his head, opens the door, and the black guy gets in the back, also wid a gun. They're workin' together, right? They rob the driver and have him drive to his house or apartment, which they clean out the jewels and cash. Nice scam. Worked thirty-two times inna row until my pal there, the cop who's moonlightin' in order to save money for his weddin', spots this couple in the act.

"Sonny there, the cop, tries to pull the black guy outta this Mercedes, an' the broad shoots him inna head. Sonny's lyin' onna ground next to the car and the black guy falls out right onna Sonny. Sonny's bleedin' like crazy but figures if he's gonna die he's not goin' down alone, so he plugs the nigger, passes out.

"When he wakes up, Sonny's inna hospital wid his eye bandaged. He's alive an' the doctors tell 'im a couple operations an' maybe he won' hafta lose his right eye. The nigger's dead; the broad got away clean. While he's inna hospital, the broad Sonny's engaged to never even comes to see him. She thinks he's gonna die anyway, right? He'd already given her, what, maybe ten, fourteen t'ousand dollars for the wedding. She's why he's fuckin' moonlightin' inna first place. So while he's inna hospital fightin' for his life she runs off wid some other guy. By the time Sonny gets out he's in deep shit 'cause the police department insurance policy won't cover him since he was off duty an' workin' for somebody else. So he needs money, he comes to me. He's suin' the insurance company, the owner of the buildin' he's guardin' that night, the cops, everybody he can think of. On top of that he's afraid to go see the broad t'rew him over 'cause he'd put six inna her. Now he's pushin' a hack tryna get back on his feet. I give him a good deal, plenya time to pay me back, right? Why not. Your dad, he helped out plenya guys."

MY MOTHER'S STORY

When Rudy and I came home from our honeymoon I wanted to get an apartment or a house but Rudy said no, we had to live near his store, near Rush Street, so we rented a suite in the Seneca Hotel on Chestnut Street. I knew the Castle boys, who owned the drugstore in the Palmer House, where we used to go often for dinner, and they offered me a job selling perfume; they wanted me to talk to customers about their line of fine French perfumes. This was to be a part-time job, more or less at my own convenience, but Rudy said no, I couldn't work, not his wife; he would give me an allowance of twenty-five dollars a week. I could go into any store and charge whatever I wanted; I could eat in the finest restaurants and never be presented with a bill; I could have my own Cadillac or any other car I wanted; but I wasn't allowed to have any cash in my hand other than the twenty-five dollars Rudy gave me each week. He was the boss.

It was a fast crowd that stayed at the Seneca in those days. Most of the guests lived there on a permanent basis or else kept a room for whenever they might need it. Eddie Danillo, who owned the Milwaukee Ace brewery, lived next door to us. Eddie was a nice guy. I knew he was connected with the Mafia, but I didn't think that was a big deal; everybody I met with Rudy had shady dealings. Danillo owned a couple of clothing stores, too, and one day he knocked on our door and gave me a box with a big ribbon on it. He said, "This is for you. I hope you like it," and then he left. There was a very nice hat in the box, from one of his stores. I liked the hat and wore it that night to dinner.

We were just leaving the restaurant when who should come in but Eddie Danillo. "Gee, that hat looks great on you," he said to me. I thanked him and said to Rudy, "Yes, Eddie gave me this hat today. Wasn't that nice of him?" "Eddie gave you that hat?" Rudy said. "Yes, why?" I asked. "Wait outside for me, Peggy," Rudy told me. "I'll be right there." I went outside and the next thing I knew there was a loud crash from inside the restaurant. I ran back in and there was Eddie Danillo on the floor with pieces of glass all over him: Rudy had knocked him down through a plate-glass window in the foyer. Rudy was calm and smiling. The maître d' was saying to him. "It's all right, Mr. Winston, we'll take care of everything, there's no problem, no problem." Rudy and I left and I said, "You're crazy. Why did you knock Eddie down? Because he gave me a hat?" Rudy stopped and looked at me; he wasn't smiling. "I knocked him down because he didn't *ask me* first if it was all right to give you the hat." "But he's in the Mafia, isn't he?" I said. "You can't go around beating up guys in the Mafia!" Rudy just laughed. "You know," he said, "that hat really does look good on you." The next day or maybe the day after there was an item in one of the newspaper gossip columns about Rudy knocking somebody through a plate-glass window, but Eddie's name wasn't mentioned. After that Eddie and I always smiled and said hello to one another whenever we met, but he never gave me any more presents.

I became immersed in Rudy's world. Most of his so-called friends I had no use for. One of his closest buddies was a detective from the local precinct named Bill Moore. What a rotten guy he was. Every once in a while he'd use me to identify a suspect for some crime or another. Of course I'd never seen the guy before in my life. "He's no good, Peggy," Bill would say, "that's the guy who did it." And I'd have to say yes, I was there at the scene, I saw it on the street, I was passing by. Oh, it was horrible. I did it because Rudy said go on, help Bill out, he's a pal. I refused to ever testify at any trials but that didn't matter, they never asked me to do that, only to identify someone in a lineup. Who knows who they were or what they'd really done, if anything, or what happened to them?

Every now and then I'd be coming to the pharmacy when Rudy didn't expect me and there would be some policemen carting him off to jail. He'd shout, "Don't worry, Peggy, I'll be back in an hour!" And he would be. This was because of the book they were running in the basement. Rudy would have to make large "donations" to the Policemen's Benevolent Association so that he wouldn't get busted too often. "Why not?" he'd joke, "I'm a benevolent guy."

Rush Street was glorious in those days: the nightclubs were flourishing, business was good; it was a twenty-four-hour part of town. It was exciting, but I was picking up the wrong values. My mother didn't like it, didn't like the life I was leading. There was a great deal of drinking and we went out every night for dinner, which I did not want; I loved to cook, I was a good cook, my mother had taught me, and I begged Rudy to let me make him dinner at home. But then he'd show up with some stranger, some drunk, and I wouldn't let him in the house. "But this guy is a celebrity," Rudy would say. I'd get angry and slam the door on them. "I don't care who it is," I'd yell, "he's dead drunk. I don't want him in here!"

There were some nice people, though, like Barney Ross, the former boxing champion. Barney used to come into the suite at the Seneca and play the piano and tell me his life story, which was pathetic. He'd become a junkie while he was in the military hospital recovering from his war wounds. Barney was on and off the hop when I knew him; I never knew if the light was on or off, as we used to say, but he was a sweetheart. A lot of boys, of course, like Eddie Danillo, were mob guys—we never mentioned the word Mafia unless we were alone—but then there were others. Dick Bagdasarian, an Armenian who'd made a fortune as a bootlegger in the twenties, lived across the hall from us. He and his wife would go out and give their dog, a poodle, to their chauffeur and tell him to walk it. Bobby, the chauffeur, would drive the dog over to Rudy's store, put it up on the counter and have a cup of coffee. Years later my son Jimmy would sit at that counter and dunk doughnuts in the coffee and feed it to the organ-grinder's pet monkey and the Bagdasarians' poodle. Another neighbor was Buddy Harvey, who was married to one of Tommy Manville's ex-wives—the eighth, I think—and I loved her. Sunny Ainsworth was her name, she was okay in my book.

One time my mother came to visit and she went to the hairdresser in the building. I came walking in and the hairdresser or the manicurist said, "Look at that young punk, with that ten-thousand-dollar mink coat. Who does she think she is anyway?" And my mother said, "That's my daughter." My folks would come and have Sunday dinner with us, but my mother was becoming increasingly disturbed by my life, and so was I.

Then I got pregnant. I remember wearing my little pea jacket and blue beret and going to the gynecologist with my mother; Dr. Marshall, who was the finest gynecologist in Chicago, a wonderful man, who's gone now. Dr. Marshall confirmed it and I was thrilled that I was going to have a child, my mother was heartbroken. "You're too young," she told me, "No, I'm not," I said. "I've been married over a year. This is great. I want a nice little girl to keep me company. I'm alone so often at night."

I really wanted my own house or apartment, I disliked living in a hotel. I knew Rudy liked it, but I wanted a place that I could furnish myself, to have my own things, my own furniture. I wanted to be able to clean my own house, not have a hotel maid. Rudy loved the fast life, living it up; he'd consume at least a bottle of sparkling burgundy or champagne with dinner every night, even on those rare occasions he'd allow me to cook a meal for him alone. There was so much heavy drinking around me! Rudy could drink two bottles of wine with dinner and then go on drinking Irish whiskey all night, until four or five in the morning and he'd never be drunk. Other people would fall out, collapse, but not Rudy. He was a prodigious drinker and the amazing thing was that he always kept his wits; he never lost control of the situation.

We lived on the sixteenth floor and one night while I was lying in bed, thinking about my life, a bird flew in the open window. I was really petrified by this bird that was madly careening around the room, going around and around. This was after I was pregnant, I already had a big stomach. I called down to the desk and asked them for help, to get the bird out. They thought I was out of my mind, or that I'd been drinking. I said no, there's a bird going wild in here and I'm not drinking or anything. The bird was batting itself against the walls and splattering blood all over the place. And I thought, this is a bad sign; I'd never been superstitious before, but I couldn't help having this thought. This is no good, I thought, what does it mean? Finally a bellhop came up and knocked on the door. He came in and looked at me; the bird had stopped knocking into walls and was cowering on the floor in a corner. I showed the bellboy where it was and then he knew I wasn't crazy, and he took it out.

The bird was the first "sign" I had that I recognized. Many years later, the night after my mother's funeral, I was sitting in my bedroom in the house on Rockwell Street with my son Jimmy when a giant golden moth appeared at the window and began banging itself against the glass. It was the middle of winter and there were no moths that I knew of, especially large golden ones like that, flying around outside at that time of year. My first thought was that it was the spirit of my mother, it was Rose coming back to see me. The moth frightened me even more than the bird had, and I remember turning off the light and waiting in the dark, hugging Jimmy, for a half hour or so. When I turned the light on again the moth was gone, but I couldn't shake the conviction that it had been a manifestation of my mother.

Rudy's older brother Bruno was an auctioneer who also owned a couple of automobile agencies and a piece of the Chez Paree nightclub. Bruno sort of ruled Rudy, he was a tough guy, too, and Rudy looked up to him; he listened to what Bruno told him. Bruno and I got along well enough; he was much older than I was, in his forties, and we never really had too much to do with one another. Rudy and Bruno and I were at a ringside table at the Chez Paree watching Sophie Tucker when I went into labor. I almost had my baby right there on the table in the Chez

Paree, but Rudy rushed me out and around to Passavant Hospital, where I had my son Jimmy—James Barry Winston, named after a brother of my father's who had died young. So I had a little boy now, not the girl I'd been certain I was going to have, and I was very happy.

Rudy was overjoyed to have a son, the first boy in the family to be born in America. Rudy had come with his family to Chicago from Austria when he was seven years old, and Bruno had yet to have children. It was a great moment for Rudy, he was so proud. Jimmy's birth was the lead item in the *Tribune* gossip column the next morning, "Talk of the Town." My hospital room was filled with flowers, all from "the boys." They overflowed into the hall and I told the nurses to please give them to the other patients who might like to have them. Everything was fine, but I couldn't get the thought of the bird out of my mind. I knew it had been a sign, but I wasn't sure of what.

ON THE RECORD

THE ROOSTER TRAPPED IN THE REPTILE ROOM

from *THE NEW YORK TIMES* (1991)

LULA HEARD THE MUSIC before she opened the door. She had been to a blankets-for-the-poor collection drive organized by the Rev. Goodin Plenty at Bayou Lacombe, across the road from where the Crab Festival was taking place. Lula Ripley, her friend Beany Thorn and several other women members of the Church of Reason, Redemption and Resistance to God's Detractors, had devoted their Saturday to collecting blankets and other donations to be distributed to the poor and homeless the next day at the tent show in Slidell.

Lula was exhausted after having stood outside in the almost 100-degree heat and suffocating humidity all day, and was looking forward to relaxing in the air-conditioned living room of her and Sailor's house in Metairie. She was more than a little surprised to open the front door and see Sailor propped in front of the TV set watching a video with the sound blasting.

"What's this, Sail?" she asked, seeing a bunch of skinny guys in weird clothes carrying on like crazed monkeys caged up for medical experiments. "Sounds like the rooster trapped in the reptile room."

"Huh?" said Sailor. "Wha'd you say?"

Lula shouted into his right—Sailor's good—ear: "I said, what're you watchin'?"

"Rock group I ain't never seen before, Peanut. Called Faith No More. Picked up this concert video down at Rubber Room Ralph's. Ralph says these guys are the best thing to come along since before the Rollin' Stones went commercial."

"When weren't the Stones commercial, Sailor?"

"I guess before we was born, honey, but Ralph oughta know. He told me after he was wounded at Hamburger Hill in Nam, and got shipped back to the States, it was the Stones' music that kept him almost sane while they had him tacked down in the rubber room kickin' his heroin addiction."

Lula clucked her tongue, a habit she'd inherited from her mother, Marietta Fortune. Every time Lula did it, she thought of Marietta, with whom she'd had her differences, and promised herself she wouldn't do it again.

"Wish I could quit cluckin' my tongue like Mama does. I hate it. Ain't nearly like tryin' to burn down a drug got itself wrapped around your soul, though. Thank the Lord that ain't never been our problem, Sail."

"Drugs is ev'rybody's problem, peanut. Sit down and listen to these boys. They can play a little. This tune's called 'Underwater Love.' "

Lula lay down on the ecru shag rug and rested her head in Sailor's lap, keeping her eyes on the screen of their 24-inch Sony.

"Sounds a little like somethin' David Bowie woulda done a few years back," said Lula. "Only he'd prob'ly been wearin' a dress and buffalo horns on his head."

Sailor laughed. "Yeah. Or Roxy Music, maybe. They had a sense of humor. Mostly it's pretty much hard rock. This Jim Martin's got a lot of Jimmy Page in him, but just when you think it's sorta Led Zeppelin-y, they'll change up in a hurry and hit you with a '2000 Light Years From Home' feelin'."

"No wonder Rubber Room Ralph likes 'em."

Sailor and Lula watched as Mike Patton, the lead singer, stomped around the stage, mock-collapsed, leaped up, asked the audience if they were even listening, then made a vulgar noise into the microphone and stuck it under his nose.

"Sailor, that's disgustin'!"

He laughed. "They gotta do that silly stuff, peanut. It's part of the program. You know how Pace had to show us he ruled his own self, when he was growin' up."

"Our son never did nothin' like this, Sail."

"No, he only did a armed robbery durin' which a couple people got shot and one died."

"Honey, he was only fifteen then and he got forced into it by them insane Rattler brothers."

"Who told him he had to hang with them maniacs, peanut?"

"Well, these boys is much older. They oughta know better, even if they are gettin' paid. And Pace changed his ways."

"I told you, Lula, all this is part of the act. The audience ain't much older for the most part than Pace was when he got into trouble. It ain't the same, anyway."

Mike Bordin, the drummer, began wailing away and Sailor, who usually hated drum solos, cringed and prepared for the worst. Somehow, though, the sound was not only painless, Sailor thought, but intelligent; interesting, even.

"Hey, peanut, this skinny white kid with dreadlocks knows what he's doin'. I mean, he ain't just a noisemaker. Not exactly Max Roach, of course, but he's expandin' their sound. Kinda African-like, almost."

"Who's Max Roach?"

"Hand me that video case, sweetheart," said Sailor. "I want to know what the name of this one is. I can't understand most the words."

Lula handed him the slipcover.

" 'Epic,' I think," he said. "Guess you could call what the singer's doin' now Talk-Rock, 'cause it ain't really rappin'. More like talkin' fast."

"Reverend Goodin Plenty says he's gonna make a rap record, Sailor. Gonna call it 'Bust a Move on Jesus.' "

"I ain't gonna look for it on Soul Beat, peanut. He oughta call it rapture, not rap."

"Faith No More sounds sorta anti-religious to me," said Lula. "What you figure a name like that means?"

"Just gotta give it up, I guess. Like you and Beany give it up for the Church of the Three R's. You know, if it ain't here, it's nowhere."

"Sail, I swear, sometimes when you start talkin' like that I don't believe you're the one I been in love with since I was sixteen. It's like, that don't make no sense at all."

"Tell me what does, peanut, and I'll be the first to buy a ticket. Look, this band is about *energy*. Like Pace'd say, they're *in*tense as hell."

"These boys don't look like them Satan-worshipin' types, at least. The guitar player might could be, though. The few lyrics I can make out just sounds like they're kinda confused, is all."

"Well," Sailor said, "they are kinda all over the place with this one. What is it?" He looked on the box. " 'Falling to Pieces.' It ain't the same as Patsy's song, that's for sure. Sounds like the singer's sayin' somethin' like 'indecision clouds my vision.' "

"In Matthew it says, 'Do you know how to discern the appearance of the sky, but cannot discern the signs of the times?' "

"Come on, Lula, this is rock-and-roll here, after all. And 'member what the Rollin' Stones said way back, 'It's the singer, not the song.' That's what's got all them little girls hoppin' up and down, as you can see."

"Yeah, I suppose. The singer is pretty cute, even if he is dressed like most the folks we collectin' blankets for."

Lula watched and listened for a little while longer, then, despite the volume, she fell asleep, worn out from her long day at Bayou Lacombe. Sailor looked down at his wife, grinned and stroked her shiny hair with the fingers of his right hand. She stirred slightly and said something, but Sailor couldn't hear the words. On the TV, Faith No More carried on like the athletes they were. The lead singer was climbing up the scaffolding that supported the band's speaker system. With his left hand, Sailor lifted a bottle of Abita to his lips, took a swig, then held it up in front of him, tilting the tip toward the set.

"Rave on, boys," he said.

ON MAGIC SAM'S *WEST SIDE SOUL*

from *ROLLING STONE* (1968)

West Side Soul, Magic Sam (Delmark DS-615)

Delmark's documentation of the Chicago blues scene, from Yank Rachell and Junior Wells to this recording of Magic Sam's, has finally made the monumental step of incorporating the West Side into the established contemporary blues genre. Sam Maghett, or Magic Sam as he was nicknamed by Shakey Jake, has been the foremost blues and soul performer on the West Side for the past ten years. His recordings had formerly been limited to singles on small local labels like Cobra, Chief and Crash. For a long time he was in a provincial (for that part of the city) R&B bag, but by 1954 he decided to get back into the blues. And it's a good thing. Magic Sam has become a living legend in the Chicago area.

This album, which includes the participation of former Otis Rush guitarist Mighty Joe Young, pianist Stockholm Slim (Per Notini of Sweden) and the ageless Odie Payne on drums, was produced by old Shakey Jake Harris himself, the great blues singer and harp player, who, during his gambling and catting days, known then as Cadillac Jake, discovered Sam playing his guitar under a tree in his backyard at 27th and Calumet.

Sam's music represents the interaction of Memphis soul, gospel-influenced Detroit pop-soul, and the standard Mississippi-cum-Chicago scheme. But new depth has been added with the inclusion of 16-bar arrangements in the style of Junior Wells and Buddy Guy's material.

The cuts Sam has chosen to record are an equal representation of new and old. "Sweet Home Chicago" has a Jimmy Reed bass line and a direct guitar progression, but Sam's vocal takes the lyrics off the line, outside of the measured syntax, and leaves diminished notes scattered throughout the song. He is an expert song stylist; his voice is capable of changing form in mid-note—like B. B. King when he's really got it on.

"I Feel So Good (I Wanna Boogie)" is Sam's famous dance tune that he uses to talk to the audience—he's famous for doing this during performances at small clubs like the Alex or Sylvio's. Sam's original performance of this song was at the old 708 Club on East 47th Street when Shakey Jake persuaded Muddy Waters to let Sam sit in on a set with his band. He knocked everyone out, screaming: "I feel all right/I wanna boogie," and was hired to follow Muddy's engagement at the club.

The track that captures Sam at his best is "All Of Your Love." His guitar work is amazing. More in the style of older Chicago blues guitarists like Smokey Smothers, Sam, like the late Wes Montgomery, disregards use of a flat pick, using his thumb instead. He's incredibly quick and gets as sharp and clear a sound from his big shiny Epiphone, which he rests on his hip while he plays, as Buddy Guy does. His runs on "I Don't Want No Woman" are as hard and true as Albert King's, but they're very different—Sam isn't as predictable.

His powerful voice trembles slightly as he marks the final cadence of each bar. "Whoa baby/whoa baby" he yells. "Mama Mama-Talk To Your Daughter" is a classic of Sam's. It hurtles along, a 12-bar compendium of hard, driving blues chording—the guitar riffs cut back like an automatic shotgun.

This is the music of the West Side. The people come and go but the music remains. It's tough, violent and gaudy like that part of the city. The only escape for the inhabitants can be found in sex, gambling, fighting and drinking—and they're all here. As Sam sings: "Come on baby/don't you want to go/back to that same old place/sweet home Chicago."

ON JAIME DE ANGULO'S *DON BARTOLOMEO*

from *WESTERN AMERICAN LITERATURE* (1975)

UNTIL TURTLE ISLAND BEGAN issuing Jaime de Angulo's books the only one available, indeed the only one ever printed in book form, was *Indian Tales,* a selection from the original, longer, manuscript (the parts published comprise only the "children's" section, plus a selection of Shaman Songs inserted into the Indian Tales text from a separate manuscript), by Hill & Wang in hardback and large-size then-expensive paperback, and recently reissued by Ballantine in an inexpensive format, which includes excerpts from an original Hudson Review article, "Indians in Overalls."

Publishing de Angulo's books is a labor of love for Bob Callahan, the founder and editor of Turtle Island Foundation, and a great stroke of luck it is for all of us that upon learning de Angulo's widow was alive and living in Berkeley a couple of years ago, Callahan decided to visit her. When he asked if Jaime had written anything other than *Indian Tales*, the widow de Angulo opened the closet and out tumbled, in Fibber McGee fashion, the treasure trove Turtle Island has titled The Jaime de Angulo Library.

Don Bartolomeo is the third volume in the series (the others so far, each of which deserves a review of its own, are *Indians in Overalls, Coyote Man and Old Doctor Loon, The Lariat*, and *Coyote's Bones;* there are to be nine books in all). I've singled *Don Bartolomeo* out for review because of the four I've read it impresses me the most with its visual power. De Angulo's fifty page novel, upon re-reading, has surprised me in that I "remember" more than he actually wrote—that is, I vividly retain detail suggested intuitively by existing passages. De Angulo's gift is swift insight to character and a straightforward calm. He doesn't waste words—the reader is immediately *there*—and, in *Don Bartolomeo,* privy to an exceptional presence, that of the last of his tribe, the unnamed (to us) narrator who is "the last of the Surenyos," those Indians who inhabited the Big Sur-to-Monterey area of the California coast.

De Angulo was an anthropologist—he taught at UC Berkeley during the "Golden Age of Anthropology" which included, at one time, Kroeber, Lowie, Radin, Sauer, Waterman, Sapir and de Angulo—and a linguist (he lived at various times during forty years among the Pit River Indians of Northern California—see *Indians in Overalls*)—son of a Spanish Grandee he grew up in France and eventually became a rancher at Big Sur. He had a turbulent life—though he loved Berkeley he was disappointed with the academy that refused him money for recording equipment in order to preserve the dying songs and literature of the California tribes, so he undertook the project at his own expense—"they don't want an anthropologist who goes rolling drunk in ditches with the Indians" he said, or something close to it.

His life was fraught with personal tragedy—while living with his mistress at Big Sur he had gone to his wife, who lived nearby, and taken his young son from her against her wishes—driving back to his ranch that night with the boy, he lost control of his car and plunged over a cliff, crashing at the bottom of a canyon. De Angulo was unhurt, but his son was pinned against his chest, dead—de Angulo lay there for hours before rescuers came. After that he withdrew from the world for ten years, riding the borders of his ranch, shooting at would-be trespassers, speaking to no one.

Don Bartolomeo has this kind of reality. A straight-told tale, each character has a powerful, longing presence. The narrator is a witness to the self-destructing *mats-haiba,* the Spaniards (he is a half-breed himself, but distinctly not a *mats-haiba*) who have taken over the country from the Carmelenyos and other local Indians. Don Bartolomeo is his uncle, brother of his father who has run off with Doña Maria, Bartolomeo's wife who was unhappy and lonely along the rugged, unpopulated coast. The narrator, whose mother is an Indian, lives with Don Bartolomeo and is raised with his sons, Aurelio and Abelardo.

Aurelio is the wild-ass handsome reckless crack horseman who thinks all women are whores—the *gran vaquero* who eventually strays from the fold. Abelardo is the plodder, a great hulking man-bear, the opposite of Aurelio, but dangerous.

The narrator lives with them like a brother, but belongs in spirit to the Indians, like the Old Lalihesi who rides herd for Don Bartolomeo and watches over the half-breed boy. The old Lalihesi and Hilahilukeni, the ancient Gagool-like witch-woman who can change herself into a bear and travel at night, are *los misteriosos*, important influences on the young narrator.

After his mother dies, the narrator is approached by the man the Old Lalihesi calls *metg*, grandfather—a powerful doctor who tells him he is a man but has no name yet, and explains how he must go about finding his true-self, and whether or not the spirits have any use for him. De Angulo's relation of the narrator's ordeal, the private pursuit of his new name, is tantamount to the most vivid and intense description of the sacred Sun Dance ceremony.

There is the inevitable conflict between the brothers, Aurelio and Abelardo,—over a woman, of course—but no ordinary woman, Concha, daughter of the narrator's father and Don Bartolomeo's wife, a woman who makes all men crazy—a wild thing like Aurelio, who comes to live at Don Bartolomeo's and "with all her flounces and red lips and her eyes" destroys everyone, except her brother, the narrator, who lives to be a very old man, the last of his tribe.

As, perhaps, was de Angulo, the last of a kind—certainly one of the last with intimate, first-hand knowledge of the California Indians. He died in 1949, but there is enough of him left in these books for all of us.

ON ROLAND BARTHES' *EMPIRE OF SIGNS*

from *THE SAN JOSE MERCURY NEWS* (1983)

"YOU KNOW WHAT I LIKED so much about Japan?" Roland Barthes said to his American translator Richard Howard. "No one ever thought of giving me a book!" So what did Barthes do but write a book about it. *Empire of Signs,* originally published in Geneva in 1970, brings together a writer and an ideally suited subject. A professor of sociology and lexicology at the College de France in Paris until he was run down and killed by a laundry truck in 1980, Barthes devoted himself to the examination of meaning as expressed by signs. Japan, he noted, was a country of signs, many-layered meanings and a value system stranger than fiction. As such it was a territory made for a man as obsessed by nuance as Barthes.

In an introductory note to *Empire,* Barthes explains that "the text does not 'gloss' the images, which do not 'illustrate' the text." Here he is referring to the use of photographs, press clippings, maps and drawings throughout the book, a method popularized by Andrè Breton with the publication of his surrealist novel, *Nadja.* "For me," Barthes continues, "each has been no more than the onset of a kind of visual uncertainty, analogous perhaps to that loss of *meaning* Zen calls a *satori.* Text and image, interlacing, seek to ensure the circulation and exchange of these signifiers: body, face, writing: and in them to read the retreat of signs."

Communication, then. In Japan, intuition is the guiding hand, the key to behavior. People say one thing, do another. Are they two-faced? It's more complicated than that. This is the order of a culture built on imitation: they took their written language from the Chinese, their photo-chemical cue from the West. The Japanese consider skillful imitation as much an art as originality. This is a tough one to swallow for most Westerners, but the Japanese have made an art out of imitation in virtually every area from religion to painting to electronics. Barthes expresses his fascination with this extraordinary ability, discussing subjects as seemingly diverse as dinner trays, travel guides and chopsticks. His view of the raison d'être for chopsticks is ingenious and informed: "The harmony between Oriental food and chopsticks cannot be merely functional, instrumental; the foodstuffs are cut up so they can be grasped by the sticks, but also the chopsticks exist because the foodstuffs are cut into small pieces; one and the same movement, one and the same form transcends the substance and its utensil: a division . . . a chopstick (also) had a deictic function: it points to the food, designates the fragment, brings into existence by the very gesture of choice, which is the index. The chopstick . . . introduces into the use of food not an order but a caprice, a certain indolence: in any case an intelligent and no longer mechanical operation. He even pinpoints the "future" of the object of ingestion, discovering its destiny not in accumulation but "tenuous dispersal." He quotes this haiku: "*Cucumber slices/The juice runs/Drawing spider legs.*

Food is of major importance in *Empire of Signs*. Richard Howard, a close friend of Barthes' as well as his translator, wrote, "the pages on Japanese meals . . . seem to me the best French gastro-texts, as he might say, since Brillat-Savarin." The most astute restaurateurs will admit that food is chosen and arranged on a plate according to how it looks rather than according to a scheme of nutritional value. The Japanese are masters of the visual, presenting meals "composed as in a Dutch painting of which they retain the linear contour, the elastic firmness of the brushwork, and the bright-colored finish." But this is by no means all: "If Japanese cooking is always performed in front of the eventual diner"—a ceremony Barthes calls the "Twilight of the Raw"—"this is probably because it is important to consecrate by spectacle the death of what is being honored."

The key word in that last sentence is, of course, "honor." Perhaps the most remarkable photograph in the book shows a man and a woman on a Yokohama dock in 1915 bowing to one another. Of only slight interest in itself, the photo is remarkable when presented alongside Barthes' unique and insightful caption: "Who is saluting whom?" In the West, he says, politeness is too often regarded with suspicion; courtesy passes for a distance, an evasion or a hypocrisy. The Japanese form, expressed most distinctly by the formal use of the bow, rather than being "exaggeratedly respectful (i.e. to our eyes, 'humiliating')," actually signifies nothing. "The salutation here can be withdrawn from any humiliation or any vanity, because it literally salutes no one; it is not the sign of communication . . . it is only the feature of a network of forms in which nothing is halted, knotted, profound . . . *The Form is Empty*, says—and repeats—a Buddhist aphorism." Barthes' final contention in this matter is actually quite profound: "Religion has been replaced by politeness." Which is not a bad idea no matter how one manages to approach it.

The streets of Tokyo, the largest city in the world, have no names. There are no written addresses except for postal purposes. Several houses on the same street might have the same "address" simply because they were all constructed at approximately the same time, in the same year, or because they all belonged at one time to one family. As Barthes writes: "You must orient yourself in it not by book, by address, but by walking, by sight, by habit, by experience; here every discovery is intense and fragile, it can be repeated or recovered only by memory or the trace it has left in you." I can attest to this: I haven't been in Tokyo for eight years, but the hand-drawn maps of paths to various houses, public baths and buildings are indelibly printed in my memory. Knowing one's way around Tokyo becomes a condition not unlike the proverbial intimacy with the back of one's hand. Either that or a continual dependence on the kindness of strangers, which in Japan entails something more than even Blanche Dubois could fantasize.

Violence, faces, eyes. The picture of a man "close to smiling." A photo of Barthes in a Japanese newspaper, the author " 'Japanned,' eyes elongated, pupils blackened by Nipponese typography," contrasted with a photo of a Japanese actor whose eyes have been cut to make him resemble Anthony Perkins. What is going on here? What is Japan? I would recommend *Empire of Signs* in particular to anyone contemplating a journey there, for no reason other than it presents Japan poetically as a country of paradox despite homogeneity. For some reason it seems to me that the French have received the Japanese message better than other Westerners: Manet and Barthes are two good examples of this. "Turn the image upside down," Barthes says, "nothing more, nothing else, nothing." Japan turned Roland Barthes on his ear.

ON ELMORE LEONARD'S *MAXIMUM BOB*

from *THE NEW YORK TIMES BOOK REVIEW* (1991)

ELMORE LEONARD'S *Maximum Bob* is Maximum Dutch.

Mr. Leonard confirms, with this, his twenty-ninth novel, his right to a prominent place in the American *Noir* Writers Hall of Fame, along with Charles Willeford, Dan J. Marlowe, Jim Thompson, the Elliott Chaze of *Black Wings Has My Angel* and John D. Macdonald. The "other" Dutch Leonard, Emil, who was a pretty fair right-handed pitcher during the 1930s, '40s and early '50s with the Dodgers, Senators, Phillies and Cubs, and from whom Elmore appropriated a nickname, won twenty games in a season only once. This Dutch has accomplished the feat in his own ballpark a solid baker's dozen times or more, a monster of a career, better than Emil's, who, after all, won only ten games more than he lost.

Nobody I've ever read sets up pace, mood and *sound* better than Leonard. Listen:

"Music was coming out of hidden speakers and the go-go whore was moving to it on the terrazzo floor, looking around bug-eyed like she'd died and gone to whore heaven. 'Mumbo on down the hall,' Elvin said. He followed her cute butt sliding side to side in a little skirt that barely covered it, no backs to her high heels clicking on the marble. She wasn't too bad looking for a crackhead junkie. Had her G-string on under the skirt to give Dr. Tommy a show."

Maximum Bob is the story of a crackpot cracker judge in present-day Palm Beach County, Florida, who resembles the actor Harry Dean Stanton and acts like the Hanging Magistrate Judge Roy Bean. He's saddled with a space-cadet wife named Leanne who comes complete with a dual personality, a twelve-year-old black girl with a Butterfly McQueen voice who lived 135 years ago named Wanda Grace, whom he's dying to get rid of; and there are more than a few uglies on the prowl who are flat partial toward seeing Circuit Court Judge Bob Isom ("Call me 'Big' ") Gibbs become bloated and bug-eyed gator gruel in the 'Glades. Bob's peculiar appellation comes, of course, from his habit of hitting an offender with the full sentence provided by law, a fact duly noted and examined by the weekly national news magazine that laid it on him.

Elmore Leonard writes in a manner calculated to keep the reader leaning. The novelist and screenwriter A.I. "Buzz" Bezzerides, author of *They Drive By Night* and *Thieves' Market,* once told me how he explained to the director Robert Aldrich, during the filming of the *noir* classic, *Kiss Me Deadly,* for which Mr. Bezzerides had written the screenplay, the way to shoot a scene wherein a man is thrown over the side of a cliff. It was better to *not* show the guy going over, Buzz said, to instead show only the men doing the job, then keep the camera on them as they watch the victim fall. This will make the viewers *lean forward in their seats*, as if they might catch a glimpse of the flier. Leonard knows how the body looks when it lands, too.

Maximum Bob Gibbs fancies himself a real ladies' man, has his eye on a cute young probation officer named Kathy Diaz Baker, wants her, tries to set her up, but she won't tumble. He tries hard to make it work, but this low-rent Crowe family keeps getting in the way, especially Dale Junior and his ex-con Uncle Elvin, an A-Number One Bad Dude fresh out of the Florida state prison at Starke. (Dale Senior has one leg—lost to gangrene following a gator bite—and his broken jaw wired shut.) Bob put 'em away, now they're tryna put Bob away. Also there's this smooth-ass cop Kathy likes, Gary, gets in between, and a dumpsterful of weird dudes such as Dr. Vasco, a crack addict-dermatologist who spends his days sun-bathing (Whaddaya mean, melanoma?); his cross-dressing Man Friday, Hector; and Earlene, the go-go whore, who can't catch any kind of break.

"Earlene walked over to the kitchen, Kathy watching the way she moved in her short skirt and backless heels in a kind of confident slouch, a low-speed sway to her hips. She kept her hand on the small beaded purse hanging from her shoulder. Earlene was looking in the kitchen now.

" 'Jesus—see that thing? He stuck it up my nose.'

"The shank made from a spoon, lying on the kitchen table. Gary edged past her and picked it up. 'I thought he didn't threaten you.'

" 'It was when I said the place looked like a rat hole? He goes, "You calling me a nigger?" I forgot that part. See, it was right then he told me he had killed a guy and was gonna do it again.' "

Florida has long been an ideal location for fiction featuring nefarious goings-on. Being the wealthiest state in the Deep South, it attracts a steady supply of transients, mostly from Alabama and Georgia, including a fair share of fugitives. I grew up there, shooting at water moccasins in the swamps with my Sears .22 rifle, working construction and laying sewer pipe alongside a goodly number of men short on history and long on mean. Once on a job building roads in Cocoa Beach, when I was fifteen, a couple of lawmen pulled up to the construction site in their beige-and-white, got out and went up to an old boy I'd gotten to like pretty well, and hauled him right off of the steamroller he was driving without bothering to cut the ignition. Turned out he was a former Georgia sheriff wanted in that state for child molestation. He grinned and gave me the victory sign with his right hand as the law stuffed him into the back seat. Leonard, a Michigander, does the place justice.

His boy Bob hires Dicky Campau, a swamp-punk frog-gigger with a large, nasty-mouthed wife named Inez, to scare off Leanne by bringing an alligator to the house. See, when Big's wife was a mermaid at Weeki Wachee Springs, a gator swam into the middle of her act and freaked her out, so maybe, the judge thinks, a repeat will make her run now, and take that soul sister Wanda Grace with her. Only it doesn't, not really. I mean, everything backfires, to the max.

Elmore Leonard is the greatest living writer of crime fiction. Find a body does it better, you call me. Hear?

FILM ESSAYS

from
OUT OF THE PAST: ADVENTURES IN FILM NOIR (2001)

BLOOD ON THE MOON

1948. Directed by Robert Wise. Starring Robert Mitchum, Robert Preston, Barbara Bel Geddes, Phyllis Thaxter, Tom Tully, Walter Brennan and Frank Faylen.

This is the truest Western noir ever made, straight out of the RKO chiaroscuro corral. Robert Wise was a graduate of the Val Lewton School of Shadows and Camera Murk (*The Body Snatcher, Curse of the Cat People*, etc.), and *Blood on the Moon* moves through the same territory as *The Leopard Man* and *Cat People.*

Mitchum plays Jim Gary, a would-be cattle rancher who's lost his herd and goes to work for his old pal Robert Preston. Preston is trying to manipulate a group of homesteaders, featuring Walter Brennan, against a cattleman, Tom Tully, in a struggle over land. What the homesteaders don't know is that Preston's cooked up a deal on the side with the Indian Bureau man, Frank Faylen (who went on to play Dobie's dad in the TV series *The Many Loves of Dobie Gillis*), wherein the two of them stand to cash in to everyone else's disfavour. Preston's a conniving snake, romancing rancher Tully's older daughter, Phyllis Thaxter, in order to get information out of her concerning a cattle drive. He hires a couple of thugs to ride with the homesteaders, and with the outfit bolstered by his buddy Mitchum, the only guy he knows who's as tough as himself, there seems no way Tully can survive.

The real romance, though, is between Bel Geddes, the younger, feistier cute-not-pretty, Annie Oakley-like daughter of Tully's, and Big Old Lazy-Eyed Hunk-o'-Man Mitchum. Mitch cuts through Tully's land on his way to join up with Preston, not knowing yet what he's riding into, and stumbles across wildcat Bel Geddes, defender of her father's domain and integrity. So they get off on two wrong feet, but of course are mightily attracted to one another and we know where this game is headed. It's the perfect play-off for the deceitful Preston and his use of Thaxter, who is made to betray her own father for the Music Man.*

Everything in the movie is dark, cloudy—even the scenes in daylight on a snowy mountain where Mitchum kidnaps Faylen after Mitchum turns on Preston and sides with Tully. There never seems to be more than two hours of available light in a day here. It predates *McCabe and Mrs Miller*, Robert Altman's moody, long-suffering neo-Western by a quarter of a century. The only later Western to come close to Wise's in terms of feel and look is Stan Dragoti's *Dirty Little Billy* (1972), with Michael J. Pollard as Billy the Kid in one of the slimiest, filthiest, muddiest movies of all time—a real little masterpiece too—little known, another noir Night of Nausea (look out the ghost of J. P. Sartre!).

Walter Brennan, who looked like he was sixty when he was in his early twenties, plays a pivotal role in *Blood*, coming back to assist Mitchum after first running out when his son is killed by one of Tully's men during a stampede instigated by Preston. Brennan plays his usual crotchety, Wicked Witch of the West/Rumpelstiltskin character—the stoic with a heart, though, in this one. Eight years before, he'd been Judge Roy Bean in William Wyler's *The Westerner*, an unredeemed, nasty son of a bitch; but here he comes through for Mitchum and Bel Geddes against Preston's hoods after Mitchum is stabbed in the stomach. Bel Geddes has a pudgy but pert nose—she's the head side of the coin on which Peggy Cummins (*Gun Crazy*, 1949) is the tail; kid-sister tough but just enough of a sex kitten to claw her way up Mount Mitchum.

A dark, cranky, realistic, serious Western with enough moonlight and blood on the trail for anyone this side of *Dragoon Wells Massacre* (1957).

THE DEVIL THUMBS A RIDE.

1947. Directed by Felix Feist. Screenplay by Felix Feist; based on the novel by Robert C. DuSoe. Starring Lawrence Tierney, Ted North, Nan Leslie, and Betty Lawford.

*A role created on Broadway and in the movie version by Robert Preston.

I got up at 3:30 in the morning to watch this movie on T.V.—the perfect time for it. The hours covered in the film are from midnight to dawn, the period during which reality is suspended, when the rational mind loses control, and everything goes haywire. This is one of the meanest, most boldly deranged exercises in maniacal behavior this side of Farmer Ed Gein, minus the dismemberment.

Lawrence Tierney is at his most vicious and amoral here. He robs and murders a theater manager in San Diego, then grabs a lift from a traveling salesman played by Ted North, a decent enough, slightly tipsy, average Joe on his way home to the little woman in L.A. Tierney, famous for his role as Dillinger for Robert Wise in 1945, and for his barroom brawls (he was stabbed in one as recently as 1973), and drunk driving arrests, is the wickedest looking big lug in B-movie history. He dresses sharp. He's got big shoulders and a snap brim fedora; evil doesn't lurk in his face, it gloats. He's a real con man, convincing the salesman, named Furgison—"Furgie" he calls him—to let him drive, that way they'll get to Los Angeles faster and safer. Right. At a gas station in Oceanside two young women approach the car. They'd met in Globe, Arizona, hitched a ride to San Diego, and are now hitching their way up the coast highway, just looking for a lift. Tierney says sure, hop in. Furgie doesn't like it—he's married, you know. How will anyone know? asks Tierney. Furgie agrees. Tierney arranges it to suit himself: the brassy blonde up front with Furgie, the better-looking brunette in the back seat with him.

Before they leave the filling station, though, Tierney insults the attendant when he shows Furgie a picture of his two-year-old kid. With those ears the kid could be a flier, says the Mean Big Guy. The attendant pays special notice to Tierney, and after they drive off he hears a description of Furgie's car, a gray convertible, on the police band: the car was spotted driving away from the scene of the robbery. The gas jockey runs to the cops, of course, and an APB goes out all the way up the coast to L.A. The kid goes along with a detective from Oceanside to help in the chase, to identify Tierney.

In the car Tierney comes on hard and fast to the brunette, telling her about his Hollywood connections, how a girl like her, with perfect lips, eyes, legs, should be a movie star; he can help her out. He frightens her but she's interested. The brassy one up front is the bad one and Tierney spots it; he likes the innocent, a naïve soul to chew up and spit out. They stop at a roadside diner but there's a roadblock ahead. Tierney rushes them all back to the car, takes the wheel and peels out, headed for a road off the highway to get around the blockade. A motorcycle cop comes after them—the cop puts on his sunglasses, at two-thirty/three A.M.!—and Tierney backs up into him, crushing his leg. The cop fires a few rounds at the speeding gray car, but Tierney gets away.

By now Furgie knows he's in trouble, but he's told Tierney about a beach house a friend of his keeps and they head there, to Newport. Don't worry about that cop back there, Tierney tells Furgie. He couldn't be too badly hurt; after all, he fired three shots after I ran him over, didn't he? So the monster and the girls take over the beach house. The old night watchman comes in and Tierney gets him drunk so that he passes out. Furgie phones his wife who hears the blonde laughing and music from the radio and hangs up on him. Furgie runs out to find someone to drive him to L.A. right away, but his car has two flat tires now, cut up by Tierney with broken whiskey bottles. Tierney terrorizes the brunette, chases her down to the beach where he beats her up and she drowns in the shallows by the pier. Meanwhile, the cops are mobilized from Dago to San Clemente. The blonde fixes herself some food and takes over a bedroom. Furgie comes back, sweating, crazed, and opens her door. Boy, she says, I'm improving my mind. She holds up a book. "Who is this guy Balzac?" she asks. "He sure can write."

Furgie's life has gone to hell, dragged down step by step by the massive-shouldered devil Tierney. The beach house is a wreck. Don't worry, Tierney tells him, conning him again, everything'll be fixed up like new. Tierney steals Furgie's wallet, his money, and I.D. The cops break in and Tierney pretends that he's Furgie, shows the I.D., imitates Furgie's signature, and almost gets away with it until the detective and the filling station kid come in and the kid fingers Tierney. The cops find the floating brunette. Tierney tears the place up and beats it out to the cop car with the blonde. They get away as daylight breaks. A patrol car chases them down outside Santa Ana and shoots them both dead. The sun comes out of the fog. Furgie's wife arrives from L.A., frantic, but he calms her. All is well. She's pregnant, she says. They laugh and embrace. The night has ended.

The Devil Thumbs a Ride is as frenzied as *Gun Crazy*, as darkly depraved as *Detour*, but simpler, more linear. (Felix Feist made only one other halfway decent film, *This Woman is Dangerous*, a 1952 gun moll-crying towel vehicle for Joan Crawford.) Tierney invests this basically stupid plot with such genuine virulence that *Devil* must be ranked in the upper echelon of indelibly American *noir*. I saw Tierney on an episode of "Hill Street Blues" not long ago, and in Norman Mailer's *Tough Guys Don't Dance* (1987), a movie he steals with ease. He's in his sixties now, fat, and completely bald. His gigantic, gleaming skull is absolutely square. In "Hill Street" he played an old police sergeant and he didn't have many lines, but that mean look was still in his eyes; that bad-to-the-bone, never-give-in visage. There is no daylight in that face.

HOUSE OF STRANGERS

1949. Directed by Joseph L. Mankiewicz. Based on the novel I'll Never Go There Again *by Jerome Weidman. Starring Edward G. Robinson, Richard Conte, Susan Hayward, Luther Adler, Paul Valentine, Efrem Zimbalist, Jr., and Debra Paget.*

Edward G. as the great patriarch is simply stunning. Gino Monetti, owner of a bank in New York's Little Italy, father of three sons, and tyrannical ruler of his family, is arguably Robinson's greatest role. Gino runs his bank as he pleases, dispensing loans at whim, taking exorbitant bites but lending dollars for little or no collateral. His eldest son, Joe (Luther Adler), whines and begs to be more than a clerk in his father's bank, wants more money to satisfy his striver, waspish wife. Gino humiliates him regularly, as he does the big goon son, Pietro (Paul Valentine), whom Gino calls "dumbhead." Max (Richard Conte), a lawyer, is the favorite son, the son most like Gino, the one Gino trusts. Joe is envious of Max, of Max's smooth good looks and way with women, and, of course, his princely position insofar as their father is concerned.

When Gino takes a fall and loses control of his bank for violating loan regulations, Max does the time in prison, protecting his father. He does seven years, and when he comes out Joe is running the bank. The old man, who for so many years completely dominated his wife and sons, who insisted on blasting Rossini on the phonograph while they ate—much to the displeasure of Joe and his wife—finally dies, and Joe begins to extract his revenge. He's afraid of Max, though, and his own paranoia and greed eventually do him in. Max's loyalty and stand-up attitude pull him through.

The cleverest parts are reserved for Max's relationship with Irene (Susan Hayward), a rich woman, non-Italian, for whom Max forsakes his beautiful young fiancée. Irene tries to buy Max, to get him to help her in his capacity as an attorney, but he turns the tables on her and she falls for him. The family crumbles, and Max can give up the rigors of carrying on in the Italian tradition more easily. Irene probably isn't even Catholic! Max is the one who moves into modern society, adopts the fast life, but with old-country values held firm. The old man may have been a monster but he was sharp enough to figure the moves. Hayward is a wastrel, unsure of the direction of her life until she meets Max. He takes over. He gets her and gets the bank, too, along with the loyalty of the big dummy Pietro. To his father Pietro was a palooka, good for nothing but being a guard at the bank and a bad club fighter; to his older brother Joe he could only be a strongarm go-fer; but to Max he's a human being.

Conte played heroes differently than most leading men; in fact, Conte never really qualified as a leading man. He was resentful that Brando got the *Godfather* role over him from Coppola; but Coppola knew what he was doing: Conte's psychic scar showed on his face and ran right down the middle. Harvey Keitel has the same scar; he's the closest thing to Conte in the movies nowadays. Even as hero Conte couldn't claim innocence or naïveté. Everyone is in his or her right place in the story of The Fall of the House of Monetti. My Uncle Les's fishing buddy Tony Grimaldi, who ran the Columbia Bank in Ybor City in Tampa, was a lot like Gino Monetti; he was tough but fair in his own way. He used to separate people into those who were "on the up and up" and those who weren't, which is relative, I know, but better than right or wrong.

KING CREOLE

1958. Directed by Michael Curtiz. Based on Harold Robbins's novel A Stone for Danny Fisher. *Starring Elvis Presley, Walter Matthau, Carolyn Jones, Dolores Hart, Dean Jagger, and Vic Morrow.*

No cracks, please. *King Creole* is a legit piece of work, and one of Elvis's best performances as an actor. Surrounded as he is by solid movie veterans, and directed by the man who made *Mildred Pierce*, among numerous other memorable films, it's not really a surprise. Elvis really could act when given the opportunity: *Flaming Star, Jailhouse Rock*, even *Love Me Tender*, show his real talent at moments. Those stupid Hawaiian hula-rock epics destroyed him—man and music—for many years.

The movie opens with El leaning over a balcony singing in response to a black woman coming down a French Quarter street in New Orleans, calling "Crawfish! Crawfish!" And there are a few other songs strewn throughout the picture; one underrated little ditty, "Lover Doll," is especially nice. But Elvis is a young guy exploited by a gangster, played by Walter Matthau in one of his better roles as a heavy. Matthau began his acting career by playing bad guys: *The Kentuckian*, with Burt Lancaster, was his first. And he did it very well. Vic Morrow is Elvis's counterpoint, his nemesis, who works for Matthau. Carolyn Jones, thin, dark, and sexy with those Walter Keane giant kid's eyes, is Matthau's moll but she falls for Elvis. He sees something in her, knows she's really a better person than she seems to be, hanging out with scum like Matthau, but his chick is Dolores Hart. Hart, of course, left acting and became a nun. This was after dating Elvis for a while.

"If you're lookin' for trouble," Elvis sings, "then you came to the right place. If you're lookin for trouble, then look right in my face. Because I'm eeeevull, my middle name is misery." Elvis's cellblock dance number in *Jailhouse Rock* is a gem; and his ability to convey hurt, emotional pain, is genuine in *King Creole, Wild in the Country*, and *Kid Galahad. Wild in the Country*, with Tuesday Weld and Hope Lange, comes closest to *King Creole* in terms of Elvis's veracity as an actor. In that one he plays a jailkid who can write, who wants to be the new Thomas Wolfe, and winds up torn between two women, one older, one younger. This was a fairly common theme for Elvis vehicles. In *Creole*, Carolyn Jones has real sympathy as well as lustful feelings for him, and he's a real gentleman. Elvis's ability to portray sullen, rebellious boys who nevertheless are polite and without malice is no mean feat. With some real words to say, an intelligent script, such as Clifford Odets's screenplay for *Wild in the Country* (which he also directed), Presley made something of it. He was a natural performer, interesting to look at, slightly stupid, and emotionally retarded, which helped make his attempts to cover up his vulnerability ingenuous. Hollywood made every mistake with him. In fact, he might have been as good as James Dean, but after 1956 he never had a chance to be alone.

ODD MAN OUT

1947. Directed by Carol Reed. Starring James Mason, Robert Newton, Dan O'Herlihy, Kathleen Ryan, and Cyril Cusack.

It's Belfast or Derry just after the war. The young and sensitive James Mason is the chief of a rebel squad, "The Organisation" they call it instead of the IRA: Johnny McQueen, eight months in prison before he escaped, and since then six months inside a safe house, hiding out. The plan is for Johnny and two others to rob a mill office for funds to support The Organisation. A pretty young woman, Kathleen Ryan, who lives in the house, is all eyes for the trembly Johnny; but he's all for the cause, doesn't respond to her attentions.

The boys don't want Johnny to take on the task of the actual robbery: he's not been out on the streets for too long, but he insists on participating. At the mill they get the loot but Johnny falters on the steps coming out; his eyes blur, he gets dizzy, and winds up being wounded by a guard and killing the man himself. As the getaway car careens around a corner Johnny falls out and has to crawl away on his own, the cops after the car. An all-out manhunt ensues. Long angle shots of wet dirty Irish cobblestone streets. It starts to rain, then snow. Dirty, poor kids begging. Chimney pots smoking. Bleak landscapes out of Bill Brandt. Everybody in this neighborhood is a Dead End Kid.

McQueen manages to get to a raucous giant barroom where the owner hides him in a private locked booth. In the meantime his cronies are turned in by an old bitch who plays both sides of the fence, informing to the cops so they'll let her run her gambling parlor. The other two robbers are shot and killed, the third planner arrested trying to help Johnny. McQueen's badly hurt, bleeding, losing the little energy he had left. The fair Kathleen goes to Father Tom, a sympathetic priest, for aid; and she makes a deal with a tugboat captain at the river to take Johnny out of town that night. A creepy little guy spots Johnny and tells his wild-haired neighbor, Robert Newton, a crazed painter, where he is. Newton lives in an old tumbledown flat with snow flurrying through the roof. He wants to paint Johnny before he dies, to capture the look in his eyes! Newton enters the film about halfway through and steals it straightaway. Kathleen is running all over, searching for Johnny; but Newton, named Lukey, gets him, and installs him in a chair under harsh light while he attempts to render his likeness. Another inhabitant of the building, Tabor, a former medical student, patches up Johnny's wound, but says he must get to the hospital for a transfusion or he'll die. Newton's in a frenzy, wrapped in motheaten tweed coat and long scarf, the snow blowing in, feverishly painting away.

Finally Johnny escapes, making his way with the aid of the creepy pal of Newton's toward Father Tom's church. The cops are everywhere, closing in. They're tracking Kathleen and keeping an eye on Father Tom. McQueen collapses in someone's yard, crawls in the street; the creep runs on ahead to tell Kathleen. She comes to Johnny, helps him toward the harbor where she's convinced the captain to wait until midnight. The clock chimes; the blizzard increases. Kathleen and Johnny are caught against a fence by the river as the cops close in on them, torches bright. Johnny tells her to run, get away. "They'll take us both," she says and pulls a gun, fires twice at the bulls, who fire back, killing Johnny and the faithful daughter of the revolution. Their bodies turn white under the falling snow. The boat goes by on the river. It's the World's End, me boy-o. Work, love, suffer.

ONE-EYED JACKS

1960. Directed by Marlon Brando. Starring Marlon Brando, Karl Malden, Pina Pellicer, Timothy Carey, Katy Jurado, Ben Johnson and Elisha Cook, Jr. Screenplay by Guy Trosper and Calder Willingham.

Brando never looked better than he did in this picture; in fact, he made certain—he was the director, after all—that he was downright beautiful, if fat around the edges, a tendency difficult for him to disguise even then. The opening scene is a beauty: Marlon, as Rio, or The Kid, is sweet-talking a classy señorita at her house, cooing in her ear and slipping a ring onto the third finger of her left hand, telling her it's the ring his mother gave him just before she died. The dark-eyed beauty melts as he insinuates his body into hers—The Kid knows he's about to carve another notch on his gun. Then Karl Malden, called Dad Longworth, who's been taking care of some business of his own, shows up and shouts that the law is hot on their trail—this is Mexico in the early part of the 20th century—they've got to hightail it pronto! Rio wrenches the ring his "mother" gave him on her deathbed off the señorita's finger, says sorry, honey, and splits with his compadre Dad, leaving her, with perspiring thighs and quivering lips, in a literal lurch.

Dad and The Kid are bandits, of course, and they take off for the mountains with the gold booty they've appropriated from a Mexican bank. They ride hard for the sierras and finally hunker down on a ridge, doing their best to hold off the troops. One of their horses goes down, they're trapped, and Dad goes for help, taking the gold with him while Rio holds his position. He does the best he can, keeps looking over his shoulder for his trusted compañero to come back for him, but the authorities close in. Dad's to hell and gone with the loot, betraying The Kid, and Brando surrenders with the bitter knowledge that his so-called best friend has abandoned him.

The Kid breaks jail eventually and, accompanied by a Mexican cellmate, picks up Dad Longworth's stale trail, tracking him to a town on the central California coast near Big Sur. It's a couple or three years since Dad left Rio for dead on the mountain and Longworth has built himself a new life—with the aid of the stolen gold—he's now a sheriff, married to a handsome Mexican woman played by Katy Jurado (sturdier-looking a decade since her svelte *la victima* in Bunuel's *El Bruto*), and stepfather to Katy's pretty, barely post-adolescent daughter played by Pia Pellicer (who later committed suicide).

When Rio shows up with not only his Mex escapee pal but a trio or quartet of low company including Ben Johnson playing the kind of badass he did in *Vera Cruz* and *Shane,* old Dad knows The Kid is itching to burn "Vengeance Is Mine" on the inside of Longworth's upper lip like you i.d. a racehorse. Not only is Dad nervous about his own safety, but that of his wife and daughter and the town bank. The sheriff pretends he's glad to see Rio, amazed he's still alive, tells The Kid a cock and bull story about how he couldn't get back to the mountain, how the gold got away and all sorts of mealymouthed bushwah. Rio just takes it easy, slow to rile, seething beneath the surface at Dad's lies. Dad knows Rio knows he's lying, and warns him to behave; this is a nice little town we got here, a good place to raise a family. Yeah, drawls Rio, I might just want to do that. Longworth snickers, says this ain't your kind of situation, Kid. Best if you moved on.

The Kid doesn't move on. He sniffs out Dad's daughter, gets a start on that, then brawls with Timothy Carey, a snarling Neanderthal thug who attacks Rio in a bar. The Kid shoots him dead (in self-defense), and for this Dad nails Rio, hauls him to a hitching post and in view of the citizens smashes The Kid's gun hand with the butt of a rifle, pulverizing

Rio's trigger finger. Dad orders him out of town and Rio limps away with his confederates to bide his time on a beach ranchito while his hand heals.

Ben Johnson and his mates—one of them is his brother—deride The Kid's attempts to shoot again once his gun hand is sound enough to rehabilitate, and they're impatient to bust the bank. They don't care much about Rio's revenge motive—until he got hurt they kept a cool distance from him, having heard about The Kid's gunfighting prowess; but now he's damaged goods and they've got big doubts that Rio will ever be of real use to them. Disrespect doesn't pay off for much in a world of killers, of course, and The Kid does come back. All of the mean business we've been waiting for is played out to no good end, and it's worth the wait. There's a particularly chilling moment when Rio's jailfriend is turned on by the bad brothers, but the scene itself is so poetically and beautifully set on the windswept, cypress-spotted sand dunes of the Monterey coast that the grisly part almost doesn't matter. In fact, the California littoral is a major player in the movie, making even the few tedious parts bearable. It's a long'un: 141 minutes of Brando's fumbling and mumbling, but it works, and often majestically.

According to film editor Paul Seydor, one of the first full-length screenplays Sam Peckinpah ever wrote was an adaptation of *The Authentic Death of Hendry Jones*, a novel by Charles Neider (1956), which was based on the lives of Pat Garrett and Billy the Kid. Neider set his story not in New Mexico, where Pat and Billy had known each other, but in California, and fictionalized Billy Bonney and Pat Garrett as Hendry Jones and Dad Longworth. Garrett had written a book called *The Authentic Life of Billy the Kid* from which, also according to Seydor (who was a great friend and confrère of Peckinpah's), Neider borrowed, lifting dialogue and various incidents. Peckinpah was hired to direct the film version in 1957, wrote the screenplay, which went through numerous vicissitudes, then was fired off the project.

Following Peckinpah's departure—he would go on to direct an unhappy version of these events, *Pat Garrett and Billy the Kid* in 1973—five or six other director/writers, including Stanley Kubrick (who found Brando to be a less-than-candid and/or trustworthy piece of work), came and went, until finally, in 1960, Marlon Brando—who owned the book rights—directed the picture, ultimately re-titled *One-Eyed Jacks*. Brando's opus isn't Billy Bonney's story—Arthur Penn, in 1958, gave it a try with *The Left-Handed Gun,* Paul Newman re-creating his role from TV's "Philee Playhouse" (though James Dean was supposed to have starred in the movie), with a screenplay by Gore Vidal; it was Stan Dragoti, in 1972, who made the best Billy the Kid film by far, *Dirty Little Billy,* with Michael J. Pollard as a whiney, mud-splattered, mutt-faced, cowardly, backshooting punk killer—but Brando did a splendid job, bringing together a story of almost-epic proportions, using the big screen to force surrender as real cinema demands. That Brando never again directed a movie may or may not have been a good thing, but with *One-Eyed Jacks* he accomplished what more celebrated directors could seldom do: he made an unforgettable film.

One-Eyed Jacks is not a masterpiece, like Peckinpah's *The Wild Bunch,* but I'll always remember Brando's Rio, The Kid, goading Malden's Dad Longworth—these two had had it out before in *A Streetcar Named Desire* (1951)—"How you doin', Dad?" The Kid asks, fake-friendly, when he arrives in Sheriff Longworth's town, suppressing his hatred of the father figure he once loved and trusted who'd thrown him to the wolves. It may as well have been the poet saying "How do you like your blueeyed boy now, mister death?"
(previously unpublished)

SHACK OUT ON 101

1955. Directed by Edward Dein. Starring Terry Moore, Lee Marvin, Keenan Wynn, and Frank Lovejoy.

The secret of this movie is that nobody has to act in it. And it's a good thing, too, because neither Terry Moore nor Frank Lovejoy could if they had to. Lee Marvin and Keenan Wynn, however, give their usual hammy, amusing performances, and the whole thing is low-key enough that nobody gets stepped on. What comes out of this silly little Red Scare spy drama from the smack-dab middle of the 1950s is an almost perfect, semitrashy set piece; everybody has a good time.

The setting is a beanery near a missile base owned by Wynn. Marvin is the short-order cook, Moore is The Tomato, and Lovejoy, as usual, is the humorless Fed out to uncover the spy. As Lovejoy goes through his "Meet McGraw" routine, Wynn works out with weights, Moore displays her lovely breasts in a sweater, and Marvin grunts and leers and makes unwholesome suggestions to her. It's as if William Inge were forced by the government to rewrite some Chekhov play, but set in McCarthy-era America, and he took twenty Valium, washed them down with Old Crow, and dashed it off as the drug grabbed his brain and put him in Palookaville.

It doesn't matter who the spy really is: everyone sits around on stools and makes comments not unlike the characters in the Arizona café in *The Petrified Forest*. People going through life half-awake, half-aware, unfinished, unsure of how to handle destiny's nagging reminders. They poke at one another, spook away, there's an occasional shove. The government guy is always the stupid one, the real pawn, the one who follows orders. All The Tomato wants is some flash jerk to drag her off down Highway 101 to L.A. where she can shop and go to the beach. Wynn is a guy who knows his limitations. Lovejoy's a blank. Marvin's the only interesting one here. This movie is a dead-on minimalist portrait of America at its most paranoid. It's the one to show the history class.

POETRY

from
COYOTE TANTRAS
(1973)

CI

Coyote stood by the river

with his lady,
where
the North Alouette
spills into the Fraser

"Write down what you see,"

said Coyote,

"just that –
"anything else

is your own fault"

CII

Coyote sat
    on a slope
above a wire corral
    on the plains,
a whitefaced sorrel
ran along the Alouette
    chasing crows

"What a racket"
yawned Coyote, nudging
    nearer the sun

"All this room
        on
        one great star—

            Who can speak?"

from THE BOY YOU HAVE ALWAYS LOVED (1976)

SONG

O fly
wouldst I
the size
of thee,
or bee,
O yes, yes
one of those,
to sleep
for ever
in a rose

HOW MANY MANGOS IN MANGO CHUTNEY

There is a broken heart
in the Chinese restaurant
sitting at a booth
with a low-tugged hat
and its eyes are on the coatrack
All night it has been telling me
to order a big meal
and get on with my soup
but I muff it
I lose the fly ball in the sun
I pull my hat lower in the booth
The sun has killed my chance of a dark day
Whoever is running on the beach
will never get to know me
There is music here
There is romance
At the crack of a bat
the shortstop breaks to his left
All of the ears in the Chinese restaurant
are not able to follow the sound
The lady with the long hands
and rouge fingernails is eyeing me
I might have known

MY FATHER

The day
he died

Pops, my mother's father, sat
in the kitchen

drinking
tea,

toast crumbs
in his lap,

crying.
Death's

boy, I looked out

the livingroom
window

for the big
blue car.

PARIS STREET

Wind up gray
schoolgirl's skirt—
As she passed
copper ringlets
touched my shoulder.
Seven years later,
agonizing over
her little blue cap!

POEM FOR A PAINTER

I have a friend
A very good friend
Who is a fine painter
Just now he paints nothing but his girl
A fat Chinese girl
With blue hair
Orange eyes
Green hands and feet
This is how he sees her
And there's no arguing it
If tomorrow she has black hair
Yellow eyes
Purple breasts
He'll have caught it right
And the wonderful thing
Is that it amuses her
Nothing more
She doesn't care that he's an artist
Or that he loves her
When her red hands disappear
Into thick blue air

TWELFTH STREET

for Butch Hall

Beautiful girl
hurrying home
down 12th Street
on a windy night
no way I'll ever
know her
run my hand
up her leg
while she's reading

POEM UT ANIMUM NOSTRUM PURGET

She lov'd Villon—
  I was a poet, but
  no Villon;

she lov'd Scarlatti—
  I made music, but
  most unlike Scarlatti;

she lov'd Renoir—
  and I did not paint.

from

PERSIMMONS (1977)

RETURNING BY BOAT ON A COLD RIVER

Along
the rocky coast

the wind
has silenced
the houses

My boat
floats
to shore

head down,
I hurry
toward home,
forsaking
the sea

Are things
any better
in the mountains?

After the painting by Chikuden

from CHINESE NOTES (1978)

Separated by a river
I try not to think of you
At least my tears
please the flowers

•

Startled by a bird
I clutch my heart
as if you'd flown
out from it.

•

This summer
more than before
storms miss land
Each morning
fresh flowers
in the green
peacock vase.

NOTE TO A FRIEND FAR AWAY

Cranes slowly
settle on
nearby pond
clouds blow through
no lovers
or friends
birds, weather
will do

A CHINESE NOTE TO MARY LOU

This backyard
is our Giverny—
Roses precise as Monet's,
leaning hollyhocks,
haystack compost,
sparrows on the
warped-plank bench.
Sleeping cats, black
and gray, in vine
tangle—orange, blue,
pink, red, brown,
green, yellow—all
below the Japanese sky.

from
FLAUBERT AT KEY WEST
(1997)

MARIA LA O

In 1959, my cousin Chris and I
accompanied my Uncle Les
from Tampa to Jacksonville,
where he had business to do.
I was twelve, Chris sixteen.
Jacksonville was a small town
then, palms lined the street
where I bought a papaya drink
from a sidewalk stand.
We ate lunch in a big hotel.
I watched people through
a long, plate-glass window
behind our booth. After lunch,
Uncle Les passed out Havanas.
We lit them and puffed away
as the three of us left the hotel
and strolled down the street.
Passersby stared at me, a small boy
smoking a big, black, Cuban cigar.
I loved the taste of it, bitter
after eating sweet *flan*
for dessert, and breathed deeply
the romantic aroma of smoke
and tropical air. Thirty-five
years later I recall the smell,
the blue sailfish shirt
I wore, the Florida that
isn't there any more.

TO TERRY MOORE

for Dutch Leonard

This morning I am not
at my best
but I woke up
dreaming of Terry Moore
red apples in her sweater
sitting on a stool
in *Shack Out On 101*
sweet Terry Moore
who couldn't act
it's so painful to watch her
even in my dream
she looks uncomfortable
I want to take her in my arms
that perfect fifties body
hair shook loose over right eye
Tell me, Terry
when you were young
were your lovers ever gentle?

A NOTE ON INSPIRATION

for Duane Big Eagle

Baudelaire kept a Creole mistress
to whom he never made love
She was six feet tall
an alcoholic and a whore
Many of his *Fleurs du Mal*
were written for her
Who's to know if she ever
read any of them or cared
that he wrote her love poems
It's likely she did not
and probable that
Baudelaire died a virgin
all of which makes
for a rather sad history
Rimbaud and Verlaine, of course
fared not much better
Of those we remember
only Villon had his way
and he was hanged
The sports and divertissements
of French and other poets
are not now so easily translated
nor were they ever

FAREWELL LETTER FROM JEANNE DUVAL TO CHARLES BAUDELAIRE

Charles, from the beginning you always
made me laugh. Sending flowers to my
dressing room at Le Théâtre du Pantheon
as if I were a real actress
not just the piece of fluff
trotted out for a few moments
in a brief costume
to make the boys' cocks hard.
You had money, you were charming
and respectful. You appeared impervious
to the fact of my blackness.
When we entered a café together
you were like a proud buck with his doe.
All eyes were on us as we paraded through
and you treated me as if I were a great lady;
you had the finest manners.
The apartment you bought for me
was furnished exquisitely.
It resembled a Kaliph's boudoir.
If only you had been a Kaliph!
That would have made my being a whore
more palatable. Expensive whores
live longer than the rest.
Nadar knew me before you, yes,
as did Blanville.
When you first brought me to your suite
at the Hôtel Lauzun I pretended
never to have been there before.
But I had, several times, with different men,
men who knew how to satisfy a woman,
and themselves.
You created me for yourself as an object
only, a stone creature whom you could idealize
and pretend to worship and torture

yourself over. It was madness!
I'm a slut, yes, perhaps worse;
a drunkard, too. But I am *real!*
I exist *here* in this time, not in
any other and I never will.
Your reliance on women such as Luchette
and Madame Meurice has stunted you.
They encourage your impotence.
"My vampire!" you called me. It's what
you wanted, begged for, demanded.
Only by cruelty could you be convinced
of anything. Being cruel is
a soul-consuming task, and one
which amuses me to a lesser degree
than you would suppose.
I plead exhaustion, Charles.
I release myself from this obligation to you.
My sweet, poetry is not enough.

THE SURREALISTS COME TO CALIFORNIA

Cruising in a Cadillac
down sunny 101
"Earth Angel" by The Penguins
on the radio
André Breton at the wheel
Louis Aragon and Robert Desnos,
who is dozing,
in the backseat
Breton shouts, "The old Dali
would have loved this!
The Dali of before Gala!"
"Man Ray was right about America,"
says Aragon
"All around us is
the evidence of inevitability"
"Inevitability is irrelevant,"
says Desnos, coming to life
"The true Surrealists of America
are the Oklahoma Indians
who buy big cars with oil money
and drive them until
they run out of gas,
then abandon them"
"Poor Eluard," says Breton
"he would have loved
to have accompanied us"
"Poor Péret," says Aragon
"he never kept a sou"
"Poor us," says Desnos
"snow, a woman's glove,
such gloomy symbols"
"Had Reverdy lived in California,"
says Breton
"he would never have written

'winter chased me
in the streets' "
"You must remember," says Desnos,
only one eye open
"this highway is a manifestation
of the route of Apollinaire"
"Yes," says Breton, "beauty
is no longer a nuisance"
"Or," adds Aragon, "a dream"

from REPLIES TO WANG WEI (2001)

POEM AFTER WANG WEI

I keep
in
my apricot chest
the willow
branch
you gave me
the morning
we parted
at Peach Blossom
Spring
brittle now
I handle it
tenderly
How can it be
you are
no longer
there
to dangle
your fingers
in the bright
green
water

IN MEMORY OF SUWA YU

Creek
crawling through
woods
How many thousands
of years
without stopping
I'm happy
to listen
longer
than that

NEW POEMS

BACK IN AMERICA

Old cowboy
crossing Oakland
street
with rodeo limp,
spotted face
and hands
boots scuffed, cracked
filthy shirt
untucked—
stuffed in left
back pocket
of faded jeans
The Iliad—
if only Homer
could see him,
headed
to dump hotel
half-pint
of bad bourbon
in bag
dreaming glories
of Greece
and his
lost
horse

ON VIEWING THE MANUSCRIPT SCROLL OF JACK KEROUAC'S NOVEL *ON THE ROAD* IN THE TOSCA BAR, SAN FRANCISCO

Lying in state, under glass,
partially unrolled to reveal
flood of words describ'd
Mississippi River near New Orleans
1947—an American Shroud,
Davia Nelson called it, like
the Shroud of Turin, holy remnant
of modern Literature, naively
woven tapestry—
                    Kerouac would have lov'd
this, I think, his own worn
Shrouded Stranger, well-travel'd,
displayed for religious purpose,
himself collapsed Catholic Buddhist
pilgrim in constant search
for the Sacred, sanctified today
here in sere mute Tosca cathedral
light, lone silver'd stream of sun,
God's finger pointed toward window
sarcophagus casket containing
phantom tome brought out by hand
half-century before by Jack Kerouac
from America's burning Egyptian heart.

SMALL ELEGY FOR CORSO

to Fernanda Pivano

Gregory Corso's buried in Rome
a few weeks ago next to Shelley
in an *acattòlico* cemetery in Testaccio
Sitting on a bench in the Piazza Cavour
I recall Nanda telling me last December
Gregory had his balls cut off
"I don't care," he told her, "I fucked enough."
Now at twilight in the Quartiere Prati
watching rich women walk big dogs
past palm trees under plum-colored sky
suddenly there's Corso ten years ago or more
at a baseball game in San Francisco
shouting at a player, "Pull up your pants!
It's a disgrace to the uniform!"
Three rows in front I looked around,
"Gregory," I said, "what happened to
your teeth?" "They're gone!" he said
"Who needs teeth after fifty?"
We met again at a wedding in Bolinas
Quietly he told me how secretly he
envied Kerouac having died so young,
only 47. "If only he could have enjoyed
himself more, but he was always drunk."
O Gregory, may you take eternity for all
it's worth, the same as you captured
your time on earth, knowing all along
there was nothing real to lose.
Roll over, Captain Poetry,
tell old Percy the news.

POEM

That the thought
of losing you
is even in my head
disturbs me
I've never cared
for anyone
in this way before
never thought
that I could make
such a mistake
to fall in love
with the real girl
of my dreams
Now it's too late
the hunter captured
by the game
You sleep
with my soul
in your mouth
When we kiss
I can taste it

A DREAM

As I told you
last night
we were walking
in a dark forest
we got lost
from each other
I had to find you
I called your name
you answered
but your voice
was faint
as if you were suddenly
impossibly far away
I followed the sound
for what seemed
like days
I didn't want
to give up
to leave you alone
in the forest
I didn't know if
you were really lost
or where I was
Finally, I saw you
walking along a path
I didn't know was there
You stopped by a tree
I waited to see
which way you would go
I heard a noise
behind me
and looked around
but nothing moved
Now you were
beside me

and we moved together
along the path
You took my hand
It's true, you said,
I'm a little lost
I followed you anyway
The path disappeared
but we kept going
This is love, I said
You turned and kissed me
Yes, you said, I know.

SHOOTING POOL IN THE DARK

Living with you
is like shooting pool
in the dark
impossible to guess correctly
which ball to hit next
or even know what stripe
or solid, number or color
is still there or where
Life with you is like
being asked to run
a neverending table
blindfolded and bleeding
from a shotgun wound
I once saw Willie Mosconi
run 91 balls in a row
shooting straight pool
at Benzinger's in Chicago
I'd bet anything
he couldn't have done it
with a hole
this size
in his heart

TRUE LOVE

Your sickness made me
a little sick, it's
true—I still
feel it
Mayakovsky got down
on his knees
and declared
his love
to his last
mistress
a few hours after
he'd met her
Remember me
at the hotel
in Paris,
on my knees
in the lift?
We're all the same
men of too much passion
and a little talent—
some a little more
than others
We fool ourselves
into thinking
we're strong
then complain
the rest of our lives
crippled by
the consequences

THE TALK

INTRODUCTION TO JACK'S BOOK, 2nd ed. (1994)

ON MAY 30, 1936, in a letter to Arnold Zweig, Sigmund Freud wrote: "To be a biographer, you must tie yourself up in lies, concealments, hypocrisies, false colorings, and even in hiding a lack of understanding, for biographical truth is not to be had, and if it were to be had, we could not use it . . . truth is not feasible, mankind doesn't deserve it . . . "

Heeding Freud's admonition, Larry Lee and I chose the rather unorthodox (for that time, 1975) method of "oral history" to capture on record the brief life of Jack Kerouac. Larry called it "a rather more immediate form of biography"; the idea being that since most of Kerouac's cronies and family members were still alive (he having died of alcoholism at the early age of forty-seven), if we could find and then persuade them to talk candidly about the subject, it would be left to us—and the reader—to sort through the revisionism and decide whose versions most closely approximated the ineluctable "truth." It was Jack's long-time cohort, the poet Allen Ginsberg, who pronounced, upon completion of his reading of the uncorrected galleys of the book: "My god, it's just like *Rashomon*—everybody lies and the truth comes out!" Allen's words are branded in my memory; I am not paraphrasing.

It was Allen's well-meaning desire to see Kerouac presented in the "best" light, owing, no doubt, to the disrespect and disservice that Jack—and Allen, among other contemporaries—had received from critics and the news media during the heyday of the "Beat Generation." Though *Jack's Book* surely presents Kerouac warts and all, it was Larry Lee's and my intention to get people busy reading J.K.'s eleven mostly ignored novels and other works. When we began our research for this biography, only three of Kerouac's books were in print: *On the Road, The Dharma Bums*, and *Book of Dreams*. By 1980, two years after the publication of *Jack's Book*, at least eight titles were available. In 1994, virtually all of Kerouac's work can be found in new editions.

Larry and I did not intend that *Jack's Book* be a "definitive" study. We assumed that more scholarly approaches would follow ours—"*Après moi*," wrote J.K., "*le deluge*"—and, true enough, that avalanche fell in short order. In fact, it's still falling. We wanted to create a conversational, novelistic (in terms of dialogue) reckoning of this man's life. We wanted the people he knew and loved and hated, and who knew and loved and hated him, to say whatever they had to say without being given too much time, too many years, to think about it. In most cases, these people had not yet spoken on the record about Jack Kerouac. Their thoughts were fresh—they didn't know what they thought until they'd told us, until they'd said it out loud. One reviewer declared, "If you're interested in listening to what the talk of the fifties sounded like, and if you believe that literature may just have something to do with life, then read this book." *That* was what we were after, the *talk*.

The novelist and journalist Dan Wakefield, later himself to chronicle the period in his memoir, *New York in the 50s*, magnanimously described our effort as "a fascinating literary and historical document, the most insightful look at the beat generation." The key word there, for us, is *document. Jack's Book* is constructed like a documentary, what Kerouac, in his novel *Doctor Sax*, called a "bookmovie." Others of Mr. Wakefield's generation decried the new attention being paid to Kerouac; they had disliked him and/or his work then, and they disliked him and it—and, by association, Larry Lee and me—now. That was all right with us; we, who cared enough about his writing to devote two years of our lives in an effort to get the Kerouac ball rolling again, expected as much.

We knew that just the mention of the name Jack Kerouac was enough to aggravate some people. We also knew that his novels had inspired thousands and thousands of readers—especially youthful readers—to get the hell out of whatever boring or dead-end situation they were in and take a chance with their lives. I'll always respect the writer Thomas McGuane for going on record about J.K., saying in an essay that he, McGuane, never wanted to hear a word against Kerouac because Jack had indeed worked a kind of salutary magic on more than a few. "He trained us in the epic idea that . . . you didn't necessarily have to take it in Dipstick, Ohio, forever," McGuane wrote. "Kerouac set me out there with my own key to the highway." Kerouac's literary standing aside, the man had the power to *move* others.

Jack Kerouac was no avatar and *Jack's Book* was not meant as hagiography. This book—biography, reportage, collage, holy mosaic, unholy mess, however it's been and will be characterized—contains some extremely emotional, confessional material; it's not dull. Dr. Freud notwithstanding, there is at least a sort of truth to be found here. The book belongs to those persons who bared their souls in conversations with us about their dead friend or adversary. Therefore, it belongs to Kerouac, which is why I titled it *Jack's Book*. These are letters to a dead man from people who for one reason or another didn't tell him what they really thought of and about him while he was alive. It was Larry's and my pleasure to provide them the belated opportunity.

I'll never forget sitting with Jimmy Holmes, the hunchbacked pool-shark of Denver, in the stuffy parlor of his elderly aunt's apartment, where he lived, and him saying to me, after I'd read aloud a lyrical passage from *Visions of Cody* that Kerouac had based on his life, and which Holmes had never read, "I didn't know Jack cared about me that way. He really *cared*, didn't he?" Or stumbling drunkenly along the Bowery in the wee hours one frozen February morning with Lucien Carr, who kept repeating, "I *loved* that man. I *loved* Jack, goddam it, and I never *told* him!"

BLACKOUT

from *HOTEL ROOM TRILOGY* (1995)

CHARACTERS

DANNY, *a man in his late thirties.*
DIANE, *Danny's wife; she is in her mid-thirties.*
BELLBOY

SETTING: *a hotel room in New York City. Mid-summer.*

[In the original production, the play was set in the year 1936.]

Darkness. We see nothing but pitch black.
We hear voices, feet on stairs. Suddenly, a beam of light coming from a stairwell off what we can barely discern as an empty hotel corridor. Now there are two beams of light streaming into the corridor as the voices grow louder and the steps are more audible. The shapes of two men, both holding flashlights, one of them carrying a bag in one arm, enter the corridor from the stairwell. Their flashlight beams precede them as they turn and walk toward us down the corridor.

BELLBOY
Watch out, for the carpet here. The edge of it. Don't get your toe caught under the edge. The toe of your boot, I mean.

DANNY *(Laughs)*
Thanks, I won't. I been walkin' in boots since I was born, practically.

BELLBOY *(Stops in front of door to room number 603.)*
You're from where? Nebraska?

DANNY
No. Oklahoma. My wife and me are from Big Eagle, Oklahoma. Outside Tulsa.

BELLBOY
You get blackouts in Big Angle? Electrical blackouts like this?

DANNY
Big Eagle. No, not really. Not too many lights to begin with. Not in Big Eagle. Tulsa's a big town, though. Ever been there?

BELLBOY
No, sir. Farthest west I've been's Jersey City. That's in New Jersey, just across the Hudson River.

DANNY
Do you mind opening the door for me? With this bag of food and the torch, it's tough to get at my key.

BELLBOY *(Quickly takes out his master key.)*
Oh, sure, yes sir. Sorry. (*He unlocks the door and stands aside.*) There you are, sir.

> DANNY *enters the room, followed by the* BELLBOY. *Lightning flashes outside the window, followed by a crash of thunder. This continues intermittently throughout.*

DANNY
Hey, darlin'. You in here somewhere?

> *Both* DANNY *and the* BELLBOY *wave their flashlights around until they locate* DIANE, *who is sitting on a couch in the dark. The lights circle and blind* DIANE *momentarily. She puts one hand up and covers her eyes.* DANNY *puts the bag down on a table, then switches off his flashlight. He sits next to his wife while the* BELLBOY *begins lighting candles all around the room.*

DANNY
Sweetheart, you okay? I got us some Chinese for supper. *Good* Chinese.

BELLBOY *(Strategically setting up the candlestick holders.)*
The best. Low Fon's the best around here. New York's got the best Chinese food in the world. Better than in China. At least that's what our Chinese guests tell me. I was never actually in China. But I guess the Chinese should know.

DANNY has one arm around DIANE as they sit together on the couch. She still has one hand over her eyes. The BELLBOY finishes arranging the candles and stands in front of the open room door, holding his flashlight.

BELLBOY
I'm sure they'll get the lights fixed soon. The candles should last until they do. There're more candles in the cabinet there, under the window, if you need 'em. The phones are working—at least they were a few minutes ago. If you need anything else, just call down. I'd recommend, though, that you stay in the room until the power comes on again. New York's not Oklahoma, you know. There're plenty of people take advantage of a situation like this. You know what I'm talking about.

DANNY
Thanks. We'll be all right. Can I keep this? (*He holds up the flashlight.*)

BELLBOY
Oh, sure, no problem. Listen, they'll have this fixed before you finish your dinner.

DANNY
Come back get the torch, you need it or someone else does.

BELLBOY
We got plenty, don't worry. Enjoy your dinner now, folks.

The BELLBOY leaves, closing the door behind him. The candlelight bathes the room in a warm, rose-colored glow. DANNY takes DIANE'S hand from her eyes, kisses it, and holds it. She sits still with her eyes closed.

DANNY
You can open 'em, honey. Come on, open up your eyes.

> DIANE *opens her eyes, blinks a few times. She looks around without moving her head.*

DIANE.
It's like being inside a Christmas tree, isn't it? Like sitting on one of the branches, surrounded by ornaments.

DANNY *(Laughs.)*
Yeah, yeah. I see what you mean. This is somethin', though, isn't it? We come all the way to New York, the city of lights, and there ain't none. Hold it, maybe that's Paris is the city of lights. But Broadway, anyway. The Great White Way, only now it's black. Or is it London has the Great White Way? Well, let me tell you, sweetheart, when I was out gettin' the Chinese? People are bumpin' into one another, runnin' to get home. Lucky thing I got into the Chinese restaurant when I did, too. Soon as the lights quit, those guys ran and locked the front door. Then they brought out big sheets of plywood and stuck 'em up by the windows. Those Chinese fellas weren't takin' no chances. They were real polite to me, though. Apologized for takin' a little longer than they said was ordinary for my order. Didn't charge me no tax. At least they said they wasn't. Man unlocked the door to let me out, said, You be careful, sir. Hurry, be careful.

DIANE
Danny, we're not in China.

DANNY
No, honey. New York. We're in New York.

DIANE
Why did you speak Chinese to that man?

DANNY
What man?

DIANE
The doctor who was here before.

DANNY
Diane, that was the bellboy. We're going to see the doctor tomorrow, remember? And you know I can't speak Chinese. I barely get by in American.

DIANE
Don't be so modest. You know Spanish, too.

DANNY
Just about twenty-five words, maybe. Like, *huevos rancheros,* and *buena suerte.*

DIANE
Si todo sigue igual.

DANNY *(Laughs.)*
What's that? What's that mean?

DIANE
All things being equal. It's an expression. You know what an expression is, Danny. Don't try to fool me.

DANNY *(Hugging her.)*
The last thing I'd ever do is try to fool you, sweetheart. You know I care more for you than anything in the world. There's foolin' around and then there's tryin' to fool. Foolin' around is what we always done best, Di, don't you think? You still like to fool around with your old Danny, don't you? Even after all these years?

DIANE
It has been a long time, Danny, hasn't it?

DANNY
Almost seventeen years. Since I got out of the service.

DANNY stands up, wipes his forehead, his cheeks. He takes a napkin from the bag and wipes his hands.

DANNY
Lord, it's warm. I don't mind the dark, but I could do with some air-coolin'.

He walks over to the windows, which are open. He leans out, trying to catch a breeze. There is none, so he comes back in.

DANNY
Could we'd be on Lake Osage this evenin', we were back home. Canoein'. Wouldn't you like that, darlin', if we were lyin' in a canoe lookin' up at the stars, driftin' on Lake Osage?

DIANE
Is it a Chinese doctor? The one I'm seeing tomorrow? He's Chinese?

DANNY comes back over to DIANE, kneels in front of her, taking her hands in his.

DANNY
Diane, listen. Forget this Chinese. The only thing is Chinese is the food that's waitin' for us to eat it in the bag there. The spring rolls and shrimp with lobster sauce and sweet and sour pork and chicken fried rice. All your favorites. The doctor's name is Smith, Hershel Smith. He's a specialist, honey. He'll know what to do. It's all been arranged by the clinic in Tulsa, remember? They said Dr. Smith is the best there is. He's expectin' us tomorrow.

DIANE
You were away.

DANNY
When, honey? When was I away?

DIANE
I'm not sure. You were, though. Away in the Sea of Red.

DANNY
The Red Sea. When I was in the navy, you mean?

DIANE
Oh, of course. When you said Lake Osage, I thought of it. I took a walk and everything was just like this. There were lights on in the dark, just small ones, shimmering lights.

DANNY
Lights on in the houses around the lake.

DIANE.
I saw you on the other side and I shouted, Danny! Danny! But it wasn't you at all.

DANNY rests his head on DIANE's lap. She strokes his hair gently.

DIANE
A fish jumped.

DANNY
What kind of fish?

DIANE
A Chinese fish.

DANNY
How could you tell it was Chinese?

DIANE
Because it told my fortune.

DANNY
You sure this was at Lake Osage?

DIANE
It jumped straight up out of the black water and spoke to me.

DANNY
You never told me this before.

DIANE
You'd just think I was crazier than I already am. That's why.

DANNY
I don't think you're crazy, sweetheart. I don't know what to call it, but it's not crazy. Maybe Dr. Smith has a name for it.

DIANE
A fish by any other name is still a fish.

DANNY
Even if it's Chinese?

DIANE
Definitely if it's Chinese.

DANNY
So what did the fish tell you?

DIANE
About the children.

DANNY *(He is looking up at her now.)*
What about them?

DIANE
All about them. Their names, their hair color, the shapes of their noses.

DANNY
What children, Diane?

DIANE
Ours. Yours and mine, Danny. All of them.

DANNY
How many were there?

DIANE
Six. Six altogether. Do you really want to know?

DANNY
I got no place to go, honey. Not without you, anyway.

DIANE
Danny, you were always the sweetest child.

DANNY
You didn't meet me until I was twenty, Di. How do you know I was a sweet child?

DIANE
You were one of them.

DANNY
One of who?

DIANE
The six children.

DANNY
Wait up. The Chinese fish told you about them?

DIANE
You were first, the largest, with red hair and blue eyes.

DANNY
Doesn't sound like me.

DIANE
The rest were girls. Five perfect girls.

DANNY
Did they have red hair and blue eyes, too?

DIANE
No. Each one of them had brown hair, brown eyes and brown skin. They looked like fawns.

DANNY
You saw them? I thought this was just a fortune the fish told you.

DIANE
Danny, these are our children! Don't you recognize them?

DANNY *(Sits next to her again.)*
Di, I love you. (*He kisses her.*) I've loved you since I was twenty and you were eighteen. Seventeen years and I love you more than ever.

DIANE
I know, Danny.

DANNY
We did have a child. Danny, Junior.

DIANE
Dan-Bug.

DANNY
That's right, Di. Dan-Bug. We called him Dan-Bug. Do you remember what happened to Dan-Bug, Di?

DIANE
Not really.

DANNY
Yes, you do. Come on.

DIANE
He was two.

DANNY
Two years old.

DIANE
How old is he now?

DANNY
Two. He can't get any older, Di.

DIANE
He might have gone in the navy, Danny, like you did.

DANNY
He might have.

DIANE
I wouldn't have wanted him to go sailing in the Sea of Red. Sailors don't come back from there sometimes.

DANNY
I came back, Di. I'm here.

DIANE
Dan-Bug's not.

DANNY
That's right, Dan-Bug's gone, baby.

DIANE
He drowned in the Sea of Red.

DANNY
He drowned in Lake Osage.

DIANE
The five fawns are fine.

DANNY
That's a pretty sentence, Di. The five fawns are fine.

DIANE
The Chinese fish was right about them.

DANNY
I suppose he ain't half-wrong most of the time.

DIANE
I'm dealing with it, Danny. I am. It hasn't been that long.

DANNY
Twelve years, Di. How long is long?

DIANE
I know this isn't China, Danny. I think I'd like to go there, though.

DANNY
That's not impossible. We can see about it. You ready to eat yet?

DIANE
Remember Rinky Dink, Dan? What happened to him?

DANNY
Yes, Di, I do.

DIANE
The woman who was driving never looked in her sideview, she said, just the rearview mirror. Knocked him sideways off his motorcycle into the road in the path of oncoming traffic. Patrolman said Rinky Dink's head hit the ground an instant before that Buick run over his back.

DANNY
He was an okay boy, okay.

DIANE

He wasn't very big, and he had a three-inch scar on his forehead that filled with red whenever he laughed or was angry. Remember? The car that crushed him didn't leave a mark. There was only a light bruise on his temple that would never heal. When Bonnie saw him in the coffin, she said, Why he looks cuter now than ever.

DANNY

When I got out of the navy, before I came back to Oklahoma, I went to visit a guy I'd met in boot camp. We'd kept a correspondence goin', and he was livin' in New Mexico, in the foothills of the Sangre de Cristo range of mountains. His name was Famine McCoy. He reminded me of Rinky Dink. Or Rinky Dink reminded me of him, I forget which.

Anyway, we were ridin' in his truck on some backroad, and we got stuck in a rut. We looked around for some timber, somethin' to get some traction from, but there was nothin' except a petrified stiff dead dog in a ditch on the other side. So we took it and shoved it under the wheel and rocked right out of there. Later we got down to the town and Famine mentioned to a fella he knew what happened and said how he felt a little guilty about abusin' that dog's body and all. Don't worry about it, the guy told him, that's what it's there for. People use it all the time.

DIANE

What kind of a name is that, Famine?

DANNY

I asked him about it. His real name was Dave, I think. He said that before he went in the navy, he became famous for showin' up on people's doorsteps just at suppertime. Every evenin', he said, he'd go out sniffin'. Just like a dog casin' garbage cans, he'd prowl the neighborhood with his nose up to smell out who was cookin' what. He got to know everybody around where he was livin' and walked the streets until he found a smell he liked, so he knew what they were havin' for dinner. He'd knock on the door, make out like he was just visiting, and don't-mind-if-I-do'd his way to a free meal.

It was his neighbors nicknamed him Famine. They got hip to him and didn't answer their doors until they'd finished eating. Forced him to get a regular job as a carpenter so he could afford to pay for his meals in restaurants. Got himself a hog Lincoln and kept all his tools in it. Told me he didn't have a muffler on it, and he'd drive up and down the streets at suppertime, real slow, gunnin' the motor real loud, so everybody'd know he was out there and that he knew they were eatin', tryin' to make 'em all feel guilty about not invitin' him in anymore.

We wrote to each other for a while after that visit. He told me he lost an eye in some work-related accident and got permanent disability payments from the government and a load of insurance money from the outfit he was carpentryin' for. He moved down to Florida, where he bought himself a piece of land, got married and had a kid or two. He was eatin' steady, I guess. Then I had a letter from his wife, tellin' me Famine was dead.

Seems he was out takin' a dump in the palmettos and felt a sharp jab in his butt. He felt around but couldn't find nothin' wrong, so he just zipped up and didn't think any more about it. That night he started feelin' real bad and actin' strange, so his wife took him to the hospital. The doctor couldn't find anything wrong with him and sent him home. Two hours later, he was dead.

Turned out a snake bit him while he was in the bushes. If he'd told the doctor at the hospital about that jab he'd felt they could have saved him, but it didn't occur to Famine until right before he faded out that it wasn't just a palmetto leaf that stuck him. Poor Famine, just when it looked like things were goin' good, too. Makes me hungry sometimes to think about him.

There is a bright flash in the room, followed by an extremely loud clap of thunder.

DIANE
My mother closed the bedroom door.

DANNY
What? What door?

DIANE
My door. That's what it sounded like when she closed it. Like thunder that's so close. I'd never allow her to put Dan-Bug to bed. I didn't want him to be frightened that way.

DANNY
Dan-Bug could sleep through anything, even a thunderstorm. He liked to watch the lightning with me, the double bolts of ground lightning like we get in Oklahoma. Did you know, Di, that a channel of lightning has a width of only about an inch?

> DANNY *stands up, takes out a handkerchief from his back pocket and wipes the sweat off of his face and neck. He goes over to the window again.*

DANNY
Too hot to eat, I guess.

> DIANE *stands and picks up one of the lit candles. She dances around the room, slowly, whirling gracefully.* DANNY *turns and watches her. She sees that he is watching and she moves gradually in his direction, writhing now, Salome-like, coming closer. Suddenly, the candle she is holding goes out.* DIANE *stops dancing and stands still for a moment, then her knees buckle and she collapses to the floor.* DANNY *rushes over and lifts her back onto the couch. She has not lost consciousness, but seems stunned and disoriented.* DANNY *sits next to her.*

DANNY
Hey, baby, you all right? Come on, now, talk to me. Talk to me, Di.

DIANE (*Very woozy.*)
I am not drunk, Dan. I haven't had a drink since you've been away. Not one. It was Bonnie who made me, wanted me to go out. But I just watched 'em. Cranberry juice and soda water, that's all I had. We were at the Cherokee and there was a good band. Played a lot of old stuff, made me cry 'cause you were away. I was sittin' on the toilet after I peed, cryin' 'cause I missed you, and Bonnie was in there with Rinky Dink doin' lines. They offered me some but you know me and drugs is not on friendly terms, so I declined. All it took was that woman's small miscalculation and Rink was dust.

DANNY
I wasn't anywhere, Di. I wasn't away.

DIANE
Oh, you were, you were. Off sailing in the Sea of Red. Do you know how it hurts your eyes to stare at the horizon? If you stare at the horizon for too long all you can see is fire. The entire line of the horizon is burning. Fires as far as the eyes can see.

DANNY
Come back, Diane. I'm here, it's okay. You don't have to pretend now.

DIANE
Danny, Danny. Can you keep a secret?

DANNY
Sure.

DIANE
When we go to see this doctor—what's his name?

DANNY
Dr. Smith, you mean? Hershel Smith?

DIANE
When we go to see Dr. Smith. Don't tell him about Dan-Bug, okay? Can we forget about Dan-Bug?

DANNY
I think Dr. Smith already knows about Dan-Bug, sweetheart. He's spoken to the people at the Tulsa clinic. They sent your medical records to him. That's how come he agreed to see you, see what he could do. I told you that, honey. I told you before we left home.

DIANE
Gee, Danny, it's so dark here. It's so hot, and there isn't any moon.

DANNY
There's a power failure, Di. The lights are out all over New York City. AC's out, too. At least in this hotel they got windows can open. Some places they're sealed shut.

DIANE
It's kind of beautiful, though, the dark. Don't you think, Dan? I could get used to this.

The telephone rings so loudly that it startles both DANNY *and* DIANE. DANNY *is about to pick up the receiver but it does not ring a second time. He waits, staring at the phone, but nothing happens.*

DANNY
Now that's spooky.

DIANE
Spooky?

DANNY
The telephone. It rang once, then quit.

DIANE
Maybe it was a signal.

DANNY
What kind of a signal?

DIANE
A message.

DANNY
Nobody knows we're here, Di. I mean, nobody knows what hotel we're staying at. I didn't tell anyone. Somebody rang the wrong room, that's all.

The telephone rings again. DANNY *looks at it and lets it ring a second time, then a third. After the fourth ring, he picks it up.*

DANNY
Hello?

He listens for a few moments, starts to speak, then stops and listens again. DANNY *hangs up. A few moments pass in silence. The telephone rings again. On the second ring,* DANNY *picks it up.*

DANNY
Hello?

DANNY listens for a moment, then hands the receiver to DIANE, who looks at him but does not talk into the phone.

DIANE
Who is it?

DANNY
He asked for you.

DIANE (*Lifts the receiver to her ear and mouth.*)
Hello? Yes, yes it is. Thank you. It is dark, yes, very dark. We have candles. Uh huh. I'm sure it's not. No, I never have. Yes, Danny went out and got Chinese. You're very kind. I hope so. Yes. Yes. Thank you. We will. Bye.

DIANE hands the receiver to DANNY and he hangs it up.

DANNY
Who was it?

DIANE
Dr. Smith. He was very sweet.

DANNY
The clinic must have told him where we were staying. What did he say?

DIANE
He just wanted to make sure that we were all right during the blackout. That we were comfortable and had food.

DANNY
That must have been him the first time, too. When the line was messed up. Someone was talking but I couldn't understand him. The connection was bad, full of static.

DIANE
He wanted to assure me, he said, that he was looking forward to our visit tomorrow. He has a nice voice, Danny, you know? A *good* voice.

DANNY
I'm glad.

DIANE
I'm going to tell him about Dan-Bug.

DANNY
I know, Di. You have to.

DIANE
I couldn't live without you, Danny. I really couldn't.

DIANE *puts her head on* DANNY'S *shoulder. His arm embraces her.*

DANNY
Jesus, honey, you're burnin' up.

DANNY *gets up and goes into the bathroom. He comes out with a wet washcloth, sits down next to* DIANE, *and uses it to wipe perspiration from her face. Then he folds it and presses it against her forehead.*

DIANE
Danny, I didn't tell you everything about the fawns.

DANNY
The fawns?

DIANE
You know, the five fawns.

DANNY (*Removes the washcloth and wipes his own face with it.*)
What about the fawns, honey?

DIANE
They have names.

DANNY
Did you name them?

DIANE
Of course. Don't pretend you don't know.

DANNY (*Laughs.*)
Me? I ain't pretendin', sweetheart. What are they?

DIANE
Thumb, Index, Middle, Third and Pinkie. Pinkie's my favorite.

DANNY
Diane, you're the one and only, that's for sure.

DIANE
Dan-Bug drowned, didn't he, Danny?

DANNY
Yes, honey, he did.

DIANE
Do you recall how it happened?

DANNY
You and me was makin' love down on the shore of Lake Osage. We thought the boy was asleep on his blanket, but he woke up and walked into the water without makin' no noise we could hear. By the time we found him, he was gone.

DIANE
It was a long time ago, Danny.

DANNY
Twelve years, Di, like I said. Not so long. It's good you can talk about it, though. If you didn't, I'd probably lose you, too.

DIANE
Me and the five fawns, you mean.

DANNY
Yeah. Them, also.

DIANE
That night I was in the Cherokee, the night Rinky Dink was killed, Bonnie said somethin'.

DANNY
What was that?

DIANE
Oh, she was wasted, I guess. But I heard her say to Peggy Worth how it was some people don't deserve to have kids, anyway.

DANNY
And you figured she was meanin' you?

DIANE
Uh huh. I didn't take it to heart right away, but then after it turned out I couldn't get pregnant again, I started in on it meanin' somethin'. There was no way I could get it out of my head. It just stuck in my brain like a knife. It got so bad that I asked 'em at the Tulsa clinic could they just do an operation pull out that knife.

DANNY
It ain't been easy on me, neither, Di. You driftin' in and out, though, I suppose give me a purpose in life since the accident. Needed to keep you from gettin' away from yourself altogether.

DIANE
Driftin' so far out into the Sea of Red I couldn't get back, you mean.

DANNY (*Looking at her.*)
I have to admit there been times lately I been feelin' a little desperate. I'm a pretty good hand, they tell me, but it comes to bakin' cakes I'm clutterin' up the kitchen. It's a damn hard thing to take, feelin' useless.

DIANE
You don't have a useless bone in your body, Danny. I'll tell everyone we know.

DANNY (*Moves closer to her.*)
If it weren't so damn hot, I'd kiss you.

DIANE
Kiss me anyway.

As they kiss, the lights suddenly go on in the room, as does the air-conditioning. DANNY *gets up and goes to the window.*

DANNY
Look at this, Di. The whole city's lit up!

DIANE *joins him at the window and they stare at the magnificent sight. They embrace and kiss tenderly.*

DANNY
Honey, what would you say to some Chinese food?

FADE OUT.

from
LOST HIGHWAY

A SCREENPLAY
(1997)
WITH DAVID LYNCH

INT. THE MADISON HOUSE. LIVING ROOM. DAY

Two men in suits, the Detectives, Ed and Al, are seated on the couch, watching the last part of the second videotape. The screen turns to snow and stays that way for several moments, until FRED *shuts it off.*

FRED
That's it.

ED
Let's have a look at the hallway outside the bedroom.

CUT TO:

INT. THE MADISON HOUSE. HALLWAY. DAY

All four of them go to the hallway, where Ed and Al look around, especially up toward the ceiling.

AL
Very strange.

RENEE
What is?

AL
The angle. The high angle shot on the tape.

ED
How'd the camera get so high like that?

AL
And smooth . . . Almost no movement—back and forth, I mean.

ED
Like you'd get if it was hand-held.

AL
Right—This just glided along.

CUT TO:

INT. THE MADISON HOUSE. BEDROOM. DAY

The Detectives enter the bedroom. Fred and Renee follow.

ED
This is the bedroom.

The Detectives look around without touching anything.

AL
Do you always sleep here? . . . In this room? . . . Both of you?

FRED
This is our bedroom.

ED
There's no other bedroom?

FRED
No . . . There is, I mean, I use it as a practice room . . . It's soundproofed.

AL
You're a musician?

FRED
Yes, I thought my wife . . .

ED
What's your axe?

FRED
Tenor . . . Tenor saxophone. Do you . . . ?

ED *(shakes his head)*
Tone deaf.

AL *(to Renee)*
Do you own a video camera?

RENEE
No. Fred hates them.

The Detectives both look at Fred.

FRED
I like to remember things my own way.

AL
What do you mean by that?

FRED
How *I* remember them. Not necessarily the way they happened.

ED
Do you have an alarm system?

RENEE
Yes, actually we do . . . but we haven't been using it.

AL
Why not?

FRED
It kept going off for some reason. False alarms.

ED
Might be a good time to try using it again.

AL
Anybody else have a key to the house?

RENEE
No.

AL
Maid? Relative?

RENEE
No, one of us is always here to let the maid in. Nobody else has a key.

ED *(to Al)*
Let's check the doors and windows . . . See if there's been a break-in.

They all leave the bedroom.

CUT TO:

INT. THE MADISON HOUSE. FRONT DOOR. DAY

Ed is checking the door for marks.

CUT TO:

INT. THE MADISON HOUSE. LIVING ROOM. DAY

Fred's POV: *he's watching Ed and Al with Renee who are outside the house, walking around the property, checking it out.*

Fred looks up through the skylight and sees Al on the roof looking down.

CUT TO:

EXT. THE MADISON HOUSE. DRIVEWAY. DAY

Ed and Al are standing by an unmarked police car with Fred and Renee. The Detectives are about to depart.

AL
We'll keep a watch on the house.

ED
As best we can.

AL
If anything else happens, you'll call us?

Al hands Fred a card. Ed hands Renee a card.

RENEE
We will.

FRED
Thanks, guys.

ED
It's what we do.

Ed and Al get into the car and drive off. Renee and Fred look at each other, warily, then go back into the house. The camera slowly pans over the front of the house as in the videotape.

FADE OUT.

• • •

INT. DAYTON HOUSE. NIGHT

MR EDDY *(phone voice)*
Hey, Pete . . . How ya doin'?

PETE
Who is this?

MR EDDY
You know who it is.

Bill and Candace have stopped in the living room—watching Pete. Pete is going crazy with Mr Eddy on one end, and his parents staring at him on the other. He waves his parents away, but they leave slowly and reluctantly.

PETE
Mr Eddy?

MR EDDY
Yeah . . . How ya doin', Pete?

PETE
Okay.

MR EDDY
You're doin' okay? That's good, Pete.

PETE
Look . . . It's late, Mr Eddy . . . I . . .

MR EDDY
I'm really glad you're doin' okay, Pete.

Pete doesn't know what to say.

You sure you're doin' okay? Everything all right?

PETE
Yeah.

MR EDDY
That's good, Pete. Hey . . . I want you to talk to a friend of mine.

Pete can hear the phone being handed over to someone. There is a long silence. Pete can hear breathing.

VOICE
We've met before, haven't we?

Pete freezes. His mind is scrambling.

PETE
I don't think so. Where was it that you think we've met?

VOICE
At your house. Don't you remember?

PETE
No. No, I don't.

VOICE
We just killed a couple of people . . .

PETE
What?

Pete can hear Mr Eddy laugh in the background.

VOICE
You heard me . . . We thought we'd come over and tell you about it.

Pete is becoming pale with fear.

PETE
What's goin' on?

VOICE

Great question! In the East . . . the *Far* East . . . When a person is sentenced to death . . . they're sent to a place where they can't escape . . . never knowing when an executioner will step up behind them and fire a bullet into the back of their head . . . It could be days . . . weeks . . . or even years after the death sentence has been pronounced . . . This uncertainty adds an exquisite element of torture to the situation, don't you think? It's been a pleasure talking to you.

Pete can hear the phone being passed again.

MR EDDY

Pete . . . I just wanted to jump on and tell you I'm really glad you're doin' okay.

The phone goes dead and Pete sits—fearfully pondering his fate. He hears a noise and turns.

Down at the far end of the hall he sees his parents staring at him.

CLOSE UP: *parents staring in the direction of the living room as if sensing something, but not seeing.*

Parents' POV: *the hall and living room beyond. There is no one there.*

DISSOLVE.

Line drawing by Barry Gifford from *Wyoming*.

from WYOMING (2000)

SOUL TALK

"MOM, WHEN BIRDS DIE, what happens to their souls?"

"What made you think of that, Roy?"

"I was watching a couple of crows fly by."

"You think birds have souls?"

"That's what Nanny says."

"What do you think the soul is, baby?"

"Something inside a person."

"Where inside?"

"Around the middle."

"You mean by the heart?"

"I don't know. Someplace deep. Can a doctor see it on an X-ray?"

"No, baby, nobody can see it. Sometimes you can feel your soul yourself. It's just a feeling. Not everybody has one."

"Some people don't have a soul?"

"I don't know, Roy, but there are more than a few I'll bet have never been in touch with theirs. Or who'd recognize it if it glowed in the dark."

"Can you see your soul in the dark if you take off all your clothes and look in the mirror?"

"Only if your eyes are closed."

"Mom, that doesn't make sense."

"I hate to tell you this, baby, but the older you get and the more you figure things should make sense, they more than sometimes don't."

"Your soul flies away like a crow when you die and hides in a cloud. When it rains that means the clouds are full of souls and some of 'em are squeezed out. Rain is the dead souls there's no more room for in heaven."

"Did Nanny tell you this, Roy?"

"No, it's just something I thought."

"Baby, there's no way I'll ever think about rain the same way again."

WYOMING

"WHAT'S YOUR FAVORITE PLACE, Mom?"

"Oh, I have a lot of favorite places, Roy. Cuba, Jamaica, Mexico."

"Is there a place that's really perfect? Somewhere you'd go if you had to spend the rest of your life there and didn't want anyone to find you?"

"How do you know that, baby?"

"Know what?"

"That sometimes I think about going someplace where nobody can find me."

"Even me?"

"No, honey, not you. We'd be together, wherever it might be."

"How about Wyoming?"

"Wyoming?"

"Have you ever been there?"

"Your dad and I were in Sun Valley once, but that's in Idaho. No, Roy, I don't think so. Why?"

"It's really big there, with lots of room to run. I looked on a map. Wyoming's probably a good place to have a dog."

"I'm sure it is, baby. You'd like to have a dog, huh?"

"It wouldn't have to be a big dog, Mom. Even a medium-size or small dog would be okay."

"When I was a little girl we had a chow named Toy, a big black Chinese dog with a long purple tongue. Toy loved everyone in the family, especially me, and he would have defended us to the death. He was dangerous to anyone outside the house, and not only to people.

"One day Nanny found two dead cats hanging over the back fence in our yard. She didn't know where they came from, and she buried them. The next day or the day after that, she found two or three more dead cats hanging over the fence. It turned out that Toy was killing the neighborhood cats and draping them over the fence to show us. After that, he had to wear a muzzle."

"What's a muzzle?"

"A mask over his mouth, so he couldn't bite. He was a great dog, though, to me. Toy loved the snow when we lived in Illinois. He loved to roll in it and sleep outside on the front porch in the winter. His long fur coat kept him warm."

"What happened to Toy?"

"He ran after a milk truck one day and was hit by a car and killed. This happened just after I went away to school. The deliveryman said that Toy was trying to bite him through the muzzle."

"Does it snow in Wyoming?"

"Oh, yes, baby, it snows a lot in Wyoming. It gets very cold there."

"Toy would have liked it."

"I'm sure he would."

"Mom, can we drive to Wyoming?"

"You mean now?"

"Uh-huh. Is it far?"

"Very far. We're almost to Georgia."

"Can we go someday?"

"Sure, Roy, we'll go."

"We won't tell anyone, right, Mom?"

"No, baby, nobody will know where we are."

"And we'll have a dog."

"I don't see why not."

"From now on when anything bad happens, I'm going to think about Wyoming. Running with my dog."

"It's a good thing, baby. Everybody needs Wyoming."

THE UP AND UP

"WHY DIDN'T YOU TELL ME dad was going to die?"

"Oh, baby, I didn't know he would die. I mean, everyone dies sooner or later, but we couldn't know he would die this soon."

"Dad wasn't old."

"No, Roy, he was forty-eight. Too young."

"I didn't know he was in the hospital again."

"We talked to him just after he went back in, don't you remember?"

"I forgot."

"Your dad really loved you, Roy, more than anything."

"He didn't sound sick, that's why I didn't remember he was in the hospital."

"It's a shame he died, baby, really a shame."

"After he came home from the hospital the first time, after his operation, Phil Sharky told me Dad was too tough to die."

"Phil Sharky's not a person worth listening to about anything. I'm sure he meant well telling you that, but he's the kind of man who if you ask him to turn off a light only knows how to break the lamp."

"What does that mean, Mom?"

"I mean Phil Sharky can't be trusted. You can't believe a word he says. If he says it's Tuesday, you can get fat betting it's Friday. Phil Sharky's a crooked cop who doesn't play straight with anyone."

"I thought he was Dad's friend."

"Look how dark the sky's getting, Roy, and it's only two o'clock. If we're lucky, we'll make it to Asheville before the rain hits. I thought we'd stay at the Dixieland Hotel. It has the prettiest views of the Smokies."

"Phil Sharky gave me his gun to hold once. It was really heavy. He said to be careful because it was loaded."

"Was your dad there?"

"No, he went out with Dummy Fish and left me at the store. He told me he'd be right back. I asked Phil if the gun wouldn't weigh so much if there weren't any bullets in it and he said if they went where they were supposed to it wouldn't."

"Baby, you won't ever see Phil Sharky again if I have anything to do with it. Did you tell your dad about this? That Phil let you handle his gun?"

"Dad didn't get back for a long time and I fell asleep on the newspaper bundles. When I woke up, Phil was gone and Dad and Dummy and I went to Charmette's for pancakes. I remember because Solly Banks was there and he came over to our table and said I was a lucky kid to have the kind of father who'd take me out for pancakes at four in the morning."

"Suitcase Solly, another character who couldn't tell the up and up if it bit him. So your dad didn't know Sharky showed you the gun?"

"Phil told me not to say anything to Dad, in case he wouldn't like the idea, so I didn't."

"We're not gonna beat the rain, baby, but we'll get there while there's still light. Tomorrow we'll fly to Chicago. The funeral's on Sunday."

"Will everyone be there?"

"I don't know about everyone, but your dad knew a lot of people. Most of the ones who come will want to talk to you."

"Even people I don't know?"

"Probably. All you have to do is thank them for paying their respects to your father."

"What if I cry?"

"It's normal to cry at a funeral, Roy. Don't worry about it."

"Mom, what was the last thing Dad said before he died?"

"Gee, baby, I really don't know. I think when the nurse came to give him a shot for the pain, he'd already died in his sleep. There was nobody in the room."

"Do you remember the last thing he said to you?"

"Oh, I think it was just to not worry, that he'd be okay."

"I bet Dad knew he was dying and he didn't want to tell us."

"Maybe so."

"What if he got scared just before he died? Nobody was there for him to talk to."

"Don't think about it, Roy. Your dad didn't live very long, but he enjoyed himself."

"Dad was on the up and up, wasn't he, Mom?"

"Your dad did things his own way, but the important thing to remember, baby, is that he knew the difference."

18 May 74

The Lost Dream

Last night I was awakened three times by a disturbing dream--
I was down on the Bowery in New York City, the waterfront
in an evil smoky grey dawn looking for a man, my father or uncle,
cousin, brother, I don't know,--who was a bum in an old torn overcoat
I finally located in a corner grocery and tried to persuade him
to come with me for Thanksgiving dinner--He insisted he was too hungry
to wait, with thirty day beard, yellow pouch of a face, ragged teeth,
unrecognizable almost--so I bought him a stale fly-ridden piece
of apricot or apple pie, and I debated taking one myself--
Somewhere nearby was Mary Lou, who met me, with her
and my stumbling bum brother whoever ghost we walked along
the dismal docks and then away from the harbor, back from the bridge,
and the light--

Barry

Postcard to Marshall Clements.

ALSO BY BARRY GIFFORD

FICTION

American Falls (New York: Seven Stories Press, 2002)
Wyoming (New York: Arcade/Little, Brown, 2000)
My Last Martini (Birmingham, AL: Crane Hill, 2000)
The Sinaloa Story (New York: Harcourt Brace, 1998)
Baby Cat-Face (New York: Harcourt Brace, 1997)
Perdita Durango (New York: Grove Press, 1996)
Arise and Walk (New York: Hyperion, 1994)
Night People (New York: Grove Press, 1992)
Bad Day for the Leopard Man (New York: Vintage/Random House, 1992)
Sailor's Holiday (New York: Random House, 1991)
Sultans of Africa (New York: Random House, 1991)
Consuelo's Kiss (New York: Random House, 1991)
Port Tropique (New York: Vintage Books, 1991)
Wild at Heart (New York: Grove Press, 1990)
Landscape with Traveler (New York: E.P. Dutton, 1980)
A Boy's Novel (Santa Barbara: Christopher's Books, 1973)

NONFICTION

Las cuatro reinas (with David Perry) (San Francisco: Gallery Sixteen, 2001)
Out of the Past: Adventures in Film Noir (Jackson, MS: University Press of Mississippi, 2001)
Bordertown (with David Perry) (San Francisco: Chronicle Books, 1998)
The Phantom Father: A Memoir (New York: Harcourt Brace, 1997)
A Day at the Races (New York: Atlantic Monthly Press, 1988)
Saroyan: A Biography (with Lawrence Lee) (New York: Harper & Row, 1984)
The Neighborhood of Baseball (New York: E.P. Dutton, 1981)
Jack's Book: An Oral Biography of Jack Kerouac (with Lawrence Lee) (New York: St. Martin's Press, 1978)

POETRY

Replies to Wang Wei (Berkeley: Donald S. Ellis/Creative Arts, 2001)
Flaubert at Key West (Lawrence, KS: First Intensity Press, 1997)
Ghosts No Horse Can Carry (Berkeley: Donald S. Ellis/Creative Arts, 1989)
Giotto's Circle (Laurinburg, NC: St. Andrews Press, 1987)
Beautiful Phantoms (Bolinas, CA: Tombouctou Press, 1981)
Horse hauling timber out of Hokkaido forest (Santa Barbara: Christopher's Books, 1979)
Poems from Snail Hut (Santa Barbara: Christopher's Books, 1978)
Persimmons: Poems for Paintings (Berkeley: Shaman Drum, 1977)
The Boy You Have Always Loved (Vancouver: Talon Books, 1976)
Selected Poems of Francis Jammes (translations, with Bettina Dickie) (Logan, UT: Utah State University Press, 1976)
Coyote Tantras (Santa Barbara: Christopher's Books, 1973)
The Blood of the Parade (London: Silverthorne Press, 1967)

PLAYS

Hotel Room Trilogy (Jackson: University Press of Mississippi, 1995)

FILMS

Wild at Heart, 1990. Directed by David Lynch. (Propaganda Films/ Samuel L. Goldwyn) Based on the novel by Barry Gifford.
Hotel Room, 1993. Directed by David Lynch. (Asymmetrical Films/HBO Television) Two plays, "Blackout," and "Tricks," written by Barry Gifford.
Perdita Durango, 1997. Directed by Alex de la Iglesia. (Iberoamericana-Lola-Sogetel Films) Screenplay co-written by Barry Gifford, based on his novel.
Lost Highway, 1997. Directed by David Lynch. (Ciby 2000/Asymmetrical Films) Original screenplay by David Lynch & Barry Gifford.
Bordertown: A Journey with Barry Gifford, 1999. Directed by Georges Luneau. (Nestor Productions, France) Documentary.
BARRY GIFFORD: Wild at Heart in New Orleans, 1999. Directed by Francesco Conversano & Nene Grignaffini. (MOVIE MOVIE/RAI, Italy) Documentary.
City of Ghosts, 2003. Directed by Matt Dillon. (Banyan Tree Productions/United Artists) Original screenplay by Matt Dillon & Barry Gifford.
Ball Lightning, 2003. Directed by Amy Glazer. (San Jose State University/Sparky & Buddy Productions) Screenplay by Barry Gifford (also act.), based on his short story.

LIST OF PUBLISHED SOURCES

Night People excerpt in *Buzz* (September/October 1992); in *Love Is Strange*, Joe Rose and Catherine Texier, eds., (New York: W.W. Norton, 1993); in *Double Dealer Redux* (September 1993)

Arise and Walk excerpt in *Double Dealer Redux* v.1 no.4 (Summer 1994)

"The Passion of Hypolite Cortez" in *Panta* [Milan] (1993); in *Exquisite Corpse* 45 (January 1994); in *French Quarter Fiction Anthology* (New Orleans, LA: Light of New Orleans Publishing Co., 2002)

Baby Cat-Face excerpt in *First Intensity* 2 (Winter 1994); in *Exquisite Corpse* 50 (1994 / 1995); in *Juice* 2 (December 1995); in *The Graceful Lie: A Method for Making Fiction* (New Jersey: Prentice Hall, 1999)

The Sinaloa Story excerpt in *Exquisite Corpse* 54 (November 1995); in *Shenandoah* (Summer 1996); in *First Intensity* 7 (Summer 1996); in *La Repubblica delle Donne* 37 [Milan] (February 1997); in *Double Dealer Redux* 4 (September 1997); in *Speak* 9 (Spring 1998); in *Excess* 1 (1998)

"Where the Southern Cross' the Yellow Dog" in *Speak* 10 (Summer 1998)

Introduction to *Texas Stories* in *El País* [Madrid] (April 1994)

"Black Wings Had His Angel: A Brief Memoir of Elliott Chaze" in the *Oxford American* (January/February 2000)

"The Strangest One of All" in Synaesthesia Press Chapbook (1998)

"The Face of the Hero" in *El País* (February 1995)

"Fuzzy Sandwiches or There Is No Speed Limit on the Lost Highway: Reflections on David Lynch" in *Première* [Paris] (2002); in *Esquire*

Japan [Tokyo] (May 1997); in *The Complete Lynch* (London: Virgin, 2001); in *San Jose Mercury News* (August 2001)
"My Last Martini" in *San Francisco Chronicle* (February 1998)
"The Tunisian Notebook" in *The Berkeley Monthly* (April 1980); in *The Boston Monthly* (April 1981); in Ten Mile River Press Chapbook (1983)
Wild at Heart excerpt in *San Francisco Examiner* (August 1990); in *Cosmopolitan* [Paris] (July 1990); in *San Jose Mercury News* (August 1990); in *El País* [Madrid] (June 1991); in *Speak-Up* [Milan] (October 1991); in *Southwest Stories*, John Miller and Catherine Morgan, eds., (San Francisco: Chronicle Books, 1995)
Sailor's Holiday excerpt in *San Francisco Focus* (March 1991)
Landscape With Traveler excerpt in *Christopher Street* (January 1980)
Port Tropique excerpt in *San Francisco Review of Books* (November 1980)
Phantom Father excerpt in *La Repubblica delle Donne* [Milan] (February 1999)
"My Mother's People" in *Response* 33 (Spring 1977)
"The Old Country" in *The Berkeley Monthly* (June 1981)
"Mrs. Kashfi" in *The Berkeley Monthly* (June 1981)
"The Trophy" in *First Intensity* 8 (Winter 1997)
"The Kid Who Torched the *Charterhouse of Parma*" in *Pangolin Papers* v.3 no.3 (Spring 1997)
"The Aerodynamics of an Irishman" in *The Fireside Book of Baseball* (New York: Simon & Schuster/Fireside, 1988)
"A Good Man to Know" in *Arizona Republic* (August 1984); in *PEN Short Story Collection: The Available Press* (New York: Ballantine Books, 1985); in *Rolling Stock* 12 (April 1987); in *Negative Capability* XIII nos.1,2 (1993); in *El País* [Madrid] (March 1995)
"A Long Day's Night in the Naked City" in *Mystery Scene* v. 1 no. 5 (September 1986); in *Rolling Stock* 12 (April 1987); *First Intensity* 4 (Winter 1995)
"The Rooster Trapped in the Reptile Room" in *The New York Times* (September 1991)
"Magic Sam" in *Rolling Stone* (1968); in *Rolling Stone Record Review Anthology* (New York: Simon & Schuster, 1971)
"Don Bartolomeo" in *Western American Literature* (May 1975); in *Open Letter* (February 1975)

"Empire of Signs" in *San Jose Mercury News* (October 1983)

"Maximum Bob" in *The New York Times Book Review* (July 1991)

"The Devil Thumbs a Ride" in *Mystery Scene* 7 (January 1987)

"Blood on the Moon" in *Mystery Scene* 23 (October/November 1989); in *San Francisco Bay Guardian* (July 1992)

"CI" in *Wisconsin Review* (November 1970)

"Paris Street" in *The Niagara Magazine* 2 (February 1975)

"Returning by Boat on a Cold River" in *The Niagara Magazine* 2, (February 1975); in *KUKSU* 4 (1975)

"Chinese Notes" in *The Berkeley Monthly* (November 1982)

"Maria La O" in *American Poets Say Goodbye to the Twentieth Century* (New York: Four Walls Eight Windows, 1996)

"On Viewing the Manuscript Scroll of Jack Kerouac's Novel *On the Road* in the Tosca Bar, San Francisco" in *Exquisite Corpse* 10 (September 2001); in *Poetry Flash* 288 (August/September 2001)

"Small Elegy for Corso" in *Exquisite Corpse* 10 (September 2001); in *Poetry Flash* 288 (August/September 2001)

"True Love" in *Shenandoah* v. 52 no. 3 (Fall 2002)

Wyoming excerpt in *Speak* (November/December 1998; January/February 1999; March/April 1999; September 1999; January 2000)

ACKNOWLEDGMENTS

Lost Highway copyright © 1997 by Barry Gifford and David Lynch used by permission of Faber and Faber, Limited, and Faber and Faber, Inc. (an affiliate of Farrar, Straus & Giroux, LLC).

Wild at Heart copyright © 1990 by Barry Gifford used by permission of Grove/Atlantic, Inc.

Night People copyright © 1992 by Barry Gifford used by permission of Grove/Atlantic, Inc.

Used courtesy of Seven Stories Press:

"I Wish I'd Made It Up: A Note to the Reader," "The Winner," "My Last Martini," "The Tunisian Notebook."

"Letter to Marshall Clements" and "The Lost Dream" from Barry Gifford Papers, M0927, Dept. of Special Collections, Stanford University Libraries, Stanford, Calif.

Used courtesy of the author:

Arise and Walk, Baby Cat-Face, The Sinaloa Story, Sailor's Holiday, Sultans of Africa, Consuelo's Kiss, Bad Day for the Leopard Man, Perdita Durango, Landscape With Traveler, Port Tropique, Phantom Father, Blackout, Wyoming.

"The Thrill of a Writer's Lifetime," "Where the Southern Cross' the Yellow Dog," Introduction to *Texas Stories,* "Black Wings Had His Angel: A Brief Memoir of Elliott Chaze," "The Strangest One of All," "The Face of the Hero," "Bordertown," "The Ciné," "The Rooster Trapped in the Reptile Room," "Magic Sam," "*Don Bartolomeo,*" "*Empire of Signs,*" "Maximum Bob," all film essays, "Fuzzy Sandwiches or There Is No Speed Limit on the Lost Highway: Reflections on David Lynch," all poetry, Introduction to *Jack's Book,* 2nd ed.

ABOUT THE AUTHOR

BARRY GIFFORD's novels have been translated into twenty-two languages. His book *Night People* was awarded the Premio Brancati in Italy, and he has been the recipient of awards from PEN, the National Endowment for the Arts, the American Library Association, and the Writers Guild of America. David Lynch's film *Wild at Heart*, which was based on Gifford's novel, won the Palme d'Or at the Cannes Film Festival in 1990; and his novel *Perdita Durango* was made into a feature film by Spanish director Alex de la Iglesia in 1997. Gifford co-wrote with Lynch the film *Lost Highway* (1997); he also co-wrote with director Matt Dillon the film *City of Ghosts* (2003). Gifford's recent books include *The Phantom Father*, named a *New York Times* Notable Book of the Year; *Wyoming*, named a *Los Angeles Times* Novel of the Year, which has been adapted for the stage and film; and *American Falls: The Collected Short Stories*. Mr. Gifford's writings have appeared in *Punch, Esquire, Rolling Stone, Sport*, the *New York Times, El País, Reforma, La Repubblica, Projections* and many other publications. He lives in the San Francisco Bay Area (and on the web at www.BarryGifford.com).

ANDREI CODRESCU's recent novels include *Casanova in Bohemia* (The Free Press, 2002), and the just-completed *Wakefield* (Algonquin, Fall 2003). He is a journalist for National Public Radio and the MacCurdy Distinguished Professor of English at Louisiana State University in Baton Rouge.

ABOUT THE EDITOR

THOMAS A. MCCARTHY, originally of Omaha, is an editor at Seven Stories Press in New York City.